D0092917

8·19   **DATE DUE**

SEP 2 0 2019

OCT 2 5 2019

Rutherford Park

Center Point
Large Print

**This Large Print Book carries the
Seal of Approval of N.A.V.H.**

Rutherford Park

Elizabeth Cooke

CENTER POINT LARGE PRINT
THORNDIKE, MAINE

This Center Point Large Print edition
is published in the year 2016 by arrangement with
The Berkley Publishing Group,
an imprint of Penguin Publishing Group,
a division of Penguin Random House Company LLC.

The text of this Large Print edition is unabridged.
In other aspects, this book may vary from the original edition.
Printed in the United States of America
on permanent paper.Set in 16-point Times New Roman type.

ISBN: 978-1-68324-003-7

Library of Congress Cataloging-in-Publication Data

Names: Cooke, Elizabeth, 1953– author.
Title: Rutherford Park / Elizabeth Cooke.
Description: Center Point Large Print edition. | Thorndike, Maine :
Center Point Large Print, 2016. | ©2013
Identifiers: LCCN 2016009749 | ISBN 9781683240037
    (hardcover : alk. paper)
Subjects: LCSH: Large type books. | GSAFD: Romantic suspense
fiction.
Classification: LCC PR6063.C485 R88 2016 | DDC 813/.6—dc23
LC record available at http://lccn.loc.gov/2016009749

Chapter 1

S now had fallen in the night, and now the great house, standing at the head of the valley, seemed like a five-hundred-year-old ship sailing in a white ocean. Around it spread the parkland, the woods, terraces and gardens; beyond it and high above was the massive slope of the woodlands and the moor. To the south and the east, the river described a wide loop; to the west, the nine-acre lake was a grey mirror fringed with ice.

Although it was early, Rutherford was not asleep. It was never truly asleep, for everywhere in that white landscape there was hard labor to keep the estate functioning. Power and influence had raised Rutherford; power and influence trailed in its wake. Just as the late-Victorian additions to the house spread outwards from the Tudor hall where the first brick had been laid in 1530, so Rutherford spread outwards from the house itself, radiating through the tenant farms, the villages, the long sweep of the valley down towards York, touching and altering everything in its path: commanding lives, changing landscapes.

On the first floor now, above the terrace, a light was shining, and the heavy curtains of the largest room in the west wing were drawn back. It was barely seven, but Octavia Cavendish had been awake for some time. She sat swathed in the Poiret dressing gown, full-length black-and-white satin, lined in sable, that William had bought her in London eighteen months ago. A fire glowed in the limestone-framed fireplace; Octavia's morning tea was laid to one side.

Around her fussed Amelie, her maid, laying out the first changes of clothes of the day: four alternatives. The lavender, perhaps, for luncheon, or the morning dress of grey velvet. A tea gown for the afternoon. And the elaborate white tulle with green appliqué for the evening. Past the gowns, on the dressing table, Amelie had already spread out the jewels that had once belonged to Octavia's husband's mother: heavyweight emeralds set in gold, and the opals, which she particularly loathed. In a room awash with silks and gauzes, Octavia looked, and felt, like some overblown rose wilting before the fire. "The lavender," she decided eventually. Amelie dipped her head in agreement, bundled up the grey velvet over her arm, and retreated to the dressing room.

Octavia got up and looked out at the snow. It was more than an hour since she had first noticed the great beech tree lying on its side at the top of the drive, and she gazed at it now, watching the men gathering below the curved steps: monochrome silhouettes against the branches and the burned-out color of last year's leaves.

She had an overwhelming feeling that she might

go outside; she might go and listen to their conversations. She might run in the snow as the children used to. She remembered running across this perfect lawn, this perfect terrace, when she had first come here with William, a bride of nineteen, alive with a happiness that had been rapidly extinguished, brimming with an enthusiasm that was not required. She remembered passing the North Lodge in the old landau on the very first day, the large carriage dipping and rolling as it turned the corner of the drive, and Rutherford had come into view, with its towers, mullioned windows and barley-twist chimneys looking so ravishingly pretty in the afternoon sunshine.

Octavia unconsciously straightened her shoulders. Of course, it was impossible to go outside. One would hardly be expected to, unless there were a shooting party or one was dressed to walk, as she sometimes did in the spring or summer. Besides which, it would not be seemly for the wife of the eighth earl to run. And she certainly could not go to listen to the talk among the servants. Still, it was unreal: the huge tree lying broken-backed. The silence of the snow for miles beyond. The ghostly atmosphere of the day. She had once dreamed, not long after Harry had been born, that all of Rutherford had vanished. She had dreamed that the grounds had fluttered for a brief second and were suddenly gone: the glasshouses, the lake, the long drive to the edge of the hills, gone in an instant, shut up in a breath, eclipsed in one long, suffocating sigh.

She wondered why she thought of that now. It was Christmas Eve, 1913; the house was entertaining for the next four days; as the mistress of the house, she ought to be too busy for such fantasies. She turned back and looked at the room, frowning and calculating. There were sixteen guests coming in all: a rather small house party, but she preferred to have simply friends at Christmas, for there were too many formal parties to host during the rest of the year.

She had no doubt that the stoical little steam train would run from Wasthwaite along the valley; but she wondered about the horses struggling along the country road to the house. There was no possibility, surely, of the Napier or the Metz going out in this weather? The Napier was temperamental at best; the wheels would slither down the incline to the gates—and as for the Metz, it had been a whim to occupy Harry, to distract the boy from his perpetual obsession with air flight. The Metz was a little green roadster hardly capable of battling through snow. However, no doubt William would insist upon his Napier, for, to the horror of the staff, he enjoyed driving it himself, and had an enormous fur driving coat, a boxlike monument of a coat, that he would wrap himself in today. The drive would be cleared, the lane, the hill—four miles of snow. William would set the ground staff to it. Four miles. Eight more guests to add to those already here. Two more trains, Charlotte and Louisa returning on the same afternoon train and Helene de Montfort before luncheon.

"Oh, Lord," she murmured.

There was a knock on the door. Amelie ran to answer it, but Octavia already knew who it would be. There was no mistaking the thunderous three raps.

"M'lord," Amelie murmured, as Octavia's husband was admitted.

William Cavendish looked uncomfortable in the yellow-and-white upholstered sanctum that was Octavia's room, but then, he always did. He walked stiffly over to her and gave his wife a small dry kiss on the cheek. He smelled of shaving soap and—rather more distantly—of dog: his spaniel, Heggarty, slept in his room. William's suite was far more spartan than hers, and Octavia rarely trespassed upon it; painted blue, with plain furnishings, it was startlingly male, with its hunting prints on the wall and the costly Landseer that he had told her was far too sentimental, but which he had bought all the same. Leaning towards her now, William seemed almost loath to bend. He was a tall, broad man.

"Will you come to breakfast?" he asked.

She raised an eyebrow. "Have you come to ask me? Dearest, how romantic."

William did not return her smile. He merely indicated the presence of Amelie with a glance.

"Leave us," Octavia instructed. The maid vanished, carrying the unwanted tea tray, closing the bedroom door behind her.

"Are you ill?"

"No, not at all," she said. "Why?"

He pursed his lips, rocked on his heels. He was twenty years older than she, and sometimes the way he stood, hands locked behind his back, was reminiscent of her own father building himself up to one of his storms of temper.

"Cooper has told me that you were downstairs this morning," he said, naming his valet.

"Cooper?" she echoed, amused. "And why would Cooper be in the least interested in that?"

William let the mild joke hang ominously in the air for a second. "Cooper is not *interested*," he told her. "Cooper has been told by Mrs. Jocelyn."

Octavia sighed. "Lord, how they gossip."

"Octavia," William said. "You were seen by a housemaid. You spoke to her."

She flung out a hand carelessly, as if to swat his inquiry away. "The heavens shall open, I expect."

"What were you thinking?"

She met his gaze. "Thank you for supposing I was thinking at all," she murmured with a smile. "But I had seen the tree. I wanted to look at it."

"Look at it? What for?"

She wondered for a second whether she ought to

explain the childlike impulse to run out in the snow, and suppressed it. "I have no idea," she said finally. "I was simply awake."

"You have perplexed the staff," he told her.

"I'm dreadfully sorry for it."

He looked at her for a while, shaking his head. She deliberately puzzled him sometimes; she rather thought that it was good for him. Besides, somewhere down in her soul, a little light still burned. It was a sense of humor. Something that neither he nor her brute of a father had ever been successful in removing.

"I shall expect you for luncheon," he said, turning away. "I am going to fetch Helene de Montfort."

"I haven't forgotten," she said. And, turning back to her mirror, she grimaced at the very thought.

In the corridors below the house, Emily Maitland had begun work that morning while it was still dark.

Her day began at five thirty, long before dawn in winter. She had woken, as always, cold in the iron-frame bed in the top-floor room that she shared with the two other chambermaids, Cynthia and Mary. In the dark, she had struggled into her clothes, feeling with her eyes shut for the fastenings of the long navy wool dress, and tying the white calico apron around her waist. The room under the eaves was icy: even her face flannel had frozen to the side of the water in the washing bowl. She poked her finger through the thin layer of ice in the jug and rubbed a few drops over her face. It would have to do.

For the last two months she had got up first, dressing quickly, and holding on to the nightstand when she needed. She had never known what it was like to be drunk, but she thought that this must feel something like it; to combat it, she had learned to pinch her throat just above her collarbone. It seemed to stop it. She had seen her mother do it, and for the same reason.

"Wake up," she whispered to the others. Cynthia—the permanently miserable Cynthia—pulled away from Emily's hand on her shoulder. "Mary," Emily prompted. But Mary was awake, she realized, moving like an automaton, twisting up her hair, pinning it under her cap.

"I shall freeze to death on this side," the girl complained. "Cyn, you take it tonight. You're like a hog as 'tis. Your hog's backside'll keep you warm." She turned round to Emily, her face an indistinct blur in the shadows. "Why is it so bloody cold?" she demanded.

"I think it snowed," Emily told her. She felt her way to the end of the room and the thin curtains. "It looks different, the light." Then, from the window, she saw the snow lying on the lead of the roof and stuck in the twists of the chimneys, fancy spirals in the half darkness.

"No wonder," Mary muttered, pulling on wool stockings from under her pillow so that her feet need not touch the bare floorboards. "No bloody wonder."

"Miss Dodd will hear you," Emily warned, her hand on the door.

"I don't care if she does," Mary whispered back. "She's got a piece of felt on her floor. She's warmer than us. Any more of this, I shall go home."

But they both knew that would never happen. Mary needed her fourteen pounds a year to send back to her father; she couldn't afford to be fired by the head housemaid for her language, and a single insolent word could do it. Mary would go to bed at night and Emily could hear her swearing into her pillow, but downstairs she was as they all were: eyes averted, heads bowed, utterly silent, scrubbing carpets and grates on their knees.

There was a narrow stair down to the first landing; beyond that, a stretch of corridor led to the servants' stair at the far end of the house. Directly below was the master's bedroom; the girls were taught to walk lightly on the boarded floor. Not an echo, not a word. It was a maid's job more than anything else to be invisible, a kind of wraith every morning carrying coal to every bedroom. Breathless, boneless wraith. Until the hand touched the hair on the back of her neck, until it stroked the flesh of her arm below the turned-up sleeve of the dress.

Emily screwed her eyes shut on the servants' stair, and stopped. The housekeeper had caught her crying here a week ago—come running up the stairs before Emily could right herself. "What's the matter with you?" Mrs. Jocelyn had demanded. "Get out of the way." Emily had done as she was told. Nevertheless, it was strange. She thought that she had forgotten how to cry. The shame and terror had wrung it out of her. Mostly she would stand in those lost moments with a dry mouth and dry eyes, staring into the future, beyond grief. He'd taken her heart, she'd thought then to herself. Taken it, broken it, left it staggering through each hour like a faulty clock trying to keep time.

She went as quickly as she could down to the basement, and met Alfred Whitley by the kitchens. "Give me the coal," she hissed at him, snatching the bucket he had brought. She was sorry for her rudeness afterwards; Alfred was willing, if stupid. His mouth always looked too big for his open, gormless face, and his nose permanently ran and he would wipe it on his sleeve. "Like a wet weekend," John Gray, the estate steward, had said. "That's what you get out of the village. They don't breed brains down there. Just muck."

Still, poor Alfred. Poor Alfie. You had to feel for the lad. Only thirteen, and with the worst of the jobs, the hallboy. Though he seemed not to care, standing in the yard cutting a hundredweight of logs, hair plastered to his head in the rain. They never let Mr. Bradfield, the butler, see Alfie in one of the boy's states: exhausted, muddy, wet, sitting on the back step with a mug of cocoa. Mr. Bradfield would have kicked his sorry hide. Mr. Bradfield liked his steps nice and clean.

Emily was dodging the butler's room now. She could see the oil lamp lit in there; there was a glass panel in his door. She hurried past with the coal scuttle, climbed a second stair, and pushed open the green baize door to the house.

This stair brought her out on the south side, next to Lord William's study, and the archive, and the library. Emily disliked it here: not so much the study, which was a pleasant little place with a fine desk and a small fireplace where she now lit the first fire, but the archive containing all the Roman relics that had belonged to Lord William's father. All the shelves had to be dusted, with their stained alabaster birds and cats, and little sculptures and pots, and bones dug up from Beddersley Hill, where they said that ancient kings were buried. They were all funny things, strange things. They made the hair prickle on the back of her neck. She hated the elongated eyes of the cat statues— two of them, one on each side of the door.

Seeing the fire catch, she put up the fireguard and went back to the hallway, crossing the marble floor under the high, vaulted arches. This was the oldest part of the house, what had been the main house before Lord William had extended the

15

whole place fifteen years ago with Lady Cavendish's fortune. They said that the money from the wool mills was the only reason that Cavendish had bothered with a bride, but Emily did not know anything about that. To her, the great hall seemed stranded in the center of the modern additions: heavy wood beams far above. Alfred had lit the oil lamps by the entrance and the main stair. They were pools of color in the dark.

Emily went into the drawing room. There was an urgent need to be fast at this time of day. There were five fires to light on this floor, and then the bedrooms by six o'clock, or soon after. Cynthia and Mary helped the maid of all work stoke up the kitchen fires, sweep out the corridors, and take tea and toast to the upper staff: Amelie, the ladies' maid; Mr. Cooper, the master's valet; and Mrs. Jocelyn. The last month they had also been helping the scullery maid—it was rightfully her job to make sure the kitchen was clear—but Enid Bliss had bronchitis and could not breathe when she got up, a fact that the three chambermaids had been trying to hide from the housekeeper.

Emily was still counting to herself as she worked. There were three sets of guests here already, so that was eight rooms upstairs. Her fingers flew over the paper, kindling and coal. Finishing, she wiped her hands on the apron, stood up, and immediately felt the familiar swing of sickness. Waiting for it to subside, she looked around. Hundreds of shapes inhabited the shadows: chairs, tables, lamps, occasional tables with flowers, others with hothouse plants; shelves with pernickety little flower-girl porcelain that Mr. Bradfield claimed was so expensive; fire screens, footrests. "I shall hoist the complete collection into the river one day," the mistress was supposed to have said, annoyed to find the parlor maids still polishing the furniture after breakfast. Or so Mrs. Jocelyn claimed. "A progressive woman," was the housekeeper's verdict. "I doubt she means it. The class of furnishings are so important."

Emily had found it funny. Not the remark, but the voice. Mrs. Jocelyn couldn't keep her Leeds accent out of her mouth, though she tried. Twenty-seven years in the Cavendish service, and there was still the broad, flat sound of Hunslet in Mrs. Jocelyn's tone.

Emily gazed into the middle distance. Had Mrs. Jocelyn ever been married, really? Every house-keeper was called "Mrs.," married or not. But she couldn't imagine anyone ever clasping Mrs. Jocelyn in his arms, holding her close, kissing that plain face. She had a ring on her finger, but that meant as little as the title; she might have put it there herself. It always flashed brightly as Mrs. Jocelyn fervently clasped her hands at morning prayers in the hall. Emily wiped a hair out of her eyes. Still, for all that, she might have had someone to love her; there might be a Mr. Jocelyn somewhere out in the wide world. Mrs. Jocelyn might have grasped what it took to make a man adore her. Which was far more than she herself had done. She gripped the sides of her skirt, her heart thudding. There was nothing to see: no, really, despite all that there was in this room, all that there was all over this enormous house, there was nothing to see. Nothing but night. She'd never be in the light again. Never, never.

She went to the drawing room door, sick in her heart, sick in her soul, sick of the rooms and the stairs and the fires and the secret hand that had touched hers, sick of him, sick of the abyss crawling towards her as if it were alive. It would writhe out there in the dark, sticky with guilt, like tar in the road that stuck to her shoes in the summer, and one day it would catch her by the ankle and drag her down. "God help me," she murmured, and turned out into the hall.

Lady Cavendish was six feet away, standing near the bottom of the main stairs.

"Oh, ma'am," she whispered. She didn't know what to do with herself. Lady Cavendish never came downstairs at this time of day. None of the family did: none of them ever stirred from their rooms until breakfast. Emily tried to step back against the wall. That was what she was supposed to do if any of the family appeared: flatten herself against the wall and look at the floor.

"Is it . . . Malham?" Lady Cavendish asked.

"Maitland, ma'am." Emily dared a glance upwards. Her mistress was looking at her amusedly. She was wrapped in some astonishing coat all lined with dark fur; under it she wore a pair of matching slippers.

"I'm rather out of place, Maitland," Lady Cavendish said, still smiling. She leaned forward. "But I've come to look at something."

Emily said not a word. Her mistress brushed past her, walked along the hall, the wrap trailing on the marble floor. Then she looked over her shoulder. "Is the door unlocked?" she asked.

The front door of the house was massive: Mr. Bradfield would open it in an hour. "No, ma'am," she replied.

Her mistress stopped. "Oh, it's tiresome," she said, as if to herself. "One is a prisoner in one's own home." She said it lightly, walking back to the stair. "I suppose in time Amelie will bring me tea," she remarked. "Will you tell her I am waiting?"

Emily stared at the other woman, aghast. The servant hierarchy dictated that no mere house-maid could speak to a lady's maid. Even the head maid would approach Amelie only in the direst emergency. "No, of course you can't tell her," Lady Cavendish mused irritatedly, seeing Emily's expression.

"If you please, ma'am, I can go to tell Mrs. Jocelyn."

Her mistress looked down at her from the fifth or sixth step up. She was such a pretty woman, Emily thought. Beautiful, in fact. "Like a bird in a gilded cage," Mr. Bradfield had once said. She looked gilded now: pretty hair and pretty clothes and very pale. Perhaps she was ill, Emily wondered. You had to be ill or mad to go wandering about downstairs at this time of day, hadn't you? But her mistress was leaning slightly towards her, putting a finger to her lips, the smile broader than ever. "So naughty of me to come down and disturb you," she said. "But I shan't breathe a word. And neither shall you."

Emily looked again the floor. Not a word. Not breathe a word. She was used to that, all right.

She could hear the swish of the gown on the steps, and then she heard her mistress's voice. "There is a great tree down in the drive," she called carelessly. "That was what I was coming to look at. I can see it from my room—it is near the house. You might, all the same, tell Mrs. Jocelyn that."

By seven o'clock, the "outsiders" were all out in the drive of the house: the head gardener, Robert March, and the three undergardeners; the carter and farrier, Josiah Armitage, his son, Jack, and the two stable boys. Alfie was sent to help them, kitted out in a stable blanket with an old leather strap serving as a belt around his waist.

The great beech tree lay on its side. It had been

in full leaf the previous year, and the remnants still clung to the branches. Robert March scratched his head and declared it a mystery. The old tree—the drive had been planted in 1815—must have been weakened at the root, he decided, though there was no apparent cause. All of them looked down the length of the drive at the five-hundred-yard stretch of beeches whose branches met overhead. "We don't want no more of the buggers down," March was heard to mutter as he and the boys took to the axes and saws.

It was cold, hard work. Once the smaller branches were removed, March set the farm boys to cut them down further and pile them in the wide loop of the drive before the house, feeling his way through the snow for the low metal wire where the grass and the gravel met. It would all do for kindling, some for hurdles; nothing would be wasted.

Josiah Armitage looked over at March: the seventy-year-old Yorkshireman was hunched over his work, great clouds of breath standing out like a halo around him. March was heavy and broad, and his face permanently florid, but Josiah knew better than to suggest he should slow himself down. March was bitter and fierce; he should have been a drill sergeant. Josiah had seen undergardeners quake under his scrutiny, and last summer March had fired a man for nothing more than going down to the village to attend his wife, who was in her fourth day of labor with their first child. The man had come back grinning, triumphant. But not for long. March had caught him by the collar and taken him down to the end of the drive and kicked him out. It was the very next day that Josiah had seen March tenderly pollinating in the greenhouse, twisting a fine three-haired paintbrush in the tomato flowers as if nothing had happened, and as if there was not a family newly desperate for want of a "character"—the passport to another job.

The garden boys and stable boys slaved under him now, hacking at the tree without looking up. At last, March straightened. "Go get the horse," he told Josiah. "Horse and hay cart both."

Josiah leaned on the ax he had been wielding and looked March in the eye. Sweat was streaming down the carter's face.

"If you'd be so kind, Mr. Armitage," March conceded.

Josiah and his son went off through the snow, wheeling out over the lawn so that they did not walk directly in front of the house. March watched them go; behind his back, his undergardeners smirked. If March was stone, Armitage was Yorkshire flint—brittle and cutting, tough as the long winters. He took orders only from Lord Cavendish; the boy Harry had almost been brought up hanging on Armitage's every word while his own father was away in London for the eight years he had been an MP. Harry was often silent around his father, and his father was short at best around his son, but Harry had talked long enough and loud enough with Armitage all his childhood, and Harry even now would have lived in the warmth of the stables alongside the horses, given half a chance. March knew that as well as anyone, and it looked hardly about to change, even if Harry was nineteen this coming year.

It began to snow a little again around ten o'clock; briefly, March saw Lady Cavendish at the window of the morning room, her hands wrung in front of her in an anxious pose. When she stepped away, the front door opened. William Cavendish, dressed in a greatcoat, came out and down the long flight of sandstone steps.

Seeing the earl walking rapidly towards him, March plucked at the rim of his hat. "M'lord."

Cavendish shielded his eyes against the snow with one gloved hand. "How much longer?"

"The shire's being harnessed," March replied.

"And what of the remaining trees?"

"Seem a'reet, m'lord."

"Get the men down the drive and clear the snow back as soon as the horse comes. I want to take the car to the station at twelve."

March nodded. He waited for William Cavendish to say something else: perhaps that the staff could take a hot drink at the back doors, or at March's own cottage in the walled kitchen gardens. But Cavendish said nothing. He simply walked away.

The shire horse came in a quarter of an hour. Josiah Armitage was on one side leading by the rein, Jack on the top of the cart. The three coming through the gentle snow—a fine white curtain and the horse itself grey with great white-haired hooves—looked like ghosts, scribbles on a grey page, until they were almost upon the drive. Then the shire—nineteen hands high and weighing a ton and a half—came into focus, breath steaming. Ice granules were forming on the condensation on the harness and the padded collar around the horse's neck. The boys stopped cutting. Alfie put one hand on the collar, reaching up to do so, and the horse turned its massive, ponderous head to look at the boy. Alfie laid his face against the warm flank. "Wenceslas," he said. "Old mate, old mate."

Octavia could not remember a time when she had not been afraid of Helene de Montfort.

Although "fear" was rather too strong a word for it: it was something much subtler than that. It was the kind of unease that one woman might feel around another, something Octavia felt in her stomach, in the tightening of her diaphragm when Helene walked into a room.

The woman was all charm, of course: perfectly charming. Helene was William's far-distant cousin, a product of the eminent Beckforths, educated, living in Paris, renowned—if Helene's own stories might be believed—as a hostess; what else would she be but charming? Octavia sighed, drumming her fingers on the curtain cord, smoothing the fabric of the huge velvet drapes. Helene was always elegantly dressed by Worth of Paris; and with her small pert face, her mass of strawberry blond hair and her little foxlike smile, Octavia had once heard Helene described—at some long-ago London party—as having "dancing eyes." Perhaps they danced for a man; to Octavia, Helene's eyes were speculative, assessing. If they danced at all it was with a lively kind of cunning.

Octavia stood in the second sitting room and waited. Helene would think it terribly funny that there was snow, of course. It would all be so delicious, so *northern* of them to have snow, to have ice, to have had one tree missing, in a pool of sawdust, right from the front of the house; it would be so divinely *gauche* of them. Octavia consciously, slowly unwound the cord from her fingers.

Here came the car; it rounded the corner by the lodge. There was a knock at the sitting room door, and Mr. Bradfield appeared. "Madame de Montfort is arriving, ma'am," he said.

"I know," Octavia replied. "Bring her straight in here. See that the room is warm upstairs. Have Amelie look after her clothes."

Bradfield raised a slight, discreet eyebrow as he left. Octavia bit her lip. Of course it was done already.

There was a noise out in the hall. The sound of the door being opened, a flurry of voices. Nash, the footman, trotting down the outside steps in that irritatingly effeminate way of his. Octavia turned to the mirror over the fireplace and smoothed her hair. How ridiculous to be annoyed at Nash, she thought. He was a very adept, very careful boy. She could hear the luggage being unloaded. Helene would purse her lips at such a fuss within a few feet of her. Service should be soundless. The front door closed with a sepulchral thud.

Helene was suddenly in the room, peeling off her long kid gloves, letting her immense coat fall, holding out both hands.

"Oh, but I'm terribly cold." She laughed. Behind her, William sidestepped the coat and Bradfield leapt to retrieve it. "Like a corpse! No blood at all! Just feel me!" Helene pressed her face to Octavia's cheek. "My dearest girl," she whispered. She was wearing some kind of adolescent perfume: all violets. She stepped back and held Octavia at arm's length. "Don't you look lovely!" she exclaimed. "What is this? Callot Soeurs? I've never seen their day dresses. How extraordinary, and how fine! So brave of you to choose lavender in winter. It makes one seem so pale. But *you*." She smiled, looking down at Octavia from her five feet, ten inches, made even larger by the huge traveling hat with its spray of pheasant feathers, "*You,* darling." She leaned close to Octavia's face as if confiding a secret. "How you carry it off."

You are a parody of yourself, Octavia thought. She knew by evening the gushing Helene would have been replaced by the meditative, intelligent Helene so full of sly witticism. But it always, always knocked her back, this first assault of words. "Helene," she said, smiling. The knot in her diaphragm eased a fraction. "Come and sit."

There was still the sound of labor in the drive outside when William went up to his room in the early afternoon.

Luncheon had been pleasant enough; the talk had been of the weather, of course. And of the Stanningfields, who were already here and who had gone out to see their relations in Richmond for the day; of Harry, who had gone with them; of the charm of Wasthwaite station, farther up the line, with its Christmas wreaths; and the jocund station master, Baddeley. The three of them had politely considered William's return journey in the Napier to meet Louisa and Charlotte coming from Manchester on the afternoon train.

Yet with every step on the stair, William cursed. He cursed himself; he cursed the wretched woman who was never out of his mind; he cursed the weather; he cursed Baddeley's cheeriness and Wasthwaite and the whole damned charade of Christmas. Looking out the window, he cursed the bloody man March, whom his father had hated, whom he himself hated, but whose cleverness with the gardens was indispensable. He cursed his own inherited characteristic to let things go, to let them heal themselves. To imagine a problem solved if he turned his back on it.

"God damn her," he muttered. "Damn her, damn her." He turned from the window and the sight of the horse with its neck patiently bowed and the cart loaded high behind it in the snow; clenched his fists, looked about himself for something to do. He had told Octavia that he felt unwell, but that was a lie. He had left her with Helene, which was cruel of him; he had caught sight of his wife's pleading expression as he walked away, and all the way through the hall he had heard Helene's grating voice.

He looked at himself in the mirror. A man of some bearing, a man absolutely of his class and nationality. The straight back, the uplifted chin, the rigid shoulders—the stance that had been instilled in him as a child, sitting in the nursery on a training chair for an hour a day, his feet tied to the chair legs, his torso tied to the wooden frame. *That such things existed,* he thought. He considered his face, looking so much now like his father: still dark haired, the same ironic self-deprecating smile, still a boyish pleasure in his eyes, and a note of humor. It was what Octavia told him was a terribly pleasing face. He looked away, leaning his weight on the flat of his hands;

then, abruptly, he snatched up the heavy china jug from the dressing table and threw it. It smashed against the wall by the bed, cracked, splintered, fell to the floor. He went over to it and kicked the pieces around, and a sound came out of him, a note of soul-destroying frustration.

What was he to do? Jesus my Lord, they depended on him. Each one of them here in this house, depended . . .

He recalled his father sitting on the bank of the river below Rutherford one August afternoon. It had been raining in the morning, and he remembered now the utter freshness of the grass, the clarity of the water. His father was sketching a plant, a drawing board on his knees. His fine tailcoat was all bunched beneath him, grass-stained. William had run to him: what had he been then, five or six? Run down the long slope to the river and tried to hide under his father's arm.

"What is it?" his father had said.

"Her."

"And who is that?"

A silence, while William had kicked stones into the river, scuffing his shoes. "Nobody."

Patiently, his father had put down the pencil. "Come with me," he had said. "Back to the house." William had refused to get up. "What is it?" his father had asked. "Is it Kemble?"

The hated nursemaid. William had begun to cry. His father had pulled him to his feet and put his hand, elaborately and firmly, in his, interlacing their fingers. "It is not obedience, William," he had told him, "that necessarily matters. It is courage."

Courage, not obedience.

Courage. Oh, Christ.

He wished the old man back now—wished it with all his heart. His father had died when he was sixteen, his mother when he was twenty-six. They had been a doting, quiet couple. It was hard to believe that they sprang from the Beckforth stock, that rapacious family who had once ruled their West Indian island and taken everything it could yield: sugar, slaves, taxes, power. William's grandfather had given Rutherford to his son because he was ashamed that the boy had been more interested in plants and flowers and Egyptian cats than living in London and being at Court. William's father had been put here, exiled here, in fact, to prevent the rest of the Beckforths laughing him out of society. It had been a shock when William's uncle had died suddenly and his father came into the title. But still, the old man had cared not at all for London: he had liked his Yorkshire exile, had grown to love it. He was interested in the farms and the gardens; he had built the great glasshouse and the orangerie. Had a dozen dogs, a stable of horses, even a racehorse that ran at York. He had been a kind, benevolent person. Never cheated a soul.

Never cheated a soul. William slumped on the

nearest chair and put his head in his hands.

When he wanted to be with his father now, more often than not he went to the archive and held his father's precious amulets and stones and trembled at them, if the truth were known—and it was hardly a truth he could tell anyone, even Octavia—that he actually trembled with passion to hold what his father had loved. He had gone in there the day he had buried William Cavendish, 7th Earl Rutherford, and flung himself down in his father's Egyptian chair and felt so utterly alone. Frightened at the responsibility of being the eighth earl, and what he was supposed to achieve from that day forward.

"Father," he murmured. "Father, for Christ's sake, tell me what to do."

The afternoon wore on; the tree was hauled out beyond the kitchen garden; the light faded. As the last drops of daylight were drained from the sky, the lamps in Rutherford were lit. All was silence in the snow-filled parkland, but downstairs in the house, the atmosphere was electric.

Emily was facing Mrs. Jocelyn in the house-keeper's sitting room.

"What on earth were you thinking of?" the older woman demanded.

"I couldn't help it," Emily replied. "She spoke to me."

"*She?*" the housekeeper repeated. "*She?*"

31

"Lady Cavendish, ma'am."

"And what were you doing in Lady Cavendish's way?"

"If you please, ma'am, she was in my way."

"I beg your pardon?"

Emily faltered. "Not so much in my way. I mean, she was on the stairs as I came out of the drawing room. She was standing—Lady Cavendish, I mean—was standing on the stairs and she walked to the door and she asked if it was unlocked. And then she said she wanted tea and I was to tell Miss Amelie. And then . . . then she said about the tree."

Mrs. Jocelyn stared at her. "And you go to Mr. Bradfield." It was said with complete disdain.

"No, ma'am," Emily objected. "I was coming to tell you. . . . I was coming to tell Cook. . . . I was in the corridor, and Mr. Bradfield—"

Mrs. Jocelyn put up her hand to stop Emily's flow of words. She sat in the upholstered armchair in front of her coal fire and regarded Emily for some time. "And now you'll tell me what's the matter with you."

The blood ran cold in Emily's veins. "Nothing, ma'am."

The older woman looked her up and down. "You've put on weight."

Emily said nothing.

"Come here."

She took a step or two forward hesitantly, and the housekeeper grabbed her by the wrist and

32

pulled her to the arm of the chair. Looking into her face, she put her hand on Emily's stomach. "Do you think I don't know what ails you?" she asked.

"I am all right."

"Who is to blame? Besides you, Emily."

"I am all right," the girl repeated.

"Jack Armitage, is it? One of the farm boys?"

Emily felt herself swaying. "It's no one," she said.

Mrs. Jocelyn sighed. "Of all the girls, I would have thought you had more sense," she complained. "I shall find it out. I shall find the culprit." She pulled Emily even closer. "What are you?" she asked, not unkindly. "Four months? Five?" She squinted at her suspiciously. "More?"

"It is not that," Emily said.

"Don't lie to me, child."

"It is not that. I've been feeling sickly. I've been eating too much."

"You?" Mrs. Jocelyn snorted derisively. "You eat nothing," she said. "Your arms . . . your hands. Look at them; you are nothing but skin and bone. You've been starving yourself so that it doesn't show. You think I don't know? What do you suppose I have for eyes? Don't you think I've seen it before?"

Emily closed her eyes. "Not Jack," she whispered. "Not anyone."

The housekeeper abruptly let her hand fall. In the fire grate, the coal hissed. "Emily Maitland," she said. "This is a God-fearing house, and God shall certainly strike you dead for your lies."

The house was feverishly busy belowstairs that night. By tradition on Christmas Eve, a table was laid in the great hall and not the dining room. A twenty-foot tree, brought from the estate, dominated one end of the hall—the Tudor fireplace, blazing with logs, the other. All the family were now home; the children Harry, Charlotte and Louisa had come downstairs first, the girls in a flurry of loose, gauzy gowns, and Harry in a new dinner suit that had been delivered just that week from London. Their voices and laughter had filtered through the house. Sixteen guests were now occupying nine of the guest rooms.

Every member of staff, aside from the master's valet and the mistress's maid, was working below. The cook, undercook, kitchen maid and scullery maid, helped by the housemaid of all work, were elbow-deep in entrées, releve, game course, entremets, all of it providing a smoky cloud of condensation as soups, fish, cutlets, meat and duck were passed from the huge black-leaded ranges to table to serving dish. The butler, first footman and two second footmen were marshaling the setting of the table and the serving of food.

For a while, the three chambermaids had had breathing space, a light meal with the rest of the servants at half past five; then the two parlor maids had been summoned to help Amelie with the ladies' dressing. Helene de Montfort had her own maid, a little Parisian girl who spoke no English, and Ida Stanningfield employed a girl who was competent and unfussy, but the others needed help with their hair and gowns. As soon as the guests came down to dinner, the three chambermaids went back to the bedrooms, putting away clothes, turning down the beds, warming them, restocking the fires, closing the curtains and shutters, replenishing the water jugs, straightening the chairs.

Emily was coming down the back stair, exhausted, when the first footman, Harrison, caught her. She wanted to avoid him, because he had tried to catch her once in the yard, tried to press his face against hers and find her mouth with his lips. He had smelled of the beer he used to pinch from Bradfield's pantry when the butler's back was turned. She had a feeling he would try to find her again tonight, when the footmen were allowed a glass of brandy to toast Christmas at midnight.

"Hello, Maitland," he said. "On your own?"

She tried to edge past him.

"Go and find March," he said.

"What?"

"Don't answer back."

"Mr. March?" she repeated. "But I'm not allowed out."

"I'm passing on a message from Mr. Bradfield."

"But he'll be in the gardener's house."

Harrison sighed. "State the obvious, won't you?" he said. "Tell him Lady Cavendish wants gardenias brought in from the glasshouse."

"In the middle of dinner?"

"After dinner, you dolt."

"But I've got to take up more water to the rooms."

"Better get a move on then, hadn't you?" At last, he grinned at her. "Don't want to disappoint, eh? Her ladyship wants to show off her prize fucking gardenias."

She pulled back as if he'd struck her. But he passed on, smiling at his own prohibited obscenity, and then adjusting his expression to one of blandness as he rounded the corner to the kitchen. In just a moment, he reappeared with Nash at his side, both of them carrying silver trays in whose polished, domed lids she caught sight of herself standing in the corridor—a patch of white apron, a glimpse of pale face. "Get off with you," Harrison ordered. He nodded in the direction of the boot room. "Take an overcoat. Look sharp."

She ran. With one of the men's coats over her shoulders she went out the back door and across the yard, slipping every other step. At the end of the yard was a gate in the wall; it opened into a corner of the kitchen garden, and to the left, in another wall, was a door to the rose terrace. There was barely any light at all here: the kitchen garden was a huge walled area some hundred yards square, bordered on one side by the glasshouse that had been built by the seventh earl forty years before. Here, the gardeners labored to produce the fashion of the moment: pineapples, melons, and strawberries ahead of the season. There were almond and apricot trees and, at the far end, palms and ferns. There was a passion for ferns just now; it was supposed to be a ladies' pastime. Still running, her shoes now wet from the snow that had settled on the swept paths, Emily arrived at the glasshouse door and pushed it open. The quickest way to the gardener's house was through here.

Once inside, she stopped, halted momentarily by the change in temperature. Despite the snow, the atmosphere was clammy; water was dripping somewhere over her head. She looked up and saw condensation in a sheet of opaque droplets over the closed windows of the roof. Running at waist height around the outside walls, hot-water pipes periodically gave off cracks of expansion or contraction. Here and there along the green avenue of plants there were seats. She had once seen Charlotte and Louisa one spring day here as she had passed outside, hurrying on some errand or other; she remembered looking through the glass and seeing how lovely they had looked, reading together while sunshine filtered down through the glass and scattered shadows and light on their white dresses. Their little terrier, Max, had been curled by their feet, fast asleep. She remembered gazing at them as if they had been spirits from another world: so pretty, so careless, so fortunate.

She started along the glasshouse path now. Perhaps she might see gardenias; perhaps, for speed, she ought to carry some back without disturbing March. What did gardenias look like? she wondered. They were the ones that smelled very nice; were they with the orchids? She stopped at a display of flowers with their pots well insulated against the slightest breeze; she looked at their curious little faces. Pretty things, as pretty as the daughters of the house, and seemingly as fragile. She reached out her own hand to touch one, and saw how reddened the skin of her hand was against the petal.

She didn't belong here. She ought not to have come; what had she been thinking? She was suddenly convinced that the butler had not sent her at all, that it was Harrison's joke at her expense. If she touched a flower, even a single bloom, she would be reprimanded; she would be reprimanded anyway for leaving the house. Mr. March would rage if she dared to disturb him. It was all a mistake, a stupid mistake. Even now they might be calling for her, looking for her, and what could she tell them? That she had been to pick flowers on some fantastical errand for which she was wholly unsuited?

She turned, and suddenly saw him standing in the shadows by the door. He had been watching her; now he walked forward.

"It is a joke," she said.

"A ruse, yes," he replied. "Even if I had to employ Harrison."

"I shall be in trouble."

"No, no," he murmured. "No, no." He put his arms around her, looking intently into her face. "Dear little girl," he said.

She tried to pull away. "I am not a girl," she told him. "You have seen to that."

He kissed her. She allowed it. She wanted to be loved for a moment; she wanted to be seen in the way that he saw her. She wanted to come into focus for someone, to have a name—*Emily, Emily*—in the way he was whispering it now. She wanted to be comforted, at least; that alone was almost worth all the rest. Just comforted and kept warm. She would have lain down with the flowers in here and been packed tight against the cold, gladly.

"You are my dear girl still," he was whispering.

She tried to pull away, holding her hands against his shoulders. "But I'm not," she said. "Don't you see? I don't belong to you."

He was smiling as if he hadn't heard her. Out of his pocket, he pulled a little package: it was a midnight blue box.

"What's this?" she asked.

"It's Christmas," he said. "I've brought you a present."

She held the box in her hand and looked directly at him. "What is it?"

"Open it and see."

"I must get back."

"At least see what I've brought you." She opened the velvet-covered lid. Inside was a thin gold chain, and each link of the chain was shaped like a heart. "Do you like it?"

She shut the box and held it out to him. "I can't keep this."

He closed his hand over hers. "It shall be our secret."

"But don't you understand? When could I wear it? The girls would see it. What would I say?"

"Say it's been left to you by a fond aunt."

She looked at him, shook her head. "Perhaps in your world," she said. "Not in mine."

He laughed. "Darling, you *are* my world. Take it, do."

She stood trembling; the air was too thick for her to breathe. "I must go away," she told him.

"What on earth do you mean?"

"I shall have to leave. I must go home," she said.

He put his head to one side, frowning. "Is someone ill?" he asked. "Is it your mother?"

"No," she said. "Not Mother."

And her mother's face was suddenly conjured

up. She knew exactly what her mother would say when she went home. *We shan't be able to be seen in church.* The church was everything; it was what had kept the family together when her father had died. It was the church that made sure they had parish relief. It was the church that gave them food. Nothing was more important, nothing, nothing, nothing, than her mother scrubbing the church steps and sweeping out the rooms of the vicarage and sending her children to the new Sunday School, and keeping them clean. Everything had to be clean. The step on the door of their tiny house in a dirty little street. Because it belonged to the church. Because they had to set an example. She and her two brothers and two sisters must go to the church school, eat the church food, clean the church brasses and pews, and arrange their faces to be good children, quiet children. Clean and respectable, their hands clasped in prayer in the back pews, brainwashed to remember whole passages from the Bible. To respect their elders and betters, the churchwardens who kept them from disaster. They were fortunate, her mother always said, to have been saved by kindness when their father died, drowning in the fluid that had filled his lungs. And so very fortunate—so very fortunate—to have been introduced to Mrs. Jocelyn, who was willing to take Emily on because she too was a servant of the church, a regular worshiper when she visited her

41

sister in the town, who had noticed Emily as a good, willing girl.

She had once told him all this. It had been last summer. The phrase had amused him completely. "A willing girl." He had drawn her close, to her astonishment and horror.

"Is there something I can do?" he asked.

She looked down at the box. "Perhaps you might look after me," she whispered.

"Look after you?" he echoed.

"If I were ill."

"But of course," he said, smiling. "And are you?"

She couldn't say the words. They were there in her mouth, but she couldn't repeat them. "If I . . ." But they wouldn't come.

"But you're not going to be ill, Emily," he said. "Not like your father. Not now that you live here." He kissed her again, looked behind him. "I think you ought to go," he admitted. "Bradfield and Jocelyn and all that."

She gazed into his eyes; he put the box into her hand. "I suppose," he said, "that I should get you into awful trouble if this went on."

"Went on?" she repeated.

He made a rueful face. "I mean, if it became . . ." He stopped. "You've been such a wonderful girl, really, Emily."

He began to walk away, got halfway down the path, and then glanced back at her, where she was standing like a statue beside the orchids. With a gesture of helplessness, he spread his arms. "Awfully pretty," he said. "Do try to wear it, if you can."

As he went away, and the door of the glass-house closed behind him, she looked down at the box, but she saw nothing.

Nothing at all.

The gentlemen had joined the ladies in the drawing room; it was almost midnight.

Octavia sat with her two daughters, Louisa fondly holding her mother's hand. Charlotte—at fifteen, this was the first time she had been allowed to join the Christmas Eve dinner—perched rigidly as if to keep herself focused and awake, a sign that she was completely bored. All three were listening to Harry tell some endless story about Blériot.

"I should love to do it; wouldn't you?"

"But, Harry, flying? It seems so dangerous and pointless."

"Pointless!" he exclaimed. "Mother, it's the most wonderful thing."

"But simply to drift about, like the ballooning people do . . ." Louisa said.

"It's not drifting about," Harry answered scathingly. "Don't you remember Beaumont two years ago?"

"I remember you going to Harrogate and getting

crushed by a great horde of idiots," William interposed.

"He flew round Britain and got ten thousand pounds," Harry retorted. "I think it was ripping."

"I heard that the Bellingtons woke up one morning in Dorking and one was stuck in their trees," Louisa said. "I mean, it was just hanging there."

"What was?" Harry said, frowning.

"The balloon. They called out to the people in it and they said they were going to Dover. Can you imagine?" Louisa dissolved into one of her peals of laughter. "It's hardly . . . well, *dignified.*"

"Do you ever concentrate on any topic of conversation for more than ten seconds?" Harry said.

"Harry," Octavia interjected. "Enough, darling."

"It's simply a fad," William opined.

"But they are sending letters by air now, aren't they?" Edward Stanningfield asked. "Very efficiently, too."

"The practical applications will be limited," William replied.

"Beaumont won three races," Harry said. "Paris to Rome, Circuit d'Europe . . ."

"And his colleague was killed," William answered. "And two others were blown up by their own gasoline tanks."

"Oh, William, no," Octavia murmured. "It's Christmas Eve, after all."

"Well," Harry said, "I shall learn how to do it."

"If I approve it," William replied. "And I am not likely to do that. There's more than enough to occupy you on the ground."

Father and son stared at each other; Louisa stroked Harry's knee as William lit his cigar.

Octavia tapped Charlotte on the arm. "Play the piano, darling," she murmured. "The sight of Harry smoldering is quite off-putting."

"I don't know what's got into that boy," William muttered as he took Louisa's place next to her.

"Youth," Octavia replied. "Just that, William. Youth."

Helene was standing in front of the French mirror that had been brought from Paris; she was engaging Alexander Kent in what seemed to be a lengthy conversation. Elizabeth Kent was eyeing her coldly from the nearest sofa. Helene wore a fabulous blue gown, remodeled, she had told Mrs. Stanningfield at dinner, from a ball gown she had worn in 1890. "I am awfully circumspect with money," she had said, laughing lightly. "Paris is so expensive."

Ida Stanningfield had been complimentary. "It's very pretty—the figuring . . ."

"It's the Bluebird satin. I had various things made. My own design."

"Bluebird?" asked the older woman. Octavia could see that Ida was struggling with the vision of Helene, trying to discern whether any of Helene's racy reputation still clung to her after all these years. Helene had once been scandalous, but only she and William knew quite how scandalous. Now, if you looked at her, one would be hard-pressed to believe it; Octavia, rather guiltily and entirely privately, always thought that Helene, decked out in her finery, looked suspiciously like a man in a frock. She had a very defined way of walking and standing; it overwhelmed one. She wished Helene would not look at William as if they shared some deliciously private joke; she thought that almost certainly Helene did it to score some obtuse point, but even now, after all this time, Octavia could not guess what that private point might be.

Looking at her objectively across the heavily laden table, the artfully arranged fountains of flowers, Octavia had thought that one had to give Helene her due, nevertheless: although admittedly rather outré, she was nevertheless gracious. Too modest to expound on her heritage, Octavia had leaned helpfully forward.

"The Bluebird plantation in Jamaica," she explained to Ida, "was William's great-grandfather's."

"Oh, I knew that," Ida rallied. "And so, the satin . . . How clever."

Octavia smiled at her. She was fond of Ida and Edward; second-generation cotton from Manchester, they might usually have been declined a place at any titled table, but her insistence had prevailed over William's obstinacy. Edward Stanningfield couldn't hook a fish in a barrel, William had declared; he was a rotten shot; his voice was too loud. As a wife, Ida was too . . . But there, William's opinion had faltered. "Ida is too jolly?" Octavia had said, with one raised eyebrow.

The fact was that the Stanningfields were trade, their immense wealth coming from Manchester cotton, and not Yorkshire wool, like her own fortune. But they were generous people; they had even built decent cottages for their workers. They had taken an interest in Octavia as soon as they had learned, twenty-seven years ago, that she had lost her father; word had traveled fast in the industry, and Edward Stanningfield had kept an eye on the management of Octavia's own mills from a discreet distance.

They were quite a contrast, she had to admit, to the other guests: the pale, ascetic-looking Lord Dalling, Humphrey Villiers, and his new wife; the Kents—of extreme poverty and enormous pedigree—who owned prime grouse moors farther north; the pretty little Gardiners, newly wed, and the Gardiner parents, all of them neighbors to the Cavendishes' London house. It was a happy party, everyone determined to be decent company; everyone sweetly complimentary of the tree, the candles, the food, the wine, the astonishing hall with its towering Gothic roof, the soft and sumptuous drawing room dominated by the Parisian glass.

At which Helene now was smugly displaying herself.

The Gardiners were discussing the coming London Season; it was the year that Louisa would be presented at Court.

"When will you go down to the London house?" Octavia was asked.

"Oh—March, I should think. Before Easter, to arrange the fittings for Louisa's dresses."

The women smiled at one another, exchanging sympathetic shrugs at this draining and expensive exercise. Gertrude Gardiner patted Octavia's knee. "Louisa can't fail to be a wonderful success," she reassured her. "And is this man Gould coming up to Rutherford later in the year?"

"What man is that?" Octavia asked.

Gertrude waved her hand. "Oh, he's been to us all, my dear. Rather dashing, you know, terribly American. He's writing some sort of book about old families." She sighed reflectively. "Good company, I suppose, but a dilettante, if you want my opinion, rattling around Europe to no obvious purpose."

Octavia smiled, recalling now. "I think William mentioned someone. The Goulds are bankers or some such, aren't they?"

Gertrude sniffed. "Trade, dearest." She glanced

at the Stanningfields, immediately realizing her faux pas. "But awfully sweet, they say. The man is . . . *quite* distracting."

Octavia lowered her voice. "Henrietta de Ray told me . . ." She glanced across at William to make sure that he could not hear. "That he's rather . . ."

Gertrude laughed softly. "Oh, he is *rather*," she replied. "You had best keep Louisa out of his way if you don't want her spirited away to New York."

The fire was drawing down; Octavia, aware that Bradfield and the footman, Harrison, had been standing for at least five hours since dinner, now nodded to William to let them go. "I think it's time to go up, darling," she murmured. "Don't you?"

The company rose, the ladies retrieving their shawls and bags. Octavia noticed how the newlyweds almost raced to the door; it was so sweet. The parents held back, Alicia Gardiner intrigued by the series of tiny framed sketches by the door.

"They were for sale in Bond Street the last time we were down," William explained. "Not my cup of tea, you know, but Octavia liked them."

"Just little portraits," Octavia said. "Lautrec."

"What is he, a painter?" Villiers asked.

"French painter of some sort," William replied, as Bradfield opened the door.

Octavia looked at Villiers's wife, a plain woman

who seemed to possess considerably more common sense than was usual in an aristocrat, and they exchanged complicit smiles.

One could feel the cold in the hall; even in an hour the temperature seemed to have fallen dramatically.

Allowing her guests to go ahead of her, Octavia paused for a moment on the stairs while Ida Stanningfield stopped to consider Octavia's Singer Sargent portrait; then she watched them go to the left along the gallery. There was a hush of doors closing to the guest rooms; along the landing, the lights were all turned down.

Octavia looked up at the huge window; it was three stories high, and the panels of glass at each side had been replaced by William's father with stained glass of vines and trees. The tracery was a very delicate color, but now the reflection from the snow shone faintly through it, framing the view of the drive and the parkland sloping away to the river.

As Octavia stood silently in the half darkness, she heard a movement below. She looked down and for a moment could see nothing, and then William emerged from the drawing room, glancing over his shoulder. He had gone back for something; she was about to call out to him. He stopped, looking at his feet. Bradfield came out of the room; the two men spoke. And then Bradfield walked away, turning to take the green baize door close to the stairs.

There was only the glow of the dying fire in the hall now; traces of its color flickered on the high stone walls. There was a murmur, a flash of blue in the doorway. Helene came out; she said something in what seemed like an urgent voice. William made a motion with his hands. The same kind of motion that he had made when denying Harry his ambitions: one flat, rigid palm facing the floor.

Octavia saw Helene grip William's arm; their heads were together. And she heard him say something. It might have been, "I shall not. I will not." The last word echoed a little, full of tension. Something shifted in Octavia's chest, a sort of low thrill of horror, of distant recognition, like the replaying of the long-ago dream of destruction.

And then Helene kissed her husband. She pressed herself against William and put her lips to his lingeringly. Octavia saw him take a step back, and then another. But, when he stopped, his arms went around her.

She turned away.

She turned away and closed her eyes. And then she picked up the fabric of her dress and tried to walk upstairs. Somehow, as she hurried, she tangled herself in the material of the several underskirts. She stumbled against the ledge of the window, put her hand out and inadvertently touched the glass.

All she could think of was that it was bone-deep icy cold, and an inch away beyond the glass was an ocean of white, and that the house was adrift in that white-cold sea where there was a scar of the cut-down tree and the long dark line of the drive. . . .

And someone walking.

Octavia leaned closer to the glass.

Out there, alone in the snow, alone in the dark, Emily Maitland was walking towards the river.

Chapter 2

*H*arry lay on his bed and stared at the ceiling. Just lately he could never get to sleep here. In Oxford, it wasn't so bad: he was inconspicuous among the rows of little rooms. He rarely went to lectures; his tutor told him that he was a Beckforth as if he would never amount to anything, which made him laugh once out of the man's sight. It was true, he supposed, for six generations of Beckforths had gone to Oxford and six had come back without an ounce of worthwhile knowledge: their wits had kept them alive and wealthy, their cunning and cruelty—not an education. And sometimes sheer laziness. Sometimes one of the generations had just lain about like hogs wallowing in their own sloth and terribly pleased with themselves, bleeding the local people dry and wasting a fortune here and there on Court intrigue and women. He didn't see why he needed an education at all; it wasn't as if he was ever going to be allowed to use it.

He flung his arms wide on the bed, still in his clothes. He had not wanted Harrison or Hardy or Nash to attend to him. Let them fuss over his father or the guests; he couldn't stand their silent, obsequious presence. God, he was stifled. He truly felt as if the air were being squeezed out of him.

For a moment, he wished for his Oxford room and the little fire where he made toast and sat smoking one cigarette after another; then he thought of the calling to dinners, the falsetto voices of the choir in chapel, and cringed.

Everything was too old. He thought that was the heart of his irritation: Oxford certainly, but Rutherford too, lying like some indolent pretty beast in the valley, too ancient and too delicate with its turrets and towers. He wanted something plain and square. A house like Armitage's: small, plain and squat, next to the stables. He stared at the dim ceiling and wondered how the Armitages would celebrate Christmas; he would bet that it was very jolly and nice. He would give anything not to endure Christmas luncheon and dinner in his own house; his father thought it wise to corner him at every opportunity, to bring him into the library and lecture him about the tenants and the accounts. William had told him that he would take him to Blessington to look at the mills in the New Year. It was a ritual that William Cavendish performed—pointlessly, Harry thought—every six months: meetings with the mill manager. His father said that it was their duty to see where some of their income came from, and to appear at least to have an interest in it.

Harry supposed that Blessington actually had a reality about it, some sense of urgency, even if it seemed the mills' primary purpose was to kill off the population as quickly as possible. On one hand, he admired the places that had been the source of his mother's fortune; he liked the perpetual deafening noise of industry, the speed, the production of something, even if it were literally woven through with the sweaty imprint of hands and the air choked with wool fiber; but on the other, he despised himself for standing looking at the rolling, shunting looms in his silk-lapeled suit. He hated the way the women looked at him, sidelong, as if he were another species. At the end of the day they went out in their crowds, arm in arm, under the street lamps, down the dirty sloping streets, while the siren wailed. The day was rigid in its shifts of hours; each person knew his place, had his or her name on the greasy slotting-in cards on the timing clock by the thumping double doors. He wasn't of their world; he wasn't one of the faces slipping away in great dry-eyed coughing drifts of humanity. He couldn't ever be anonymous. He was the owner's son or the seventh-generation Beckforth from some second or third wife two hundred years ago, carrying a cousin's name. He had duties; he had a place. But he had nothing to do.

He got up and went to the window. When he was younger he used to go up on the roof and look out over the grounds and the hills, like a little god of privilege sitting among the Tudor chimneys, watching the harvest teams in the fields slowly turning crop to stubble, the carts swaying, the horses merely oblong blocks of color far below. There would be moments of freedom in the exalted open air. Now he never went there. He felt like the whole of his existence was dragging him down.

God, if only they would let him go. If only his father, not to put too fine a point on it, would let him go. Things were happening in the world: not just the aeroplanes, but automobiles. He would like to travel, see something of humanity. If only he could be let off this leash. One of the fellows at the university had said that he was going to America, and Harry's own ancestors had routinely taken the grand tour. In fact, a great-uncle eighty years ago had been notorious for traveling around Europe, going to France and Portugal with choirboys, building up a giant collection of erotica. No one had stopped him; his mother had even encouraged it. His letters had been published; Harry had read them in the university library, and discovered a man of doubtful associations and extraordinary taste—but he had been allowed to do it, which was the point. He'd taken off with his little scandalous retinue, and bought up culture by the ton. His name had been synonymous with everything hateful, and it was no use his own father rolling his eyes and pretending that it was nothing to do with their family, for it was. Harry let out a giant sigh. His life was peppered with such injustices. Suffocation appeared to be his due, his lot. It made him thoroughly sick.

He had only to look at his father's study and the archive to see how much gadding about his own grandfather had undertaken. And yet all his father wanted him to do was sit in Oxford to no discernible purpose, and hang about London during the Season—as if that weren't hell on earth, with all its gaudy finery and old dames prodding one with the tips of their umbrellas and saying what a fine young man one might be. God save him. He should like to see America; he should like never again to wear some stiff collar and stand about in society feeling an utter idiot, with mothers ogling him in the cause of their marriageable daughters.

The only thing that had made him truly alive in the past year was her. He would never have thought to let her go if the chaps at Oxford had not warned him against her: against getting too far involved, against what she might become. It had been their idea to give her the gold chain, although it broke him almost completely to see the terrible dismay in her face as she held the box. It had cost him dearly to walk away.

All last summer had been like a waking dream. The heat had brought the staff out, after lunch and before supper, to stand where they thought no one could see them: in the shade of the yard, letting the cold water of the pump run over their hands. He had crept up to her room one afternoon when he knew she wouldn't be there, and found her underclothes in the scratched chest of drawers. He had held them to his face while he leaned from the window and saw the edge of her shoulder in the yard, the curve of her face, her hands smoothing the cold water over her hair, taking off her cap. Just a blur of hand, cheek, neck while he buried his face in her clothes, and at the same time was terrified that someone would come up the stairs and find him there.

It had been the hottest summer for years: there had been a drought through June, July and August. The river had run down to a trickle, a thing that was almost unheard-of in the Dales. He had been there that Sunday when she came back from her mother's. It was a twelve-mile walk: she had forbidden him to come with her, even part of the way.

"Someone might see," she had said.

"Who is there to see?" he'd demanded.

All he could think of was getting her down in the soft rolling turf, in one of the many hollows on the moor side, down among gorse and heather and grass. She'd denied him; he kicked the day away walking around in the parkland.

But she had come back. The path dropped from the hill and down through the trees, and there was shelter in among the shrubs by the side of the river for half a mile. He had waited for her there. Even then, at five o'clock, it had been stiflingly hot.

"Don't you know you're my life?" he had asked her. He had absolutely meant it at the time. She filled his mind, obsessed him. She had been carrying a little bag of cakes that her mother had made; he could smell the cinnamon on them. Even now the smell of cinnamon filled him with guilt and a kind of blind crawling need. She hadn't replied. She had tried to get away. "Won't you love me?" he'd asked. "Not at all, Emily?" His hand on her waist, her throat. Finally she had kissed him, and they had dropped to their knees in the shade of the trees.

Far away now, down in the house, he thought he heard doors closing. He listened: feet in the hallway, and then the muffled slam of the green baize door. Perhaps they had been putting out the fires in the downstairs rooms? He glanced out at the snow, and saw lights far down in the park; pushing open his window, he was met with an icy blast of air. Voices muffled by the snow could be faintly heard, the lights dipping and disappearing, dipping and disappearing. Someone was running out there in the dark.

Amelie was waiting for Octavia as she reached the yellow-and-white room. She stood by the dressing room and allowed the maid to unlace the gown and take off her shoes and stockings. She stepped out of the petticoats, sat down on the chair, and let the girl's deft hands unroll her

59

hair, putting the padding in the satin-lined box, unpinning it and letting it fall past her shoulders. Not a word was said; in the deep recesses of the room, over the slow-burning fire, the mantelpiece clock chimed the quarter hour.

It was Christmas Day.

Octavia sat there and stared at herself in the mirror.

She was thirty-nine years old this spring. She was twelve years younger than Helene de Montfort. She had expected rage, but felt only embarrassment—that, and disappointment. For all Helene's reputation—and Octavia had learned, early on, the story of the elderly patron with his wonderful house at Bergerac, and later the accounts, related to Octavia second- or thirdhand over some hostess's tea table, of Helene's having been seen in the company of Jules Cheret, even that she had been the model in the Olympia posters—Octavia had always assumed that Helene was far fonder of seeming to be outrageous than actually capable of being so. She was, by her own admission, craving of the right company, and she could not have been accepted as well as she was if all the rumors had been true. Helene was a tease—that was certain; she enjoyed shocking people. But as for whether she had a heart that could be won or broken—whether she was capable of some grand passion—that was another matter.

Octavia remembered one spring afternoon years

ago when she and William had been in Paris for the Exposition when it had first opened in April 1900. They had taken afternoon tea at the Ceylon Pavilion—it was the place to be seen. They had met Helene there by arrangement, and she had made such an entrance, resplendent in a painted chiffon dress and wearing the most enormous hat. Octavia had felt quite the frump: an obviously English frump in an ocean of French fashion. Helene had talked that afternoon of the latest painters—of Maxim's and the Moulin Rouge—as if she knew them, was one of their intimates, and Octavia remembered William almost brushing away her accounts. "So much silliness," he had said afterwards.

"You don't think Helene is rather superb?" she had asked him as they dressed for dinner. They had still been close then, friends; they talked together.

"Not at all," he had replied. "She merely thinks she is superb. That is something quite different."

Had he meant it, or was it a smoke screen? Had they been lovers then, these Beckforth descendants, sharing the same subtle faults, the same selfishness? Octavia lowered her eyes from her own reflection. She was still, despite the thirty-nine years, naïve, she told herself. Society was awash with *affaires de coeur*; it was an unspoken accommodation. She had heard the gossip, especially in town, of Lady So-and-So with her younger lover, and Lord So-and-So parading not one, but two mistresses in public. When the old King had been alive, it was all the rage: country house parties had begun to have cards attached to the doors saying who slept within, so that lovers could find the appropriate room under the very noses of their husbands or wives. It was even said that at some houses, a bell was rung at six a.m. to allow the guests to return to their own bedrooms before the maids found them in the arms of their lovers. She and William had even seen it themselves. But they had never indulged. As far as she knew.

Amelie began to brush Octavia's hair. Well, in this perhaps she had been as naïve as always. Was naïveté something that one might scrub from one's soul? If so, she ought to find the precise way of achieving it, for it seemed to have blinded her. She wondered how many of her friends had seen Helene take William's hand when her own back had been turned at some gathering or other. Had that happened? Had she been utterly fooled? Had he met Helene in London? He was often away; he would pay the usual afternoon visits in London. Had Helene been waiting for him somewhere, in some friend's house? Surely they had not sunk to a hotel; and yet, without a hotel, which friend had turned a blind eye; which women knew among their endless train of acquaintances?

Octavia took a breath. Now her imagination was

running away with her. She must not allow it. After all, what exactly had she seen? Helene demanding a kiss, William responding to it. It might have been only a moment; she had not stayed to see where it ended. Perhaps he had pushed her away; perhaps Helene had meant it as some sort of joke; it was exactly her kind of teasing humor. And what had he said to her? "I will not," or, "I cannot," or some such thing; he had been in the very act of denying Helene when she had pressed her face to his.

"Is there anything else, ma'am?" Amelie asked.

"No, nothing," Octavia murmured.

Amelie was gone in a moment or two, but still Octavia stayed seated by the mirror. She ran over those moments on the stair again: the sight of Helene and William, and her own turning away towards the window. She had been sure that she had seen the maid that she had spoken to that morning walking out there in the snow, and yet when she had unwound the skirts that had tripped her, and looked again, there had been nothing. The shadow of the trees, and that was all. She rested her head on her hand on the elaborate dressing table; she really ought to go to bed.

There would be the usual Christmas gathering from the area tomorrow: it was a tradition that the house gave presents not only to the servants but to the estate workers, which encompassed the entire village. She doubted that, even in the deepest of snows, the locals would forgo their dinner laid out in the tithe barn and the theatricals that followed. Mrs. Jocelyn would be at her door before break-fast. She got to her feet.

It was pitch-black by the river, and the noise of the current was loud. There had been so much sleet and rain before the snow that the Wastleet was carrying far more water than usual.

Looking back at his father, Jack Armitage could see the older man running through the six or seven inches of snow, the lantern held high above his head, following the mark of her footprints. Far behind him, the lights of Rutherford were almost all out.

"Over here!" Jack shouted. "Here!" He could quite clearly see where she had gone; it was unmistakably towards the water. The bank was steep, and there was a great gouge in the mud, as if she had slipped. "Emily!" he yelled.

His father was next to him now, breathing hard. "Where is she?"

"I can't see."

They both held up their lights. Two circles of yellow appeared on the black and foaming water. Bitter cold rose from the river, an icy mist.

"She's gone here, don't you reckon?" Jack asked, pointing out the bank side.

"Scrambled down, or fell," Josiah agreed. Jack could see that his father was shivering; the wind

64

had picked up. Snow granules blew into their faces. "That bitch. That woman."

"Mary Richards says there was never a word. She sat in the corridor and was told to go to bed."

"And that bitch Jocelyn never harping on at her? Nay, don't credit it. She's drove her to this."

Jack stared at him. "What was it?" he asked, guessing at the answer. "Not him?"

"I told thee," Josiah muttered. "I told thee what would be." He screwed up his eyes against the weather. "But that she would do this . . ."

"Happen she went home to her mother," Jack said. "The bridge is a bit farther down."

"With no coat and no hat? You reckon she was making across the hilltop in this?"

The two of them staggered, slipping and sliding, along the bank in the snow. Soon it flattened out a little: they were coming to the bend, the great lazy loop of the Wastleet as it encircled the park. Jack knew that somewhere quite close was a spit of sandy gravel; sometimes in the summer he had come here when he was a boy and played in the shallows. His heart seemed to contort itself in his chest: an odd motion, a kind of strangulation, because he knew that just opposite the gravel, across the twenty yards' width of the river, the water was suddenly deep under the trees; he had been warned against it many a time. He could read the same fear now in his father's face.

"Emily!" he shouted. "Emily!"

His father gripped his arm. There was something there, midstream, in the water; he could hear something now above the noise of the river.

They both saw her together, the noise of the river deafening now; she was standing just at the end of the gravelly shore, up to her knees in the dark, swirling water. The reflections of the lanterns played over her; she looked around at them. He thought she looked as if she had taken leave of her senses: wild, lost, a fragment of a thing. The sound of her crying was drawn out, high-pitched, faint, but she seemed unconscious of it, as if the crying had taken hold of her, as if she were in the grip of it like the horses could sometimes be driven in circles, gnawing at their flanks, kicking their heels as if a devil were on their backs.

"Emily!" he shouted. "Emily, for God's sake!"

She shook her head and looked away, taking a step forward. Jack knew that the gravel bank dropped sharply away; there were large stones for a while, and then the current was strong and fast. "Emily!" he repeated. He stepped down onto the shoreline.

All at once, he heard other voices behind them. He looked and saw Sedburgh, the eldest of the stable boys, coming through the snow. At his back was the unmistakable figure of March. Jack grimaced. March must have seen the lights at the stables; Sedburgh would have blithely told him that a message had come from the house. He would have wanted to know what was going on. Jack watched the old bastard come trudging on, face like thunder.

Jack looked back at Emily. She seemed to be swaying midstream; her hands were outstretched as if to keep her balance.

"What's this?" March yelled.

"Leave the lass; leave the lass," Josiah was saying. "We'll fetch her. Don't be frightening her."

March glared at him. "I have to find out myself, do I?" he demanded. "And never tell me? Is that it? Never tell me?"

"It's none of your business," Josiah replied, and March immediately grabbed his arm, swinging the other man around to face him.

"Staff are my business. You, him"—he indicated Jack with a wave of his hand—"the boys—"

"Not the house," Josiah said, wrestling his hand away.

"It's more mine than yourn!"

"One of the girls come running to the stables," Josiah shouted. "One of the maids, saying they'd looked all over. What do you want me to do, think on it all night? Raise the whole house up? What?"

There was sudden cry from the river.

Emily had lost her footing; she was sinking, arms out at her sides. Her black dress ballooned around her, and to Jack's horror he saw her lean back and the water plucked at her and pulled her down.

He plunged in.

She was only a slip of a lass: her body moved quickly out into the current. Only a slip of a lass; he couldn't shake the thought. He hardly knew her, had seen her about the garden once or twice, carrying a tea tray almost her own size, seen her scurrying, like they all did, head down. Poor little thin, frightened girl. Fury drove him on.

The cold made him gasp. His heart thumped like a drum. He struck out from the shore, thanking God for the stolen hours down here in past summers, knowing where the largest rocks were. Somewhere behind he heard his father shout, but the noise of the water soon swallowed up the sound.

Pushing hard, he came within a few feet of her; the dress was dragging her progress. She didn't struggle; she was staring up into the sky. He made a grab for her, and missed. He tried to reach her hand, but it floated from him. At last, he got hold of the hem of the dress, wound the material around his wrist, and hauled her into him. The water played with them, pulling them from one side to another.

"Emily," he called. "Help me."

She turned her head and stared at him, and her mouth worked a little. He couldn't hear what she was saying. He found her waist and pulled her alongside him, and turned back for the shore, water pouring over his face, down his neck. The current was so fast that he could feel the gravel churned up in it. She was a deadweight, so heavy for a girl so small. For a moment she kicked against him, and then suddenly went limp. And then there were others in the water, up to their waists: Sedburgh, and the second footman, Nash, all gasping, all pulling and dragging, all stumbling. They landed in the shallows, the three men trying to gather up the unconscious girl. And then Jack's father was there, turning up Emily's face, opening her mouth, putting his fingers down her throat. She retched and coughed, then opened her eyes. Jack realized only then, as he helped Nash raise her to her knees, that she was pregnant, the rise of her stomach obvious now through the wet clothes on her pathetically narrow body.

Jack looked up to the bank, and Harry Cavendish was standing there, held back by March.

Jack stood up, water pouring from his clothes. There was a pile of blankets that Nash must have brought, and he went over to them, slipping, staggering, snatched one and gave it to his father. He stood in the falling snow for a moment, staring down at his feet.

And then he climbed the bank, stood up, and crashed his fist into Harry Cavendish's face.

It was still called the tithe barn, although the Church had relinquished the tithe payment fifty years before, and instead of housing hay and farm machinery, the medieval building had been—for a while last year, at least—the place where the Napier had been kept. But the car had its own new garaging now, and the long stone structure with its timber-frame roof comfortably hosted the Christmas celebrations. It looked quite lovely lit by oil lamps and warmed by the big portable oil stoves from the school; the stone of the floor, rubbed smooth by generations of feet, had been covered by matting. Cut holly hung from the walls, and the trestle tables that were used for the harvest supper had been brought in and covered with red paper cloths; down the whole length of them hung Chinese lanterns that they sometimes would light in the summer and hang in the gardens. A tree, not as tall as the one in the house but handsome nevertheless, stood at the top near the door.

William was sitting alongside Octavia and his guests, waiting for the usual theatrical from the village children. There was a nativity play, and the singing of carols: he couldn't help noticing that however prettily the little girls were decked out in their pinafores and large hair bows and polished boots, some of the boys fidgeted and ran their hands around what were obviously paper collars, staining them with the muddy marks of Christmas cake. Octavia murmured with appropriate senti-mentality at the figure of Joseph, hands like hams clutching a shepherd's crook, letting in real shepherds' sons to gaze at the baby Jesus—a porcelain-faced doll with a painted Cupid's-bow mouth and, William saw to his amusement, a few brown ringlets of artificial hair. Occasionally, a child's eyes would dart back to one parent or another, only too aware of the instructions to behave or speak up.

William smiled to himself. "Don't go mithering theladythelord," he had once heard a villager say, cuffing his hapless child, who had stepped out in front of them at York Races. He wondered whether they all saw him like that, a kind of collective noun forever tied to Octavia, *theladythelord.* "Don't mither them." Don't bother them, don't speak to them, don't complain, don't fuss. He looked over them all now; even the lady pianist hammering away at "Hark! The Herald Angels Sing" was occasionally glancing over at him with an expression of trepidation. They saw him as some sort of fixed being, a symbol, a caricature. Octavia too, perhaps, in her great wool-and-velvet shawl with her pretty little straw-colored boots under a cream dress. They were both a sort of monument, he supposed: not real in the same way that the laborers were real, all of them red faced now with their pints of porter in hand, yelling out the hymn. He'd seen the same men sweating as they had hauled in the Christmas tree; caught a group of them once fighting in the fields while the threshing machine poured steam into the summer afternoon; heard them cursing and slipping about on the straw; seen the same men a week later contentedly fishing in the Wastleet. They would look up as he passed, and pull off their caps by way of respect; but he didn't think they saw him as a man like them. He lived at the edge of their highly colored world.

The hymn came to an end; another song began. The children were passing along a garland that they had made: Union flags and hand-drawn animals. Camels and donkeys. Palaces with domes. Pictures of cups of tea and railway engines and soldiers on horseback. He realized that it was an homage to the Empire. In his father's day it had always been said that the sun never set on the British Empire, and a thrilling quarter of the world had been ruled from London. Now he felt that the old world was running out of steam, like a massive engine running down. Australia and Canada were now dominions, not strictly part of the Empire. One day, he felt sure, India itself would pass out of their hands. There was a shift somewhere: he could see it when the men looked at him with their sense of distance. One day, he thought, they might prod him to see whether he was flesh and blood. As Octavia clapped politely, he thought of the same men prodding her too, or the women unraveling that great velvet shawl and weighing it in their hands, as if Octavia were some doll they could stroke and admire and steal from.

He frowned and looked into his lap. This, he thought, was all Helene's fault. Her wry sense of humor, her idle threats, her little caresses and kisses were a form of prodding and wheedling too. She had spoiled the happiness of Christmas for him, made him feel a dolt in his own house, made him feel like a one-dimensional cardboard representation of himself rather than an actual person. That was where this damned feeling had begun. "You are set in your ways," she had whispered last night as he had tried to extricate himself. "I shall prize you out of your comfortable life, William, and see how you like it." All said with her reptilian smile.

He looked up and applauded loudly. He would show himself to be real, a decent host. He got up and made a cheerful speech, and handed out the Christmas gifts: sides of ham, and woolen blankets made at Blessington, and to each family a token to be exchanged for kindling at the farm. He shook hands and was curtsied to and smiled at shyly by the women. The men stuck their chins in the air and took the gifts without deference, because no Yorkshireman took charity. It was understood that the Christmas handouts had been earned. Everyone smiled; more songs were sung; the noise level rose.

William looked across at his daughters clapping and laughing. The dancing would soon start. He would wait while they took two or three turns about the floor, but then they would all retire to the house and allow the village to let down its hair. He smiled at Louisa's profile in particular; she had the light coloring of the Beckforth line, blond haired and fair skinned.

"Don't you think I look like Dorothy Gish?" she had asked, pirouetting about this morning and striking poses from the silent films they had seen.

"Dorothy Gish has dark hair," he'd responded. Of all his children, she was the favorite; she had always been so good-natured, so lighthearted.

She had come up to him and taken his hands. "Why, you *do* know," she'd said, delighted. "And you pretend you don't. But you know Dorothy Gish!" She'd laughed. She was laughing now.

Somewhere in the background, he noticed Helene watching Louisa too. He turned away.

"Where is Harry?" he asked Octavia, as they rose to leave at last.

"He had an early breakfast, I'm told," she replied.

"And went where?"

"I don't know," Octavia admitted.

William sighed as he offered his arm to her.

Mrs. Jocelyn was waiting for them when they reached the house. She stood in the great hall, a statue in black with the chatelaine keys of the kitchens and storerooms about her waist. Octavia raised an eyebrow in surprise.

74

"May I speak with you, ma'am?"

They were taking off their coats. "Is it the dinner?"

Mrs. Jocelyn's eyes flicked briefly to William. He shrugged and walked away to his study. Mrs. Jocelyn watched him go; Octavia walked in the opposite direction, to the morning room, where she went to the window and gazed out at the lake. Mrs. Jocelyn came in behind her and closed the door.

"Well, what is it?"

The older woman actually wrung her hands; Octavia had never seen her betray a moment of anxiety. Her housekeeper's normal attitude was one of rigid, stoical calm. "I am sorry to bother your ladyship with such a thing, but it will be necessary to call the doctor."

"The doctor? For whom?"

"For one of the maids, ma'am."

Octavia turned back from the window. "Why? What is wrong? Who is it?"

"It's Maitland, ma'am. She . . ." The house-keeper blushed. "I thought it best not to bother his lordship."

"And why not?"

"The girl is very ill."

"Good heavens. But surely not enough to call Evans out here on Christmas Day?" And then the image of the girl from the night before came back to her, of Emily Maitland walking through the

75

snow, and vanishing almost as soon as Octavia had noticed her.

"I'm afraid so, ma'am."

"Well, what is it? Influenza?"

Octavia was rather fascinated to see the shade of red that Mrs. Jocelyn blushed: her whole face became suffused. "It's a . . . a woman's matter, ma'am."

"A woman's . . . ? What on earth do you mean?"

"The girl is expecting a child," the housekeeper replied. "That is . . . she's having a child."

"A child?" Octavia walked over to Mrs. Jocelyn. "Maitland?" she asked. "Wasn't that the girl I saw yesterday morning?"

"Yes, ma'am."

"But surely not!"

Mrs. Jocelyn looked her mistress squarely in the eye, summoning up courage. "She took herself to the river last night," she said. "Jack Armitage and Nash and one of the stable boys pulled her out."

"My God . . ." So it *was* the girl. Octavia's heart sank. She had seen her out there after all, and done nothing, told no one.

"She was terribly cold, ma'am. We put her in my own room. She couldn't be warmed, and then . . ." She paused. "She began with the child at two o'clock this morning."

Octavia stared at her. "Do you mean to tell me,"

she said, "that you have had a girl in labor in this house for the past fourteen hours, and you have not informed me of the fact?"

Mrs. Jocelyn had the grace to bite her lip. "I thought it might be over very soon," she replied.

Octavia regarded her levelly. "You thought she might miscarry this child, and you would tell me after the event?" she asked. "Or simply not tell me at all?"

"I thought it best not to say."

"I see." Octavia looked the housekeeper up and down. "This is disgraceful. How could you allow this to happen?"

"She hid it well. She is only six months gone, ma'am."

"Six months? Then the child will surely be dead."

"I think so, ma'am."

Octavia considered. "Who has attended her? Anyone at all?"

"Mrs. March came to see her just now."

"And said what?"

"She thinks it's breech, ma'am."

"Oh, for heaven's sake," Octavia murmured. The gardener's wife had had seven children, but was now in her sixties—hardly a modern-day authority on the subject. She thought a second. "Does Bradfield know?"

"Only that she's taken ill."

"And that she went out to the river?"

"Yes, ma'am."

"And what explanation have you given him for that?"

"That it was over a lad, your ladyship."

Octavia looked at her. "Well, there's truth in that, at least," she commented. Bradfield's room was at the opposite end of the house from Mrs. Jocelyn's; it was possible, though not probable, that the situation could be kept from him for tonight, at least. "Do we know which lad?" she asked. She saw Mrs. Jocelyn hesitate for a second, and waved her hand. "No matter," she said. "Send word out to Evans."

"Yes, ma'am."

"And don't bother his lordship with this just yet."

"No, ma'am." The housekeeper made for the door.

"Oh, it really is too bad," Octavia murmured irritatedly. "I shall find him out, Mrs. Jocelyn. You'd better let that be known. If the father belongs to the house, he shan't be employed here another day. And neither will she. Tell Evans to come see me when he's done."

"Yes, ma'am." Mrs. Jocelyn began to open the door.

"And you and I will discuss your lack of supervision in this matter at a later date," Octavia warned.

There was not a word of reply.

• • •

He had gone out at first light, initially with no
purpose at all in mind, but later up the broad slab
of the moor side Harry had thought that he might
go as far as Penyghent if he could find anyone
with a cart going that way, and that he might at the
same time see Emily's mother.

He had never been there, but he knew the
village, and he knew that her mother's house was
by the church. She would be at home, certainly;
after all, it was Christmas Day. The snow had all
stopped, the sun was out, and he thought that it
would not be far after all: twelve miles, and half of
it downhill. Harry could still see tracks and the
drystone walls, and the view from the top of the
moor stopped him dead. The sky was a brilliant,
high blue; the valley, two miles wide, was a huge
arc surrounded by fells. He could hear sheep at a
farm below, and the barking of a dog; he could
even see the dog, a faint wiry mark in a far-off
field.

He had climbed Penyghent a dozen times. The
peak was like a sleeping limestone lion. You could
breathe up there; you could lie flat and look up
into space, and that was all there would be, the
space and nothing else. And no one else.

Unconsciously, he nodded to himself. Yes, he
would go down and see her mother. That was
what a man was supposed to do, see the father
or mother. There was no father now, and so he

imagined himself standing in some narrow little kitchen with some woman he had never met, saying that he would give her daughter money. This was the plan, such as it was, in his head: that he would give enough money to look after Emily and the child. Marriage was out of the question; his family would never allow it, and, more to the point, he would not allow it himself. Marriage was an impossibility, but he was not a barbarian. He would see that she had a comfortable place to come back to, see that the child was cared for. He would keep it secret, of course—as secret as he could. His parents must not know. That much, with luck, he could persuade Emily's mother to do: keep a secret, and take the little money he had. Until such time. Until such time as . . .

But he couldn't get his mind to finish the sentence. Until such time as he was older. He came into his trust fund when he was twenty-five. Until such time as . . . he was twenty-five, then. He would find Emily a nice little house and he would visit her occasionally, and if she wanted to marry some local man, well, then, he wouldn't stand in her way. He would find it in himself to be obliging about it. He would be a patron of hers. A faint smile came to his face. That sounded all right, at least. One could be a girl's patron without scandal, without a reflection on himself, surely. The villagers might gossip, but if Emily's mother was quiet, and Emily was quiet, then they could tell some story other than that Emily had been abandoned by the real father and that he was kind enough to care about her.

And his parents would never know. He frowned to himself. Was that likely? That they really would never find out? That they would never know that one of the maids had tried to commit suicide on their own grounds, and that she was pregnant? Josiah had said that they would keep her downstairs until she was more herself, until she had recovered somewhat, but that then she would be sent home. Mrs. Jocelyn, he had added darkly, would have to know. Harry had winced at this information. Jocelyn would certainly tell his mother that Emily had had to go, even that she had been fished from the river, that she had been distraught. But if the housekeeper were sensible, she would not tell the whole story. If Jocelyn cared anything at all for Emily she would simply tell her mistress that the girl had gone home for some family reason. Neither Emily nor Mrs. Jocelyn would want the mistress of the house to know that a maid had become pregnant. It was a shameful matter, one that he had heard before that the staff might cover up completely in order that the girl might get another character later on, the first mistress never knowing the real emergency that had taken her away. He considered the whole thing as he walked. It depended upon Armitage's and Jocelyn's not breathing a word. That was the truth of it. The servants might protect their own—might try to salvage Emily's reputation, might hide her away, might even tell less than the truth to his mother for that reason. But would they protect him? Would Jack Armitage, who had called him a filthy name, protect him?

He shoved his hands deep into his pockets, shivering despite the climb. Below him, the dog continued to bark and the sun blinded him. He stood on the ridge overlooking the valley, and he thought of the history of the family, littered with mistresses and illegitimate children—of a great-great-grandfather who had sired more children outside marriage than in it, and of others who wore their wives out with giving birth. He had always thought of those ancestors as being nothing more than shades of history. He had rather pitied their old-fashioned lives, and the grotesqueness of their morals. All the same, they had been rather fine, above the law, above what society considered right, so far gone in their own selfishness that they almost made a code of their own peculiar, distorted moral code, one in which a man might not be all bad as long as his wife was kept ignorant, or his mistress had the good grace to die before having too many bastards. His class was full of such cases, and he had heard other fellows talking of their own dusty scandals. It was said that Lady Cunard's chambermaid had been seduced five or six years ago, and that someone in the family—some woman, some young daughter, or so he understood—had said that it was "all very eighteenth century and droit du seigneur and *rather nice*." Rather nice, as if it were some charming little custom, like giving out the Rutherford gifts at Christmas.

He laughed sourly to himself. Yes, like giving out gifts. Which in his own case he had taken rather to extremes. He put a hand to his forehead, choked at his own dark sense of humor. It was all right for other people to talk about it being *rather nice* in that stupid careless way, but it wasn't rather nice at all; it was bloody. He tried not to think of Emily's face, averted beneath him last summer, eyes closed, lips parted. And of her face last night, so deathly white.

Well, he was a Beckforth after all, it seemed. He had been predictable enough to seduce a servant. For that was what it was, and he was as slothful and disgusting as the rest, no better than them. He was *one* of them, as if he couldn't extract himself from their legacy.

He glared down at the ground, fingering the split in his lip where Jack Armitage had hit him. He would have hit Armitage back if it hadn't been for Josiah's grip on his arm, and then the sight of Emily, being carried and then wrapped in blankets, had also stopped him. Nash hadn't looked at him, and neither had Sedburgh; only Jack was staring at him. "Come away," Josiah had urged him. They had taken Emily in one direction, towards the house; Josiah pulled him in another. He had sat in the stables until Josiah was satisfied that he was in command of himself. He had been told to go to bed, like a child, by a servant. Taken to the side entrance by the same glass-house where he had met her. Climbed the stairs and lay in a nightmarish sleep all night.

When he woke at six he realized that the maids would be bringing coal to the bedrooms before long, and he had got up and dressed and gone out of the house. He hadn't even felt cold until he was halfway through the woods and out onto the back of the moor and could see Rutherford below him. He had thought for a moment that he might go to his father and tell him that Jack Armitage was not to be trusted, and that he had struck him in a drunken rage—and almost in the same instant he had imagined William's look of disbelief.

Damn it all, Harry thought, all the same, those long-ago ancestors might have killed a man for less. In fact, in the Caribbean they had. Or at least, so he had heard. And who was Jack Armitage to call him names? He had probably wanted Emily for himself. That was probably the entire explanation.

He looked down into the valley now, and out towards Emily's mother's village buried some-where there, five or six miles farther on, and he knew that it was futile. He didn't want to follow

Josiah's advice—"Be still; let it go on; leave the girl alone"—because he had thought that it was the kind of thing that one said to a coward. And then he realized that he was just that: a coward. He was the kind of man whom Jack Armitage could strike and draw blood, and who wouldn't strike back or breathe a word to his father about it, and Jack knew that. He knew that because he knew *him,* had known him all his life. Jack knew that he hadn't the nerve to do the right thing, to go and see Emily's mother. He would just retreat back into his own guarded and privileged space and deny he had ever known her. Sooner or laterEmily would get better and be gone. He would never see her again.

He felt suddenly sick at the realization of it. At the easy way out, the obvious solution. He would deny it all. It would be his word against a servant's. Against, perhaps, two or three servants. And what could be done about it? Nothing. Nothing at all.

And long after Emily was gone and away somewhere else, long after, in years to come, she was married with her own family, and a grown woman with no hint in her face of what had happened to her, he would still be at Rutherford.

She would change and be elsewhere. But he would not change. He would still be here. He would be exactly the same.

And he would still be a coward.

He might have got back to his own room before dinner if he had not been met by Louisa on the stairs.

It had got dark; the candles and lamps were lit; it was barely an hour before the meal would be served. She ought not to have been out of her room, but she was, and when she saw him coming dressed in his coat, she ran down to him.

"Where on earth have you been?" she asked. "Father's been asking after you."

"For a walk," he said.

She caught his arm. "Hold on," she commanded. "What's happened to you?" She touched his lip.

"I've been out on the horse, and the blighter caught me as I was putting on his bridle."

"*You* were putting on his bridle?" she asked, astonished.

He tried to get past her. "I've got to change."

"And you've been out all day?"

"What does it matter?"

"There's been something happening."

He turned to look at her. "What do you mean?"

"I saw the doctor come."

He felt himself reel a little. "For whom?"

She put her head to one side, regarding him. "I don't know," she told him. "Someone downstairs. There's been a lot of rushing about, and Mother said I was not to go and see Father. Now, why do you suppose that? He was only in the library."

"How should I know?"

"I thought you might," she murmured, and touched his hand. "Are you sure you're all right? You look awfully done in."

At that same moment, they both heard a heavy step on the landing above them. They looked up to see William looking severely down at them.

"Where have you been?" he demanded.

A beat of silence followed. Louisa, glancing from one to the other, answered, "He's been riding, Father."

William's face betrayed nothing. "Come to my room, Harry," he said. "At once."

Belowstairs, despite the preparations for the evening meal, the clatter of plates, and the ceaseless movement up and down to the dining room, a kind of eerie gloom hung in the air. Nothing had gone right; what ought to have been the best day of the year was spoiled. Bradfield stood near the kitchen with a face like thunder; occasionally he would stare at the girls and Cook as if they might be harboring more secrets, something else of vital importance that they had not told him. Everyone avoided his eye, and said nothing.

It had been midmorning before the butler even knew that Emily Maitland was in Mrs. Jocelyn's room. Word had spread among the lower staff, and in the end it was Harrison who let it slip that he had been out in the snow and that Emily Maitland had been the cause. From there, the truth tumbled out. Bradfield went to Mrs. Jocelyn's room, demanded to see Emily, and had retreated only forty seconds later.

Lunch came and went; silence took hold. During the servants' meal, the bell rang on the electrical board that had replaced the old system of bells in the corridor. Mary had gone to Mrs. Jocelyn's room. "Stay with her," the housekeeper had ordered, "while I fetch Mrs. March."

The housekeeper's sitting room had been warmed by a fierce fire in the grate. Hesitantly, Mary took two or three steps across the carpet. Emily was propped on a daybed, her face white, and both hands clutching the blanket over her.

"Now, then, our Em," Mary murmured.

To Mary's horror, Emily began to make a noise. It was like nothing she had ever heard before, and she had heard enough where she came from, brought up in a back-to-back terrace where one family's noise became another's, meshed together by paper-thin walls. She had heard women giving birth—heard the yelling—but she had never heard a woman keeping it in like this until what came out of her mouth was a thin single note that made her want to cram her hands over her ears.

She knelt at the other girl's side. "Don't take on," she said. "Mrs. March is coming."

Sweat was streaming down Emily's face. She

looked at Mary like an animal cooped up in a slaughtering pen. There was a smell on her too: some visceral heat that had nothing to do with the fire.

"What can I do?" Mary whispered. She took Emily's hand and was sorry at once; the other girl's grip nearly broke her fingers. "Is it bad?" she said, although she knew the answer.

The clock ticked loudly over the mantelpiece; Mary glanced at it. It was a solid black slate thing with columns at either end, funereal, morbid, Victorian. In a glass dome alongside it were two stuffed songbirds. The whole lot stood on a piece of yellow velvet hung with tassels.

The long keening sound stopped.

"Why'd you never tell us, Em?" Emily had closed her eyes. "Who was it?" Mary asked. "Where is he? Shall we ask him to come?"

Emily shook her head. She was panting now.

"Shall I damp down the fire?" Mary asked. "Are you too hot? What shall I do?"

The minutes passed. Mary's feet cramped from crouching alongside. She stroked Emily's hand. The clock struck half past one. All at once there was a sound in the corridor and Mrs. March was ushered in. There was a blessed moment of cooler air before the two older women crowded over Emily. Mary stood back; her eyes ranged over the songbirds, the clock, the little shelf of books. The Bible and *Pilgrim's Progress*; a hymnal, a book of psalms. Mary looked up at the wall, at an engraving and the title underneath it: *Elisha Raising the Shunammite's Son*. She didn't know who Elisha was, and she didn't care. She just wanted Mrs. March to go away and leave Emily alone.

At last, the older woman stood up. "Lady Cavendish will have to know," she said. "The doctor must come."

"God have mercy," Mrs. Jocelyn said. "She'll have my guts for garters."

Mary stood transfixed while the two women exchanged a grimace, as if their bad fortune at having to confess Emily's state to Lady Cavendish were worse than Emily's suffering. In that moment, Mary hated the housekeeper as she had never hated her before; it was all she could do to look silently at the floor as they passed, Mrs. March telling her to pour Emily a glass of water and to make sure that she drank it.

Mary went over to the bed with the glass trembling in her hand. "It'll be all right," she said. "The doctor will come. He'll be here soon."

Emily looked at her. She said something. Mary moved closer. "I can't hear you, Em."

"The box," Emily muttered. "There's a blue box."

"What box?" Mary asked.

"In the glasshouse."

Mary frowned, perplexed. "What do you mean?"

"Look for it."

"But I can't go to the glasshouse, Em." She looked hard into Emily's face, wondering whether this was the kind of delirium she'd seen in her little brother when he had scarlet fever. He'd talked of all sorts of things he had never seen and never would see, ships and castles. Emily gripped her hand. "Look in the glasshouse," she hissed. "Find it."

"All right," Mary promised.

Emily seemed to relax. "He gave it to me," she whispered. "You get it. You have it."

"A box?" Mary asked. She wondered what she wanted with a box; what Emily wanted with it, come to that. Nevertheless, she agreed. "Don't you worry; I'll get it," she said.

Emily put her head back on the pillow. "What time is it?"

"It's two o'clock."

"I ought to get up."

"Nay, you can't do that."

But Emily was upright again, grimacing, her gaze oblique, unfocused, her mouth set; she began to try to swing her legs off the bed, shuffling forward.

"Don't," Mary begged. "Oh, don't do that."

"I've got to walk," Emily told her. There was a sudden panic in her tone. "I must get up." She got one foot to the floor; she gripped Mary's arm. "Help me."

"Em, I can't. You must stay."

For a second, Emily stared at her; then her eyes slipped away to that distant point at which she seemed to have been looking just a few seconds before. It was as if she were listening to something that Mary could not hear. Then, "Oh, God," she whispered. "Oh, God." Her eyes rolled back in her head; she fell sideways, half on and half off the daybed. The hand clutching Mary's arm relaxed, and two high spots of color, jagged circles, flushed Emily's cheeks. Her deadweight fell back, her head brushing the wall and the upper half of her body pressing down until, despite Mary's efforts, she slithered to the floor. As she fell, she took the blanket with her, and on the bed Mary suddenly saw a trail of blood.

She jumped to her feet, aghast.

"Mrs. Jocelyn!" she cried out. "Mrs. Jocelyn!"

While he stood in William's bedroom, for the first time Harry felt truly cold. Snow that had adhered to the hem of his coat was dripping now onto the Indian carpet; he looked down and saw the wet, dark patches among the flourishes of knotted flowers, the blue medallions of silk and wool. William paced backwards and forwards, and then stood with his back to the fire. Above him, the Landseer with its pathetic dog on some Scottish hillside cast a sickly sentiment over the room.

"For God's sake, take off your coat," William ordered. "Don't stand there like a fool."

Harry did as he was told; he looked around for somewhere to hang it, and finally took it to a chair by the door. He felt his father's eyes boring into his back, and was infinitely colder, though he recognized that the room must be warm. He longed to shove his hands into his pockets; they felt too large for him. He turned to face William.

"Suppose you tell me how you came by that swollen lip."

Harry opened his mouth to speak, but was not quick enough.

"And no lies about a horse. I am not Louisa."

Harry stared at him, trying to determine what his father knew. He felt a crawling sensation of pressure, the need to blurt out everything. He wanted to say that he would marry Emily, absurd as it was, and despite all his thoughts that day. For a second this seemed paramount; he thought of people like Featherstonehaugh, the baronet, marrying his dairymaid eighty years ago—those Regency scandals that boys had talked about at school, the butt of jokes. But jokes that had always had a thread of envy in them; to buck the system would be a delight, wouldn't it? He heard his own thirteen-year-old voice in his head. "One in the eye!" To marry a dairymaid, a housemaid, what did it matter? A sort of crazed idea rattled in his brain, pressed down on his tongue as if it were going to leap out of his mouth. He realized that he was shaking not from cold now, but from the sensation of standing on the edge of a precipice where everything hinged on his next reply.

"You were down at the river last night," William said. "Armitage has been here. You might as well know that."

Harry tried to get a hold on the carousel, slow down the circularity in his head. "Jack Armitage struck me," he heard himself say.

William looked wordlessly at his son for a while. "Perhaps you'll share the reason with me."

"I don't know, Father."

"I see."

"Really, I don't know," Harry continued. "I was looking out; I saw lights outside. I went down there and they were trying to get a girl from the water, one of the maids. . . ." William said nothing. Harry took a step towards him, trying to smile. "I mean, what was she doing?" he asked. "I only wanted to know what she was doing. I asked Armitage."

"You asked him?"

"Or . . . or rather, he said . . ."

"You asked Armitage who this girl was?"

"I could see that it was one of the maids." He tried to blot out Emily's face, the shape of her under the dress. "And suddenly Jack Armitage struck me. I don't know why. He never said a word."

William's face did not betray a single emotion. "Then perhaps, if there was no reason, I should get rid of them."

"Get rid of whom?"

"The Armitages."

Blood beat in Harry's throat. "No, I . . ."

"I can't let it go, Harry."

"I wish you would, sir," Harry replied. "I mean, it was a rotten thing, you know. The girl and all. I don't know if Jack even knew that it was me standing there. He had been in the water; it was snowing; I don't know that he saw that it was me at all."

William still had not moved an inch from his position before the fire. "Armitage said as much," he replied. "He said that Jack had been angry, but did not say at whom, or why. He claimed not to know."

Harry did not dare say a word.

"Harry," said William. "You must tell me now if there is something between you and Jack, something to make him do such a thing."

"Nothing," Harry said.

"He simply lashed out at you?"

"He was coming out of the river. I don't know that he even knew . . ."

William waved his hand. "All right, all right." At last, William shifted his position; he walked up to his son and looked him hard in the face, assessing him. "Have you something to tell me?"

"No, sir."

"The truth, Harry."

"No, sir."

"You didn't know this Maitland?"

"No, sir."

"You've seen her about the house, though?"

He found himself shrugging. "One sees them all, I suppose, at some time or other."

William nodded, and then moved so close that Harry could feel his father's breath on his face. "Did you know this girl?" he asked in a low voice. "I'm asking you, Harry. Do you hear me?"

"No," Harry said.

"You swear this to me on your honor?"

"I did not, sir."

"You understand what I mean?"

"Yes, Father."

"You are not responsible for this unholy drama?"

"I am not, sir."

William assessed him a moment longer. Feeling sick, as if he had been cut off from the world—his word of honor, on his *honor*—Harry managed to take in a long breath.

"The girl had a child this afternoon," William said. "A daughter, not expected to live."

The world dropped under Harry's feet, and he dropped down with it like a lead weight. For a second he closed his eyes and, opening them, was surprised to find himself still standing. William was gazing at him acutely. "Dreadful thing, under this roof. Your mother is most upset."

"Mother?"

"She went down to see the girl." William sighed with complete exasperation. "Down to Mrs. Jocelyn's room, if you please, with the doctor."

"The doctor came?"

To his intense relief, William turned away and walked back to the fire, where he stood with his hands behind his back, staring down at the flames. "It's no concern of yours." He flexed one fist. "Damned stupidity," he muttered, "utter wasteful stupidity." Though whether he was talking about Octavia, or the girl, or Mrs. Jocelyn, or anyone else was hard to tell. When he looked back at Harry, his eyes ranged over his son; there was a fleeting look of unease that did not quite amount to distrust. Then it was gone. "Get along to dress," he instructed. "And make yourself pleasant at dinner, for God's sake. It's Christmas Day, after all. The guests are not to hear of this bloody disgraceful business. Do you understand?"

"Yes, Father." Harry moved towards the door. At the threshold, he paused a second, and said, "What of the girl, Maitland? What happened to her?"

William looked over his shoulder. "She died" was his unemotional reply. "Two hours ago, at half past four."

Chapter 3

T hree months later, the family were in London.

This was the year that Louisa was presented at Court: a ticket to the wider world, a passport to an eligible marriage in society.

It had been a bright start to the Season, though not everyone was in town. It was still only March; Easter had not come, but despite the glorious sunshine of the morning, it was now almost impossible to believe, Louisa thought, that there was any world worth seeing out there in London beyond the windows streaming with condensation.

She looked over her shoulder and saw herself in a series of reflections in the floor-to-ceiling mirrors of the dressmaker's. A fire roared at either end of the room, and between herself and the other two girls and their attendant mothers, the seamstresses were on their knees, endlessly unpicking and pinning great swathes of white tulle and satin. Octavia sat with Charlotte, trying to interest her reluctant younger daughter in the fine distinctions of various styles; Charlotte, by way of reply, leaned her head on her mother's shoulder and feigned sleep.

Louisa considered her own reflection objectively: not half-bad, rather tall, delicately pale. Her presentation gown was cut low on the shoulders, revealing a pretty décolleté; the sleeves were a froth of embroidered gauze. All the same, she wished that she were not fair; it seemed so uninteresting somehow. She would much rather be Lily Elsie or Daisy Irving or Gertie Millar, with their thick dark hair drawn up off the neck with artful little bands and tiaras. Of course, she had not been allowed to see any of these women perform; she knew of them only from gossip and from the newspapers, because they were beyond the pale as actresses, and Irving was worse, being in moving pictures.

Louisa envied their lives nevertheless. She would love to sing in the music hall or on the stage like Lily Elsie. They said that all London had been at Elsie's feet six years ago, that men had sent her replicas of her stage jewels in real gemstones, that they crowded the stage doors and the corridors of the theaters. It must all be rather exciting. She too wanted men to die at the sound of her voice, to breathe their last when she sighed. It would be delightful to have a trail of expiring lovers in her wake; just the sight of the few who now followed her and Mother as they shopped on Oxford Street, and gazed at her at suppers and concerts—as if she couldn't see them! it was too funny—all of that, all of the gazing and following, was simply the soup course to the main. She wanted to be adored; she fully expected it. Adored, not gazed at; drive them mad with desire, not just be followed. And she would be remote and careless as they died at her feet—she would be so awfully good at it.

London in the Season was unashamedly a marriage market on a huge scale. It was what all the piano lessons, the deportment classes and the learning of French had been for: to ensnare a baronetcy or, failing a title, a fortune. All rather unnecessary—Louisa felt that she could do that without recourse to the Season at all; in fact, a day at Ascot alone ought to do it—but then, one had to be seen. One had to *see*. One had to attend the breakfasts, the lunches, the teas, the dinners, the balls; one had to be thrown into the stream to see whether one could swim, as it were. She, and hundreds of other girls flooding Hyde Park and the Royal Academy and the Court drawing rooms and Derby Day and Henley, she and hundreds of other girls in their hats and riding coats and tea dresses and boating suits and Royal Enclosure lace and crepe. It was rather like a very long race—one that she had been especially designed to win.

Some days when she got up, the excitement of it all was palpable. The house on Grosvenor Square bustled with it; those servants whom they had brought down with them from Yorkshire seemed brighter, more alive than when they were holed up in the middle of nowhere at Rutherford. Oh, she might never see the old place again, and be perfectly happy! London was so much brighter: so many more people, so many theaters and concerts. And so frightfully gay. The streets heaved with horse-drawn omnibuses and carriages, pedestrians and bicycles. One might look out of one's window at Rutherford and never see a carriage, but here! Progress could be slow along the choked streets, but it was such fun to sit in one's carriage and gaze out at the people on the pavement. And when one stopped and the carriage door was held open, the crowds parted. Her mother had taught her this. Don't stop; don't look to left or right. Descend the step and walk straight forward; don't slouch or hesitate. Simply look ahead. The doors of the shops would open as if by magic to admit them; her mother would barely look at the liveried doormen who held them open. One had to be gracious, of course; that was only polite. One must nod just a little at the doorman, or the footman who opened the carriage door, just as one must always say, "Good morning," to the staff, but nothing more was necessary.

Louisa fondly saw herself as a flower being held up to be admired by everyone who passed, and then smiled ruefully at the analogy. Well, what if one did think of oneself as a flower? God knew that when she was twenty-three or twenty-four she would be regarded as firmly left on the shelf; flowers bloomed and glowed for a limited period; she must take advantage of it. When she and her mother had walked into a soiree the other evening, there had been a current of subdued whispers of admiration; Mother was lovely, of course. But it was she, the Honorable Miss Cavendish, the pretty little rose—it was she who drew the eye. She knew it, and basked in it like a contented kitten lying on a cushion. She didn't mind admitting it, and why shouldn't she? For it was simply lovely to be Louisa.

As far as the presentation dress was concerned, she had shown a photograph of Lily Elsie to her mother and begged that her Court dress be at least embroidered the same: coils of flowers and petals across the low neckline, and the organdy across her breasts sewn with little dashes of diamanté, like raindrops. Her mother had said it was too gaudy, and that a Court dress was enough with its enormous train, and the flowers that she would carry, and the veil that hung down her back, without hundreds of hours spent sewing cabbage roses into the seams.

Louisa had sulked at that for some time. Her mother's dress in 1891—Louisa's grandfather had managed to get a Cabinet Minister's wife to introduce Octavia at Court despite her background in trade—was still encased in a linen shroud in her wardrobe. It was vast; the train alone was twelve feet long, and it had two thousand pearls on the bodice and hips. It was the dress that had helped ensnare Father. And yet here *she* was, sweltering in front of the mirrors with Madeleine Grosvenor to her right, the great gawky bulk of a girl absolutely reeking of privilege—look at her now, the corset tightened around that piggish waist, primped up like royalty herself—and yet Louisa Cavendish was destined to be Cinderella in her plain little frock. She might as well die.

"Darling, don't pull such a face," her mother called, her soothing voice falling amid the yards of satin. "There's only one more fitting to go. Then we shall have tea."

Louisa looked down at the seamstress. The girl, head bowed, was pinning the last of the hem; one hand was flat on the floor as she considered the hang of the gown. For a reason that she couldn't fathom, Louisa had an urge to step on that hand, to flatten it, to hear the girl squeal. Astonished at herself, she blushed, caught in a sort of fright. "Do hurry up," she said to the bowed head. "Or I shall fall down. I'm terribly tired."

The girl smiled. Louisa thought idly, and with some surprise, that she was very young, perhaps too young to be competent. She was tiny—rather bony and thin—and spotless in her grey-and-white-striped dress of the couture house. The head dressmaker advanced; the job was done; the dress was removed. The little seamstress labored out with her gigantic burden of material that nearly swamped her, and through the open door Louisa glimpsed a room full of benches and sewing

103

machines and a girl wiping her hands, seemingly bathed in sweat.

Out came the final fitting for the day: a ball gown, the eighth that had been made this spring for Louisa, and the most beautiful confection of palest pink that barely clung to her shoulders and dropped, petticoat after petticoat, to the floor. Each petticoat was silk, and the gown was silk, so that it draped on her, and yet when she moved, when she danced, there would be the endless whispering seductive rustle of skirts.

"You look very nice," her mother said. "What do you think, Charlotte?"

The younger girl pulled a face. "Puffy," she opined.

"It is perfection," ventured the dressmaker.

"Yes," Octavia agreed. "It is indeed perfection."

Nothing less would do.

They walked out onto Bond Street, into the blessed coolness of the afternoon. The day was fading over the rooftops, casting a milky grey and yellow light; it was almost four o'clock. Louisa's father had asked for the carriage—he was at the Houses of Parliament to see an old colleague—and so a cab was hailed for them; all three crammed into it as quickly as they could—it was rather cramped, and they laughed as they squeezed together through the narrow step at the front.

Claridge's, the great hotel on Brook Street, was

104

midway between Hanover and Grosvenor Square, and close to their London house. Its new red-brick facade—it had reopened only fourteen or fifteen years ago—was a favorite of Octavia's; it reminded her of the color of Rutherford. She swept into the foyer and looked around her.

"What are we stopping for?" asked Charlotte. "I'm hungry."

"I promised to meet Hetty. I wonder where she is?"

"I've never yet seen Mrs. de Ray anywhere but at rest in front of a tea tray at four o'clock, Mother."

Octavia smiled. It was true that the woman whom William had first introduced her to in London, the wife of a diplomat, had embraced the English afternoon tradition wholeheartedly after several postings to less hospitable climes. As a young woman, Hetty de Ray had confided in Octavia, she had been forced to tolerate any amount of tea balanced on the back of a yak in some Nepalese outpost, so now that they were in London for good, she had vowed to repay a thousand uncomfortable Far Eastern afternoons with a permanent seat in Claridge's deeply upholstered chairs.

Charlotte was right: Henrietta de Ray was in the center of the tearoom, a vision in lilac taffeta. Beside her sat her daughter, Florence.

The women embraced; the daughters exchanged smiles.

"What are you doing tomorrow morning?" Florence asked.

"I don't know. There are two invitations to breakfast. One at the *Porrets'*." Louisa shuddered at the name of the dreadfully ugly American steel heiress.

"Come riding with me in the park."

"All right. Charlotte must come too, though."

Charlotte smiled at the mention of an activity that would at last take her out of doors, and the morning was arranged efficiently. The girls sat back and listened to their mothers reel through a dozen dates, notebooks opened: this gallery they would go to, that supper to be abhorred. This dinner, that ball, most emphatically *not* that lecture. The investments of thousands of pounds of other mothers were thus considered and disposed of. Charlotte took no notice; she would be expected to stay at home for most events. All of them agreed, over a fanciful tower of cakes and small sandwiches, that Easter, just a week away, was likely to be crowded.

Hetty de Ray leaned across the table to Octavia. "What do you think? Mrs. Canford is in town."

"Good heavens."

"As if anyone would have thought he would let her out!"

"Let who out?" Louisa asked.

The older women sat back as tea was poured.

"She was one of the King's," Florence said. Her

mother shushed her, widening her eyes and inclining her head in Charlotte's direction. "Well," Florence muttered. "She was."

"She must be ancient," Louisa replied.

"Her husband locked her up in their pile in Kent because she ravished somebody's son," Florence added. "He was twenty and she was thirty-nine."

Hetty rolled her eyes at Octavia. "I simply do not know where she gets such gossip from." She patted Charlotte's knee. "Close your ears, darling. It's all too trivial for words."

The older women smiled at each other. Octavia liked Henrietta; she was pragmatic and light-hearted. For eighteen dutiful years she had moved from one ambassadorial post to another, as a stoical wife of the diplomatic corps. The longest she had spent anywhere was a four-year sojourn in Naples, where, Hetty had explained, her husband, Herbert, had sired another family, a gaggle of children to a very nice woman, by all accounts. When Hetty had first told Octavia this, Octavia had been aghast.

"Weren't you devastated?" she had asked.

"I certainly was," Hetty had replied equably. "It was so unimaginative of him."

Hetty and Herbert had three sons, all now married and abroad in the service of George V; Octavia had once or twice wondered whether Louisa might marry one of them if a title could not be secured. They seemed dull, dutiful boys, exactly the kind to keep Louisa in check.

"What happened to the Italian woman?" Octavia had inquired of her friend.

"Given an allowance," Hetty had told her. "Awfully tiresome."

It was not as if Henrietta herself ever suffered financially from her husband's dependents, for money poured in from their Lincolnshire estates and some sort of ghastly mining affair in South America. Octavia, still with her father's clattering mills shut up in her heart, tried not to think about the mines. It made her think that all of them—all the favored wives, the upper-class families— might be standing on quicksand: the quicksand of others' toil. If she allowed herself, she could still hear the interminable thump of looms in her head together with her father's thundering voice. She closed her eyes and listened to the distant music of the string quartet. It was so much nicer not to know, actually. She wished she didn't; she wished, for a passionate second, that she were Louisa.

"You're not listening," Hetty said.

"I'm so sorry."

"Sweden."

"Sweden?"

"Herbert is going to Stockholm. The Olympiad, you know, in the summer."

"Oh, of course."

"Official representative. His Majesty."

"How wonderful."

Hetty smiled. "No, darling, it isn't wonderful. I

can't imagine anything worse. But he's as pleased as punch. And so I was thinking of Italy. For the girls."

Florence had already gripped Louisa's arm, privy to the secret. "Should you like to come with us?"

"Not Venice, of course," Hetty was saying. "Not in the summer. But the Adriatic. We might come back through Switzerland. I thought it might be fun. And Charlotte too, naturally."

At this, Charlotte piped up. "Oh, I'm afraid I'm invited to Brighton with a school friend." She looked at Octavia imploringly. "Katherine, Mother. You said it would be all right. They have a sea bathing box and everything. Oh, please!"

Octavia nodded. "I haven't forgotten," she said. She smiled at Hetty. "William is in Yorkshire from August. I must be there."

"Mother," Louisa pleaded. "What about me?"

Octavia looked at her eldest daughter. Well, what was to be lost by it? It might well be the last summer before Louisa settled down. "I don't see why not," Octavia murmured. "Thank you, Hetty."

"You won't come with us?"

She hesitated for a moment. "I should love to, but no," she replied. "The shooting starts on the fourteenth. William will expect me at home."

She had a duty to him, and it was their tradition. There would be several weekends to be spent as a hostess. Venice and the Adriatic faded; she looked across at Florence's and Louisa's hands clasped in delight, and smiled philosophically.

The spring took Rutherford by surprise.

It was unseasonably warm in the days before Easter—so warm that they began the cleaning early, opening the windows. It was like early summer, color springing out in the hawthorn on the lanes, and the grass an almost hallucinogenic green after the snow. Blossoms came to the apple trees in the orchard. On the driveway the beech uncurled their first small fists of leaves; the narcissi in the gardens looked already faded.

Mrs. Jocelyn was down in London, along with Mr. Bradfield, the parlor maids, the cook and the first footman, Harrison, but the engine of the house ticked on; the head housemaid, Dodd, was still there. Under her eagle eye all the winter curtains were taken down; the windows were cleaned; the thickly upholstered cushions were taken away to the laundry along with table runners and antimacassars; the great Persian and Indian carpets were taken outside to be beaten free of the dust and stains of a whole year that the scattering of tea leaves and relentless brushing by the maids had not been able to remove. Too heavy for the laundry lines, the carpets were carried by March's gardeners to the field fences. There in the bright sunlight, beaten with brooms and sticks, the orange and gold and blue medallions of the

Kashan and Tabriz became more plainly visible.

In the rooms of the main house, Mary Richards and Cynthia Wright were joined by the maid of all work, Betty; they worked from one wall to another, side by side, scrubbing the stone floors with soap and water. The wood floors in the morning room and the library and study shone from Jackson's Polish, the furniture from lavender cream, or linseed oil and turpentine; in the kitchens the copper pans were scoured with the mixture of sand, salt, flour and vinegar. With Cook no longer there—Mrs. Carlisle had gone, complaining and fearful, to London after hearing the merits of a Parisian chef discussed by Helene de Montfort, the insistence being that every decent house ought to employ one—the staff ate meals brought in by Mrs. March: suet puddings for the most part, more oil than meat; bread and cheese; "cold comfort" made from bacon fat; potato soup; lardy cake. Cynthia would mop it up with relish, but Mary turned up her nose; it seemed that the Marches survived on fat. For supper came bread and dripping, the fat from beef roasts that had been skimmed off and left to cool in the big ridged white bowls in the scullery. It was, to Mary's mind, disgusting stuff. She wondered whether the mistress knew what Mrs. March served them. She wondered, also, where the food went that she was sure they ought to have eaten. She imagined it stuffed into Mrs. March's larder, with all the fat little March children cramming their faces. "Little bastards," she muttered to herself.

"Who's that?" Cynthia asked her, huffing at the exertion of making Brunswick Black. They had set to the task of mixing up asphaltum and linseed to make a varnish for the kitchen range.

"Nobody," Mary answered. "Moths in the carpet." Cynthia agreed in her dogged way.

They looked up; Nash was standing in the doorway. Sleeves rolled up, he was smiling. "Come along to the scullery."

"I don't think so," Mary said.

"Not to work. Come and see."

It was half past three in the afternoon—still an hour and a half before their customary break. Mary looked at Cynthia, who didn't need a second telling; the black-lead brushes and leathers were already flung back in the box. "We're not done," Mary objected. But Cynthia was halfway out the door.

In the scullery sat Enid Bliss, thin as a whippet, in a uniform that had swamped her since her bronchitis of the winter. Sitting next to her was her mother, and on the other side of the narrow table sat Enid's brothers and sisters, looking like a set of Russian dolls descending in size to the smallest one, a little girl who was Enid's image, all cowlike brown eyes and scrawny hands, with her hair scraped up under a wool hat. They had come up from the village, three miles. In the middle of the table was a fruit cake the size of a dinner plate, and one of Cook's giant brown teapots, and a set of the servants' tea plates and cutlery. Alfred Whitley hovered in the background, his gaze fixed solidly on the cake.

"Oh, you'd be for it if she could see you," Mary murmured.

"Well, she can't," Nash responded. "Dodd has gone to York."

"York? What for?"

"Something her ladyship saw in London. To bring it back here."

"What kind of thing?"

Nash just smiled. "You'll see soon enough."

Mary sighed exasperatedly. "Where's Mrs. March?"

"Out," he said. "So get this eaten before she can lay her hands on it."

Mary sat down, awash with delicious guilt. Her arms ached, her knees ached, her back ached, everything ached; people said every housemaid had housemaid's knee, but that hadn't caught her yet. It was her hips and lower back—too long in the body, "like a bloody dog," the overseer at the mill had told her. "Too long to get under without a clout," trying to thump her as she wriggled under the loom to catch threads. She smiled to herself, thinking, *Well, I'm out of that, and look who called who a dog, you bloody mastiff,* and gratefully inhaled the scent of the tea and cake. She wondered at the cursing that came into her head all the time, whether she really felt it or not; it was like some rotten thread of anger; she always tried to suppress it. She wished she could wake up happy, like Miss Amelie or Miss Louisa; they always looked like cats that had got the cream, all pleased with themselves and pretty. She looked across at Mrs. Bliss, who, like her, had perhaps never been pretty either. Not that it seemed to bother her.

"I made it," said the older woman, all red-faced pride. "I were given the dried fruit at Christmas and I thought, 'Well, they've gone away; they're out of sight; I can go and get Enid proper fed.'"

"We'd swing for it." Cynthia grinned.

"See all, hear all, say nowt," Mrs. Bliss responded. The cake was cut.

At six o'clock, the carpets were brought back in.

Nash helped in the struggle through the great hall with them, though no one might have expected him to. The long roll of the Tabriz was set down inside the drawing room. Without curtains, the room looked almost empty, full of light, stripped of comfort. The furniture was under white sheets. As the undergardeners went away, Nash closed the door and stepped up to the window, and looked along the drive.

He came from the village down there in the valley; it had a church, and Old Wharton Farm, and a rectory where the new reverend seemed to like to hide himself, a faltering Oxford theology graduate with no feeling for his flock; it had twenty or so houses collected around the village green. That was all. It was a place that had always seemed to him half-asleep in the vast rolling edge of the Vale of York. Farther up towards Richmond was a military camp, but Nash didn't like to go either to the camp or the town. He liked his world quiet.

Sitting down in the empty whiteness of the room, he got out the book from his pocket. He had taken it from the master's library. He looked at the spine. It was a handsome, worn red leather with the title engraved in gold: *John Keats.* He had looked at it before, keeping the words in his head: *who fears to follow where airy voices lead,* and, *a thing of beauty. . . .*

He liked poetry. Lord Cavendish wouldn't miss the book; he could keep it, except his scrupulous honesty wouldn't allow it. He'd replace it later, when everyone had gone to bed.

"What are you doing?"

Nash jumped. Mary was standing in the doorway.

"Reading."

Walking over to him in the half-light, she looked like a ghost for a moment. As she came closer, he was glad to see her open, smiling face. She leaned over him. "Reading what?" She took the book, leafed through a few pages. "You're a dark horse," she commented.

"Do you like it?"

"What?"

"Poetry. Do you like it?"

"I don't know. I never had time. There's not much where I come from."

They regarded each other: chambermaid and footman, who were usually kept separate—even separate when they ate downstairs.

"You're from one of the mills," he said.

"The worsted mill at Blessington, yes."

The mistress had a policy of bringing the occasional housemaid from the mills. It was a charitable act of rescue; everyone knew that. Emily had been from a mill town too. He had even heard visiting staff say that it was strange of Lady Cavendish: that nobody would want a mill girl anywhere near a good house, as if they might run off with the cutlery or eat their way through the kitchens. The way that people talked about the mill towns, you half expected some sort of feral animal, not a person. Certainly not a girl like Mary, with her steady, appraising gaze.

"How long have you been here?" he asked.

"What—never noticed me?"

"I've noticed you. But how long?"

"Two years." She seemed to be laughing at him, her mouth tucked up in a private little smile.

"And how long in the mill?"

Abruptly, she sat down in the covered armchair. She picked up the narrow skirt of her uniform and spread it about her as if it were a ball gown. "Coo, this is nice," she murmured. She smiled. "Going to report me?"

"No."

She continued looking at him, assessing him. "I was in the weaving rooms with my mother," she said. "I was six. They give me a box to stand on."

"At six?"

"What was you doing at six?"

"Going to school. Helping plant out, and then at harvest. Cleaning the roads."

"Cleaning roads? Why?"

"That's what my father did."

"That's not much of a job."

"No, not much," he agreed. "He was sixty-six when I was born. Had a wife before my mother. Fifteen children."

"Fifteen?" Mary raised up her hands. "Fred Fernapackpan!"

He started to laugh at the nickname. It meant—well, what his mother would call "backward at coming forward," a reluctant lover—something that his father had certainly never been. His father had died when he was seven; he had a vague memory of the horse-drawn hearse, with the horse draped in black, tied up at the churchyard gate. And throwing himself down in the shade of a

117

spindly tree by the grave, realizing that his father would never be there again to take his side, and the thought had set him crying so loudly that his mother had to drag him to his feet and give him a hefty smack across the face. There ended the soft regime of his feckless, loving father, and there began the reign of his swift-handed mother. "He was not that," he murmured. "No, I should say not. He had love to spare."

He looked up; Mary was regarding him seriously. "Do you ever think of Emily?" she asked.

He nodded. "I think of Christmas night."

"You were at the river." Mary crossed her arms tightly in front of her. "I don't think of much else."

They were silent for a few moments, both recalling Emily polishing in this very room—so slight, so fair. So quiet.

She looked at Nash. "Do you ever talk to Jack Armitage?"

"Armitage? No."

"Do you think . . ." She leaned forward.

"What?"

"It doesn't matter." She sprang to her feet. "I'm forgetting what I come to tell you," she said. "Miss Dodd is back, riding in a wagon off Daight's stores in Richmond. Sat up next to the driver looking like the queen of Sheba with a bad head." She put her hands on her hips. "And now you can tell me what the bloody heck's in the back of the wagon."

• • •

The next morning, it was revealed in all its glory.

Two men came all the way from York in another cart, bringing a large drum of gasoline, which they stacked next to the machine that had been delivered the night before; then the whole cart was taken to the front of the house. The main door was opened, and the carpets that had been beaten outside the day before were spread out again in the great hall.

"What's it about?" Cynthia wondered.

"Dodd said it was to do with cleaning."

"Well, that were a waste of time then yesterday," Cynthia observed. From the green baize door they surreptitiously watched as the same under-gardeners hauled at the carpets to straighten them.

"Dodd says they wanted airing and beating first," Mary muttered.

One of the men came in from the wagon. He was carrying a length of flexible hose that reached all the way from the wagon, up the steps, and through the door. He turned back and raised his hand, and then pressed the end of the hose to the edge of the carpet. There was what seemed to be a thunderclap from the drive outside. The long hose was transparent; they saw something moving in it. Behind Mary, both Betty and Enid were plucking at their dresses. "Come away," they were saying. The booming of the engine outside was echoing round the great hall like a banshee.

"It's eating it," Betty screeched. " 'Tis a serpent!"

"Don't talk so ruddy daft," Mary retorted. She ran forward, clapping her hands over her ears as she got closer. The nozzle of the hose moved along the massive rug; behind it was left a lighter stripe. Over the noise, Nash caught her eye; he was shouting something.

"What?" she yelled, but couldn't hear the reply. He walked over to her, grinning, and caught her arm. He maneuvered her into the drawing room. "What is it?" she shouted.

"Puffing Billy," he told her. "It sucks up the dirt." He took her to the window, and she saw the dirt and dust coiling along the hose and into the bags of the machine. The cart was shaking under the pressure from the piston pump. "One cleaned the carpets in the Abbey for the Coronation."

"It sounds like the devil," she told him.

"Aye," he agreed. "It does. Costs the devil too. Lady Cavendish saw it last week, Dodd says. Sent a letter. Some big place in London had a *party* to watch it being done. Watch the dirt go up. Thirteen pounds to clean a house."

"But they was all beaten and cleaned yesterday."

"This is proper cleaning, though."

"Good God," Mary said. She walked away, back out into the hall, paused for a while to see the clean streaks in the Tabriz, thought of how long, and with what awful effort, she and Cynthia would take to clean like that. Proper cleaning, he had said. Like a machine could do it better. A frown came to her face.

Thirteen pounds, she thought.

Thirteen pounds was what Enid was paid for a whole year scrubbing pans and dishes in the scullery. Mary looked back at the girl's face framed in the doorway to the stairs, a place where normally she would never be, a place where she would probably never be again until next year, when the family was away.

Thirteen pounds.

For a bloody machine, for a day.

Just for the hell of it, in the pandemonium, Mary dropped her hands from her ears and screamed and screamed.

William stood for a while on Westminster Bridge, and looked down at the Thames.

Night was falling; all the clerks and bankers and little shopgirls were rushing towards Waterloo Station across the bridge, to the trains belching soot and smoke. Carriages jostled one another, the breath of the horses and their dung stinking in the gaslit shadows, and with the omnibuses and the motor vehicles combined, it was appallingly noisy. He had come along to take the air before going home, but he wondered whether there was actually a breath of clean air to be found anywhere in London.

A hundred years ago, Wordsworth had been in

this same spot and written that "Earth has not anything to show more fair," but he couldn't see it himself. He wished that he were at home in Rutherford. The poet had called London a mighty heart, and it was certainly that—but a great sluggish heart, as turgid as the river beating and rolling under the boats. He had tired of London long ago—been excited as a boy, of course, and probably in the first few months as a Member of Parliament, but now not at all. He had been routinely elected—the nobility always were—but today things were different. People were being elected whom one would never have seen in Parliament in Victoria's heyday—working men, and liberals of the most wishy-washy sort. People who even condoned the women's movements, wanted them to have a vote, wanted them—God forbid!—in the House itself.

He didn't think of himself as old, but he was certainly too old for such nonsense. Thank God that Octavia didn't subscribe—she had little political feeling—but he should like very much to nip Charlotte's support for the suffragettes in the bud. It was all idealism; he tried to tell her that—but his youngest daughter was a determined child. He rather approved of her militarism— it was an old Beckforth trait, after all—but it was to be eradicated in a woman. If you gave women freedom they might all become Helene de Montforts, and then the world would go to hell. He sighed, turned his back to the river, and leaned against the parapet, watching the mass of humanity go by.

He had been at the Derby last year—that was enough to put anyone off the suffragette cause. Fortunate enough to be in the King's party— he knew the trainer of the King's horse—he remembered Anmer's jockey being brought into the ambulance room at the back of the grandstand. The King himself had gone down to see how his man was. A fractured rib, a bruised face, concussion: fortunately, that was all. The plucky little chap was back at Newmarket three days later, as right as rain. He might, of course, have been killed—like the "brutal lunatic woman."

The Queen had called her that, and the Queen was right. The Derby had been almost over, the crowds pressed fifteen deep against the rails, and Anmer had been coming up third from last. The woman Davison had dodged under the rail and run out into the race and tried to get hold of the reins of Anmer; the horse, the jockey and Davison herself had gone flying—they had seen Davison cartwheel over, her hat rolling from her head, her feet in the air like a rag puppet, having taken the full force of the horse. Anmer was perfectly all right, thank God; it was a very decent chestnut and it got up and ran on, riderless, to the end of the race. Davison lay there unconscious; crowds ran onto the track in a fury—it was, after all, an insult to the King. They had all stopped, however, when they saw the blood running from her mouth and nose. The woman died four days later in Epsom Cottage Hospital, senseless, with a letter from her mother at her side talking about "the cause."

William snorted to himself at the memory. Women and their causes. Helene and her cause, her objectives. It was a kind of cancer of the spirit once women flung themselves out into society; they could not cope alone. Their very independence spread misery among their daughters and sons. There were several examples in his own family history of wives who had determined to be separated from their husbands, and what had it got them? Lonely deaths in far-off dependencies, living scandal-strewn lives. Wives and daughters needed to be at home, under a common roof. Boys might stray; they might sow their wild oats.

He thought of Harry as he was last night at the Partington ball. He had felt quite comfortable until he had seen his own son with a party of raucous fellows causing a rumpus at the end of the room. Once or twice they had removed themselves after being talked to; he had glimpsed them outside, each with a champagne bottle in his hand and smoking a cheroot. He had not known that Harry drank much at all; he rarely touched a drop at home. Eventually, around midnight, in the haze of the dance floor, he had watched Harry come back into the first room beyond the buffet. His son had stood for a while in the center of the floor, alone. For a moment William thought that he might have been seeking out his own family; then, with a stab of disappointment and chagrin, he saw that he and Octavia and Louisa were not the objects of Harry's attention at all, but Isabelle Canford, who, like Harry, was standing alone.

He had seen them regarding each other, seen Harry approach her, seen them talking. He had been able most acutely to put himself in Harry's place, for he had known such women before in the 1880s: women disregarded by their husbands and who, having provided the heir and spare, were out on the town. He recalled one long-ago night in a theater box, remembered, foolishly, how padded the woman was in her clothes, and how that had never occurred to him, all the skirts, the rigidity and formality of her; he remembered the thick opera cloak wrapped around her in the carriage and his own youthful fumbling—even the steps to the little London house that she secretly owned were etched on his memory.

He had watched Harry take Mrs. Canford's arm and hold her hand. Canford himself was very old now; even his imprisonment of his wife had relaxed after her scandalous affair—he was ill at home, a subdued old man of eighty. And now here she was, circulating confidently again in society, and rather pretty still despite her forty-nine years. Both women and men gazed after her as if she were some exotic bird. The woman he had taken in the carriage long ago and afterwards in the secret little house had been twenty and already a mother twice over to her fifty-year-old husband. She had been another woman like Mrs. Canford—lonely, and desperate to be loved.

William had an urge to go over to them, through the crowds, and take Harry's hand away from hers. There was something unpalatable in it, for really Isabelle Canford was old enough to be Harry's mother, even his grandmother. One would not think so to see her, of course; she looked barely forty. As he watched, he saw a man he recognized come over to the couple; it was Gould, the heir to a vast American fortune, who had asked him a few weeks ago whether he might visit them at Rutherford. William frowned and regarded the trio: Gould—tall, blond, elegantly fashionable—had amassed a reputation for being rather too charming to one's wife, and William wondered now whether that was actually true, or just the empty gossip of London. Then he saw Gould laugh at something that Harry had said, saw the man also glance at both Harry and Isabelle Canford. Gould seemed to make a decision, nodded at Harry, and stepped back. Well, that was one conquest that he had evidently given up on; his nod had been a gesture of gracious defeat. Despite himself, William smiled at his son's victory over the dashing American.

Watching still, he noticed Isabelle whisper to his son. He resolved not to interfere. After all, there could be no better introduction for Harry. She would be instructive and kind—better than some whorehouse in the West End. His heart had ached a little. He had surprised himself, and resolved to think no more of it.

At the same moment, he had seen Octavia notice Harry; his wife had pulled herself upright in her seat, glanced across at her husband, and made a grimace. She was worried about Harry, she had told him that morning. People talked; they said that Harry was up to all sorts of scrapes. He had dismissed it and reassured her, and now, perhaps, he would have more reassuring to do once the evening was over. He had smiled at his wife, glad of her beauty, her quietness, her calm. His own history never crossed her mind, or, if it did, he was sure that she dismissed it. Their marriage might be dry now—she submitted to him, and that was all he could ask—but at least they were decently together.

Women, he thought, needed to be contained. They could, if not constrained, be dangerous, tempting, indecipherable beings. In the noisy darkness of the bridge, he put his hand momentarily to his head.

If only it were possible to contain Helene de Montfort.

He turned and walked down towards Parliament Square, where his own carriage was waiting.

• • •

Jack Armitage stood outside the village pub, eyes closed.

He had been waiting so long that he was half-asleep in the sun, leaning against the immobile flank of Wenceslas. Now and again the horse shuddered, but otherwise it too might have been asleep, its head bowed. There was not much to hear in the deserted lane; the grass was already high in the verges, and beyond the drystone wall the fields stretched away. Out there in the new greenness of the year, the Wastleet came skirting the village just as it skirted Rutherford, clear and shallow—down here it had none of the depth that it achieved near the great house. Jack was thinking in an idle way of some little girl he chased across the fields once—all he remembered now was the heat and the sight of her long hair flying—and then the image of Louisa came into his mind. And then Emily. He opened his eyes.

John Gray, the Rutherford land steward, was coming out of the pub, wiping beer from his mustache with the back of his hand. Jack thought him a stuffed shirt in his tweed breeches and jacket and waistcoat—yes, stuffed was how he looked, full of self-importance—but for all that he was a good man. Jack straightened himself up.

"If you take the wagon to the quarry, they'll be waiting for you," was all his instruction.

Jack touched his cap. "Aye, sir."

Gray walked away to his own horse and swung himself up onto it. Jack watched him; they said in the village that Gray had some aristocratic blood—had been born on the wrong side of the blanket somewhere in Sussex. You could hear the southerner in his voice, but Jack didn't know whether the story was true. Gray kept himself to himself, and his family out of everyone's way down at the gate lodge.

Jack took Wenceslas's bridle and led the horse down the road. They reached the curve of the river and the medieval stone bridge that crossed it, and the quarry came into view, a little place not above two acres, chipping a band of limestone out of the sand and clay. With the sun overhead, the light was blinding, a white world. Dust rose. Wenceslas barely shifted as the stones were hauled up rollers and into the back of the wagon. "For the house drive?" someone asked him. "Aye, right enough," Jack answered. The snow had taken away a lot of the drive's edges. This would make it all neat again, which was what Rutherford was, in his opinion: neat and tidy, trimmed and cut, an unreal place. He preferred the stables. And he thought of Louisa again in his dogged, dreaming way. He wondered who would contain her and keep her in the neat edges she was supposed to fill, and her image became tangled up with the running girl. He wiped the sweat from his neck and wondered whether it was warm in London.

He had been told once, by one of the house-maids who had gone there for the Season, that the women all looked like princesses: that they dressed up every day in much finer clothes than they wore here, and that there were dances every night, and that she had seen Lady Cavendish come in from a party at night and there had been fresh orchids in her hair and pinned to her dress. And that she had stood in the hallway and pulled off the orchids and thrown them to the floor as she took off her wrap.

The maid had rescued the orchids and kept them in a vase, where they had bloomed in the kitchens. And he thought of those flowers, and imagined Louisa in all sorts of gowns, and her turning to look at him, as she had often looked at him kindly when he had saddled her horse for hunting, or for going on to the parkland, and that this time she would have orchids in her hair, just like her mother, and like the orchids growing in the glasshouse. And then the idea of the glasshouse shattered the dream as Emily's face came back to him, pale, motionless, rigid, as they put her in the shuttered motor van that had smoked and snaked its way down the drive, taking her away to be buried. He stood up, slammed the back of the wagon shut, and took Wenceslas out of the yard into the green, deserted world of the road.

They trudged on down past the pub, its windows now closed against the afternoon and its curtains drawn. It was only when he was well past it that he heard someone calling out behind him. He stopped and looked; the publican's daughter was coming up the road after him, holding a leather pouch.

"Is it Jack?" she asked.

"Yes."

She held it out to him. "Will you see Mr. Gray? He left this behind him, his tobacco pouch."

He took it. And then from the pub came the unmistakable sound of a child crying.

"Oh," the girl said. " 'Tis the bairn."

They regarded each other. He tied the horse to a field gate and walked back, ducking into the cool interior of the pub. It was only two rooms, centuries old, low ceilinged. The girl took him to the back, where a kind of dairy house was attached. He recognized the room; there was a stone plug in the sloping floor, and the well of the floor was covered in water from an underground spring. Milk churns from the farm stood in the water, waiting to be collected and put to Richmond. In the far corner, on a stone windowsill, was a basket, the kind that he and his father kept bran in at the stables. He walked across and looked into it, and a squalling, red-faced child looked back at him, fists clenched. The girl took the baby out and held it in the crook of her arm, glancing up at him.

"A fine lass," he said at last.

"Aye," the girl agreed. "When she quiets."

As if in obedience, the hiccuping cry stopped,

131

and the color faded in the face, and all at once it was a tiny version of Harry Cavendish looking up at Jack—the same eyes, the same shape of forehead, the same color hair.

"Well, that's his image," Jack murmured.

"Aye, but best not say it," the girl replied.

He looked for a while, turning the tobacco pouch over and over in his hands. "Did Mr. Gray come to see it?" he asked.

The girl made a huffing sound of disapproval. "She's got a name."

"Oh, aye?"

"It's Cecilia," the girl said, pronouncing it with elaborate care.

All was still. He could hear the water faintly lapping on the floor against the metal churns. "Cecilia," he repeated.

"Reet fancy, though, bain't it?" The girl leaned forward, imparting a secret. "It were the grand-mother's."

"Whose grandmother's?"

"Hers," the girl replied, cocking her head in the direction of Rutherford. "*Her* mother's."

"Lady Cavendish?"

"Who else?" the girl said. "She comes here and pays us."

"Eh? Does what?"

"Pays for her keep."

"Does she indeed," Jack murmured. "Does she."

When he went back along the green lane, past

the hedges, past the fields, he felt no surprise, though he had never known where the baby had gone until today. His father had said far away, but now he knew it was a lie to stop him from seeing Emily's child, to stop him from thinking of that night, to stop him from thinking of Harry Cavendish. "Keep away," his father had warned him. "Mind your work. That's all you have to do. Don't cross them."

But *she* had not kept away.

She came to see her, and named her for her own mother.

She knew. And had, after all, kept her grand-daughter close.

William reached the London house at six o'clock, to be met in the doorway by the de Rays and Louisa. There was a carriage standing outside— he presumed it belonged to Mrs. de Ray—and it was confirmed by the woman marching towards it, Florence and Louisa in tow, like some flounced and beribboned massive barge towing two smaller boats.

"Good evening," he said.

Mrs. de Ray inclined her head by way of acknowl-edgment. Louisa caught his arm. "Where have you been?" she asked, all smiles. "We're going out to the Chathams' party. Mother says she's not coming. Are you?"

"No," he told her. "I've been to the House."

"Oh, pooh," Louisa retorted. She lowered her voice. "Florence's mother seems in a bit of a bate."

"Over what?"

"I'm sure I don't know, Father," Louisa said, gathering up her skirts. "There's been a visitor in with Mother, and when Mrs. de Ray came they had some sort of confab and Mother said to go on without her. I haven't been in there. I don't know who it is."

He regarded her levelly. "I do wish you wouldn't use all this jargon—'confab' indeed."

She laughed and kissed his cheek. "You really won't come?"

"Who is the visitor?" he asked.

"I told you that I don't know," she told him. "Mother kept the doors shut."

He frowned. As Louisa got into the carriage he noticed Mrs. de Ray looking at him. It was a baleful glare, and the smile froze on his face. It came to something to be snubbed on one's own doorstep.

Inside, Bradfield stood waiting for him, taking his coat with downcast eyes.

"Where is Lady Cavendish?" he asked.

"In the drawing room, sir."

"What the hell's she doing in there?" he demanded. "Why isn't she going out?"

Bradfield said nothing. As William made for the drawing room, the butler merely walked ahead and opened the door.

Octavia was sitting in a chair in the center of the room. He stood in the doorway, thinking immediately that she was ill; her face was deathly pale. She looked almost absent, and for an awful moment he thought of his own father in the moments after his fatal stroke, head cocked to one side as if listening to faint music before he died. Then Octavia turned her head and stared at him.

He stepped into the room, Bradfield closed the door, and it was only then that William noticed the figure standing at the far end of the room. It was a young man, hands clasped behind his back. He appeared, from his stance, as if he had been looking out the window through the heavy drapes at the carriage leaving outside.

"William," Octavia said. Her voice was a low monotone. "I'm told that you know who this is. I'm told . . ." She hesitated. He saw that her eyes were full of tears.

The young man stepped forward. He bowed slightly from the waist. "Lord Cavendish," he said, with a slightly satirical air. The lisp in his voice added a childish edge; William had an eerie sensation of having stepped onto a stage where the blackest comedy was taking place. He turned back to Octavia. "Dearest—" he began.

She held up her hand to stop him. "This," she went on, "as you know, is Charles de Montfort."

And then he realized, watching de Montfort walk towards him across the room, that Helene had carried out her threat. She had sent their son to London to see Octavia, to confront them both.

And that while he had been out that afternoon—sometime perhaps when he had been standing on the bridge idly watching the world go by—his marriage had fallen irretrievably to pieces.

Chapter 4

*O*n the day that John Boswell Gould was born, there had been an earthquake in New York City. It was August 10, 1884, and the noise rattled through Long Island and Connecticut and Pennsylvania, shaking the windows on Brighton Beach so much that the diners rushed out from the restaurants, and the telegraph officer on Coney Island asked where the explosion was, thinking that a powder mill had gone up. People in Greenpoint ran to the vast oil works, expecting to find an accident, and the animals in the Central Park menagerie paced their pens, disturbed, heads down, staring at the ground. Farther west, they said that the Housatonic River boiled and shook.

John was born at the split second of the second aftershock, in a Fifth Avenue mansion, right across the street from the Goulet brothers' magnificent houses. Only four months before, John's mother had been in there marveling at Mary Goulet's gold drapes and the fourteenth-century-style dining room, but the scent of the flowers had made her feel doubly sick. She was sick all the time while she was pregnant, she had told him. "And the stench of those damn flowers, those damn waterfalls and pastures and mountains and *roads* of damn flowers, John, I near passed out," made her ill for the rest of her life at the sight of lilies.

And so he came into the world while Fifth Avenue cracked and rumbled, and while he grew up, New York grew up with him, just the same as him, leaping headlong, roaring down the world driven by the railroad and financier families that sweated the rest of the population. The streets got paved, the Astor slums flourished, and Little Italy heaved with doubling and redoubling torrents of immigrants. John Boswell Gould, in his fancy school suits, watched Waldorf build his giant hotel on the corner of Fifth and Thirty-third; then the Astoria right next door. John had watched the workmen crawling about in the scaffolding of the Gothic towers like flies on fanciful facades.

He had gone to Harvard with Mike Vanderbilt, and he knew Vincent Astor, and he had sailed at the yacht club where Jay Gould, his distant cousin who knew how many times removed, was reviled behind men's hands and behind his own back, everywhere. "You a Gould?" he was asked. Sometimes they spit on the ground. "You a Fisk?" he'd reply. "You a Crocker?" They called them robber barons: the Fisks, the Vanderbilts, the Crockers, the Villards, the Harrimans, and they were all mad, in his opinion. Crazy mad like foxes, smashing banks and brotherhoods and businesses, and building up their vast fortunes—their hundred-million-dollar fortunes, their two-, three-, four-hundred-million-dollar fortunes. And their sons, some of them, went crazy too in their fathers' footsteps, clinging on to slums or railroads or steel mills like weasels, or building casinos in the South of France, or getting divorced because they couldn't satisfy their wives, or going crazy in quiet confused ways, unable to hold a candle to the sledgehammer-wielding thugs who had been their fathers.

So he would say that he wasn't really a Gould. He told himself that he was cut from a different cloth despite his money. He was second and third generation, and he had ideas of his own. His father, Oscar, had bought a department store—a good one too, a great one. It had all the New York ladies buying their linen there and their Tiffany glass and their inscribed dinner services and the trousseaux for their daughters. The waves of lace and silk and linens, and the floor after floor of furniture, had been enough to send John Boswell to Harvard, and let him spend his summers at the yacht club. It was where he had met J. Pierpont Morgan.

You could smell J. Pierpont coming a mile away by the trail of his Havana cigars, and God help you if you looked at him too long or tried to take his photograph, because the old man had some kind of illness that put a nose the size and shape of a bagel on his face. They had names for it—names they called it behind his back—but the real name was rhinophyma. It didn't stop

J. Pierpont from owning half the railroads in the country, though, or keeping all the banks in his pocket; and it didn't stop him from being commodore of the club or having a big black steam yacht on which John Boswell had sailed; and it didn't stop him from bellowing like a bull or being a force of nature, all of which John heartily admired. And John Pierpont Morgan, with his grotesque rhinophyma nose, was the real reason that he was here in England at all.

John Gould stood back now and surveyed Rutherford, the house seemingly silent and dozing in the early July afternoon sun. He had come to England before Christmas aboard the *Laconia*, and, following his plan, he had seen other Tudor houses: Kentwell Hall and Long Melford and Burton Agnes. Yesterday he had been at Moulton Hall, the manor house built in 1650 and only a few miles up the road, near Richmond. The country around here reminded him of parts of Vermont; it was surely strange to think that the English places had already been old—ancient, their history indeterminate, the families who had once held them a thousand years ago now lost in time—when the *Mayflower* had nudged a shoreline on the other side of the Atlantic.

He had seen William Cavendish in London in March just before the Season began, and told him that he was writing a book, and asked whether he might visit Rutherford and look at the beautiful library. Cavendish, to his mind, had taken an age to reply, putting his head to one side and frowning, looking down at him as if from a great height. But then, John had found that was the way of the English. They distrusted a man if he didn't own a title going back at least six centuries. Gould had a famous name, all right; they recognized that, and the word "Gould" had opened a good few doors to him that might otherwise have been closed. He had been admitted to numberless London drawing rooms, charming the ladies—those bored aristocratic ladies, how they blushed to be so ruthlessly charmed!—but the men . . . ah, the men were a different matter. They would ask him whether he rode, whether he shot, whether he hunted. They would ask what *manner* of trade his family was in, as if they were asking what *manner* of contagious illness he was carrying. And when he answered that he was just traveling, they frowned; if he dared to mention that he was writing a book, they shied away from him, as if the possession of a brain were a dangerous, incomprehensible treason. He had smiled to himself at it all. No doubt he was puzzling; he puzzled himself, in fact. He would agree with anyone who considered him feckless, for "feckless" he rather liked; yes, feckless was good—he was feckless and footloose, impatient, easily bored; he had a curiosity in his soul that he couldn't get the better of. It had led him all over: into houses, across seas. But he wanted to know people—yes, perhaps that was it most of all. He wanted to know people. And for a man it was, in any aristocratic household on this side of the great pond, seemingly like admitting to being a traveling freak show all his own.

He would be thirty years old in nearly six weeks' time. Thirty was the age that his father had warned him would be the time to settle and prosper. And so he thought of his birthday as if it were some dimly clanging chime of doom, sonorously slamming the door of adventure in his face. He would avoid his father's metaphorical eye on the subject, he had decided. Life was too good as a charming wanderer to change for a life sentence as a besuited purveyor of fancy goods in New York. He took the hat off his head in the hot sunshine now, and twirled it in his fingers, laughing quietly at the picture of himself selling drapes to dowagers while he slowly choked inside a wing-tipped collar.

He put his head to one side and wondered idly whether Rutherford Park was as impressive as the other houses he had seen. It was superb; it was beautiful—but he thought maybe too much so to be impressive; it was smaller by a couple of wings. However, he liked all the lawns, and he admired the sweep of the river. He liked the big broad terrace that faced him now. He had come around the side, finding no one on the drive, and he had decided against ringing the front doorbell. He wanted to see what Rutherford looked like when you caught it unawares.

He walked across the grass from the side of the river, seeing the groups of houses beyond the giant glasshouse. It must be inordinately warm in there, he thought. Somewhere far off he could hear some kind of motor running. He looked at his watch: it was half past three. London had not been as hot as it was here; even the moors that stretched up and away shimmered straw-colored and grey, bleached.

Then he saw a woman come out from the house.

She was dressed in a loose white gown, and was walking so slowly that she looked as if she were drifting. With the thin trailing dress and the large hat weighed down with silk flowers, she looked, from a distance, like a discarded rose floating across a stretch of green water. He stayed where he was under the chestnut tree and considered her, both hands on his hips. After a moment or two of pacing to and fro along the grass, the woman stopped. From the gap in the garden wall behind her, a maid came out, carrying a tray, and behind her a man with some sort of board that, once they reached the woman, was revealed as a folding table. They stood hesitantly behind her; she waved a hand. Soon a cloth was laid, and tea was provided, and the servants retreated; at the garden wall he saw the maid look back, frowning before she disappeared again into the house.

He walked across the lawn. Seeing his movement suddenly, the woman looked his way, but she did nothing.

When he got level with her, he took off his hat. She gazed up at him and he smiled back. It was the smile that always disarmed the ladies, but it had no effect now. "I guess there's no one to introduce us," he said. "I'm sorry to trespass on your afternoon. I'm John Boswell Gould."

She was still regarding him with a glacial expression.

"I wrote you from New York," he said. "In the spring."

"You still have me at a disadvantage, Mr. Gould."

"I'm an historian."

"Is that a profession?"

He laughed. "Not with me. An interest."

She raised her eyebrows, spread her hands. "I don't remember."

"Lord Cavendish was kind enough to invite me. I'm writing a book on English houses."

Some faint light dawned at last. "You're the American Gould."

"That's correct, ma'am."

She held out a languid hand. "Octavia Cavendish." He took it, a very pale offering; there was no pressure. "The railroad Goulds?"

"Distant. We don't usually admit that we know them. Not all good families have great backgrounds."

"In that," she said, "I would agree with you."

She withdrew her hand and told him to sit down; she poured the tea. All the time he watched her guarded face, the measured pace of her hands, as if moving at all were a struggle to her. He wondered whether she was ill; he had heard that she was a beauty, but there seemed little of it now. A beauty had some life in it, some spark. Octavia Cavendish looked dried out somehow, exhausted. Perhaps it was the heat.

"I'm afraid Lord Cavendish isn't at home," she told him. "He's in Paris."

"In Paris in July?" John replied. "That's against the law."

She looked perplexed. "Is it?" Then she nodded. "Ah, a joke, of course."

"What takes him there?"

She looked off towards the long sloping lawn. "Diplomatic work, and a family matter," she said. "My son is in London and my daughters are away," she continued slowly. "One in London and one in Brighton. You'll find the house very empty, I'm afraid."

He gave her his most practiced smile. "Well, I hope to be a diversion for you." She said nothing. "I was in London at the start of the Season. I had the pleasure of meeting your son several times."

145

She considered this. "Perhaps you move in the same circles."

He held up his hands. "Oh, I'm too old to be in his orbit," he told her. "But he's an engaging fellow."

She almost smiled. "What a turn of phrase," she mused quietly. "His engaging nature is becoming quite the talking point."

"I assure you I don't gossip," John replied. "I leave that to others. Everyone in London tells me I'm after their wives, for instance."

"And are you?"

"My God, no." He smiled broadly. "But women are much more entertaining than men. At least they talk about something other than dogs and horses."

"Well," she murmured, and looked away from him across the grass. "I hope to be more interesting than a horse. But I can't guarantee it."

John looked for some time at her reflective profile. She seemed very lonely, and it did not surprise him. All this great house and nothing but her in it, with what he guessed would be a small army belowstairs. What did she do all day? he wondered. Walk about staring at her gardens? Sit down alone at dinner? She looked as if nothing at all would interest her; she was just a stuffed doll sitting in a pretty dress. He'd met a thousand women like her, empty vessels in their wallowing pond of riches, with beautiful faces and nothing at all—nothing *at all*—to say. He felt a ripple of disappointment; his mother had said that Lady Cavendish was supposed to be good company.

"I came to look at the library more than anything," he said. "If that was still convenient." She turned her gaze back to him. "I'm doing a kind of study of English titled families. Tudor history right up to Georgian."

"And are Americans interested in all that?"

"They are indeed."

She shrugged. "How extraordinary," she murmured. She tossed her head slightly in the direction of the house. "There are acres of records as dull as ditchwater," she told him. "Cavendishes stretching back into the dark ages. I don't envy you."

My God, he thought. *Is there anything at all that matters to you?*

He was put in a guest room that night, a room that looked out towards the great beech-lined drive. When he came down to dinner, he found that he was alone, that Lady Cavendish was "indisposed" and had taken to her room.

The butler—a laugh a minute if ever he saw one—was stone-faced; her ladyship often took dinner in her room, he was informed. She sent her apologies. At one end of the formal dining table, John tried to engage Bradfield in conversation. There was nothing doing. Over the soup and the main, Bradfield gave nothing away. By the time dessert came around, Bradfield's supercilious tone politely told him that he might burn in hell. It was not his business, Bradfield answered to John's interested questions, to know what Master Harry was doing in London, or whether Master Harry might return anytime soon. It was not his business to know whether Lord Cavendish would come back from Paris this month. Bradfield in addition did not know anything about this unsettling fiasco with the Austro-Hungarian Empire on the Continent. When John asked the old man whether he knew that some Serbian archduke had been shot two weeks before, and that a London newspaper had the headline "To Hell with Serbia," and that British ministers were squawking about London like chickens with their heads cut off—or at any rate the British equivalent—the dry response was merely that Serbia was not Bradfield's concern. The butler added, with a slightly raised eyebrow, that the Balkans had been at war since 1912, and probably would continue to be at war indefinitely.

"And you don't think you'll be dragged in?"

"No, sir," Bradfield replied, as if the suggestion were preposterous.

John thought about Princip, the boy who had shot Franz Ferdinand and Sophie—the boy who was Harry Cavendish's age. He thought about Duchess Sophie throwing herself across her husband's body and taking a bullet in the stomach, and of Franz Ferdinand gasping that she should stay alive for their children. And he considered that maybe the British were about to get a mighty jolt out of their great houses and stupefied lives, because he couldn't see Lady Cavendish stirring herself to throw a hand over her eyes, never mind destroy herself for her husband. They all sat in their fine places and read the cricket scores and complained about the servants. They picked up a newspaper only to fan themselves against the heat. In London, he could feel something black gathering: clouds on the horizon thick with destruction. But you wouldn't know it here. Kaiser Wilhelm, he thought, had been right when he'd had his little rant in 1908. The English *were* as "mad, mad, mad as March hares."

Eventually, John took the hint. Still watched by Bradfield, whose disapproval was tangible enough to cut with a knife, he got up, walked back through the magnificent hall hearing the echoes of his own feet, and took himself resignedly to bed.

There was still no sign of Octavia Cavendish the next morning, so he went into William Cavendish's study and then into the library at the back of the house.

He stood for a moment taking it in: the floor-to-ceiling shelving that ran right round the room, the French doors to an orangerie, and then out into the garden. Through an open window, there came the scent of roses in the warm, midsummer air; sunlight dappled the room. He wandered around, gazing at the titles on the spines of the books— vast three-foot-tall encyclopedias and atlases in leather bindings, with the titles picked out in gold, crumbling editions of Dryden and Pope, the ubiquitous complete works of Shakespeare, dozens of estate books arranged by year, beginning in 1750. Carefully he took one down, walked over to the long library table and opened it.

Here were the lives of the Cavendishes laid out in expenditures through the centuries. Mortgages and rents occupied most of the entries, but there were household ones too: *sugar, jam, nutmeg, saffron, chocolate salup, oil of almonds, tincture of myrrh* . . . He wondered what the hell they used myrrh for. Wasn't it to wrap bodies? He ran his eye down page after page. *A pair of everlasting shoes, five shillings* in 1755 made him smile; *a beehive, one penny;* and then, *gave Fanny Thoms three shillings for making my gown,* written in a sloping feminine hand later the same year. Nice gown, he thought to himself: it was worth thirty-six beehives.

Noted in the lists were the payments for staff: the stillroom maids, the laundry maids, the cook maids, the maids of all work, the parlor maids, the housemaids. He sat back in his chair and thought of the master of the house taking his pick from a whole population of them. They were of varying distinctions, he thought. Was it beneath a gentleman's dignity to take a maid of all work? Could he seduce only upstairs maids? He started to laugh to himself. Perhaps the fellow went outside the house, to the field hands, the milkmaids, the dairymaids? Or maybe the washerwoman, paid sixpence in 1761, or the "weeding woman"? He'd heard how women who worked in these places were fair game; he wondered whether they were still. What was William Cavendish doing in Paris? What did he do with the gaunt, sad woman who was his wife when he *was* here?

He leafed through the years: bills for the coachmen, the housekeeper, the huntsman, the nurse; endless entries for malt and cider and brandy and wine; for asparagus, for scissors, for soaps, for a carriage, a compass, and hunting dogs; for mahogany chests and great beds and Turkey carpets; for ducks and chickens; for saddlers and tailors. In one of the margins someone had written, *Honesty is no match for villainy.* He puzzled over its meaning. Who was the villain—the tradesman, the master, the maid, the wife?

Just as he leaned over the book, frowning, the door opened. Octavia Cavendish stood on the threshold. "So, you are here," she said.

He got to his feet. "Good morning. I hope you're recovered?" he asked. "It's a fine day."

She glanced out the French doors as she walked

over to him. "So it is," she observed. Coming to the table, she asked, "What are you looking at?"

"I've been distracted by beehives and ever-lasting shoes," he said, smiling. "These ancestors of yours enjoyed themselves."

"Yes," she murmured. "They are good at that."

She looked him up and down—to his mind unsettling; he started to wonder whether he had shined his shoes, her inspection was so lingering. He had stepped back to let her see the book, and had a moment to observe her now at close quarters. He'd spoken in the past tense—"they were"; she'd spoken in the present, he noticed: "They are good at that." This morning, she looked a little more alive. Rested, anyway. Her skin was so pale. Her hair was caught up somehow in a loose roll; she wasn't fashionable—she might have cut the vast mass of dark coils if she were— but he could see that there was no affectation.

"Well," she murmured. "Well." She turned and walked along the far wall, looking up at the shelving. "What did you particularly want to see?"

"I was told over in the States about Beckforths," he said. "By a man called Morgan."

"And who is he?"

"He's over in Egypt right now," he told her. "He's a banker. He's a lot of things, actually. But he's got a house in Khargeh. The Temple of

152

Ammon, you know? He wrote me that he can hear the jackals howling at night. He said it was just like the bank."

His joke fell flat. She merely murmured, "The fashion for Egypt and all that. Yes, I see." Then she paused thoughtfully. "Has he been in London? I think William may have met him at his club. Some years ago, when William was last in Parliament. Does he have . . ." She waved her hand close to her face. "It's rather . . . what would one say . . . ?"

"The nose. Yes, that's him. He comes to London," John confirmed. "He's a regular traveler."

"I hear there're a lot of Americans in Luxor and Cairo."

"Yes." He grinned. "We infest everywhere. Like fleas."

She rewarded him at last—at *last*—with the ghost of a smile. "And are you a flea?"

"You'll be scratching in no time. Maybe you're scratching already, with my coming here?"

"And why would I do that?"

He waved his hand at the library. "Centuries undisturbed," he said. "Picking it over, shaking off the dust."

"My God," she replied. "Shake it off all you like. It deserves it."

There was a beat or two of silence. He felt like he had stepped into something: some dark, unexpected pool of water.

"You're from Yorkshire yourself?" he asked. "Another house nearby?"

"No," she said. "I'm an outsider, Mr. Gould. Just like you."

She sat down at the library table, arranging the folds of her thin cream dress carefully around her. She wore some kind of lace collar with a point hanging down her back almost to her waist; it looked as if that heavy Brussels lace alone were worth a fortune. And then, with a jolt of surprise, he saw that her feet were bare. He struggled with the sudden juxtaposition of the heavy, all-covering lace and the glimpse of naked skin, but she was already talking.

"I'm one of those whom they marry to keep the houses paid for," she was saying. "Every now and again they take up with some common woman with money, with a fortune. They install us so that they can pay the staff."

He stared at her, shocked. A creeping tide of color had risen on her throat. She put her hand to it almost immediately.

"Well, I guess . . ." he began. But he couldn't think of anything to say. She had sounded so bitter.

They were interrupted by a footman at the door, carrying a tray. "You'll have coffee?" she asked.

They sat while the sun crept round the garden outside. She barely touched the tray. He tried to think of some innocuous subject.

"You'll go to Egypt too?" she asked eventually.

"Yes."

"As a guest of this man, this Mr. Morgan?"

"Yes. I find him inspiring. He put me onto history."

"You're inspired," she murmured, as if envious. "And do you have a family, a wife?"

"I wouldn't inflict my life on a woman."

"Why, what sort of life do you have?"

"A selfish one. Traveling, pursuing things that interest me." He got up and went over to the first shelf he had seen as he had come into the room. "Like this," he said. "Look at this. *Travels in the Chinese Regions, 1822.*"

"They sponsored exploration," Octavia said. "They paid people to go looking for them, to find trade routes or bring back botanical specimens. We have trees in the garden here brought back from China."

"See, that's what I like," he told her.

"They were everywhere," she said. "But the Caribbean mostly. Doing I don't know what."

He glanced around at her. "And your family?"

She gave a short, soft laugh. "We dirtied our hands. We stayed where we were and built wool mills. We ran them. We still do."

"*You* do?"

"My managers. Or rather, as they are now, my husband's managers."

"And this is. . . ." He paused, wondering whether

155

he should say it. "Excuse me, but this is what makes you a common woman?"

She didn't answer. She looked at her naked feet.

"I guess I shouldn't say it," he murmured, "but you know those Beckforths were pretty darn common to start off with. The first of them being a horse catcher and all."

She glanced up. "A what?"

"The first colonel, the one who got to Jamaica whipping three slaves ahead of him. He'd been at sea. God knows if he stole the slaves. But he couldn't get work, so he sold himself as a horse catcher." He saw that Octavia was smiling. "Must have caught a lot of horses. They made him governor. It's all in the library at Oxford University. The great-grandson put his diaries there."

"They were the richest men in the Caribbean," she countered. "And that great-grandson built a very famous house in England. He was an art collector. His father had been the Mayor of London."

"That'll be the man with fourteen illegitimate children by two mistresses?"

Her glance skittered away from him; she pushed away her coffee cup.

"They started marrying real well," he continued, anxious to get her smile back. "There was a daughter who married an earl, and then that art collector—well, he was fine. Filled his house with choirboys and made them dress in harem pants. And he seduced his cousin's wife. But that's really no surprise, because her husband didn't do a whole lot but build a ten-mile wall round his house and shoot things. And that same cousin brought a boy from Italy and kept him in his house until the boy escaped when he was eighteen, and dashed away to France, where he went crazy one day and murdered an Italian countess for wearing a green dress. And then there's his wife—the one who got seduced by the harem-pants man—her mother left her father, and her sister got along just fine with her coachman, but not before her husband filled the house with his prize pigs and gave them whole damned great sofas to lie on and tucked blankets round them at night. . . ."

Finally, she was laughing. "That's not so," she said.

He gestured at the library. "Got to be here somewhere. You want me to find some family letters?"

"No, no," she murmured.

"And then there's Jamaica," he added. "You think your hands are dirty with the wool mills? Did you read anything here? There's half a dozen volumes right over there. The lives of slaves. The rebellion of 1831. They executed them all kinds of dirty ways. They said they weren't human. But it was them, the plantation owners. It was those people who weren't human." He sat back in his chair, seeing the mixture of humor and dismay on her face. She began to frown.

"Excuse me," he said. "I'm sorry. I've really no right."

"This part of the family here, William's family," she said slowly, "were the ones who didn't want slaves."

"I appreciate," he answered.

"But no, you don't," she told him. "William's father was an extraordinarily kind man. He was given this house because he didn't want part of that trade. And because he wouldn't sit in Parliament."

"I'm sorry to correct you," John said, "but the money that bought this house came from Jamaica and all the misery out there." She held his gaze. "But who am I to talk?" he asked. "Money trickled down to my father from the fine art of clubbing union workers unconscious when they went on strike. Esteemed cousin Jay had a filthy character, they say." He spread his hands apologetically.

She stood up slowly. "Mr. Gould," she said, "you are welcome to read through anything you find here, since William has given his permission." She walked to the door, where she turned briefly. "But I think it rather below the belt to insult his family. Despite everything this year, I am proud of our place here."

And, before he could answer, she was gone.

Leaving just the one phrase in his head, and it rattled around in his head all day long.

Despite everything this year.

Two hundred miles south, Harry was in London, standing in front of St. Martin-in-the-Fields and looking at Trafalgar Square. He had come from the Gaiety along the Strand, and was staring at the blackened column of Nelson, thick with its years of soot in the midday sun. He was waiting to keep an appointment with his father.

His hands were plunged into his pockets, and he wore a bowler tipped back on his head and a sunflower in his lapel. He'd almost bought a checked waistcoat to set the lot off. If the cheap ensemble didn't make his father's blood pressure rise, however, then nothing would; he wouldn't need a bookmaker's waistcoat to see William's fury etched in every pore.

He was thinking grimly that it would be jolly fine fun if his father would knock the hat off his head. He'd rather enjoy a fistfight with the old man. He was sure to come off better; he'd had his share these last few months. He would give anything to see William's top hat roll in the muck under the wheels of the omnibuses; he'd like to see it trodden on by one of the delivery carts trotting round the square, weaving in and out of the lumbering buses with their lurid Dewar's advertisements snaking up their outside steps.

William was coming from the Royal Exchange. He had let Harry know that in the letter from his club yesterday evening. *I shall be engaged at the House until eleven, and thereafter at the Exchange,* he had written. And followed it with a veiled reference to their having to speak about money. Of course, the old man meant debts. *His* debts. Harry had penned a reply saying that he'd meet his father in the street, knowing that would be beneath his dignity. Well, if he didn't come, what of it? He doubted anyway that he would look the old man in the face, such was his contempt. He hadn't laid eyes on the lying bastard for nearly five months.

It was Charlotte who had started the story, of all people.

He had gone to the London house on a whim that morning last March; the kind of whim that drove a fellow home to see whether his mother would lend him money. He remembered feeling bad even then—not sleeping for thinking of Emily's face—and had probably been drunk all day; since Christmas he had been trying to make life jump, to make it live, to fill it with something to make the blood run hot. As a result, he had felt tired: slow to catch on, hands thick, brain filled with mud. He wasted his days with God knew what—anything. Nothing. Women, sport. He had almost cried when he had first seen Louisa in her presentation dress, because she had looked so very virginal and clean: laughing and bright, nothing clouded in her face. He couldn't remember when he had last felt clean like that. Some days he had felt as if Emily were still clinging to his neck, haunting him with that aghast expression of that December night—that horrible look of humiliation. He fought it off, occupied himself, roared and fought and gambled. It was fine. Very fine. All told, he was a very fine fellow. He'd knock anyone down who said otherwise.

He had hardly got in the door that night—with the footman looking like someone had died—before he saw his youngest sister on the stairs, first putting one foot on an upper step, and then back again in a private little dance of indecision.

He'd thrown his hat in Charlotte's direction. "What are you hopping about for?" he'd asked, grinning. "Go on up or come down, one of the two."

Charlotte had put her finger to her lips and indicated the drawing room with a twist of her head. "Mother and Father," she'd whispered, stricken. He had stopped and listened. He could hear voices: his father's uppermost. But he couldn't hear the words. "What's the matter?"

Charlotte had gazed at him. "Where have you been?"

"Out and about."

"There's been the most awful row."

"What for?"

"I don't know," she had confessed, looking agonized. "Somebody was here last night. Father came home, and . . ."

"And what?"

"There was a man."

A smile had begun to spread over Harry's face. "This sounds rum," he said, and made straight-away for the drawing room, ignoring Charlotte's calls to come back.

When he had opened the door, William had been standing by the fireplace, where a fire burned. It was the only bright spot in a room steeped in grey; no lights had been lit. The freezing March day seemed to have invaded the room despite the blaze from the hearth.

He caught William saying, ". . . a necessity." Then his father saw him.

Octavia was standing by the window. To his astonishment, she was weeping. He had never seen his mother cry. Laugh, yes; wipe her eyes at some absurd story. But real tears? Never. He was across to her in half a dozen strides. "Mother! What is it?" Octavia had taken his hand briefly; in a curious gesture she tried to stroke his arm, a gesture of pleading restraint. Harry had turned back towards his father. "What has happened?" he asked.

William took an age to answer; then, "Come here and sit," he said. "Sit with your mother."

Octavia had guided her son back to the couch;

162

William stayed standing. In retrospect, it was one of the things Harry couldn't forgive: that William stood over them, every inch the patriarch, the figure of authority, while they were forced to sit beneath him looking up into his face. He might have sat opposite. He might at least have brought himself to their level.

"There is news," William had begun slowly, "which I had hoped never to have to share with you."

At Harry's side, Octavia let out a gushing sigh that might have been disgust. "Is it Louisa?" Harry asked. "Where is she?"

William had waved his hand dismissively. "It's not Louisa."

Harry had looked from one parent to the other, mystified. His mother was looking away, towards the fire.

"I have a son," William said slowly. "That is, I have another son. He is a French citizen."

"French . . . ?" Harry smiled involuntarily. It was ridiculous.

"His name is Charles de Montfort. His mother is Helene de Montfort. He came here last night."

Harry stayed for some time looking at his father without saying a word. He was trying to work it out. Helene de Montfort was a reasonably regular visitor to Rutherford; she was some sort of distant cousin, his father's age. Maybe a little younger. All very French. She always emphasized that. All the little French phrases, all the names dropped. *That* awful woman? "She was at Rutherford at Christmas," he said slowly.

"Yes."

"At our table. In our house." In the ensuing silence, he rose to his feet. "How old is this . . . this Charles?"

"He is twenty-one this month."

Harry looked back at his mother. She'd told him years ago that he was born a year after she and William were married. He was nineteen now. And so . . .

As if he had read his mind, his father said, "Charles was born in Paris a year before your mother and I were married."

"In Paris," Harry had repeated. He'd clenched his fists at his side. "And you were not . . ." He struggled to find the words. "Not married . . ."

"There was never any question of that," William said.

"Why not?"

"Because she was poor," Octavia said bitterly.

Harry rounded on her in astonishment.

"That is incorrect," William said. "Helene was not the type of person . . . I was not sure . . ."

"Of what?" Harry demanded.

An expression of awkward distaste crossed William's face. "Madame de Montfort had many acquaintances."

To Harry's horror, his mother began to laugh. In

the circumstances, it was an awful sound. He saw that, at last, his father had begun to blush—if blush it was—the dull red tide flooding his face. Anger. Embarrassment. It was hard to say which.

"Oh, yes, a great many *acquaintances,*" Octavia said. "Despite wanting to be called Madame, she was always very keen to impress her popularity upon us, if I remember. Or to impress it upon me." Octavia shuddered. "Madame de Montfort, who was no *Madame* at all, and how very scandalous she was as a result. How very fascinating that made her! There was so much talk. No one ever knew if it was true. . . ."

"I doubt that it was," William said.

Octavia turned a ferocious, scathing gaze on her husband. "And you know that for a fact, I suppose?" she asked. "That she was perfectly well behaved? In the face of all talk to the contrary?"

"That is all it was. Talk, hers and others."

"You defend her, even now," Octavia hissed softly. She bit down hard on her lip. William said nothing at all. Octavia looked back at Harry. "She had a patron," she told her son. "That much I know. That much I was *told,*" she said, glancing at William. "This *hearsay* maintained that she had a patron with a house in Bergerac. An estate there. She had taken herself off and we heard nothing of her, and then when she reemerged it was said that this man had committed suicide."

Harry looked back at his father. "What for?" he demanded.

"I really can't say."

"He discovered that she had a son," Octavia said. She had begun to cry again, soundlessly.

"My God." Harry breathed out. "When was this?"

"In 1893, or 1894," Octavia said.

"And you heard this then? What, from others?"

"I heard the gossip. I heard the rumor she had a child. But I never thought that . . ." She left the sentence hanging; then, straightening her shoulders: "She had never mentioned a child to me."

Harry got up from his mother's side, walked halfway across the room, and turned to William. "She had your son; she kept it secret, hoping to . . . what? Marry this other man? He found out, and . . ."

"It is hearsay. I have no idea what happened."

"But why didn't you marry the woman?"

"This is not your business."

"I should jolly well say it is," Harry expostulated. "I should jolly well like to know why you wouldn't acknowledge a son. I should say that was of some profound interest to me."

"It was not discussed."

"A bastard! Not discussed!"

William's face froze. "I'll remind you that your mother is present before you use such language."

Harry laughed out loud in surprise. Then he took a breath. "Do excuse me," he answered with excruciating emphasis.

William was glaring at him. "It was not . . . such an outrage—if you like, if that is what you would imply—in Paris. Such were the times. Such was the society. And Helene did not want to live here. She wouldn't have me. I was never entirely sure . . . not entirely sure that the boy was mine. But she told me that he was."

"You asked her to marry you?"

"It was never the case that she would accept me. It was not the life she wanted."

"But you . . ." The blood was beating in Harry's temple. "So, for one reason or another, you came home. And married Mother and never told her." He looked between the two of them. "That is a disgrace."

"Harry," Octavia murmured. "You are judging something that you know nothing about."

He looked at her, hearing the grief in her voice. "What does one need to know," he asked, "other than that?" He turned away, saying—almost to himself—"She's been here a lot. I remember her even when I was little. She . . . she played boules with me out there once, on the lawn at Rutherford; she taught me . . . and I showed her cricket, when I was beginning to play cricket. . . ." His voice trailed away. His father's mistress had been coming to the house for years, watching him.

When she had a son of her own hidden away. His father's son. His half brother.

He looked at William. "You kept this secret," he said. "All these bloody years."

William stiffened. "I don't intend—"

"But she came to our house!" Harry exclaimed. "Came here, and to Rutherford. She sat and ate our food and lorded it over the bloody servants . . ."

"Be quiet," William said.

"Be quiet!" Harry repeated. "Is that what a gentleman does? Be quiet about it?"

"I should think you have little room to maneuver on the subject of being a gentleman," William retorted.

"What?" Harry said. "What?"

"Harry," Octavia warned.

"I mean, I beg your pardon, sir?" Harry shouted. "I am at fault in some way?"

"You have behaved . . ." And William, at last, seemed to grasp the folly of his argument, which was about to be based on his son's profligate spending. He literally backed away as Harry strode forward.

"Are you to lecture me, sir?" Harry demanded. "Perhaps on women of a certain kind? Spending one's money on them? Following the horses? What? Do tell me, sir."

"Please," Octavia said, unheard.

Harry's face was livid. "And this . . . son . . . came here last night to say what?" he continued in a dangerous monotone. "To do what? To ask what?"

"He won't come here again," William said.

And, almost in the same second: "He came to ask for money," Octavia replied. "For what he believes is his inheritance. And your father has refused him."

"What else would you have me do?" William said.

Octavia looked at her husband levelly. "What did he mean by what he said to you as he left?"

"What was it?" Harry asked. "What did he say?"

His mother glanced at him. "He said that he would make your father understand what it was to be ruined."

William gave a derisive snort. "The boy has inherited his mother's dramatic gifts," he said. "He is not ruined, and neither is she. There are plenty of those willing to support her."

Neither Harry nor Octavia replied to him. Octavia dropped her gaze, and, when he saw her distress, William's stiff-backed dignity briefly deserted him. He leaned towards Octavia, put out his hand. "My dearest . . ."

She shied away from him, and looked up again at Harry. "Helene came to Rutherford at Christmas to demand money for Charles. Your father refused her. And so she sent her son . . . their son . . . to see *me*."

William's hand dropped to his side. Harry

walked up to his father until he was barely an inch or two from him. "You subjected my mother to this humiliation," he said.

"It was never my intention."

It was as if Harry had not heard him at all. "You subjected my mother to this humiliation," he repeated. "On top of your deceit." And he had turned back to the sofa, and taken his mother's hand.

It was at this remembered moment, at the very moment when he saw himself again walking out of the room and out of the house all those weeks ago, that Harry noticed a cab stop on the intersection of the Strand with the Square. A man got out and paid the fare, and shielded his eyes against the sun.

He was wearing a top hat, all right. The last man in London to wear a top hat in daylight, by Harry's reckoning. Harry watched him objectively until William's gaze lighted on him and the older man raised his hand.

He waited while his father walked over. In the time it took for William to reach him, Harry had the chance to consider that there was something different in William's walk, his bearing, some hesitancy. Perhaps he was nervous, Harry thought with satisfaction.

William drew level with him. He held out his hand, and, after a moment, Harry reluctantly took it. If William had an opinion on Harry's clothing, he didn't mention it. Instead, he gave a small, polite smile. "Are you hungry?" he asked.

"Not remotely."

"Shall we go to Brown's?"

"I don't care," Harry said.

William eyed him almost with distrust. Then he gave a slight wave of his hand towards Brown's and, after a long moment, Harry followed him.

That afternoon in Rutherford, Octavia was thinking of the very same evening in February that Harry had been remembering.

She was alone in her bedroom, and had been asleep, and had woken up to see the long voile curtains billowing gently in the breeze from her open window. Octavia had lain there while a dream rapidly escaped her: something concerning the Ponting exhibition of the year before—of standing before the photographs of Scott's exploration in a gallery where the national grief was tangible. The Antarctic landscapes had made an impression on her of such bleakness and extraordinary beauty; they were scenes that needed no titles. She sat up, conscious of the coldness in the dream, and its loneliness, and she put her hands to her eyes.

She swung her legs out of bed and went to the window and let the sun stream in on her face. She was aware of the significance of the dream;

she was aware of this cold great gulf that had opened up in her life. She sighed, and thought that she must pull herself together. Wasn't that what her father might have said? "You must pull yourself together, Octavia." For a second, his grip was on her arm and his cigar breath streaming over her face. "What the devil are you crying for? You must shape yourself. Stand straight." My God, her father. Of all the memories that she wanted in her life at that precise moment, he was the last—he, and his selfish admonishments ringing in her ears.

And yet she knew that she must try to rouse herself out of her lethargy; she was succumbing to it all too readily. Depression was in danger of drowning her, and she must resist it. She kept going back, over and over again, through the scene in the house with William and Harry after Charles de Montfort had left. And she kept returning to her conversation with Hetty de Ray some forty-eight hours later.

Hetty had not railed against William; she had not even seemed surprised. She had sat listening calmly as Octavia had stuttered out the truth.

"You must understand something of what I'm feeling," Octavia had murmured.

"You mean my own dear husband's Italian menagerie?" Hetty had responded. "Ah, well, my dear, of course it is maddening. But what is one to do?"

Octavia had bitten her lip in an effort not to cry. "But William," she had whispered. "Of all people."

Hetty had smiled sadly. "You mean that he is so respectable?" she had said. "Darling, they are quite the worst."

"And with such a woman!"

"Well," Hetty had replied equably, "what other sort of woman would it be, after all?" She had shrugged disdainfully. "You ought to really thank God it is someone like that. Imagine if it were some pretty little thing of a good family who was desperately in love with him. How much *worse* would that be!" She had nodded sagely. "It's much better that Helene is already disgraceful."

Octavia had shaken her head. "I can't be sanguine about it, like you. I don't find it funny."

"You're quite mistaken if you think I do," Hetty had told her.

The traffic had streamed past Hetty's drawing room window; and at that second Octavia had felt a sudden and violent rush of loathing for the city. She had felt claustrophobic, as if at any moment she might leap up and run from the room. Hetty must have seen something in her expression, for the older woman had got up and crossed to the sofa where Octavia was, sat down next to her, and held her hand.

"The worst of it is, I feel that everyone must know," Octavia whispered. "All of society. When

I go out with Louisa, I sense everyone's eyes on me. Perhaps they've always known. Perhaps it's been common knowledge, and I've been an utter fool."

Hetty had shushed Octavia into silence. "You must put such ideas out of your head at once," she had retorted. "My dear, I pride myself on gleaning as much gossip as possible out of our dreary days, and I have to tell you that I've never heard a word about William and Helene de Montfort."

"It might have been going on for years," Octavia had replied. "I simply don't know. I can't bear to ask William." She had raised her eyes to Hetty's. "In fact, I can't bear to speak to him, or even to be in the same room."

Hetty had nodded. "Of course you can't."

"And he's going to Paris almost immediately."

"What on earth for?"

"Some visit to the embassy."

"And to see this woman?"

Octavia had nodded. "I suspect so." She sighed. "I can't stand the Season anymore," she had murmured. "I want to scream at it all. I've little patience with Louisa; I shall spoil it for her, I'm sure."

The two women had sat in silence for a while. Then Hetty had rung for tea to be served, and the silence continued all the while it was brought. When the parlor maid had at last vanished and left them alone, Hetty had turned to Octavia. "If you can't bear it here, go to Rutherford," she had said.

Octavia had looked at her, surprised. "Leave London?"

"I rather think you should," Hetty had said decisively. "Dearest, you look like a perfect wet weekend. People haven't talked about you yet, but they surely will if you persist in drooping about. Leave Louisa here with Florence and me. Go home and recover. Don't wait about here for William to return; let him find you." She had leaned forward and smiled conspiratorially. "And make sure that you exact a very heavy price for his indiscretion. A month in Monte Carlo at least, and a rather important piece of jewelry."

Remembering now, Octavia smiled to herself. Of course, Hetty knew that it was all so much more serious than an indiscretion. But if she was anything, Hetty was the flagship for fortitude. "You must be dignified," had been her parting wisdom. "Rise above it."

Octavia had taken her advice. She had come back to Rutherford; she had left Louisa in Hetty's care. She had come home and tried to put it all into proportion, and she had failed. She would imagine William in Helene's embrace, and the black clouds of misery would drop down on her.

She envied John Gould. She envied his ability to go freely about, pursuing whatever interested him, with no apparent obligation to anyone. She envied him this wonderful ability to shake the dust from his feet. She envied him his good humor. He seemed so absolutely fresh, somehow, as if he had stepped from a bandbox, polished and gleaming. He breathed life; his face was full of interest.

And then it came to her: he was the mirror image of herself twenty years ago. He was the picture of what might have been in a parallel universe. She might have had that life, if she had been a man: free to travel, free to form friendships, free to explore—she might have been him, twirling his hat in the sunshine and smiling broadly at the absurdities of English history and the very kind of family in which she was now imprisoned.

Imprisoned . . . She straightened herself, stepping back from the window.

Shaking her head at her own thoughts, she rang the bell for Amelie.

It was the next morning when Mary Richards held a letter in her hand and stared at the handwriting.

Mr. Bradfield looked down at her with his usual inscrutable expression. It was breakfast time in the servants' kitchen—she sat at the table with her untouched bread and tea in front of her.

"Well, open it," Mrs. Carlisle prompted. They all

watched her. Deep inside her, a small, dark note became a constant drumming: it was pure fear. She opened the envelope and took out the single sheet of paper. *Blessington Rectory,* said the address at the top. She saw the first words, and the drumming became a thunderous roar, closing off her oxygen, making the room swim.

Mary, like Emily, was a mill-town girl.

Cook said it was a Christian kindness on Lady Octavia's part. Most were very grateful, but Mary was not. She carried her resentment silently; she nourished it. She often thought to herself during family prayers that she was probably not a Christian at all, but, just the same, it was really not her fault that she had been lost from the fold.

She had been introduced to the devil at an early age; he was the overseer, and he belonged among the hellishly clattering looms. Mary knew that if she ever came into contact with Lady Octavia— if she would ever meet her on the stairs one morning as sad little Emily had done—she might want to drag that particular Christian soul back over the moors and introduce Lady Octavia to Satan himself. Still, she tried to be a good girl. Not because of Mrs. Jocelyn's dour Presbyterian warnings about damnation—how could that touch her?—but more to do with keeping the job she had. To lose it would mean she'd be forced to go back. To lose it would be to step back into Hades.

Sometimes at night she would lie awake with a hard little knot in her chest, as if she had swallowed a stone. It wasn't envy; she didn't envy Lady Octavia's listless life this summer; nor did she want to be like Louisa. She could see they were constricted in their own way—caught in a net, much like her, forced to behave in a certain fashion and with no freedom to break from it. No, the knot was made up of something else— pity and anger for Emily, exhaustion, and a fierce desire to *do* something, to make a mark. She wanted to be elsewhere with a passion that made her skin itch and her very bones ache from frustration. She was in a cage; she knew that much. But somewhere there had to be a way out.

She would lie and think of Nash—romantic, sensitive Nash with his downcast look and his thin, long-fingered hands, and his secret stolen books of poetry. There was not a romantic bone in her body, but she knew why he read Keats and Shelley. He was free when he read them— somewhere else. A person with a soul, a heart. He would look at her occasionally, and her blood didn't run any faster, but she recognized a fellow captive—recognized that *elsewhere* look. He was better than anyone knew; he had a fine quality. And then, as she was alone with these thoughts, the hard little knot would increase. Where could Nash put his fineness, so unappreciated? And where could she go with her anger? Her mind ran around it all like a blind man inching around a room looking for the way out, the unmarked door.

After breakfast Mary stood in the backyard for a while and then ran to the stables. It was forbidden, of course, but just at that moment she didn't care. Passing from the bright light of the stable yard into the shadows, she saw Jack Armitage dreamily grooming the little pony that used to belong to Miss Louisa. He seemed lost in his own thoughts, a smile on his face, until he looked up and stared at her. She was out of breath, and taut with embarrassment at having to ask anything of a man she hardly knew. "Do you know how to get to Blessington Mills?" she asked him. "I have to go now. I have to go."

He hesitated. "If Mrs. Jocelyn says so."

"Jack, please." Jack relented, seeing the anxious look in her brown eyes. She had a plain, open face and was short—almost tiny—but gave off an aura like a little powerhouse, a fierce determination.

"Best ask her."

Mrs. Jocelyn read the letter from Canon Wesker while Mary waited, hands clasped in front of her. Eventually, she raised her eyes to the girl. "Your only sister?" she asked. And she had the ledger of employment in front of her that told her when Mary had come, how many were in her family.

"Yes," Mary replied, looking behind Mrs. Jocelyn at the locked linen cupboards, thinking how often she'd stood here to be handed bed-

179

sheets and coverlets and pillowcases. How many hours she'd spent in this house and never asked a favor, anything extra. Mrs. Jocelyn knew that Mary's wages supported her family—or what remained of it: her younger sister and father. She knew that it was a year since she'd been home. Yet the older woman made a great show of considering the address of the rectory on the letter, her lips pursed. Mary felt like running across the room and slapping her, shaking her. *Let me go, let me go. . . .*

"It would only take two hours if Jack took me over the tops," Mary blurted out at last. "The train doesn't come till three, and then there'd be a wait. . . ." She hated to beg.

"If any more of the family were home, it would be out of the question," Mrs. Jocelyn told her. "I must ask Lady Cavendish. Go and wait in the scullery."

Oh, God, Mary thought. *You old bitch.* She knew as well as anyone that for half the time now Lady Octavia couldn't be disturbed. Something had happened—none of the maids knew what— in London; neither the master nor young Harry ever came home; the daughters kept away. Lady Octavia was a ghost, and so Jocelyn was never going to consult her. She'd make Mary wait all day and then tell her no.

Mary ran back to the stables, stowing her cap and apron in the kitchen on the way, and taking down her shawl. She heard Mrs. Carlisle call out, but ignored her.

"What's Mrs. Jocelyn say?" Jack asked.

"She says it's all right," Mary lied.

She had never even ridden on a horse, and if her mind hadn't been elsewhere she might have liked it, seeing the world spread out around them now on the two-hour journey. She clasped her hands tightly around Jack's waist, afraid at first, but soon getting used to the motion. Eventually, she rested her head against his back. On the top of the moor you might have been a million miles away, in some tropical land; the moor was almost burned away with the heat, and a sandy path ran through it as straight as a die, and the country for the last hour was a heat-drugged, soporific division of orange heath and blue sky. She did not care whether she ever reached home, because she knew what she would find when she got there. She knew that she would smell the town, and she was right: as they came over the last brow, it was underneath them in a smoky haze. The pony's hooves began to slither as they started the descent, and by the time that they reached the lane, grit was in the air: grit, smoke and dust.

Jack stopped by the pub beyond the beck. Except for the smell and taste of the place, if you turned your back you might still have been somewhere pleasant. The beck rushed over pebbles and there were sheep in the field opposite, staring walleyed at them. She would think of the little bridge afterwards as the division between heaven and hell. In the dappled light and shade beneath a line of ash trees, Jack let the pony drink from a water trough.

"You'll be all right?" he asked. "You want me to come down?"

"Go home," she said.

"I can't do that."

"I'll be the night. I'll find a way back. Go home."

He hesitated, turning his cap in his hands. "I'll wait till six."

"Do as you must," she replied. She started to walk, but after a moment turned back to him. "Thanks for bringing me, Jack," she said. "But please go back now."

He gave her one of his dogged, thoughtful smiles. "I'll come back at eight tomorrow morning," he told her.

She walked down the hill.

Once, this had been a green valley, and only a village. Then someone—she didn't even know his name—had built a water mill, and, taking in used clothes and blankets from the workhouse, started to shred them, combing out the strands, washing them, making them back into yarn. They called it "shoddy." And the shoddy mill grew, and other mills were built, and a hundred years ago Lady

Octavia's father came here and built the great grey stone blocks by the river—five- and six-story mills that housed the spinning rooms. And he built the long lines of spinning sheds, and the scrubby little streets of back-to-back houses where the floorboards were laid over bare earth. And in no time at all it had become filthy.

Mary had been born down there in one of those houses, and she had only the vaguest memory of her mother—a kind of sketched profile as she always saw her while she worked: hands flying, head cocked to one side like a bird's, a band of dark brown hair pulled tight. The memory was hazy now, frost on glass. As for the house, cold and damp was the most she recalled, and a clothesline across the only bedroom, with a sheet hung between her parents and the children, and all of them in one bed, stacked head-to-feet. In winter, everyone froze, and their breath hung in the upper room in a barely dissipating opaque cloud. They had nothing; they were always in debt. In summer, the rats ran along the wall of the privy at the end of the street, and the river stank, and in the mills the wool fiber clung to their clothes and skin. They breathed it in, and they combed it out of their hair, and they shook it from their hands.

One day when Mary was working in the packing room, standing on her wood box next to her mother, they heard something strange. It was the shriek of the clocking-on whistle in the middle of the day, and soon after, a silence that hollowed out the air, making every worker in the room look to the door. Mary had started to shiver without knowing why.

In a few minutes, the overseer came; he went into the glass-walled office, and then he and the manager came out and walked to their bench, and took her mother's arm. Her mother had gone white. She had walked only a few paces with them before she had fallen down in a dead faint.

The cottage hospital was set back a little from the narrow road three-quarters of a mile from the mill. There were railings in front, and a patch of grass, and a wide turning circle for the wagons. A large, white-columned door was much too big for the single-story building behind it. Mary went in and gave her name to the starched and stiff-necked woman, all disdain, who manned the desk, but when she heard Mary's surname her expression softened a fraction. The woman got up and took her down a corridor and through another door. And there, sitting on a wooden bench outside the public ward and looking sick with terror, was Mary's father.

"Don't get up, Father," she said to him as he struggled to rise. She kissed him swiftly on the cheek and sat down by his side. "What have they said?" she asked. "What are they doing?"

"There's not much can be done," he told her.

Francis Richards was forty years old and had been the sole parent to his remaining two children for ten years. It showed in his face: the awfulness of the responsibility, the shock of his injury, and the way that drink had blurred his features, flattened his sallow face. He sat with his cap in his lap, gripped by the stub of a fist that had lost all its fingers. He had been a doffer once, replacing broken threads and empty bobbins on the vast and deafening machines. On the day that the siren had screamed and the work stopped, the cause had been Mary's younger brother, Joseph. He was a scavenger, his job being to lie underneath the loom to retrieve fallen threads, and although he had been only eight he knew well enough to lie flat, to crawl as Mary used to do. But Joe had reached up for some reason, and his father, seeing him caught, acting on instinct, had reached down. Joe was dead in half an hour, but Francis had only lost his fingers. But that was like saying he had lost his life, because he had been a weaver. Mary's mother hung on for another year, fading inch by inch with a disease of the lungs that the doctor had called *congestion* but that Francis, thick and stupid with drink at night, had called something else. "Fucking cursed wool," he would say, looking about himself for something to strike, to slap, to punch. "Fucking cursed fucking wool."

He looked at Mary now, took in her neatly

pressed clothes. "You're doing all right," he said appreciatively. His eyes filled with sentimental tears.

"Never mind that," she told him. "Where's the doctor?"

"He was here first thing."

"And said what?"

"What I just told you. There's nothing to be done." He started to cry. "Oh, Mary."

She stood up. "We'll see about that."

She stepped forward and pushed open the door to the ward. There were twenty beds on each side, lined up with military precision. The linoleum floor gleamed. In the center stood a stove belching out heat despite the summer day outside. She strode down the ward, looking left and right, until a nurse caught her up and grabbed her by the arm. "You're not allowed in here."

"I'm Mary Richards," she said. "Where is my sister?"

"You're not allowed to come in. I've told your father."

Another woman was coming up the ward now. Their uniforms crackled on them like waxy paper; the ward sister's elaborate cap danced over her head in a complicated arrangement of wings. Mary tried to move, but the first nurse was holding on tight. "Diphtheria is highly contagious," she said. "And you may be carrying disease yourself."

Mary glared at her. "Hose me down, then," she said. "Do what you like."

She had by now seen Sarah: a familiar face in the far corner. And she could hear her thirteen-year-old sister's tortured breathing. There was a bowl of something by the bed: eucalyptus and turpentine; her cough sounded metallic. "Sarah," she whispered.

"It's not allowed," the nurse repeated. The sister stepped in front of Mary; she was taller and broader. "You must get out," she said. "If you don't want to be like her."

Mary wanted to kill her. "I haven't got it," she retorted. "And you haven't got it. So how did she?"

The woman tilted her chin. "There are many causes," she replied.

Mary nodded. "I know what the causes are," she said. "Dirty mill work and dirty mill houses."

"Are you a nurse?"

"No, I'm not a nurse," Mary said. "But I know who gets it and who doesn't." She gave the woman a savage look and elbowed her way through. She walked to the bed and squatted down at Sarah's side and felt for her sister's hand under the tightly pulled sheet.

"Don't touch her," the sister warned.

Mary took out Sarah's hand and rubbed it between both of her own. "I'm here, I'm here," she murmured. "What have you done to yourself, eh?"

Of all of them, Sarah looked like their mother. She had thick brown hair; the rest of the family—Francis included—were mousy or fair. And Sarah's hair was drawn back now just as her mother's had been to avoid the loom and, later, to get out of the way of the finishing: a near-black wing across the forehead. Sarah wriggled her fingers a little, pointing at her throat. Mary could hear the high-pitched thread of air on every breath.

"Yes," Mary said. "But it'll be over soon. It'll get better."

Sarah's nose began to bleed. Mary reached to dab it with the end of her own sleeve, searching in her pocket with her other hand all the while to find a handkerchief. And then suddenly there was far too much blood, a stream of color against the white bed, livid in the afternoon light. The nurses pushed Mary back.

By the time she went back out to her father, she had cleaned herself up a little, careless of the fury of yet another nurse that she had contaminated a bowl of water. She had been made to swill out her mouth with antiseptic, and scrub her hands. She had been lectured and manhandled to the doors of the ward, numb with shock.

To her bewilderment, it seemed to be forty minutes later, judging by the clock over her father's head; she felt very weary, and the monochrome colors of the hall fought in her vision, a series of meaningless rectangles, and patches of light from the windows. She put up a hand to steady herself, and her palm slid along the painted wall; she looked at her father, and thought of the stories he told of his own father—a man crippled in the right knee by arthritis after being a piecer in the cotton mills. Of how he'd come to Yorkshire because he thought the work would be easier. And of a story he had told of a girl working a drawing frame who, like Joseph, had got caught in the shaft and drawn into it, and of how she was turned around and around on the shaft until it broke all her bones and her body jammed the gears. And of how, when Joseph died, Francis had said that his father had made the journey over the Pennines for nothing, and that wool was as bad as cotton, and they were all beasts made to be broken in one way or another. And of how angry she'd been even then, because she hated the way he talked, all beaten down, without any dignity.

She knew he thought that she was cruel because she hadn't cried, and because she'd got this look on her face, determined and sullen, after the accident, and after her mother died. Even now she couldn't bring herself to weep or put out a hand to help him stand, though she could see the dawning realization on his face as he looked at her, and the hard stone knot was back in her chest, an immovable, furious, choking weight.

"We're to go down to the other end of the hospital," she said. "We're to wait there."

189

"Why?" he asked. "Is she being moved?" He'd got to his feet at last, and swayed from side to side, the cap still clutched in his hands. "What's at the other end of the hospital? Is it another room?"

She couldn't bring herself to be kind; it seemed to be outside her abilities. "It's the mortuary," she told him, and took his arm and hauled him forward, a deadweight dragging his feet as he doubled over helplessly with grief. It was as if someone had struck him; he suddenly began whimpering. "Stand up straight. Don't let them see you cry, Father," she said, hissing the cruel instruction in his ear. "Do you hear me? Don't you dare give them that."

Chapter 5

*I*t was half past four in the morning when John Gould walked out of the great house. There was a faint dawn light as he opened the library doors and, passing through the orangerie, he was out into the garden. The roses were densely lined on either side of him—pale deep ranks of cream and apricot and pink. All around them hovered the seductive memory of yesterday's scent; he reached out and touched the nearest petals, trailed his hand among them. To his right was a cobbled path, perfectly laid in herringbone with terra-cotta edging. Everything was heavy with moisture; it had rained in the night.

It felt wonderfully fresh, as if the world had been newly created. The sky above was already blue, and as he stopped and looked down the broad flights of steps towards the lawns, he had a moment of complete well-being. He felt as if the house were his, just for that second: the house, the parkland, the distant woods, the rising hills. The valley was hushed; it was as if nothing could ever touch this idyll. Hard to believe that there were cities or strife anywhere in the world while standing here; it was a charmed kingdom all its own. He walked forward and rested his hand on one of the stone urns on one side of the steps, and noticed a pattern of bluebirds around the rim; he wondered whether it was the Beckforth bluebird, like the Jamaican plantation. And he wondered whether the story was true that the bluebirds were unlucky.

He considered Octavia Cavendish's luck, being alone here. She had been absent again at dinner last night, and it had disappointed him—irked him somewhat. He prided himself on knowing women—liked them, actually—but he was baffled at her obvious attempts to keep herself apart. Did she not like *him?* Surely that was not the case. Everybody liked John Boswell. In fact, he made a point of being damn likable; he was good company—he had been told so. He was easy to get along with. But perhaps Octavia Cavendish despised Americans. Or her husband's wishes, or . . . Well, then, what? Maybe she despised life. He was used to women smiling more—smiling at him, at least. He would like to be able to condemn her as cold, but could not. There was another woman, he felt, hiding under the surface.

Involuntarily, he looked up at the windows. He didn't know which one was hers; they were all closed. He turned away and went up the brick path and through the gate, walking fast along the walled garden path beyond. Two boys were already at work here, among the immaculate rows of vegetables; he raised a hand to them by way of hello. Octavia had said that there were fifteen gardeners, some just for the kitchen garden, two just for the plants in the house, some just for the flowers in the glasshouse. Gardeners and under-gardeners and boys, a seemingly mute population; he glanced back and saw the boys looking at him—perturbed, perhaps, because they had been seen. He knew that they were meant to be invisible to the inhabitants of the house. He couldn't resist a private smile—he supposed it was all to give the impression that these giant places ran along by magic, smoothly gliding without sweat, without effort. What a world. At home, he knew all the servants by name. They were Josh and Edwin and Eddie, Kate and Millie, Thomas and Si. Here, the only person Octavia called by name was her maid, a pert little Frenchwoman with a seductive face. God, it was strange. Beautiful and deserted and enchanted, straight out of a storybook, complete with kings and dukes and princesses. He came from a loud world yelling its price by the yard, and this summer he had descended, like Alice, through a looking glass, into a peculiar landscape of unwritten rules, where tradition lay inches thick and you could turn up a book that had *August 1612* written across the top of a page by a long-dead hand. The world behind the glass, the world down the rabbit hole . . . He looked back at the house, now touched by the first sunlight, the entire south front lit with a glowing, tawny light, and he shuddered for it. God save it from the brawling world, he thought. God save it.

He was coming to the stable yard, with the enormous glasshouse on his right; the head gardener lived here in the grey stone building beyond, he had been told. Past the pretty tiled roof were various outhouses, all looking prim and neat, as if they had been scrubbed and painted fresh. At right angles to the small garden attached to the first house was a massive barn. He glanced up at the sloping roof as he passed; at the far end was another gate.

As he hesitated, wondering which way to choose, a man came out of the very gate he was facing. He was about sixty or so, broadly built, dressed in breeches and a thick jacket. He was carrying a water bucket. Seeing John, he stopped and touched the rim of his cap. "Early up, sir."

"Yes, I am. I was wondering about taking a horse out."

Josiah Armitage looked him up and down, then took the bucket up again and cocked his head for John to follow.

They went into the pristine yard; there were stables on three sides. Glancing up, John saw that the clock tower said barely five. The old man went down the line, opening the half doors. In one of the stables he could hear voices: boys larking about, it seemed, laughing. "Shift yerselves!" Josiah called. The laughter stopped; two heads ducked out, and just as quickly ducked back in again.

Smiling to himself, John stopped and looked in the first stable: a grey shire turned its head to look back at him.

"That's a fine fellow," John said.

"We got him, and three t'other," Josiah told him, coming back. "And two Suffolk Punch. But the carriage horses was sold a year back. We had two good pairs, grey and black. And a four."

"Sold?"

"There's no call for carriages."

"I guess not. But what a shame."

"The young want automobiles now. We got an old landau; we got two little barouches for the ladies. But they never get out now."

"Master Harry. I suppose he's got a car?"

Josiah pulled a face of disapproval. "It'll all come to nowt. There's no style to it. 'Tis too much speed. My Jack looks after that Metz like a babe."

John was stroking Wenceslas's head; the horse blew warm, sweet-smelling breath into his hand. Then John looked up at Josiah. "I heard a child in the house this morning."

Josiah opened the door, murmuring to the horse. "There's no bairn there, sir."

"I could have sworn it. I heard crying."

"None but her ladyship home. Her and you."

"No children with the servants?"

"None allowed."

Armitage seemed so absolutely sure, that perhaps he had imagined it, after all.

An hour earlier, he had opened his eyes suddenly from sleep. The sound of a baby screaming had been close by and piercing. He had listened intently, thinking he heard it again. He was certain that there were footsteps, a door softly closing, more muffled sound. He had sat up in bed, rubbed a hand over his eyes. A child's cries, and the too-familiar dream. It kept coming to him these last two weeks, and woke him every time with a horrible, crushing presentiment.

He had looked out at the perfect peace of the Rutherford drive, and thought of Quebec and a familiar stretch of coast, where the St. Lawrence broadened out and they put the pilots ashore before crossing the Atlantic. It was where he himself had been on a ship not three months ago. And it was now barely two weeks since the *Empress* had foundered there. He had crossed over several times on board a little Quebec ferry that ran from just north of an uncle's ranch; it was a busy shipping lane, and it felt very big. He'd been across the English Channel a couple of times, but the Channel didn't feel like the St. Lawrence: massive, fast churning, icy cold. The last time he'd taken the ferry it had steered through fog, blowing its whistle constantly, and other passengers had called him out on deck, because the whales would surface in such weather. He had imagined them under the tiny boat, moving mountains in the water, navigating the blind and deep reaches of the Channel, and he had always felt very small, very fragile—just a speck on the ocean in the rolling fog.

The *Empress of Ireland* had left Quebec harbor on the afternoon of May twenty-eighth, and she had collided with a Norwegian coal freighter in the early hours of the next morning. The smaller ship had hit the liner amidships, like a screwdriver piercing a can; those in the lower cabins, fast asleep with their portholes open because of the claustrophobically poor ventilation inside, drowned almost immediately as the *Empress* had rolled to starboard. Those in the upper cabins had scrambled to the deck, but only three lifeboats were launched before the ship tipped further; seven hundred had got out somehow, through portholes onto the side of the listing vessel. For ten minutes or so in the dark, in the fog, passengers and crew had clung to the slanted hull. They thought that she was aground because she was immobile in the water; they thought that she had hit a sandbank. And then suddenly the stern tipped up and she sank like a stone: up at the stern, and then fallen to the depths. More than a thousand had died in fourteen minutes.

He'd heard about it as soon as the *Laconia* had docked in England, and he'd leaned up against the pier where he was standing, feeling sick. Henry Seton Kerr had been on the *Empress*. He knew him. He'd heard him speak at his geographic club. He'd seen himself as Henry Kerr. Now he saw himself at the bottom of the St. Lawrence. He saw the water rushing into a cabin, the door stuck against the force of the water, the gangways rapidly submerged.

And he'd been dreaming of just that: gasping for breath, and the air becoming water, and water filling his mouth and throat and lungs until there was no air at all, only the salt and the sensation of the heart swelling with the few panic-stricken seconds of flailing for oxygen. He'd felt water rolling about his body and then the ship tipping— the tipping of the ship under his feet and the utter realization that this was the end, so sudden, so unimagined, no heroic gripping to a rail or saving of some other poor soul, or survival in the sea. None of those dramatics, just the ignominious thrashing and gasping and dying, and being rattled about in the cabin like a piece of loose luggage, fingers grasping at nothing.

Everyone talked about the *Titanic*, but to his mind the *Empress* was worse somehow. Perhaps because he'd just come across that ocean himself. Perhaps because it wasn't ice, but a dirty little coal freighter that had taken the *Empress* down. A mess over navigation lights, and the crew making a mistake. Not nature, not ice, but humble little idiocies had ended a thousand lives.

That was what human beings were taken down by, he thought: not giant chaos, but trivial mistakes. Wrong turns, careless inattention, stray words, fleeting looks. Worlds turned on such things: small things overlooked. Moments of seeming inconsequence that, in retrospect, had awful significance. That was what would bring them all down, he had thought. The petty little prejudices. That, and idiot politicians.

He had got up suddenly, needing to get out. He wanted a clean, new day. He'd have to stop thinking about ships sinking. He'd have to get over this irrational fear, the old drowning fear. He wouldn't go back to New York on a slow ship, he promised himself as he hastily dressed. He'd go back on something like the *Mauretania*; she was the fastest thing afloat. Failing that, her sister, the *Lusitania*. British boats built to beat the *Kaiser* class. They'd get him home all right.

"You mun take out Springer, if you've a mind," Josiah said.

He was brought back to the present in a flash. "Springer?"

"Spring-heeled Jack the Third." There was a smile of pride.

"Your horse again?"

The fingers touched the greasy rim of the cap. "I brung him on some, sir, aye."

It was eight o'clock when he came back down through the trees by the river and saw Octavia Cavendish standing at the side of the water.

It was full bright daylight by then, and he brought the horse to a walk and was going to call to her—he was perhaps a hundred yards away—when he saw that she was reading a letter. She took it out of the envelope; she paced backwards and forwards; and then, to his surprise, she threw both letter and envelope into the river. It hardly moved; the water was low. She was leaning over the parapet of the bridge when she suddenly noticed him and looked as if she'd been caught in a crime. He dismounted and came over to where she stood.

She was dressed very plainly and rather bizarrely, with a walking coat thrown over what he guessed was a nightgown or peignoir—all its heavy ruffles showed beneath the coat and trailed on the ground. She had on a little hat; it was slanted—her hair was falling down onto her shoulders.

"Is everything all right?" he asked.

"My husband is coming back," she told him, gripping the balustrade of the bridge, staring down at the slowly circling letter. He was curiously charmed by the incongruity of it—the incongruity of her, the mistress of the house, looking for all the world like a girl who had been playing in a dress-up box. For a second, he thought that he glimpsed another Octavia: much younger, hapless, confused, struggling to find an image to suit her. He wondered whether this was a glimpse of the real her—as she used to be, the girl Cavendish had married—and he felt a small lurch of sympathy, and something deeper, more profound—a connection to her.

He stared at her, bemused, not knowing what to do. Wasn't that good news, William Cavendish's return? It ought to be, but was evidently not. She turned to him. "I suppose you think I must be mad to be out like this," she said. And she waved carelessly at her clothes.

"No, of course not," he said.

"Don't be polite," she countered. "If you thought me an idiot, you would be right."

"I don't think you're an idiot at all," he replied. "In fact, I was just thinking how charming you seemed." Her mouth dropped open; she laughed rather dryly. He realized that she was unused to compliments. Then it occurred to him, with a rush of dread, that perhaps she had decided he was being facetious. "Can I help at all?" he asked. "Is there anything I can do?"

"The problem is"—and she looked up the river—"I've lost my place. I had some sort of place. I don't know where I should be. This is my home, and yet I don't know why I am here."

"Is it your son, perhaps?" he asked. "The problem?" He was grasping at straws. He'd heard the rumors of Harry Cavendish going off the rails, though he had assumed it couldn't be as bad as all that. Young men regularly went off the rails. It was what they were supposed to do before they became fine upright citizens. It was what, after all, Harry Cavendish's ancestors had seemed to do for whole lifetimes, in some cases.

She looked at him. "Harry?" she asked. "My God, if it were only that!" She put her hand to her head, evidently distressed.

"Not your daughters?"

She shook her head. "They are both with their friends," she murmured. "Just now I thank God for it."

Confused, he looked around them for somewhere to sit. "Won't you rest a bit?" he asked. "There's a seat back a little way." She followed where he led; when she stumbled, he held out his hand. She took it, and then just as rapidly dropped it. The warmth of her, the softness of her, was impressed on his skin. He felt himself flushing, desire prickling along his hands and arms like vertigo; the patched reflections of light through the trees momentarily confused him, jangled his senses as if he really were standing on somegreat height and looking down into a chasm. It was dreamlike; he actually felt himself swaying on the brink of a drop. It was so sudden and so peculiar that he took a breath and regained reality, but he was left with an insupportable urge toput his arms around this woman. He did not dare, however.

In a few yards they were on the bench looking

at the river. Far beyond it, across the park, Rutherford was a pretty rose-colored picture, sun reflected in its windows. He glanced at Octavia; she was looking at it too. He wondered whether she knew the effect she had had on him; seeing her distracted expression, he doubted it.

"Do you have a family?" she suddenly asked.

"I have my parents. I have three brothers."

"All in New York?"

"Yes, all there."

"Living together?"

"We rub along."

"Tell me about them."

He shrugged. "Well, Father has the business. . . ."

"What kind of man is he?"

"Oh, a nice sort of fellow. Cheerful. He likes to sail best of all; he taught me that. We have a house on Cape Cod, and . . ."

"All your brothers too, all sailing?"

"Yes, and Mother's family. Full houses, you know. Parties and things all year. Mother has the Theosophical Society that we tease her about. It occupies her time. We had Indian visitors last year; she's always talking about the White Lodge and all that."

"White Lodge?"

He waved his hand. "To tell you the truth, I don't get it at all. It's a kind of religion that doesn't believe in religions." He laughed. "I don't know. It's all the fashion. We torment her about it. She takes it in good part. There are people coming and going all the time."

"It sounds very nice. And your father allows it?"

He raised his eyebrows. "It's not a question of allowing. He doesn't allow or not allow. He laughs at it all, generally. He's . . . well, he's a good example to follow."

She considered him acutely. "A fine man," she said.

"Yes."

"How good," she murmured. "How good to have someone so jolly." She looked away. Her hands were twisting in her lap. "My father ran a business too," she said slowly. "My mother died when I was small. I became his companion. I was to be there every moment. Not at the mills, but at home. Waiting."

"You must have been a comfort to him."

She began to laugh. It was the eeriest thing he had ever heard. "Companion?" she repeated, as if testing the curious word. "His companion? No, not that. I was to listen. Just stand and listen. I was told that I was particularly ineffectual at my task, but it was required of me nonetheless. Every day. For hours. To stand quite still. He would come home at luncheon, and then again at six. I had to be waiting. If not . . ."

Her head was inclined away now from Rutherford; she was gazing again at the water.

"If not?" he prompted.

She shook her head, closing off the subject. The talk of her father seemed to have let loose her inhibitions, driven by a darkness he couldn't fathom. "You are more fortunate than you know in your family," she told him. "I wish that we might be able to boast of such a thing." She turned to look at him. "You talked the other day of the Beckforth scandals," she said. "Do you have any in the Goulds?"

"Probably," he replied. "But not any I know."

She kept his gaze. "I'm afraid there are those that I do know of here," she said. He could see that she was ready to be outspoken, that some subject was gnawing away at her. Abruptly, she waved her hand at the river. "Did you know that we had a girl drown here at Christmas?" she asked. "Or almost drown. She was taken out of the water and brought into the house. It was snowing. She died the next day."

"Lord. How terrible."

"She was a housemaid here. She died having a child. It was my son's . . . my son's daughter. My granddaughter." She gazed up at the sky, seemed to give up her hesitancy and looked back at him unflinchingly.

He could find nothing to say. Which, he thought, was probably just as well.

"I don't have anyone to consult," Octavia continued in a soft voice. "I don't know, truly, whether I have done the right thing. The child is alive. I have called her by my mother's name, Cecilia. When my husband is away, I bring her to the house."

The crying child, the footsteps along the corridor. "She was here this morning," he said. "I heard her."

"She can't be here when William is home because he doesn't know," she continued quietly. "Or at least, he professes not to know." He could see her fingernails digging into the palm of her hand; she was frowning deeply. "I am faced with a problem I cannot solve; I have brought it on myself," she murmured. "I shall be criticized for taking the child in, for showing any kind of acknowledgment, of course."

"Shall you?"

She glanced up at him. "Naturally," she said, as if being obliged to ignore one's grandchild were, indeed, natural. He began to pity her intensely. "You see, William won't speak about it because Harry told him on his honor that he had nothing to do with the girl who died, and William took his word. He won't hear otherwise. A gentleman's word . . . his son, you understand?"

"I guess so. . . ."

"We might have been able to discuss it if . . ."

"If what?"

"It doesn't matter."

"I'm very sorry," he told her.

She turned to look at him. There was a flash of

defiance. "One might get used to disgrace, don't you think?" she asked. "As you said, the family is mired in it."

"I didn't mean . . . That is . . ."

She stood up and looked away, dismissing his stumbled apology. The next words were softer. "She's such a pretty little girl," she murmured. "So like Harry at his age. I expect I must find a solution somehow, but I really don't know . . . The servants talk. They see the woman from the village coming and going. My maid hints at there being talk at the downstairs table. And so one has the situation that . . . when William comes home, he may hear what I've done."

"But you'll be able to talk frankly about it, then?"

She shook her head.

"Is there anything at all I can do?" he asked. "Anything at all to help you?"

He had unconsciously held out his hand to her. This time she took it and kept it in her grasp, looking down at his fingers, and she pressed her other hand over his. "You're very kind," she murmured. There was a frisson—a jolt of electricity, it seemed to him—between them. She felt it too; he could see it in her face, a passing expression of surprise. They looked at each other. She dropped his hand as if it were hot, blushing. "I think"—and she gestured helplessly down at her clothes—"I think I must do something about this. It really won't do at all." She seemed to shake herself. "I really shouldn't be out here weighing you down with such things. What time is it?"

"About eight." She stepped away; he moved after her. "I'm not weighed down at all," he said, smiling. "It's an honor that you would confide in me."

She appraised him. "Yes, that's what I've done," she said. "I wonder why. Perhaps because I have no one else to speak to." There was a hitch in her voice; her eyes abruptly filled with tears.

"Sometimes it's a relief to speak to a stranger, an outsider," he offered. He rifled through his pockets and found a handkerchief; she took it and dried her face.

A silence dropped between them; he was only a foot or two from her. Tension drummed in his chest; he wondered whether she felt it, sensed it. She seemed quite childlike in the way that—like the bare feet beneath the gown in the library that day—the veneer of the great lady could drop away and show the vulnerable girl beneath. He wanted so much to comfort her, and struggled with what he felt were inadequate responses. He wanted to somehow show her—show the frightened girl who had waited for her father in dread, show the unhappy wife who wanted to love her grandchild freely—that she could trust him.

"I admire you for looking after the little girl," he said. "Truly I do, whatever gossip it might cause. It's a noble thing." She glanced at him. "I'm sure your husband will agree."

She stroked back a stray hair from her face, and squared her shoulders. "I wish I had your confidence," she replied quietly. "You must excuse all this," she said. "I don't cry, generally. It doesn't achieve a great deal, and in any case, it spoils the complexion."

It was said with such a pitiful attempt at gaiety that it wrung his heart. "I assure you, I'm not at all embarrassed," he replied. "And you might like to know that your complexion hasn't suffered one iota, Lady Cavendish."

They smiled at each other. It was the first true, natural smile, the first one shared. He would always remember it.

Louisa Cavendish sat in the Palm Court of the Waldorf Hotel, and felt mightily pleased with herself.

It was four o'clock, and the place was full. It was extraordinary, she considered, gazing at the crowds below the palms and the arching glass roof, what kind of people were allowed to come to the tango teas; it seemed that as long as one was able to pay one's five shillings, one might be let in. Louisa sighed, holding her skirt to one side while an absolutely gargantuan woman in an orange frock edged past her.

Louisa gazed after the fright with something

akin to pity. At least she knew how to dress, she thought, in her daring frock with the tulip skirt, and with the feather of her hat upright so that her face was not obscured; just imagine that woman trying to be seductive in the tango while the best part of an ostrich lolled down over her face; it was too funny. Some women had no idea at all.

She sat back in her upholstered chair, but only far enough to show her figure to greater advantage. It had the desired effect; one or two men at nearby tables cast brief, admiring glances in her direction. Louisa had to suppress a deliciously naughty smile. Mrs. de Ray and Florence had no idea that she was here today; she had told them she was going to an exhibition at the Tate. Florence had actually put her in a taxicab, saying that she had had enough of art for a lifetime, and it was only when the cab was out of the square that Louisa had allowed herself to laugh. It was wicked of her, of course, when they had been such absolute bricks—she would make it all up to them somehow—but she must be allowed at least one adventure. And tea at the new Waldorf wasn't *such* a scandalous event; it was rather tame, in fact. She rearranged the folds of embroidered pale turquoise silk across her knees and smiled to herself.

The de Rays were terribly good fun, actually. They might even approve of a little dalliance if they knew; Florence for certain would be green with envy that Louisa had managed an after-noon of harmless romance. When the trip to the Continent had been abandoned—all this talk of war by Mr. de Ray, without a thought for how it had ruined their plans, had put a stop to that—they had still been kind enough to chaperone her at all the largest occasions, but there had not been a single improper moment with a man. And Louisa rather thought there ought to be at least *one* before she went back home for the summer.

It was lucky that the de Rays had been able to look after her, because of Mother. Mrs. de Ray had told her with quiet firmness that Octavia had some sort of female exhaustion, and normally, of course, Louisa would have gone back to Rutherford with Mother and supported her; she would have been glad to, really, had not Mother told her to remain.

Mothers were terribly useful, and of course Louisa adored her own, but at the larger occasions they were the equivalent of a stone around one's neck. They were quite capable of frightening a perfectly good-looking prospect away, tut-tutting on about titles and names. Which sounded mean, because Mother was not a stone at all; she was good fun, if one did not count the expression on her face since the spring: that plastered-on smile. Recently, Mother had been absentminded at best, rather remote from the gaiety of some of the dances and dinners. Once or twice, Louisa had caught an actual expression of pain on her mother's face; and she hadn't indulged, as she usually might have done, in jokes about the chinlessness of one earl against the horrible halitosis of another—which was half the joy of the Season. One divided the aristocracy into droves of the murderous, the appalling, and the faintly bearable while the mothers assessed their incomes or compared their country estates, but Mother had not seemed up to the game.

After a while, Louisa had gone with her mother to the railway station and waved a dutiful good-bye amid the clouds of smoke and steam. Mother had been brittle and bright and chatty; she had said how much she was looking forward to the fresh air of Yorkshire. "When your father comes back from Paris," she had said, "you must go out with him, Louisa. You must be seen out with him. You are his daughter." Louisa had thought this rather odd. "I should think Harry ought to be seen with him rather than me," she had replied. Octavia had given her daughter a very straight look. "Harry will come round in time," she told her. "I want you to accompany your father should he ask it."

Louisa had watched the train go with mixed feelings; Father ought to be in London, not on some mysterious mission in Paris. It was something to do with the Foreign Office, Mother had said; but there was more to it than that— though what, Louisa could not imagine. He had gone almost immediately after that awkward time in March when her parents seemed to be silent with each other. They had fallen out; that was obvious; now her mother wanted Louisa to take her place on his arm about London.

Florence said that marriage was always like that eventually—her parents were frosty at best, but her mother had never allowed it to depress her. "A woman must keep her head and heart up," Mrs. de Ray had advised both girls when the subject of marriage had been discussed one evening. "And spend as much money as one can on hats. Millinery is an appropriate replacement for misery."

The letters that had come to Louisa from her mother since were jolly: reams about the house, all the usual things. And Louisa had put her mother's empty smile to the back of her mind. She would soon be home to be with her, she thought—back to the hunt balls with the chapped and ruddy faces of Yorkshire's finest bearing down on her; home so that she could hike halfway up the mountains to have lunch with Father on some boggy shoot. One particular ham-handed and gangly unfortunate had already been pointed out to Louisa as a good marriage: his family owned half of Northumberland. Louisa had pointed out to her mother that the man had all the personality of a dead fish, and the subject seemed, fortunately, to have been shelved.

Her father had been rather brutal about it: "One doesn't need a personality when one has an income of four million pounds a year, Louisa. The Abernethys have had sense enough to keep their fortune."

"That's because they're horrible misers," Louisa had countered. "Everyone knows it. They've only held one dinner, and that was absolute death. They had the most dreadful Hungarian violinists, and the wallpaper was brown. I'm not living with a man who thinks that constitutes culture."

William had at least laughed at this, which was hopeful. He seemed to have lost the knack of cheerfulness since Christmas.

As she was thinking this, she suddenly saw Maurice, coming back through the tables to their corner seat. He at least never mentioned politics; he was simply fun, always smiling, always . . . well, rather *personal*. It was so thrilling. Her heart did a little skip of excitement.

She had met him outside Her Majesty's Theatre in April for the opening of *Pygmalion*; at least, it was where she had first seen him. She and her mother and Florence had been waiting in the crowds, looking for their cab; they had been standing on the steps. It was just a few days before Mother had gone back to Yorkshire, and the conversation had been screamingly funny— all about the word "bloody," spoken on the

London stage for the very first time that night. The audience had laughed for more than a minute, stopping the play in its tracks. Now, all around them, they heard society women saying how very *bloody* it was to wait for one's driver. Mother, who once might have been the first to join in the joke, had merely looked irritably away. At first, Louisa had thought that the tall and handsome man in the crowd had been staring at her mother, but, in an instant, the stranger had given Louisa such a raffish and pointedly direct smile that she had felt herself blushing. He had vanished, but when she saw him again at the Derby, she had immediately recognized him.

He had walked straight up to her as she had watched the horses in the paddock; he might almost have been waiting for her to be momentarily alone. "Did you like the play?" he had asked.

It had taken a brief moment to place him; then, "It was fun," she had replied.

"Mrs. Pat a little past it?" he said, naming the leading actress. His accent and the common way he spoke were at odds; she associated the French with sophistication.

"No," she replied. "Not when she's married George Cornwallis-West."

"He's dashing, I suppose."

"A man must be."

He'd raised an eyebrow, touched his hat, and

turned to go. When Florence came back, Louisa had tried to locate him in the crowds, and failed. "You've imagined him," Florence had teased.

Afterwards, he had turned up in the oddest places: in Bond Street once, standing in the rain at the corner of a street as their cab had gone by, and then opposite the house one Sunday morning. In May, she had seen him when they were out riding, and then again at the mews where they took their horses. In Gamages one day, he had appeared again. "Are you haunting me?" she had asked him outright. "For if you are, I think it very rude."

He had bowed to her, taken off his hat. "My name is Maurice Frederick," he said. He stood beside the tiers of pale gloves on display—gloves and feathers and silly little purses—and seemed so at ease. "And you are Louisa Cavendish."

She'd stared at him. "I'm afraid I don't know you."

"I am an acquaintance of your brother's."

"My brother?"

"He has not mentioned me?"

"No."

"But then, you don't see him very much."

She'd taken a step back. He was very disconcerting; he talked as if he knew everything about the family—but then perhaps he would, if he was Harry's friend. "I must be going," she'd replied.

"Might I walk with you a little way? Just to the door?" He had offered his arm. "I assure you I shall not disgrace you between here and the street."

She had blushed; it was as if he had read her mind—she had been wondering whether to take a stranger's arm might be some kind of embarrassment. Or whether to refuse would make her seem gauche. After a moment's hesitation, she had complied. "Are you French?" she asked.

"From Paris."

"My father is there at the moment."

"Indeed?" he said. "But the Balkan situation, of course."

Louisa knew nothing then about a Balkan situation, so she said nothing. They reached the door to the street; she put on her gloves. Maurice looked at her appreciatively—rather too appreciatively, perhaps. "I doubt very much that your father would approve of me," he told her.

"And why is that?"

He had given a very Gallic shrug. "I am nothing. I have no money, you know."

She had tried to be modern. "I don't think that matters."

"Does it not?" He had considered this. "But no influence either. Very sad. And I must work."

"You do?" she'd asked, intrigued. "What at?"

"I'm a clerk at the French Embassy."

"Oh, but that sounds rather interesting."

"Is it?" he said, and laughed in a charming fashion. "I must remember that."

A few days later, when she had mentioned Maurice Frederick to Harry at breakfast, her brother had frowned. "I don't know a Maurice."

"He knows you."

"I daresay," Harry drawled. "But have a care, little one. Where have you met him?"

"In all sorts of places."

"Nice places?"

"I don't know any other."

"And he claims to know me?"

"He seems to know all of us. He works at an embassy."

Harry had raised an eyebrow. "He works? You mean he is in the diplomatic corps?"

"I don't know," Louisa admitted. "No, I don't think so. He's French."

"French?" Harry repeated. He'd got up and thrown his napkin on the table. "How wretched for you, dearest. And how perfectly vile for him."

But as she sat here now and watched Maurice Frederick negotiate his way through the Palm Court, cutting such a very attractive figure, Louisa had to admit that if Maurice was anything at all—and she was not quite sure of herself in the matter, admittedly—he was certainly not, and never could be, vile.

Maurice smiled as he reached the table and sat

218

down. "You look delectable sitting there," he said. "I am the envy of the room."

She laughed. "You say the most outrageous things."

He held up his hands in a gesture of mock alarm. "It is not outrageous. It is true."

She liked his brazen charm. At least he didn't beat about the bush; he made no secret that he admired her. There would be no ham-handed fumbling with Maurice, she thought, and immediately blushed at herself, and tried to change the subject. "You were an awfully long time."

"Was I?" he said. "I apologize. The bar is full of Americans."

"I suppose that's no surprise. They claim to have invented the tango."

Maurice smiled. "The tango came from Marseilles," he told her. "From places of ill repute." He raised an eyebrow to signify how shocking this might be. "Places where ladies are not ladies."

"Places that you have been?"

"I? No, never."

"But Paris is shocking, isn't it?"

"If one looks in the right places, I suppose."

She propped her chin on her hand. "I should love to see it, nevertheless. I think it's boring that Father has never taken me. He could, you know; he's over there all the time."

"Ah, well," Maurice murmured. "Perhaps it is

not a city to see with one's father. It is a city to see with a lover."

There it was again: his directness, covered with that easy smile. She was sure that she should not respond, but she couldn't help it. "Well, I haven't got a lover, so I simply can't go," she told him.

He leaned across the table and whispered, "Such a loss to Paris."

It was at this moment, rather to her relief, that tea was delivered to the table. Louisa gazed at the delicious display with perfect satisfaction; the array of tiny cakes and sandwiches was so beautifully displayed. "Oh, why can't everything be as nice as the Waldorf on a Wednesday afternoon?" She sighed.

This time, Maurice actually burst out laughing. Affronted, she glared at him. "What have I said?"

"Nothing, my dear," he told her. He pressed a napkin to his mouth to stifle his expression.

Louisa bridled. "I can't see what's so awfully funny."

"It is just . . ." He stopped as if to frame his words. "With all this talk of war, you are so refreshing."

She shrugged. "That's just what I mean," she countered, lifting the silver teapot and starting to pour. "It's all so unnecessary. Mrs. de Ray says that even the Prime Minister thinks so." She put the pot back on its stand. "Why can't everyone just be nice to one another? What is war, when you think about it? Just men posturing as usual. The King doesn't want it either, so why should anyone else? I should think the King ought to know what's what, after all."

Maurice was looking at her intently. She couldn't read his expression. She thought that, just for a second, she saw something dark cross his face, something calculating, but the impression soon vanished. He smiled broadly. "You are right," he told her, tasting the tea and fixing her with one of his direct glances over the rim of the cup. "There are a great many devious people in the world, and others suffer because of them."

"That's so," she said triumphantly. And she gazed about herself at the colorful crowds. "Everyone is so happy in summer," she decided. "And you know, it could always be July at the Waldorf. It could always be like that everywhere, all the time, if people simply put their minds to it."

He suddenly put down his cup and reached under the tablecloth, snatching at her free hand and pressing it tightly. She began to smile at the naughtiness of it; then her expression changed. "That is really rather painful," she said.

"Aren't you a precious little rose?" he asked.

She frowned in confusion. "What have I said?" she asked.

"Do you know anything at all of the world?" Still the fingers were insistent, digging into her wrist.

She tried to pull her hand away. "Maurice, don't."

A smile twitched at the corner of his mouth. "No," he said, as if confirming something to himself. "No, of course you don't. How lovely you are." And under the table, he dropped her hand.

She sat for a few seconds staring at him, perplexed, not knowing whether she should laugh or cry, not knowing whether he had been complimenting or insulting her. She rubbed her wrist; it was the first time that anyone had touched her in such a way—possessively, urgently.

She bit her lip and dropped her eyes, her heart beating uncomfortably fast. In the corner of the room, the string quartet began to play.

In the hectic rush of the London morning at eight o'clock, Harry almost missed the train from St. Pancras; he had run into the railway station with only a few minutes to spare, and the great steam locomotive had already begun to move when he finally sat down opposite his father in first class.

William neither smiled nor spoke; he merely nodded. As Harry sat down, making a great show of indifference—trying even now to impress upon the old man that his presence here was a great favor—he had privately thought that his father looked exhausted.

William had spent the previous night in the Midland Grand at the very entrance to the station, but all its Gothic splendor had not helped him to sleep. In fact, he had not slept more than a few hours of any night of the past seven; there was a clenched feeling in his stomach that would not go away. It was not Harry; though the boy's debts and his absences from Oxford had meant stern words when he had seen him a few days before, and Harry had accepted the admonitions of his father with something like relief, he thought, or perhaps his son was simply exhausted by the life he had been leading. At any rate, Harry had left off his usual truculence and obeyed his father, agreeing to return to Yorkshire. Their meeting had ended with an uneasy, awkward truce of sorts. And now here the boy was, half-asleep and across from him, lounging on the train seat. William regarded him with a troubled, puzzled expression. He wished fervently that he knew what was going on in the boy's mind.

He had never really expected his son to make a go of Oxford, and so the news of his failures there had disappointed but not surprised him. But it was neither Harry's debts nor his disgraces that concerned him now, and it was neither Harry's debts nor his disgraces that had made William insist that Harry come back to Rutherford with him. It was what was happening across the Channel.

William had been backwards and forwards between Paris and London for weeks in his capacity as an unofficial courier for the foreign office, and he had that circularity of feeling, like a prisoner on a treadmill: always moving, always traveling, but without purpose or result.

He looked at Harry, who was sitting forward in his seat. The early morning sun was full on his face. The boy—William could not think of him, even now, as anything but a boy—turned suddenly to look at him, waving his hand at the platform passing by. "You see all this?" Harry asked. William, puzzled, looked; there were horse-drawn vans in a line, their arched roofs and panniers printed with the words TRAVEL MIDLAND FOR COMFORT and MIDLAND PARCELS AND POST. Closest to them—then just a blurred and fleeting impression lost in the steam—was a horse drawing a flatbed wagon of straw and milk. "All this," Harry said, "won't be here in a year. Horses. Straw. Feed. All the horses will go." He sat back in his seat. "Do you know how many horses there are in London, Father? Two hundred thousand. There used to be a lot more. But I'll wager you there'll be none in ten years. None at all."

William had hardly heard him beyond "won't be here in a year"—it was the worst thought in his head springing to life. How much was it possible for England to change in the coming year, if what was dreaded in Whitehall might actually come true? He closed his eyes, trying to fight the sensation that he had had for days—that Europe was hurtling towards conflict while England lumbered along, blinkered and heavy, in its wake. The English were in their sleepy summer, like carthorses dozing in the shade, while the Serbs progressed headlong. It made him apprehensive for his own country.

Five years ago, taking this very train, William had seen a man loading a whole pack of beagle hounds into the guard's van; he had been taking them to Derbyshire. The British were marvelous at such things: the sometimes bizarre maintenance of the status quo. He and Harry would sit later in the dining carriage with its heavily padded seats, silver cutlery and lace antimacassars woven with the letters M and R and feel quite safe on the sleekest, fastest network in the country. But William was afraid that it all might be an illusion. It might be crushed in a few weeks; there might even be a war on English soil. Opening his eyes, he met Harry's intrigued gaze. He took a calming breath. "No doubt," he murmured. "No doubt."

William had come back to Dover four days ago and written at once to Octavia. Despite all that had been said—or not said—William wanted to be with her before the news broke, as he was sure it would. There was going to be a war, and he wanted to be in Rutherford. The Boer conflict had been bad enough, but it had been far away in South Africa; this time it would be different.

France was only twelve miles across the Channel; he had no doubt at all that the Hun would soon be staring across it.

All the same, he would say nothing to Octavia about the actual depth of his fears, and certainly nothing of a dramatic sort to the children. He saw it as his sacred duty to protect his family, and part of that protection would involve keeping what he knew—all his premonitions and worries, all his inner knowledge of the machinations of power—to himself. To tell them of those urgent, troubled meetings of the last few weeks would be to push them into the same anxiety that he himself felt. He would not do that. He would preserve calm at Rutherford for as long as he could. That was his role, the most important role of his life.

To a lesser extent, he had felt it had been only right to warn Helene of the probability of German invasion across Belgium. He had seen her last week. They had eaten at Maxim's, but it was not as it was; the customers were now merely gaudy. Helene was wearing some garish costume in green and gold with a neckline that showed, to his mind, far too much. The place was choked with too many tables, and even in the hundreds of shaded rosy lights, Helene had looked used up. A few years ago he might have succumbed to her, but now they were more like two old adversaries. Her habitual smoldering, teasing looks were meaningless and outdated to him now. She merely wanted to score points; she never kept a man. She had no interest in keeping them. Catching them, yes; bleeding them dry, using them up. But keeping, no.

At Maxim's this time, he had told her to go to London.

"You think it's not safe in Paris?"

"It would be safer at Claridge's."

She had laughed. "An influx of officers might be rather interesting."

"Helene," he had said. "Get yourself out. Charles too, if necessary."

"Charles *is* out," she'd told him. "He's working in London."

It was news to him. The boy had said nothing about being employed in England when he had come to the house—quite the contrary. He had implied that he was visiting briefly from France, and would be going back at once. "At what?"

"For a private bank. Or some such thing."

He'd sat back, the wind knocked out of him. "May I ask where?"

"You may not. Since you choose not to support him, he has a right to look for honest employment. And since you choose not to acknowledge him, he must make his way without you."

He considered her defensive expression. "Do you have anyone looking after you?" he asked.

"What do you mean?"

"Don't waste my time, Helene. Do you have someone with any influence?"

"I have many friends with influence," she'd replied airily. "If you think I shall founder simply because some pompous little archduke has been killed, you're wrong."

"It'll be war. You realize that?"

"Nonsense," she'd replied, and raised her glass in a mock salute.

Helene, Octavia, Harry, Louisa. No one, it seemed, cared. Louisa had refused to return to Rutherford. "I shall come up in a fortnight," she'd told him. "A week before the shoot starts. I promise."

He doubted, however, that there would be a shoot. He closed his eyes again, and the scenes of the last few days rolled out before him like images captured on a cinematograph.

He had been called to the House of Commons a week after the assassination of the archduke; Grey had met him in the bar. He liked the Foreign Minister very much; Edward Grey was the first viscount of Falloden and had been at Balliol, William's own college at Oxford. William had been to Falloden Hall—it was less than a day's journey from Rutherford. Before his meteoric rise to the dizzy heights of a Cabinet Minister, William had always thought that Edward might go back home to Falloden one day and write the book on English birds that he had always talked about. His first wife was long dead; he had no children. He had always seemed a man of curious, innocent passions; but nowadays he was always tense.

"Do you know what Nicolson wrote to me the other day?" he had asked William. Nicolson was his undersecretary. "He said that this storm will soon blow over."

"And will it?"

Grey had stared into the depths of his brandy glass. "The Serbian newspapers have printed reports of the mass murder of their countrymen in Bosnia."

"Is that true?"

"Of course not. But there is talk of a final reckoning with Serbia. The Kaiser refused to go to the archduke's funeral for fear, he said, of being assassinated. Ambassador Tschirschky has said that the Serbs must be disposed of. The cauldron is being stirred, William."

A day later, William had seen Karl Lichnowsky, the German ambassador, at White's. Lichnowsky was always immaculate, always refined; he exuded calm, but he had not been calm that day— he had talked of his cables to the Kaiser being rerouted. He had asked Grey to offer to mediate. He had told William what he was about to write to his own Foreign Office: that if war broke out, it would be the greatest catastrophe the world had seen. William had seen Lichnowsky's long-fingered hands clutch momentarily on the arm of the chair in which he was sitting. It was this image above all—of Lichnowsky's elegance showing strain—that he would keep secret from Octavia and Harry. That, more than anything, told him how very dangerous the political situation was at the moment.

A piercing whistle now broke William's chain of thought; he opened his eyes and looked out the window. Harry seemed to be asleep, and William almost wished that he would remain so for the foreseeable future. He had gone to Paris knowing what so many others did not: that the Kaiser had pledged support against Serbia and Russia, and that France and Britain would be Russia's allies, and that Austria was about to attack Serbia. William had carried a personal message to their own ambassador in Paris: *The Serbian crisis makes my hair stand on end,* Grey had written. William had handed over the letter, listened to interminable arguments, and sat in endless meetings.

And he was back here now, traveling north, leaving Grey to his frantic cables. He had originally planned to go to the review of the fleet in Portsmouth, but even while packing his case for the visit, he knew that he would not go, despite the King's presence. William didn't want to see ships. He didn't want to hear Churchill saying that it was the greatest assemblage of naval power ever witnessed in the world.

He wanted only one thing.

He wanted to go home, and to take his son with him.

Those of the staff who had stayed at the London house had come back to Rutherford the day before. In the soft fading light of evening, the trap had come up from the station loaded with luggage, and, sitting on the back among it, the new chambermaid hired in London and the under-cook, Catherine, had dozed with exhaustion all the way home through the lanes, past the farms and fields, and all the way up the Rutherford drive, where the last of the sun, barred with long shadows, lay over the lane. Harrison and Mr. Cooper brought up the rear in a motorized taxi-cab and, as they neared the entrance, they saw Mr. Bradfield come out onto the steps.

The second footmen, Nash and Hardy, stood behind him, but it was Mary Richards who caught Harrison's attention. She looked fresh, straight out of a bandbox, starched and clean after his two days in the dirt of the train and seven months in the bedlam of the city. He sprang out of the cab, opening the door for Mr. Cooper, taking up his suitcases. There was a flurry of activity in the great hall for a while. Harrison covertly took the opportunity to kick the hallboy out of his way. "You don't change, do you?" he muttered to Alfred. "Still a great slobbering runt."

The maids had been taken to the back of the house. Mary was ahead of him as they descended the stairs behind the green baize door; the ribbons on her cap fluttered in front of him; he could hear the swish of her skirts against the narrow walls. At the dogleg bend above the kitchen, he caught her arm. She looked up at him and tried to pull away. "Miss me?" he asked.

She managed to retrieve herself from his grasp. "It's not improved your manners, then," she said, "being with the master."

"The master?" he replied, laughing. "He's been with his tart. We've not seen hide nor hair of him lately." He cocked his head in the direction of the house. "What's *she* been doing? Bradfield wrote to Cooper there was some American here he'd have to valet for as well as his lordship."

"I don't think he wants looking after," Mary said. "He looks after himself."

"Not a gentleman, then?"

"Gentleman enough. More gentleman than you. Get out of my way, please."

Harrison had stepped in front of her. He leaned down. "Giving me orders," he murmured, angry. "That's perky of you."

She looked him straight in the eye. "In case you've not noticed, I'm not Emily Maitland," she told him. "You can't bully me."

"Here you are defending her American friend. I'd have thought you hated her, after this summer."

Mary looked away. "It's none of your business."

"Her mills, they are. Her filthy houses. I heard all about it."

"Let me by."

"Did she say anything to you, after?"

Mary was staring at the ground. "She said that she was sorry for our loss. She called me up to the morning room."

"Very nice," he said, "for her to find the time."

He let her go, watching her run down the remaining steps. He could hear the raised voices in the kitchen: Mrs. Carlisle laying down the law already for the undercook. He heard Catherine faintly protesting that she had done her best over something, and Mrs. Carlisle's patronizing tone in reply. She had come home two months ago to be with her ladyship, as Louisa spent most of her time at the de Rays' home and his lordship was in France.

Harrison caught sight of the maid of all work and the kitchen maid scuttling like frightened mice down the corridor to the stillroom, sent for the drinks and desserts; he heard Bradfield's door slamming. The smile turned to a satisfied smirk on Harrison's face; he was home with a whole book of scandal on the doings of Master Harry. It would entertain the servants' table when Bradfield's back was turned. He had a winter's worth of disgrace to share with them: Harry rolling in drunk at three o'clock in the morning,

Harry and his chums kicking in windows in Regent Street, and knocking a policeman's hat off his head. Harry taking a boat on the Thames and swimming in the Serpentine. There was a delicious fund of it to keep the parlor maids' eyes and mouths open in shock.

And there was even more entertainment to be had. The new parlor maid, Jenny, was thin and tall and anxious and eager to please. She had an East London accent you could cut with a knife, and he would have to correct her. He would see what she would do for him if he barked loud enough when they were alone. He knew which room she'd been given—next to Dodd, where the head housemaid could keep an eye on her, out of the clutches of dark little Mary and her Bolshevik cheek. It was girls like Mary, he thought, who caused trouble; he'd had a basinful of suffragettes, with their placards and white dresses and lilies held in their hands and their messages—"Give Me Freedom." He snorted to himself. Women didn't need freedom; they needed a man to rein them in like a rider reined in a fretful horse. He'd heard his lordship say something of the sort more than once. Women needed their hearts broken; that melted them. That taught them. He'd seen Master Harry break a few; saw it in their faces as he handed them down out of carriages or cabs—sad little hopeful faces at the few dinners her ladyship had organized before she came home.

He took off his coat and walked down the stairs.

The table had been laid for a late supper; it was a hurried affair, past the usual teatime of five. Mrs. Carlisle was complaining that dinner must be served as usual upstairs at eight. Harrison sat himself down.

"Who is this Gould?" he asked. Bradfield was still in his room; otherwise he wouldn't have dared to say it.

"Mr. John Boswell Gould," Mary corrected.

"What's he come for?"

"He's an historian," Mrs. Carlisle said. "Writes books. Came over here on the *Laconia*."

"He's very nice," Mary commented. "Polite."

"I wouldn't get on a big ship," Cynthia murmured. "If the *Titanic* could sink, so could anything."

"Never mind the *Titanic*," Mrs. Carlisle told her. "We all had enough of you weeping about that at the time. There won't be another sinking."

"Still, I wouldn't go near the sea," Cynthia said.

"You won't get a chance, so stop harping on it," Mary told her tartly.

"Whatever ship he came on, he makes himself at home," Harrison said. The plates clattered; the tea was poured. He began to laugh. "And he charms ladies, so I hear. Especially wives."

"Does he?" said Mary. "How would you know?"

"Popular in town. Popular all over. Certain titles."

"That's enough of that," Mrs. Carlisle countered.

"I expect *she* likes him."

"She's hardly ever at dinner," Nash said. "So I doubt it."

Harrison looked at him. "Do you indeed?" he replied scathingly. "So knowledgeable. Such a man of the world."

"Mr. Gould is in the library most of the day."

"I saw them walking in the park twice," Cynthia piped up. "I saw her taking his arm."

"Enough," Mrs. Carlisle reprimanded.

"Did you now," Harrison replied.

He said nothing else; he sat straight-backed, the fingers of one hand slowly drumming the table.

The heat of the day had not seemed to ebb; John sat in his room and counted the lazy minutes until dinner. In his hand he held the letter he'd received from Pierpont Morgan's household. Egypt, he had been told, was not a great place to be; travel was difficult. The British—who puffed about over there as if they owned the place— had become fractious with permits. Houses in Cairo had been deserted for weeks; a cold wind of unease was blowing.

He sat with his elbows on the windowsill and looked out into the canopy of the beech trees, planning where he could go. He could go overland through Switzerland, or he could try Rome, or he could go south to Spain. Someone in New York had told him that Spain and Morocco were worth seeing, and they were outside the fire burning in Europe, at least at the moment. There were no Prussians marching up and down in Cordoba or Andalusia. Perhaps he would go there; he could ride in the mountains. He could stay somewhere different from Rutherford, somewhere simple and whitewashed and remote. And drink a lot of wine. And go home from Lisbon.

And go home.

He knew in his heart that he didn't want to do that, however. What he wanted more than anything else was to stay here and watch Octavia Cavendish stirring the sugar in her coffee. He took his elbows down from the windowsill, brushing the sleeves of his evening jacket and shaking his head at himself.

She was already in the sitting room, waiting for dinner when he came down. She stood with one hand on the lid of the piano, a book in her hand; as he came in, she looked up. She was next to one of the lamps, and she wore a red dress—the deepest, most vibrant scarlet.

"What are you reading?" he asked her.

"Someone called . . ." She checked the cover of the book. "Stein."

"Gertrude Stein?"

"You sound shocked."

"I'm shocked it's found its way to Yorkshire."

She smiled, putting it down. "You think we're all cavemen here, I suppose. Compared to New York."

"Not at all," he told her. "Cavemen? At Rutherford? Hardly. But Stein."

"Rooms and objects . . . it's a very curious work."

"But you like it?"

"I like that a woman has written it."

They stood companionably by the window and looked at the evening light; the gardens were so still, so perfectly arranged that he felt even to speak would be to destroy the heavenly illusion.

Next to him, Octavia was grateful for his silence. She had been afraid that he would somehow refer to that morning and cause her embarrassment. She stole a look at his profile: the rather aquiline nose, the fine features, the shock of thick blond hair. John sensed her gaze and turned his head. His eyes were a pleasing and unusual color, she realized: hazel, more green than blue. They had an interesting expression. His reputation was for charm, but he was not charming in the empty way she had expected. Those eyes, like the rest of his face, showed both kindliness and curiosity; they were aspects she had rarely seen in a man. He smiled at her now, and a thrill of pleasure ran through her; his look was frankly disarming. She held his gaze for a long moment.

Behind them, Bradfield announced dinner, and she looked away from John, inexplicably flustered.

They went into the dining room. Their places had been laid at either end of the table, and it was like calling down a corridor to talk to each other. At the end of the main course, John took up his plate and cutlery and walked down and sat within a few feet of her. "I'm sorry," he said. "But it isn't charming to shout. I apologize to you, Bradfield."

He had turned to address the butler. Bradfield bowed stiffly. The dessert was served. Outside, the summer evening had darkened, but the heat remained. The flames of the candles flickered in the faint breeze.

"Lord Cavendish is home tomorrow?" he asked.

"Yes, in the afternoon."

"I must leave soon," he said. "I don't want to be in the way of the family."

To her own surprise, Octavia felt an acute and sudden rush of disappointment; she looked up from her meal. "Leaving?" she asked. "For where?"

"I can't decide."

She felt hurt, almost a childlike hurt; it surprised her with its intensity, this unbidden feeling. She wanted to keep him here, at this table. And in the same moment, she knew she couldn't say what she wanted. "I'm sure William would like to see you," she replied. "He would be dismayed that you had come and gone without talking to you." It was mere bluster; she had no idea whether William would care to see Gould or not.

"Yes, of course," John was politely replying. "I must thank him for his hospitality."

"We have a summer festival at the end of the month," she told him. "You ought to see that. It's the . . . well, it is a kind of harvest festival, but Rutherford has always had the party before shooting begins. It's . . . You would like it—" It sounded like a plea; she heard it in her own tone, and abruptly stopped.

They sat in silence. Her gaze darted from the table to the windows as she fanned herself with the napkin. "I want to go into the garden," she said. She stood up; Bradfield opened the doors. They walked down to the morning room, where the French windows had already been closed. There was a comical crossover of servants as the footmen tripped over themselves to reopen them. As they stepped out onto the terrace, the heat from the stones was reflected back at them. She waved Bradfield away. "We shall walk a little way, there's nothing we need," she told him. Bradfield retreated into the house.

They went as far as the steps at the front of the house, and then back again through the garden. It was almost fully dark now, and John could see her more as a glimmer of soft fabric and an approximation of shoulders, neck, and half-averted face in the shadows.

She was intensely aware of him at her side, but

did not look at him as she asked, "Do you think I'm an exile here?"

"An exile?"

"I mean from the world. From places that you travel to, from the people you know. From the Steins of the modern world."

"Not at all. You know a great many people. You have traveled. And Rutherford is a world in itself."

"Not such a great one," she said, "compared to some. There are larger houses and greater titles. We're not so impressive."

"I'll beg to differ on that one."

"It's true. You must know it. You've seen Wentworth Woodhouse?"

Wentworth Woodhouse was forty miles away. "Yes, I've seen it," he said.

"It has sixty indoor servants. The estate out-doors has more than three hundred staff."

"And they have a tiger."

She turned to him. "I beg your pardon?"

"A tiger. A boy that rides on the coach in livery. Or they did. I don't know if he's still there now. They must have an Armitage over there who's complaining at the coach houses being turned into motor garages. Perhaps the tiger has become a mechanic."

They had gone into a tiny walled part of the terrace, where an elongated pool was surrounded by an Italianate veranda. She sat down there, gazing at the water. He hovered nearby; there was barely room for two on the seat.

"I've never known anything else," she murmured. "I was the daughter. Now I'm the wife. I've simply moved from one protectorate to another. I'm a possession."

"That can't be true."

"A figurehead, then."

"You've created a lovely home. You've made a family. That is more than a figurehead. That is real."

"Is it?" she asked. "I look at what women do—even the girls cleaning the rooms; I read such books, and I . . . I long to go out, you know, and do anything at all. Milk a cow. Mend a road. Dig a ditch." He burst out laughing; she smiled in return. "It's true. Even something as simple as . . . I would like to tend the gardens, for instance. But I am not supposed to. I may pick the flowers. I may say where they're to be planted. But I can't work. I can't do anything of value."

"You have enormous value in yourself."

"Do I?" she said. "Charlotte talks of going to art school; did you know? She would like to work. William abhors it; he ridicules it. But I know what she means. She wants to see the world, to be independent. She would fly an aeroplane if she could. Just like Harry."

"And would you?"

She laughed softly. There was a pause. Then: "I rather think so. Yes."

He leaned on the stone pillar of the veranda and looked down at her.

"I wanted to do so very much when I came here," she said. "My father had always told me that I had no talent, no worth. I was in love with William, and I thought he saw something better than that." She paused. "But I learned that I was too sentimental. One could not be romantic; practicality was everything. The role to play again. Expectations. I couldn't intrude on the garden, because that belongs to March. I couldn't alter traditions here; William would not countenance it. I had my children, of course, but I was not required to enjoy them. A nurse was employed. I used to shock her by sitting on the floor of the nursery and playing with the girls and Harry. One was not supposed to, you see? You were meant to have the children brought to you just before dinner, and that was all. I used to fish with Harry, too. That caused a terrible row."

"But why?"

"Oh, 'one was the wife of a Member of Parliament.' All that."

"This was William."

"Yes. And the wife of the lord lieutenant of the county, when he had those roles. One did not take off one's shoes and wade in the river."

John began to laugh. "Sounds fun to me."

"Yes," she said quietly. "It was fun."

"But your husband surely appreciates you, your character, your wishes."

"I used to rather fondly imagine so," she said. "But my husband, as it turns out, has a life of his own." A steely edge had come into her tone.

"As a Parliamentary adviser, I hear."

"I don't mean that," she replied. The darkness lent her cover for the secret that now came flooding out; she slightly averted her face. "I mean that he has another son. Another woman. In Paris. He has known her for many years. Before we were married. And after."

John was shocked, though not as shocked as he might have been some years back; he had learned that many English aristocrats favored a mistress. The old King had had several; his wife had even entertained them to tea. In John's experience, the titled man who was faithful to his wife here was in the minority. And yet his heart bled for Octavia now, the Octavia who had not been allowed to even take off her shoes, when apparently William Cavendish had been taking off far more in gay Paree.

"I didn't know about the son at all until he turned up at our London house this spring and asked for money," Octavia was saying. "He wanted an inheritance, and William wouldn't give it to him. He wanted to be part of the family, and William denied it."

John was struggling for the right words. "To protect you, surely," he managed at last.

She looked up at him. "He thought he could keep us apart, you see?" she said. "But things can't be kept apart. They can't be molded." She paused. "They change, John," she told him finally. "People do. Times do."

"And . . ." The garden was pressing in on him, so much so that it seemed to be taking the air out of his lungs. He was painfully aware of her proximity and his own desire to touch her. She sat there like a ghost, so slight in the darkness. "What will you do?" he asked. He was trying very hard not to think of William Cavendish playing the British diplomat in Paris while all the time he had some woman tucked away in one of those fancy belle epoque apartments. God damn the man. God damn him to hell.

"I don't know what to do at all," Octavia admitted. "I am completely lost."

Two hundred miles away in London, Louisa was dreaming of her mother and of Rutherford.

She thought that she was in her own bedroom there: the apricot and pink and cream confection of colors that she herself had chosen. She was sitting in her low armchair, dressed in only her nightgown, and she had the sensation of waiting for someone—someone who had promised to be with her. On her dressing table she could see a reflection of herself in the looking glass, and the image was of a much older version of herself—tired, perhaps, dispirited, or disappointed.

It seemed that it was only with a great effort that she could raise herself from the chair, and she walked to the table to see herself in a clearer light. Looking down, she saw the items in front of the glass quite clearly: the silver-backed hairbrushes, the cut-glass scent bottles, the little silk-backed notebook she had taken to her very first dance. There too was the Royal Worcester plate on which she sometimes left her rings. She saw its familiar elongated shape, but in its center was a calling card that she had never seen before. She saw her hand, almost disembodied, reach down to the card and pick it up. *Maurice Frederick,* said the elegant printed script. And it came to her with a devastating clarity that the person she was waiting for was Maurice, but that he would never come. He had merely left the card, as one might do with an acquaintance.

A quite horrible sense of loneliness, one that she had never experienced, suddenly permeated the dream. She felt that this was a state of mind out of which she would never recover; below her, in the house, she could hear footsteps and voices, but she knew that she would never again be able to join them. In the kind of bottomless panic that only a nightmare can produce, she rushed to the window, pulled back the curtains, and looked down. There on Rutherford's terrace was Maurice himself. He was looking in each window very carefully, running his hand around each lock and frame as if he wanted to gain admittance.

When he had finally tried each one, he walked back until he was underneath her window again, and then he looked up. She called to him. She tried to make a signal that he should come to the front door and ring the bell. But he seemed not to understand her. All that happened was that he raised his hand, sadly, and turned and walked away. In no more than a breath, he had vanished.

Louisa woke up abruptly with a sense of horror.

She got out of bed and went to her own window there in the London house, and looked down into the street. Everything was as normal; a dawn light was beginning to break. Maurice was not there, of course. He was not looking up at her, or turning away. And yet she had the curious notion that he had been there at some time during the night, staring up at the house, keeping some kind of strange guard upon her, or trying to find a way through the locked doors and windows, as he had in the dream.

Trembling, she went back to the bed and sat on the edge for some time.

All that she could think of was that feeling of isolation and loneliness that the dream had brought to her: the sense of being cut off from the close and sociable world that she knew so well. She wondered what she might feel if she had no father, no mother, no brother or sister. She wondered what it might be like to be utterly alone, waiting for someone or something that might never happen, or a wish that might never come true.

Her eyes filled with tears. It was Maurice's world, she realized. Alone, without apparent family or friends. How might it be, she wondered unhappily, to move by oneself through places populated by others—others who were always in groups, or families, or in marriages or partnerships? It was how she saw him, and it was how he inevitably portrayed himself: as a perennially lonely stranger.

She got back into bed and pulled the covers around her.

In a moment or two, she turned her face into the pillow and softly whispered his name.

The summer night fell at Rutherford, but it was not a complete darkness. When John went to his room, he turned down the lights immediately, and undressed, and stood looking at the parkland bathed in full moonlight: an empty stage, a monochrome picture. He went to bed with the curtains open and the light falling across the room.

Somewhere below him in the house a clock struck midnight, then one. He had never felt less like sleep. William Cavendish and his son were at

York; tomorrow they would be here. He imagined the older man showing him the volumes that were kept under lock and key in the library, on glass-screened shelves. He tried to imagine himself being polite, but couldn't see it. He imagined far more vividly socking the old goat in the eye, and then cursed himself. It was none of his business; why should he care? Marriages went on like this; they had their own shape, each one with its own peculiar tensions. He asked himself whether he could be faithful to a woman for a lifetime, and doubted it. But then, that was the reason he hadn't married. He believed in keeping a promise; if he couldn't keep it, he would never make it.

He closed his eyes; through the open window he could hear the barking of a fox somewhere far away, up on the hills. He pushed the sheets down; it was still stiflingly warm. For a long time he considered simply getting up and dressed and leaving during the night, walking all the way to the little station. What was it, four or five miles? He didn't want to see William Cavendish. He didn't want to see him stand next to Octavia.

He rolled onto his side and looked at the little clock on the bedside table. Ten past two. The soft clicking of the pendulum began to annoy him; it was ticking away his life. He ought to have moved on, left before now. He ought to have gone. He thought of Octavia standing at the bridge yester-day morning, the dark wool coat incongruously drawn over the innumerable folds of the night-gown. He thought of her naked feet below the hem of the skirt on that first day she had sat with him in the library. He clenched his fists and screwed his eyes shut, retreating into the old trick his mother had taught him to get to sleep: to count backwards through presidents. The Goulds didn't count sheep at night; they counted the men they'd got into office. John started now with Woodrow Wilson, conjured up his long, aquiline face. Taft, Roosevelt . . . Taft, Roosevelt, McKinley . . .

It was no use.

He got up and pulled a dressing gown around him and went to the door. When he got out into the corridor, he could sense the huge house all around him, a great sleeping beast. He felt suffocated by it; he wanted to get out suddenly. He walked down the stairs, and at the curve above the great hall he stopped to look at the portrait of Octavia. It was massive—he judged it was not less than ten feet by six—and Octavia seemed to be rising above him in the swathes of satin gown like some extraordinary incarnation, at once both more real and less real than the actual woman. He tore his eyes away and went on down, padding through the hall, looking up at the vast timbered ceiling, its detail obscured by the dark. It ought to have been inspiring, but it was oppressive. He made his way to the dining room, and through that to the doors to the same terrace where he and Octavia had walked earlier that night, and where he had been at first light that morning.

Out in the dark, he sat down on one of the terrace walls. This was no use at all. He hadn't come to England to fall in love with someone else's wife. Especially not an unhappy wife. A carefree woman who yearned for a little affair—maybe . . . maybe he could have happily got himself embroiled for a few weeks, though carelessness with women was not in his nature. But this. This bloody fever. That was what the English would call it: bloody. And it was. They were right to use that word; it was bloody in all its meanings. It was like being struck, opened up, exposed, and seeing your own gore splashed on the stones under your feet. He didn't want another man's wife. He didn't want anyone. He was a traveler, a free soul. He was . . . He put his head in his hands, a gesture of defeated helplessness. He didn't know what he was, and that was the truth. He had no idea any longer.

It must have been more than an hour before he walked back upstairs. On the galleried landing he paused for some time.

And then, with his heart thudding like a hammer in his chest, he went to Octavia's door and opened it.

It took a moment for his eyes to accustom themselves to the shadowy dimensions of the room. He could see then a canopied four-poster bed with huge yellow-and-cream curtains; the walls too seemed to have a kind of creamy figured paper. He could smell flowers and Octavia's scent. He stood stock-still, wondering whether he had really lost his mind; he had never done such a thing, despite his reputation. He thought he might choke from his own labored breathing. He fumbled behind him for the handle of the door. And then he saw her.

She was not in bed. Octavia was sitting by the open window, partially obscured by the dressing table and its ornate looking glass; what he had dimly supposed was a portrait on the far wall suddenly materialized into a living person; it was her, hands calmly folded in her lap, staring in his direction.

"I'm sorry," he whispered. "Very sorry."

She stood up. She was wearing some other, less ornate gown than the one that had been under the coat that morning; it was a silvery color, and it made a sound as she walked towards him, a sound like indistinct whispering voices. She stopped by the looking glass. "Come here," she said.

He did as he was told, and crossed the room. Standing next to her, he saw that her thick dark hair hung down her back. "I've been watching you in the garden," she murmured. "You've been there such a long time, John. What were you thinking about?"

"Leaving," he told her truthfully.

He reached out tentatively for her hand, and suddenly she had stepped into his arms and pressed her face to his, not in a kiss, but with her cheek against his. She had been crying; he could feel the wetness of the tears.

And then she turned her face, and he kissed her, and was astounded to have the kiss passionately returned. It was the warmth of her that amazed him, so different from the woman he thought he had understood when he had first seen her, seemingly entirely inanimate and passive; it was the strength of her—he could feel the deter-mination, the need. So much need. So much need.

"I can't go," he told her, taking her hand and kissing her palm, her wrist. "I can't go without you."

She gently put her hand under his chin and lifted his head from her wrist and looked him full in the face. "Then take me with you," she said.

Chapter 6

It was one o'clock in the afternoon when the Napier delivered Lord William and Harry back to Rutherford, coming straight from York. Watching the car's arrival from the morning room, Octavia was still holding William's letter in her hand; it had been set discreetly by her plate at breakfast.

I am anxious to be home, he had written. *Tell Jack to bring the car.*

When the Napier came into view, she could see the small plumes of dust from far down the drive. She straightened herself, put a hand to hair, and looked around the room. Everything was blue about the day: the bright blue of the sky outside, the blue-and-white Chinese porcelain in the display cabinets, the vast sprays of blue delphinium, the blue and gold on the spines of the books, on the figures in the carpet, on the blue-and-yellow edges to the enormous curtains that had been pulled back. She looked at her hands, at the ring that William had given her. Blue sapphires, the Bluebird sapphires and diamonds in a tight band above her wedding ring. She had once danced around this room in anticipation of William coming home. How many years ago was that? Eighteen, twenty? Danced around, dragging the great awkward bustled dress of the day, with the sapphires blazing on her hand. It had been a carriage that she had been watching for then, and when William had at last arrived she had run out onto the steps and thrown her arms around him. "Now, now," he had said, in kindly admonishment. "The servants, dear. The servants."

This room had been red and gold then, heavily tasseled wherever she looked. At least she had changed that, even if William had stopped her from clearing most of the furniture. "That was my grandmother's chair," he had protested as they had progressed through the rooms trying to choose what remained and what was to go. "That was my great-uncle's Canterbury. For heaven's sake, that must stay as it is." His frowning face. "Don't touch that, Octavia." On and on, unbending. "One needs such things."

"This?" she would plead, holding up some ancient, moth-eaten tapestry cushion. "This?" A piece of furniture that was not as old as it looked: the "Jacobean" sideboard that was half Georgian and half Victorian; or tapping her fingers on the outlandish ormolu clock with its serpents and cherubs locked forever in gilded combat. "This, William? Oh, please, do let's modernize *something*." But he had been impervious to her need for change. He let her alter only the color scheme, and then only to his family's color. The blue of the bluebirds.

255

She had always supposed that Rutherford would remain in the Beckforth and Cavendish way, and that she would eventually mold herself to the house until she became part of it. She had tried, God knew. And occasionally succeeded. She had once heard William say that Rutherford had calmed her—it had been at some long-ago dinner—and he had smiled at her down the long table in his indulgent way, in that rather patronizing way, and she had responded with a smile as she was supposed to. He had meant it as a compliment—of that she was sure—but she had much rather that Rutherford had energized her, or that she could have energized it—beyond her money, of course. Beyond the rebuilding. Beyond the physicality of the building, beyond the relaid bricks, the redrawn gardens, the vast extensions to the great hall, the engineering of the double sweep of the staircase.

She wished that Rutherford had been allowed to give her what she longed for—freedom, the ability to choose, the ability to create or command. But it had given her structure and tradition. A great weight of tradition and a husband who clung to his status, which she had rapidly learned must become her own will and wish: to reinforce the house, the Cavendishes, the family. To become a Beckforth in her heart and soul. To be calm. *Calm.* Her mouth curved a little at that twisted compliment now. Calm was what

William always wanted. Calm and order. Order above all.

The day that the glasshouse foundations had gone in, William had turned to her and said, "This is what my father would have admired," with a tone in his voice almost—but not quite—of gratitude. Relief, perhaps. Relief that he was at last able to make the changes that Rutherford needed. The glass went up, and the shutters and pulleys and blinds were installed, and the hot-air channels that blew such warmth into the place so that even when snow stood outside there was pleasure and light. All those precious things were imported to Rutherford because he had married her, and just that one sentence, with its intonation of pride—"This is what my father would have admired"—served as her thanks. She had been pleased, of course, that Rutherford glowed in its renaissance, pleased to see her husband strut in the funny ponderous way he had when surveying his glorious kingdom. The pleasure of ownership. His ownership of Rutherford, and his ownership of her.

And all those years she had wished for . . . well, what? It was a nameless thing, this desire she had nursed over the years. So formless that she had not known whether it even had a name.

She stood now and watched the car draw up outside. She stayed where she was; no running now. No throwing her arms around him. She saw him get out and look up at the house; saw Harry unfold himself from the same seat. She saw how tall and rangy Harry was, much more of a man than he had been at Christmas. She watched the two of them come forward, William wearing an irritated expression, Harry a careless smile. It was only on seeing the smile that a ripple of anxiety went through Octavia. She recognized the bravado in it.

She walked slowly into the great hall.

"My dear," William said. He stopped in front of her and waited for her to incline her face for a kiss; then, somewhat disconcerted by the lack of her usual response, he took her hand and raised it to his lips instead. "You look very well."

"Thank you," she replied, and held out her arms to Harry.

As she pressed her face to her son's, an absurd question came into her mind. She almost asked him, "Would you like to go to America?" It stepped into her mind quite easily: herself and Harry and the girls on some great Pullman train heading to California, or standing in San Francisco, or on the streets of New York— reinvented quite, as if they might draw themselves entirely anew and become some other family.

Harry pulled back. As if he had read her mind, he asked, "There's some American here?"

"Yes," she said. She wondered whether she

was smiling far too much. Harry looked at her curiously; then: "I hope there's a good lunch, Mama. There was no breakfast to speak of. Father hared out of York as if the place were on fire."

He walked away; she looked at William. It seemed to her that the night with John Gould must be emblazoned on her: it must be obvious—how could he fail to see it? She could feel the heat under her skin and in her hands. She wanted to say, "He has done things you've never done." There—that was the utter shameful truth. She wanted to say it. Not just experience it, but to actually say it to her husband. The urge thundered in her head. She wanted to ask why William had never cried out her name or wept with happiness. John Gould was a perfect stranger, in reality, and he had wept because he had been in her bed. She had a violent desire to shake William out of his torpor. She wanted to ask him why he had never brought himself to love her in that dazed way that swept everything else aside. *My God,* she thought to herself, aghast, *you have stepped across the Styx. You're dead and alive at once.* She wanted to laugh, or scream, or both. But instead she looked at her feet, and she took a breath. And then, with what she hoped was expressionless calm, she looked back at William.

"I wanted to be home," her husband told her. The servants were standing in a row at their backs; Mrs. Jocelyn, flushing with pleasure, had marshaled the maids and footmen, and now William turned to them. "It's good to see you all," he said. "Good to be together again at Rutherford."

"We are not all together," Octavia remarked. "Louisa is coming up with Charlotte in a day or two. Half your family are absent."

If he was shocked—she had never before corrected him in front of the staff—William did not show it. He paused only a fraction of a second before agreeing with her. "Soon, then," he murmured. "Quite so. Soon."

After lunch, Octavia went to her room, leaving William in some interminable sparring match of words with Harry that she had barely registered. She sent Amelie away and walked into her adjoining dressing room and stood there, leaning on the sill, waiting until she saw John Gould walk out from the library below. He went down the terrace and out onto the lawns, walking briskly. Only when he was some fifty yards from the house did he momentarily pause and look back straight at her window. Briefly, he touched the brim of his hat. To any other eyes, it was simply an alteration to the angle in the afternoon sunshine; to her it was the confirmation of an arrangement. Smiling, she kicked off her shoes and undid the broad sash of the dress, twisting to find the fastenings. In ten minutes she planned to be walking across the same stretch of lawn for the same stretch of woodland and the paths to the fields below the moor.

In the bedroom, she heard the door open.

"It's quite all right, Amelie; I shall manage myself," she called. There was no reply. Snatching up a wrap, she looked out into the room and saw William standing there.

"I thought you must be resting," he said.

"I am going for a walk."

He looked at her, puzzled. "Indeed? Then I shall come with you."

"There is no need for it," she told him.

He walked to the window and gazed out. He must have seen John, for he turned back and asked, "What do you make of Gould?" Getting no reply, he went on. "I apologize for his being here. I had forgotten I had invited him. His letter confirming his visit was waiting for me at the club only when I got back from Paris."

"It's no matter," she said.

"He seems to be a cheerful fellow."

She shrugged. "I rarely see him."

He let it go, watching her intently. "Octavia," he began, "we must go forward together. We must progress."

She spread her hands. "You see me here."

"Yes," he said. "You retreated, did you not?"

"I left London, yes."

He looked at his feet, and then took a chair.

"Of course, I mean no criticism, but to leave the girls with friends, during the Season . . ."

"And to go to one's mistress in Paris and leave one's wife alone during the Season," she replied evenly. She paused. "Of course, I mean no criticism."

She noticed William's hands, the fingers spread widely over his knees as if to prevent himself from standing up. "I went to stop this business with Helene," he said.

"Perhaps you should have stopped it some years ago."

"Indeed I should." He had been frowning, head down; now he looked up. "I did not know she was pregnant until the child was born," he said. "And I had not seen her for many months. Even then, she merely wrote me a note. She was with another man by then. It was not . . ." He paused, trying to frame the right words. "She regarded it as an inconvenience. The boy was put to a nurse. I don't believe that this man in Bergerac ever saw Charles, nor knew of him. It was a secret she kept."

"Badly kept."

"As it turned out," he agreed. "I have never heard the complete story. Whether you choose to believe me or not, I am not Helene's confidant; nor have I ever been. I was merely one among many."

"What a pretty picture you paint," Octavia said.

He said nothing.

Octavia was still standing by the door of the dressing room; she now leaned against the doorframe, regarding him. "And yet you are quite sure that Charles is yours."

"We discussed this in London, Octavia."

"Oh, yes," she retorted. "Helene has convinced you that he is yours, and you have accepted it."

"It is not that I believe it. It is that I can't disprove it."

Octavia looked at him coldly for some time. "And so you have paid her for the last twenty years. You have allowed yourself to be black-mailed."

"I gave her an allowance because I could not disprove that I was the father, and because she is of my family. And because I felt it was the most honorable thing."

"Honorable!" Octavia exclaimed. "Honor has nothing to do with it, William. You have paid her money in the hope that she would be quiet."

"That is unfair," he replied. "If it was not the most honorable, then it was the least dishonorable, if you will. She has no legal claim on me."

"Other than that you have supported the boy for twenty years. That is quite some precedent."

"It is not proof."

She started to laugh. "Is it not?"

"I have given her money. I admit a dalliance with her."

"And you have been there almost every year."

Husband and wife stared at each other. Fury spiraled up in Octavia's throat; it was all she could do to hold her temper down. It was as if John's touch had sprung open a lock; all the things she wanted to say to William now rushed to her lips; there was no holding back. She felt free; felt as if she had nothing to lose. In fact, she felt as if her marriage were a sorry, decayed thing next to the experience of the night before; she had no idea why she had tolerated it for so long. It was all she could do not to turn on her heel and run out after John across the lawn. She fought down this impulse as best she could, but the truth was that the sight of William, and the awful confession about Helene—the tawdriness of it, the dirtiness and dustiness and plastic glamour of Paris, the whole prolonged lie of it all—was unbearable. "Tell me the truth," she said. "You cannot have gone to see her every year and nothing has happened between you."

William's eyes widened in shock. Then his expression closed, but it was not quickly enough. She had seen into his past as clearly as if she had been there with him.

"You have been with her after we were married," she said. "Don't deny it."

"I have gone to Paris for the Foreign Office. You know that. I have not been to exclusively visit Helene."

"But you *have* seen her there," she insisted. "You have been lovers."

"I . . ." But he could not deny it. He stared at the floor. She felt a momentary, sour sensation of triumph—she was right.

"How often?" she demanded.

"Octavia, it is years ago."

"How often? Every year?"

"No, no . . ."

"And even now?"

He leapt to his feet. "No."

"Then how often?"

He made a despairing gesture. "Perhaps . . . I don't recall. . . ." His shoulders slumped. "Perhaps the first five years or so."

Octavia regarded him. Moments of tension passed like years. Eventually, she found her voice, and it was glacial. "And you invited her here," she said. "I wonder she didn't bring the boy with her."

"She invited herself," William murmured.

"But you did nothing to put her off."

"Nothing puts Helene off," William replied hotly. "You know that yourself. She is impervious."

"You might have found a way, to prevent my humiliation."

He gazed at her, then put a hand to his forehead. "Yes," he admitted. "I might have done that more successfully than I did. I have been at fault."

"You let her sleep under this roof, and at the London house, knowing that she had once been your mistress—was your mistress still—"

265

"She has not been my mistress for a very long time."

"How do I know that?" she demanded. "How am I to take your word?"

"Because I give it to you, Octavia."

They were within three or four feet of each other, staring into each other's eyes. "Your word is worth nothing to me," Octavia said softly.

It was as if she had hit him. He took a step back, grasped the rail of the chair behind him. She remained where she was, though she straightened up, not leaning anymore.

"Whatever you said or did not say to Helene, whatever you did or did not do, she has evidently told her son that you are his father, and you cannot prove that it is a lie."

There was a long pause. William had flushed a deep red and was looking at his wife with horror. She was staring him down. It was not the woman he knew; the woman he knew would have been in tears by now, and accepted his word instead of denying it.

"What have you promised Charles?" she asked.

"Nothing at all."

"No acknowledgment, no money, no gift?"

"Nothing."

"And he has accepted that?"

"I don't know what he accepts. He is not living at home, but in London. I don't know where."

"Is he estranged from his mother?"

"I don't know."

"You have seen Helene, I suppose, and asked her?"

"Yes," he replied. "She tells me nothing. She thinks me beneath contempt."

"Well," Octavia said coolly, "we are of the same opinion, in that case."

William shook his head. "Octavia, please . . ."

"You have not been honest with me all our married life," Octavia retorted. "And I do not believe that the issue of Charles will ever go away. The boy is dangerous, because he has been rejected."

"His mother has filled his head with nonsense," William countered. "Built him up with expectations that her own past make impossible to fulfill. Now, as age overtakes her and her lovers become few and far between, she tells the boy that he must expect an inheritance from me, when she has made a fool of me all these years."

"She has made a fool of us both," Octavia said.

William grimaced. "Yes," he admitted. "That is true. She is the most devilish woman alive."

Octavia looked away from him, glanced at the window. "I must go out," she murmured.

William walked back to her. His voice was low. "Octavia, I think it unfair to punish me for something that happened so long ago." She made no reply; she was gazing out the window towards the wooded hills. "If you find it impossible to forgive me for my own sake, then for the children."

She looked back at him. "You enlist the children in your own cause?" she asked. "You want this for yourself, William, for your own peace of mind in your own home. It has nothing to do with the children."

"It certainly has," he objected. "I have excluded Charles for the sake of my own son. Our son."

"You are defending your position of authority."

"I am defending Harry."

"No, William. You are merely pushing Helene's son away to defend yourself, in an attempt to erase him and his mother."

"Isn't that what you want?" William asked.

She gave a strained, ironic smile. "Yes," she said. "I wish it could all be erased."

"Well, then . . ."

"But it can't be," she added.

"And you will let this come between us for the rest of our lives," he said, "ruining the atmosphere in this house, taking yourself out of my company?"

She began to laugh. "*I* have ruined the atmosphere?" she repeated incredulously. She held up both her hands in a gesture that stopped him in his tracks. "Let me make one thing perfectly clear, William," she said. "I am not, as you claim, punishing you for something that happened long ago. I'm well aware that you had a life before we met, even if I did not. I accepted that before we were married, although you did not confide in me whether my guess was correct. I accept that you may have been protecting me in that lack of confidence. I would not think of punishing you for a previous life."

"Octavia—" he began.

"I haven't finished quite," she interrupted. "It's not that I couldn't forgive you even for siring a son, if that is what really happened, although forgiveness for that would be hard enough." She paused. "But what I don't understand, William, what I will never understand and can't forgive, is that you never told me the truth. Worse still, you exposed me to the very woman involved, asking me to admit her as part of the family when you knew how little I liked her."

"I was at a loss to know what to do," he admitted.

"You let the situation run on."

"Yes."

"Hoping it would solve itself somehow?"

"Perhaps."

She saw by the bowing of his head that this was a terrible admission for him—an admission of weakness. In the past, this confession would have melted her heart. As it was, she only felt momentarily sorry for him. She let the moments beat out, aware of her own piercing need to be out of the room, out of sight of him, to be with John.

"I have had plenty of time to consider while

you have been away," she said calmly. "I have decided to make changes."

He seemed not to have heard her at first; then he frowned distractedly. "Changes? What changes?"

"I am going to Blessington tomorrow with John Gould. I am meeting Ferrow there. I want to build new houses."

"Ferrow?" William echoed. "Ferrow is the manager. He has nothing to do with housing."

"I am going to build behind the spinning sheds."

"*You* are going to build?"

"We will have a hundred new houses running up the hill; they will draw on Broughton Beck. When they are finished, I will demolish the houses on Town Row and rebuild them with proper sanitation."

William was staring at her as if she had suddenly grown two heads. "But you have no money," he said.

"That is correct," she replied. "But you will create an account for me and I shall be the sole signatory."

"I shall do no such thing."

She appeared not to have heard him. "While you were away," she said, "it was necessary for me to give my condolences to one of the maids, whose sister had died of diphtheria. There has been an outbreak in the town. I am determined that it will not happen again."

"And what gives you the idea that the mill houses have caused diphtheria?"

She eyed him coldly. "Don't oppose me, William," she said. "My mind is made up."

"The money is not mine simply to hand to you," he said. "There is the board. . . ."

"The board is run by you, and don't suppose me stupid enough not to know it," she said.

"And you . . . you have arranged this?"

"I shall meet Ferrow tomorrow."

"Then I will go with you."

"John Gould is coming with me. You may accompany us if you wish."

Fury crossed William's face; he made a visible attempt to check it. "Since you are so determined, you and I will go to Blessington. You will see what an ill-formed idea this is," he said slowly. "And as for Gould—if he still finds it necessary to involve himself in issues that are none of his concern—*he* may accompany *us*."

There was just one hour in which Mrs. Jocelyn took to her room during the day, and that was the hour after the end of luncheon. It was generally the case that her door would be propped open so that even while she rested her feet, she might still see the staff coming and going, but this afternoon was different. After routinely scolding several of the parlor maids for dust that she had found on the upper frame of the breakfast room door, she went along the corridor and shut herself in, saying that she was not to be disturbed.

As soon as the door was closed, Esther Jocelyn got down on her knees and began to pray. She clasped her hands in front of her, lowered her head and shut her eyes. Above her the black slate clock ticked on its yellow velvet runner; she pressed her fingertips to her eyelids and whispered her favorite religious text from Ecclesiastes, one that she had found apt to repeat to her staff on many an occasion: *Whatever your hand finds to do, do it with all your might, for in the grave, where you are going, there is neither working nor planning nor knowledge nor wisdom.*

"Neither knowledge nor wisdom," she intoned quietly. "Neither working nor planning . . ."

She opened her eyes and looked up. She had not been thinking of work for the last two days; she had been thinking of pleasure. She had been thinking of pleasure and the dreadful consequences of it, and of how she, Esther Jocelyn, might be a vengeful spirit.

Long ago and far away, one Sunday afternoon she had seen angels. She might have been four or five years old at the time, and her parents had taken her out to Hunslet Moor, dragged her along following hundreds of shuffling feet in drizzling rain. She had heard the fair a long way off as baffling waves of music, and then, as they had walked through the entrance gates, she had been hoisted onto her father's shoulders. He read out the signs to her—" 'The Fine Art Gallery of Fat

Ladies,' " and, " 'The Oriental Dancers from the Harem' "—as the crowd murmured at the shocking displays of blancmange-pink stockings, and a woman with a great moonlike face and a dress of innumerable folds and flounces stared back at them. Esther remembered not her fatness but her color: a red mouth and black eyes and wispy pale hair and the gaudy—though dirty—tartan frock with its green ribbon crossing the woman's mountainous chest.

Her mother had guided them away through aisles of shooting galleries to the carved-wood carousel, and then farther still to the flatbed cart with a curtain backdrop of painted mountains, where actors thundered biblical scenes and where Noah came onto the cart last of all, leading two dogs on silver strings and carrying two trained doves on his arm. In the finale, the angels came down, lowered from the tented roof. Esther had been put down by then, and she sat among the scuffling feet, and under the cart she had seen the sequins dropping from the angels' clothes and scattering on the wet grass.

It had grown dark by the time they came to the booth for the Parachute Queen. There was a balloon of grey tarpaulin and underneath it a square basket, and into the basket stepped a man with a captain's hat, and a boy, and a woman with high-legged boots and a green knickerbocker suit. As the balloon rose into the air, the woman waved a flag, and Esther watched the flag get smaller and smaller until the balloon itself disappeared into the low cloud. The rain was coming harder now, and there was a sizzle of electricity in the air, and as the torches were lit all over the fair, down from the cloud came the Parachute Queen, the air billowing the peplum skirt of the suit, and the little flag waving.

On the way home, the angels that had floated over Noah and the green-suited parachutist became tangled in Esther's head, until the angels floated on parachutes, and she dreamed of dogs on silver strings flying about the sky, and the sequins of the angels landing with a deadly thud and bumping along the ground, rolling as the basket of the balloon had done until it came to a stop at the very edge of the fairground.

She had wanted to be a painted angel so much, and for a while she had dreamed of running away from the dreary grocers' shop that her father ran and joining the fair as it went about the country. She would have scrambled into the balloon basket in an instant and drifted about the sky, waving angel's wings instead of flags, and descending in a lightning storm of glory.

By the time she was fourteen, her father's business was failing, and Esther had been given enough money to buy a uniform and go into service. For a while she had toiled in a large house in Dewsbury, where the owner was a coal merchant and the house stank of coal dust, but after a year she had found a job as a companion and housekeeper to the widow of a vicar. The elderly lady could afford only one servant, and by luck Esther had sprung into the job. She had been obliged to wear ordinary dress after a while; the lady, having no children, took to her as a surrogate daughter. It was here that the keys of a house had first hung around her waist: the keys to the outside doors and the pantry and the garden gate.

She never went out, except to church. And it was only kneeling in church that she felt anything at all; a thrill something like the excitement of the parachute lady and the sequined angels took hold of her when she sang the hymns. She was raised up in her heart; she came back to earth only when her solidly shod feet hit the pavement outside the church when the service ended.

Esther Jocelyn had come to Rutherford when she was forty years old. She had no family; her parents were long dead, and her single brother gone to Canada. She came to the house when Lord William was still unmarried, but nevertheless middle-aged, and she had made herself instantly indispensable. Lord William, it seemed, reserved his smiles only for her in those days; he appeared to be lonely at Rutherford. She knew that he went to Paris, and the rumor that he had a woman there, but she didn't believe it. He was too good for that. The house never gave him a moment's anxiety from the day she had walked in the door; the hiring of servants, the arrangement of dinners and shoots, the necessities of the kitchens—all that she had taken from his hands.

It had been a terrible shock when he had told her that he was to be married.

He had called her into the library as usual one morning after breakfast; she had stood with her pen and paper, ready to note down any engagements or alterations to the menus. There had been a very successful dinner party two days before, and a dozen houseguests; she had been primed to accept his usual compliments. He had looked up from his desk as she had entered.

"Mrs. Jocelyn," he had begun. He had waved his hand at a chair. "Won't you sit down?"

It had shocked her; she never sat. He smiled broadly at her and waited until she was settled. "I suppose you recall our guests," he had said. "Those who stayed with us just recently."

"Yes, of course . . ."

"Miss Bairnswick in particular?"

Miss Bairnswick. The frail beauty whom the maid—so she was told—had had to coax out of her coat as she sat in her bedroom. All eyes, all quivering hands. Bradfield reported that she had said barely a word all during dinner. Esther had admired Lord Cavendish for taking pity on her, alone now in charge of the Blessington mills.

"Yes, indeed," Esther had replied. "Poor child."

William Cavendish had raised an eyebrow. He began rearranging the papers on the top of his desk, dropping his eyes. "Quite so—a sorry situation."

She waited, confused at his evident embarrassment. Had the maids failed in some way? Had the Bairnswick girl complained? Surely not. She looked consumptive; she looked as if she had been kept indoors all her life. Perhaps Lord William felt some kind of responsibility for her, Esther had reasoned to herself; after all, the responsibilities of such an industry as the girl's father's were great, and it might be argued that Blessington was almost a neighbor. It had been kind of his lordship to invite trade to the house, but she had no doubt that it would be merely a passing gesture.

"I expect Miss Bairnswick to be coming here again," William had said, at last meeting her eye. "I expect her to be here rather soon."

Esther had frowned. That was certainly an inconvenience; she had planned for a thorough cleaning of the guest rooms. It was November, and she wanted everything to be perfect for Christmas. Besides which, Lord William never had anyone other than gentlemen to stay in the autumn; he was interested in nothing more than the shooting, and forbade wives to accompany their husbands. Rutherford had become known, in its cold and drafty state, as a man's house.

It was a reputation that Esther Jocelyn had

particularly enjoyed. In the dilapidated great hall and in the Tudor rooms upstairs, she was the dominating—and for many months of the year, the only—female presence other than the maids. In her secret heart she was almost Lord William's wife—or at least his *house*wife. She worshiped him with silent, uncritical devotion; she belonged to him and to Rutherford, and she was convinced that it would never alter; they had a life together.

William was standing up behind his desk; she gazed at him now, perplexed.

"Miss Bairnswick and I are to be married," he told her. "Next month, in London. I hope we have your congratulations, Esther."

It was the first time he had used her Christian name. That was all she could think of at first as she had descended the stairs. She had no recollection at all of what her reply had been to him; she had, she hoped, said all that was necessary and polite. But she could not remember doing so. She remembered only the curious and unfamiliar light in William's eyes, and realized that he was . . . She had been about to say "happy," but it was not happiness. It was accomplishment. There was no romance in it, she had concluded; she knew him well enough to realize that. But he was certainly pleased. She had had to stop on the curve of the stairs beyond the green baize door and breathe deeply at the thought that she would have to tolerate the birdlike and beautiful Miss Bairnswick, and no doubt would be expected to teach her the way that Rutherford ran.

She had gone into the kitchen and given Cook the menus for the day, and then she had gone walking through the stillroom and the laundry room and the storerooms. She had not quite registered where she was and what exactly she was doing until she had seen Mr. Bradfield in the butler's pantry. He had been fastidiously cleaning the silver that he did not trust to the kitchen maid, his back turned to the door, his shoulders hunched in that familiar and unbending way.

"He is getting married," she had said, in a daze.

Bradfield had turned, looked at her, and briefly nodded. "He's told you, then."

"Did you know?"

"I've heard from *them*," he said. "My brother is in service in Blessington. *She* has been talking. He has said nothing to me."

They nodded conspiratorially at each other; it was *she* from then on. Not Miss Bairnswick, and not, for some time after the marriage, Lady Cavendish, but *she*. It was *she* who had upset the apple cart; *she* who had come in as a stranger. *She,* the little frightened one who had, as it turned out—rather rapidly and to Mrs. Jocelyn's disappointment—a mind of her own.

And though Esther Jocelyn never spoke a word

of it to a living soul, her new mistress was also the *she* who had taken Lord William away from her.

Esther Jocelyn sat back on her heels now, her hands still clasped to her chest.

She looked up at the mantelpiece and the two songbirds under their curved glass dome. Two little bluebirds perched on a branch, forever facing each other. It had been a present to her from Lord William on his marriage, and although when he gave it to her he had said that he hoped she would always look favorably on the image of the two Beckforth bluebirds, and that they would remind her of her master and mistress, she had always favored another identity for the smaller bird of the two. She had imagined that he had given her an image of themselves—he and she—as they used to be: two sitting alongside each other, facing out-wards, sealed forever in beautiful companionship.

Esther Jocelyn got slowly to her feet.

She stood for some time gazing around her, first at the birds, and then at the religious texts that she herself had embroidered and that were now framed on the wall. She looked at the picture of Elisha raising the Shunammite's son, a Bible card illustration that she had bought on her annual holiday. She thought of Lord William on the day he had announced to her his engagement; of the birth of the children; of the quiet and predictable way that Rutherford went on from year to year. She thought of her duty to maintain it. And of how pleasure—the pleasure of painted angels and flying through the clouds—was empty and perishable. Painted angels falling—that was what pleasure was. It was show; it was theater; it was illusory and dangerous. It was her duty to protect this house against temptation; to defend it against the call of the devil. And it was her duty to protect William Cavendish most of all.

Early this morning, she had gone to the library to make sure that everything was in place before Lord William had returned. She had lingered for a while, running her fingers along the spines of the books, taking a handkerchief from her pocket and polishing the desk and chair to a deeper shine. Stepping back out into the great hall just before she knew that the maids would come to sweep out the rooms, she had looked up at the Singer Sargent portrait of Octavia.

It was then that a movement on the gallery above had caught her eye.

In the six a.m. shade of the summer morning, she had seen Octavia Cavendish walking softly along the upper corridor. She had seen her look back over her shoulder, and heard another door opening; in a moment, John Gould had appeared. He had said something to Octavia; he had caught her by the wrist. And then he had kissed her.

Esther had pressed herself back against the library door.

And she had been thinking all day of her four-year-old self, lying on the rainy grass so many years ago, seeing the sequins falling through the cracks of the wooden cart stage, and realizing that every angel had feet of clay.

Louisa sat on a bench in the shade of a tree near the Long Water in Kensington Gardens. She read the letter from her father once again; it gave her train times to return to Rutherford, and the news that Charlotte was being brought back from Brighton, where she had spent the summer with friends of the Stanningfields. He said that she must come at once, that it was important that the family should be at home. Carefully, she folded the single sheet and replaced it in its envelope, and looked out over the water towards Hyde Park.

She had brought Florence with her today, but had sworn her to secrecy. "I have to meet Maurice Frederick," she had confessed the night before.

Florence's eyes had widened. "Is it wise?"

"Please don't question me," Louisa had replied. "I should like you to walk with me and then leave me for a quarter of an hour. Surely that isn't too much to ask?"

Florence had considered her friend. A change had come over Louisa in the last two weeks; she was much less frivolous than usual. Her sunny nature seemed to have been replaced by an excited irritability. She spoke less but objected more. She had not wanted to join the family on trips, and explained it by feeling ill. And yet Florence was convinced that Louisa had been out on her own despite declaring herself to be sick; the cook had hinted at it several times—that Louisa had not taken luncheon, or not been in the house for tea. Worried, she had taken Louisa's hand.

"Won't you tell me what it is?" she had asked. "You may trust me."

Louisa had bitten her lip. "I can't say."

"It's Mr. Frederick who is making you unhappy; that much is obvious."

There had been a long silence. "He is going back to France."

"Oh?"

"He fears there will be a war. He says he must go and see his mother. She is alone."

"Alone?" Florence had repeated. "Has he no other family?"

"None at all," Louisa said. She had gripped her friend's hand tightly. "I must say good-bye, do you see?" she whispered. "Father wants me to go home, and Maurice is leaving. There won't be another chance. He is going the day after tomorrow."

Florence had sighed. "I suppose I might walk and look at the new statue in the gardens, the one of Peter Pan."

Louisa had smiled and kissed her. "Thank you," she had said.

"But . . ." Florence had paused. "Do be careful, dear. You will, won't you?"

"Yes, of course," Louisa had replied. "Of course."

There was a little tea stall in the gardens; Louisa could see it quite clearly across the way. Through the trees, she watched Florence walk slowly, stop at the railings by the river, and then glance back. Louisa raised her hand briefly. She saw Florence go to the seats, sit down and order something. She put up her parasol and angled it in Louisa's direction, as if to indicate that, while nearby, she would still afford her friend some privacy.

Maurice came precisely at three. The distant clock was just striking. She thought, as he walked up to her, that there seemed to be no anxiety in his face; he was completely in command of himself. She admired him for that. He touched his hat and sat down at her side. They sat together for almost a minute without speaking until he turned to look at her. "I am sorry for this," he murmured.

"It's not your fault."

He shook his head. "Ah, but it is all my fault," he replied.

"It's been both of us," she said. "Isn't that true?" Despite her determination not to do so, Louisa began to cry. She thought her whole body might break with misery; she couldn't breathe.

Seeing her distress, he quietly took her hand.

"Must you go?" she asked. "Might you come with me to see my parents before you leave?"

"There would be no use in that," he said. "They would despise me for even knowing you."

"That's not true," she said. "I would make them like you."

He frowned at her. "Louisa," he murmured, "I do not know what the future holds. In a few days I think reservists will be called to the army. . . ."

"No," she said. "Not if you're in England with me."

He now gripped her hand in both of his. "Darling, if my country is at war, I must fight. I can't hide here."

"But you have a job in the embassy. Surely you don't need to go." She looked away from him, fumbled in her bag for a handkerchief. "My father might be able to do something. Speak to someone."

A faint smile came to his face. "Your faith in him is charming, but even your father has no jurisdiction over a French national."

"You are laughing at me."

"Not at all, not at all. You are an innocent, darling. It is what I love."

She gazed at him. "I can't see why there has to be a war. What is it to do with France? What is it to do with us?" She took a hitched, painful breath. He lifted her hand and kissed it. "We might . . ." She stopped nervously. "We have never been alone. Not really alone. We might go to a hotel."

He remained where he was, eyes downcast, her hand still pressed to his mouth. Then he lowered it into her lap and looked up. "I could not do that."

"But why not?"

"It would be wrong, dear. For you especially. But for us both."

They looked out at the Long Water, and farther down to the curve of the Serpentine. A nursemaid walked by holding the hands of two small children; as they watched, the boy darted forward and picked up a stick and began to dance around the nurse and his sister, grinning, capering, pretending that his stick was a sword. A sort of coldness swept through Louisa, a premonition of stark horror.

"What will your mother do if you enlist?" she said softly. "You will have to leave her alone too."

"Yes, that's true."

"Will she be frightened?"

He paused. "Yes, I think so," he said eventually. "I have heard it said in the embassy that if war is declared, there will be a march on Paris. It will be an objective: take Paris and dominate Europe."

"But it will be defended, surely."

"We will try."

Louisa shuddered despite the heat of the day. Not Maurice. She imagined him there in uniform, a gun in his hand, or a rifle. *Please, God, not Maurice.* Perhaps, like the little boy who was passing them now, it would come to barricades and sticks and stones. "I wish I were a child again," she said. "One never thought. There were no dangers then. Only games."

"You were protected from them," he observed. "But they were there."

She looked at him sympathetically. He had confided in her how his mother had been abandoned by his father, and how she had never seen her husband again. He himself had no memory at all of him, Maurice had said. He had grown up so acutely aware of this absence, this loss. Louisa had thought of how her own father had been a constant presence; she had told Maurice so, and of how she suspected that she was his favorite; how he indulged her. She had seen envy cross Maurice's face before it was replaced with sadness.

"Will you write to me?" Louisa asked.

"I don't know if letters would reach you."

There were people passing, but neither of them noticed this time as he put his arms around her. He kissed her forehead, her fingers. She wished that he would kiss her properly; she pressed against him. He moved away, back in his seat. Looking at his profile, she thought how lonely he must be, alone here in London, knowing no one, never invited to anything. He had rejected her pleas to come to the de Rays' one evening, to be intro-duced; he seemed determined to live apart.

In this, she felt unutterably sorry for him; she wanted to change that loneliness so much. When she had asked him about it, he had merely shrugged. "I have always had to make my own way," he had told her. "And it seems that I always will." It had pierced her to the core.

The clock that had chimed three now chimed the quarter hour through the trees. Florence would be coming back soon. He would be gone. The thought filled her with dread and panic. "I want to come with you," she said. "I want to come to Paris."

"No. Impossible."

"It's not impossible," she said. "We could be married here in London. This week."

"No," he repeated. "It can't be done."

She stared at him. "Don't you love me?"

"You know the answer to that. But it is not a matter of love. It is a matter of practicality."

"But don't you see? If we are not married we may never see each other. I would go home, and . . ." She stopped. The prospect of this for the first time was unbearable; she could never sit in Rutherford and live an empty life. She would rather die, and that was the truth of it. She would rather go to a foreign country. France was only across the Channel. Maurice had told her about his city; she wanted to be part of it. She wanted to be part of him. It seemed that centuries had passed since she had left home.

She looked at Maurice and knew she would be safe. Surely they would both be safe. He had been careful not to take advantage of her; it would not be any different if they were married. He might not have a fortune, she reasoned to herself. But he had honor.

"I can be with your mother," she ventured. "We can wait together. She would be glad of a friend, surely?"

He considered her. "I think your own mother would prefer to see you more," he said. "What is she going to say, Louisa?"

"Mother worries much more about Harry. He's her favorite."

"Nevertheless. A mother is close to her daughters. It would surely break her heart to lose you."

"No," she told him. "It might break Father's heart, though."

Maurice gazed into the middle distance, seeming to weigh this. "As for my mother," he mused finally, "once you were there she would not want you to leave, it's true. She would be most enchanted to see you."

"You see?" she said. "How perfectly it would work? You mother needs someone with her. My mother has a husband, and Harry and Charlotte. She has all sorts of people around her. The servants too. But your mother is alone. We could wait together for you."

"If Paris is invaded . . ."

"It won't be invaded," she declared. "And what could happen to us if it were? We shall all be together. I shall look after her, Maurice, I promise." Louisa began to wring her hands. "I could be useful," she said. "I haven't ever been anything other than . . . well, you know . . . I'm sure everyone at home finds me amusing. I know Father does. Everyone else . . . Oh, well, Harry, you know, laughs at me. . . ." Her voice trailed away. "I'm rather the comic turn. I don't mind, but they think I can't be trusted with a decision. Not even about whom I ought to marry. And I have the dreadful feeling that they shall marry me off, Maurice. I shall be installed somewhere in the back of beyond in a huge house, and that will be my life. And I can't think . . . I can't imagine . . . I would always think of you. . . ."

"Your mother is right," he said gently. "You must marry well."

"But I would be marrying well," she protested. "I can prove that to them. I would be marrying a good man."

He regarded her for some time with something amounting to sorrow. "You have no idea what you are getting yourself into, I'm afraid. I am not a good man, Louisa."

"Of course you are!"

He became very still, looking into her face. "There will come a time when you will think badly of me. That is the way of every love affair. And then you'll be sorry that you have forfeited your huge house in . . . as you say, the back of beyond."

She began to laugh. "And all the wet winters and the dozen dogs and cold rooms and the wind whistling over Norfolk and some dreadful sweaty-handed man who has all the finesse of a . . ." The comparison evaded her. "Well, no finesse at all." She straightened her back and gave him a broad smile of triumph. "I am coming to Paris with you," she said. "We can be married there with your mother as a witness. Isn't that fine? Isn't it the solution?"

He turned away, looked back to the Long Water. "Your friend is coming back," he said tonelessly.

"Maurice," she pleaded. "Maurice, don't leave me here."

He looked back at her, shook his head slowly. "You want me to break your father's heart," he said. "You want me to do that."

She was trembling; she did not know what else to say. She realized that she had somehow lost control of herself, but she could not help it. She thought that perhaps ever since she had seen him standing in front of the theater that night, she had lost her way. Rutherford assumed all the proportions and shades of a dream, rolling away from her, fading, disappearing.

"Please take me to Paris," she murmured.

And by way of reply, Maurice Frederick suddenly grasped her hand.

Chapter 7

*H*arry stood in the crowds at the Yorkshire Show, clutching a copy of *Flight* magazine in his hand. It was the last week of July, and in contrast to the preceding weeks, the weather was rainy and overcast. Harry had bought *Flight* four months ago in London after the Aero Show at Olympia, and it had been in his pocket ever since, the turned pages now dog-eared and the print blurred from repeated reading. The grainy black-and-white photograph with the magazine article showed the new Blackburn monoplane, and now Harry was standing jammed in the crowds waiting for Blackburn himself, the builder and the pilot. Even when the rain began to get heavier—that slow, drifting Pennine rain— nothing altered the expectancy of the hundreds of men edging the wide lane.

Harry wanted to speak to Blackburn; he wanted to shake his hand. He looked down at the newspaper momentarily, an envious feeling in his gut. So many men already had a pilot's license from the Royal Aero Club. He felt that the chance to fly was slipping away from him with every passing day. His father be damned; the Blessington mills be damned. He had no interest in that or what his father supposed was best for him. Flying was what he wanted. If need be he would buy one of Blackburn's Type 1s and be a passenger in it, just as Dr. Christie was. Christie had no license, but he flew with Blackburn all over the country. Last year the doctor had been in the Wars of the Roses race with Blackburn, easily beating the Lancastrian entry, an Avro biplane that, next to the Blackburn Type 1, looked like a Victorian grandmother fastened into her corset, all strings and whalebone and fabric. Next to it, the Type 1 was a beautiful twentieth-century bird. It had a sleek aluminum body and a near forty-foot wingspan, and the compartments had been edged comfortably with leather. It would be like sitting in a motorcar; the cockpit even had the steering wheel of a car.

Harry had wasted all year in London trying to erase that winter's night at Rutherford. There had been girls—cheerful, bawdy, walking arm in arm with him home from East End pubs; there had been an artist's model who had frightened the life out of him with her recklessness; and there had been two wives who had taken no luring, no lying, no payment, no seducing. They had been shut away in dead marriages, hungry for the kind of lovemaking he had to offer. Hungry too, as it turned out, for the tears he often shed. They would hold him to their breasts as if he were a child, until, suffocated, he was forced to break free. And he never knew how to do that properly. He would often step out into the dark feeling dejected and sick. To those who clung, he was cruel, he supposed. He simply never knew how to get away from them with any kind of grace, prizing off their fingers and slamming doors. He never had words. The tears came unbidden, and whatever depth of feeling they came from was unidentifiable, locked in a box somewhere. He told himself that he didn't need to feel, that it could only make things worse. Instead, he had shouted louder and got drunk quicker and endured more rooms and hands and clinging fingers and slaps and groans in an effort to drown out that echoing emptiness.

It was not as if he had not tried to occupy himself with other things. He had gone to the Anglo-American Exhibition at the Great White City, looking at the displays. He had hoped that it would inspire him to do something more than sit in White's on St. James's Street and stare at the women walking past. He had seen the working model of the Panama Canal, and the replica of New York City, and the scale model of the Grand Canyon. He had gone to the *Wild West Show* and watched the girls on their horses. Everyone had been talking about it, but he had found that nothing really moved him as much as the small out-of-focus photograph of the Type 1. That had got under his skin somehow, and sat there, itching to be scratched.

London had been killing him, killing the heart

and soul inside him. Or what he had left of a heart and soul. He was, he found, desperately glad to be back in Yorkshire. He had had this sense of suffocation for so long. He had been choking to death, and all the noise—the screams, the sighs, the sound of his own feet running up or downstairs rattling on cheap boardinghouse floors, all the pandemonium of London streets, all the drunken yells, all the sounds of his own gasping sobs—had become so much unbearable noise. And just there out of reach—there as he woke, barely able to register her face, but feeling her in every pore— would be Emily, with the gold chain lying in the palm of her hand and a look of misery on her face.

The waiting now among the crowds began to irritate him. How long was it going to take? He had been here for an hour already. The plane had to be brought along the lane to the field, pulled by a team of men. It would be ungainly on the ground on its perambulator wheels, swaying from side to side. He had been told that was how it looked: like a grounded swan unable to glide, its wings outstretched, or like a child's arms trying to balance as it tried to walk. A stumbling progress. And yet it would be so different when it took off; then the swan became itself, a remarkable thing, an astonishing thing. The child ran; the bird flew. And he wanted to see it. He wanted to feel it. He wanted to be away from the ground.

Rain ran down his neck and under the collar of

his coat; the bodies of those closest to him, smelling of wet clothes and beer and cheap cigarettes, were nauseating. The crowd began to joke among themselves, stamping their feet, hooting in imitation of trains. "Pick up thar feet, get up thar speed." Then, "Here she comes," he heard one man say. He elbowed his way to the front. "Watch who yer treading on," growled one man.

And there she was, and Blackburn himself was walking alongside, freely swinging a flying helmet, laughing and talking to a newspaper reporter. He looked handsome, dark haired and square shouldered. As he came close, Harry stood abruptly in front of him. "Mr. Blackburn," he said, and held out his hand.

Blackburn hesitated only a moment before responding.

"My name is Harry Cavendish. I want to fly."

Blackburn smiled. The crowd pressed forward as the monoplane passed, and the words "The Blackburn Aeroplane Co., Leeds" wheeled by over Harry's head, written on the tail. He wiped the rain from his eyes. "You're flying to Leeds today."

"I'm flying half-hourly, back and forth." Blackburn was walking briskly; Harry almost ran to keep up with him, pushing away others who nudged him in the back. "Take me first."

Blackburn stopped a moment and looked him up and down. "You're in a fine rush."

"I'm in the same rush as you," Harry said. "Take me on the first leg to Leeds. And back again."

Blackburn was smiling. "That's not possible."

"I've got my ticket."

The pilot patted his arm. "Then wait in the queue, lad," he told him. "My first passenger, bless her soul, is the honorable Lady Mayoress of Leeds."

It was one in the afternoon before it was Harry's turn.

The rain had stopped by then; the clouds had parted to show a watery sun. Blackburn had made several trips and, after the last, had stood by the plane, taking off his helmet and blotting at his neck with a scarf. Harry walked up to him, his ticket in his hand.

"Ah," said Blackburn, "so here you are."

"I've been waiting all my life," Harry blurted out, and immediately cursed himself for sounding like such an awestruck boy. Blackburn merely smiled. "I was at Olympia in March," Harry continued hurriedly. "I saw this plane then. I've followed you. I know you flew cross-country last year. I wanted to come to Harrogate and Wetherby."

"Why didn't you?"

Harry hesitated. "My father thinks it's a waste of time. And I wasn't in Yorkshire. I had to . . . I had to go away."

Blackburn raised an ironic eyebrow. "It's the

future," he replied simply. "Get up. We'll go."

Harry thought that his heart might stop beating altogether as he stepped into the passenger seat; it was lurching all over the place in his chest. And then the engine started and Blackburn tapped his shoulder. Harry put on the helmet that was given to him. It was too big; he pulled on the strap to tighten it. Suddenly they were rolling forward, bumping over the uneven ground of the field. He knew that Blackburn had got his license in a Bristol Boxkite, and he couldn't imagine anything less like it than the Type 1. As the grass blurred away and the wind rushed into his face, Harry thought that Blackburn must have felt as if he were sitting literally in one those old box kites that he used to play with as a child, for the pilot had no compartment. He merely sat among the canvas-and-wood frame just as if a dining chair had been randomly stapled onto an airborne tent. But this was so different; they were encapsulated, part of the machine. Harry looked to his left and right; the wings were extensions of his own arms. He felt a primeval surge of power, as if he himself had become superhuman and were about to step into the sky. He suddenly gripped the edge of the passenger compartment.

And then the ground slipped away. They were up, into an empty space without signs or roads. There was no containment; they were alone. Wind buffeted them, bouncing them gently; the strips of cloud tore past. Below him, Harry saw the show grounds in a series of squares with the oblong white dots of marquees; the trees and woods looked like small sponges on a lumpy green board. He saw the show ring and the lane on which he had stood as mere scribbles of white, and then far away he saw Bradford itself and the Pennines rising up, and the drift of smoke around the cotton mills, and then the plane banked and the city evaporated. For a second he was hurtling not only out of the familiar landscape but out of himself, unfettered and unrestricted. For the first time in months he felt the tension in his chest slacken and then fade completely, and he felt Emily's grip on him—on the innermost part of him—disappear. She wasn't up here in the clean air; she was down there on the ground, deep down in the river. She was under the soil somewhere—he had never found out where. He had never been told, and he had never known what happened to the child. He did not even know whether it was alive or dead, and that thought had been the one that had driven him out into the long nights in London. He had had a child, but he had no idea whether it had lived for a day or a week or an hour. But up here he was alive, and what should have been guilt, the horrible sick guilt that always filled his throat, could no longer touch him. He was out of the reach of the memories.

He closed his eyes momentarily and felt the

skimming engine and the vast sky holding him up. The nightmares couldn't touch him now—he was too far up; he was moving too fast. The wind tore at him as the plane banked. He was soaring; he was rushing. A tingling sensation ran from his face and down his arms—vertigo, extreme, exhilarating. He yelled out, and looked back at Blackburn, and saw the older man smiling. Harry gave him a thumbs-up sign, laughing, and for the next twenty minutes that was all he did, yell and laugh and feel the vertigo racing around his system, taking his breath away.

Jack Armitage walked down through the fine drifting drizzle towards Rutherford. It was midmorning, and Gray, the estate steward, had sent him back after they had walked the first fields by the village. The third cut of hay lay sodden on the ground; Gray had said that they would wait until the wind got up before collecting it. Better weather was forecast for later in the day, and Jack was to go and fetch Wenceslas back after midday with the wagon.

Jack sang to himself quietly as he walked. He didn't know the name of the song, but one day last summer he had heard it coming incongruously over the wall of the orchard. It had been just before tea, and, coming around the side of the garden wall, he had seen Louisa sitting at a table with Charlotte and a gramophone player on the white cloth between them. Louisa had been laughing and Charlotte, in a low voice, complaining at the music. Jack had been transfixed; it was late in the afternoon, and the sun had slanted across them. Louisa, turning the handle of the player, looked like an angel in a white dress with a broad yellow sash around her waist, and the straw hat heavy with wax flowers tipped back on her head. "You must listen," she had been saying. "It's very easy."

"I shall never learn," Charlotte had told her. "Ask Harry. Ask Mother. They're better at all that."

Louisa had suddenly looked up and caught sight of him, standing where he shouldn't have been in the gateway through to the yard. "Jack!" she had called. "Come here!"

He had put a hand on his chest.

"Yes, you, Jack!" she said. "Don't dawdle. Come here and dance."

He had been struck dumb. He couldn't dance, and it had seemed, at that moment, that he couldn't move. He ought not to even to be looking at them. But Louisa did not care. She had stamped her foot just as impatiently as she had done as a child waiting to be handed up onto her pony. "Jack!"

He had walked over bashfully, dragging his feet, suddenly aware that he reeked of the stables. The music had begun again. Louisa was holding out her hand. "Do you know it?" she asked. "It's Al Jolson, the American."

"That I don't," he had mumbled.

She had put both hands then on her hips. "Really, you are as bad as Charlotte," she had said. "Come here."

"Nay, I must go to the yard."

"Don't be ridiculous," she'd retorted. "I shall only want you a minute." She had dragged him to her side by his wrist, and then put one hand in his and positioned the other on her waist. "It's not ragtime," she said. "It's different. Slower. Listen."

He heard the words crackle out of the speaker, but they seemed random to him. He kept looking at the hand on the soft cloth of her dress, and then down at his own outsize leather shoes with their thick brown laces. Above them, fruit hung in the canopy of the trees, green apples in a waving sea of green leaves. He allowed himself to be led around much as he would lead an unwilling horse, by a mixture of gentle pushing and cajoling words. She was nudging one of his feet with hers. "Step back," she was saying. "Now forward. It's only a waltz, Jack." She had looked up at him, smiling, laughing. "Can't you dance at all?"

That did it. He grasped her and set off under the trees with his own racing version of her leisurely waltz, swinging her around, clutching her tightly to him. She threw her head back and laughed all the louder, and in a few steps he was lifting her off the ground. The scent that she wore overwhelmed him; the fabric of the dress slithered in his fingers; as he let her down he found the sash in his hand, and suddenly she was standing still in front of him and he was holding the sash like a rein. She gazed at him steadily and then pirouetted so that the belt wound her in closer to him, and she tilted her face upwards. It was almost more than he could bear, because she was so close, and because she had that aura of innocence about her.

He remembered when they were both children, and Louisa had been taken over to the Stanningfields' in Manchester, the family known to her ladyship who had the cotton mills; she had come back—she must have been eight or nine—and run into the stables still in her town clothes and said to him, "But you'll never guess, Jack! There are tiny little houses all side by side, and some of the windows are stuck together with paper and the women stand in the doorways." He had stopped what he was doing and asked who it was she was talking about now. "The people who live there," she'd replied, mouth open in mingled delight and horror. "The babies have no shoes. And they shout, even the children. The houses are tall." She'd held up her hands over her head. "Ever so tall, like the drawings in Daddy's book. The Dickens book—what is it?—oh, *Oliver Twist*, Jack. Just like that!" It had exercised a weird fascination over her for weeks, this vision of what life was really like in all its muck and poverty. Afterwards, she'd said that his lordship was furious that the Stanningfields had allowed it. But Ida Stanningfield had been going on some mission of mercy, some do-gooding tour of workers' streets. "Imagine it," Louisa had said to him. "Just imagine!"

She was still like that, a kind of refugee in a wide world; never believing anything could be bad, never understanding why a soul could be negative, polluted to its core; never reasoning why women stood miserably on doorsteps or babies crawled in the dirt. It made him fearful for her. He imagined her running out into London and soaking up everything it had to offer, like a drunk in a bar, drinking in everything put in front of her. She would never change. It made his heart ache.

Behind them that afternoon, the voice on the gramophone had murmured, "Someone handsome, someone true," and Louisa sang the rest. "But I never thought of you." He had abruptly released the sash; she took it from him and carefully retied it. She was humming the tune while he stood rooted to the spot. Sunlight was playing over her face, and Charlotte was peering inquiringly at them both over the pages of her book. The needle of the gramophone bounced on the edge of the disk, and Louisa turned away. He watched her, and she tilted her chin for a second so that he saw her profile and realized that she was still smiling. And then he had turned and gone away, out over the grass, out through the gate, along the path to the yard. And he had gone into the stable and seen Wenceslas there half-asleep, and he had walked over to the great horse and buried his face in Wenceslas's neck, his fists bunched at either side of his head. But the tune kept repeating itself: *But I never thought of you.* He knew that. He knew it only too well. She never thought of him.

He stopped now just beyond Gray's house at the entrance to Rutherford. The line of beech trees was ahead of him, and at his back he could hear Gray's two small children playing in their walled garden, and the gentle murmur of their mother's voice. On either side the wall that edged the park led away, but to this side was the footpath that led eventually to the river. He followed it. The day was close, the sky low, as if the rain might start again. The house, a quarter of a mile away, was a rosy-colored toy in a great green expanse. He sang the song quietly to himself as he walked, and wondered when exactly Louisa would come back. She had been in London much longer than had been expected. There had been no chance at a repetition of last year in the orchard, for neither Charlotte nor Louisa had come home. There was only her ladyship and the American, and neither had gone out from the house much. The horses stood aimlessly in the stables most days, and the car immobile. Sometimes he would see Lady Cavendish and Mr. Gould walking in the gardens and sometimes in the park, but more often than not the house had remained shuttered, closed up as it had been during the Season in the spring, curtains drawn across windows. It was as if the whole place had gone to sleep until Lord William had come back with Harry.

At the thought of the son, Jack stopped. He remembered Harry's voice in the car when he had driven them home: it had been both strident and defensive. Lord William had been saying something about Austria and Serbia, something about Paris. Jack had caught Harry's tone of dismissal more than his words. He didn't seem to care for his father's opinions.

Jack would have dearly loved to have stopped the car. He would have loved to wrench open the door and drag Harry out of his comfortable seat and throw him in the gutter and drive away. They had passed the village church, and Jack knew that Emily was buried there, close by a yew tree but with no marker and no stone. He would have liked to pull Harry straight through the churchyard gate and over the grass and held his face to the weeds growing over her grave. There was a broken body and a broken heart under there, and Harry was the man who had done all the breaking. Jack seethed as he listened to Harry's voice, and he had gripped the steering wheel tighter as the miles passed. He had watched Harry get out at Rutherford and lope up the line of steps to the door. By all accounts, her ladyship had held out her arms to her son once he was inside; Jack wondered whether she had told him that he had a daughter.

Jack pulled a disgusted face here now on the winding footpath. He doubted that Harry would even care about the child growing up in the rooms over the pub in the village; he doubted that he would ask after her or go to see her. They said that she was more like Harry than ever. She would have her first birthday in five months' time. But she was unlikely to see her father, and she certainly would never have a mother. Jack kicked a stone along the path and followed it, increasing his pace, reaching the stile to the woodland and climbing it rapidly.

It was the longest way round to the yard, probably more than a mile. To his right, the river meandered for a while and then struck out towards the lake and the house. He climbed upwards through the larch and pine that had been planted by Lord William's father. A kind of murky darkness was in there under the crowded trees; rain still spattered from branches far above.

He was climbing towards where the path met the track coming down from the moors when he caught sight of something moving a few hundred yards ahead of him. He stopped, thinking it was deer. Whatever it was—it was still two or three hundred yards away in the gloom—seemed to stumble and fall. It was a mingled shape and color: first cream, then brown. He narrowed his eyes, perplexed.

He walked slower, and came to a bank where the ground sloped away. The planting of the larch stopped here; beyond them it was all pine. Somewhere in here he knew that Lord William's father had planted sequoia, a few precious trees bought from a dealer who had come back from California. He knew that they had their own small plantation, spaced far apart from one another in a long line and guarded from deer by a high wire fence. Mr. March had told him when he was a boy some years ago that he was not to go up there; the sequoias were valuable; it was not a playground.

But someone was there now. Someone or something. Jack stepped down off the bank and walked among knee-high rhododendron that had been cut back but that were growing again, thin, yellowing, searching for light. Here and there a pale mauve flower clung to the branches. And then he saw what it was ahead of him, and stopped dead.

It was Lady Cavendish and John Gould. For a second, he thought that she must have fallen, and then the idea came to him with a desperate shock that Gould had attacked her or hurt her in some way, and he was in the very moment of leaning forward, preparing to rush to her, when he saw that she had not fallen at all, and neither was she being attacked, but that she was talking—they were both talking—and that her arms were around the American's neck. And that there was nothing needed from him. And he stood half-hidden between two trees, realizing that, had they turned their heads, they would have seen him. And knowing that they were not going to turn their heads, or hear him, or care.

He got back to the stable yard just before one o'clock.

Out of breath from running, he put his hands on his knees and leaned forward. A door slammed, and his father called him; he looked up but didn't move. Josiah walked over to him.

"What's up with you?" he asked. "You've missed your dinner." Jack straightened up and shook his head. "Did yer see Mr. Gray?"

"I did."

"And what's he want?"

"The team brought down to Brooker's Field."

Josiah eyed him. "You've taken yer time, lad."

"I went up by the woodland. I seen them there."

"Seen who?"

"Her ladyship and the American."

"What? Out walking?"

"They weren't walking when I saw them," Jack told him, giving his father a significant look.

The older man drew in a breath. "His lordship's out. He's gone over to the Kents to see about a shoot in August."

"I know that," Jack responded. "He's out all day."

"You've got it wrong," Josiah said after a hesitation, protest in his voice. "Not her."

Jack thought of the American, his trousers pushed down to his knees, rutting like a farmyard animal out there in the open, and of her grip on him, and the fine lawn coat he'd seen her wearing yesterday spread out on the ground underneath them both. "I'm telling you, Father," he said. "I've seen them. And I'm not wrong."

William Cavendish walked out onto the Green Bridge at Richmond, twenty-five miles from Rutherford, and looked out over the River Swale. It was now late afternoon, and the slanted sunlight had that old-gold look more common to late summer, coloring all the trees along the river. He had spent all day with the Kents, drawing into Richmond's marketplace in the Napier only at five o'clock, and had decided to take a walk that always calmed him, along the river and up to Castle Walk, which would give him a panorama of the way he had come.

The conversation of that morning was on his mind. He had asked Hamilton Kent what chance there might be of Harry joining the Princess of Wales's Own.

"Has the boy expressed an interest?" Kent asked.

"He ought to join a Yorkshire regiment."

"That's not answering the question, old boy."

Kent smiled, lighting his cigar after lunch. "And you think it'll come to that?"

"Within weeks."

Kent had raised an eyebrow. "Of course, you know more than I do, up here in the sticks," he observed. He tapped his leg, indicating an injury from the Boer War. "Counts me out of most things."

"We'll be at war within the month."

"You think so? The Prime Minister shows no sign of it."

"Churchill will be the coming man."

Kent snorted derisively. "Don't trust a man who crosses the floor of the House."

"He's built for war; Lloyd George is not."

"Hmmm," Kent mused. He had two sons of his own, both in the army. "Mobilization, then."

William gave a slow shrug. "Two days ago, Serbia received an impossible ultimatum from Austria. Mobilization can't be far off for us."

"You've spoken to the Prime Minister?"

"Briefly, on the telephone."

Kent smiled. "I thought you despised the instrument."

"So I do," William replied. "I won't have it in the main house, only the library."

Kent began to laugh. "Determined to be an anachronism to the last."

"I hate intrusion."

Kent nodded understandingly. "But we will be

intruded upon, you think. As a country. Does Grey say so?"

"He fears it. The Austrians are determined to crush Serbia. Churchill has ordered the fleet to war stations; Russia is mobilizing on Austria's border. France will follow. And if France follows, so must we. We are allies."

Kent hissed softly to himself. "Hard to believe."

"It *is* hard to believe," William agreed heatedly. "Damned bloody whirlpool. Damned Kaiser. He's at the mercy of his advisers. I would wager you a hundred pounds that he knows only half what's going on. We're standing at the edge." He took his voice down a tone. "I'm sorry, old chap. Your boys and so on. I expect they have told you."

"They tell me nothing, and quite rightly." Kent considered William. "As for Harry . . ."

"He would buckle down to a good officer." In fact, William had come to the conclusion over the last few days that this was what Harry needed: some structure to hold him tight, to give him discipline. He bucked against his father's rule, but William had an idea that Harry would respond to other orders. Besides that, he knew that his boy had the ferocity of determination that would make him good military material. And he was trying very hard to ignore that soft voice in his head that would rather have Harry at Rutherford, growing indolent perhaps, but safe.

"What does Octavia say?" Kent asked.

"Like most of the country, she's oblivious."

"Good," Kent said. Like William, he was of the old school that women, and wives especially, should be protected from reality. "But Harry . . . last December all he spoke of was flying."

"There's no regiment for pilots."

"There's the Royal Flying Corps." Kent leaned forward and tapped William companionably on the knee. "It won't stay on the ground, you know," he said. He waved his cigar skywards. "It'll be up there. Any war at all from now on."

"It's too risky, too underdeveloped. The machines are simply toys."

"You're out of touch, William. The machines will catch up, if they haven't already," Kent said. "And boys like Harry will be in them."

William stood now and watched the water flowing. Above him, the keep of the castle was an enormous solid rectangle dominating the skyline; the pretty little streets, Millgate and Frenchgate and Lombards Wynd, circled it. He had always loved it here. This was what England was about: ancient churches and medieval houses, strongholds and permanence. The castle itself had been here since the twelfth century and it was inconceivable that it could change, or that the flag that flew above it would alter, or that the ineffable peace that hung over the town could ever be shattered.

He had come here as a boy and paddled about in

the river just as children were doing now—although he always would stand apart from the town children, afraid to mix, unsure of himself; and then there was always the traditional walk on to the Culloden Tower. Richmond's history was also Rutherford's, for somewhere in the depths of time—nine hundred years or more, give or take a century—the same Duke of Brittany and Earl of Richmond who had built the castle had also had drawn out the boundaries of Rutherford's estate. It was all of a piece, indivisible.

He wondered whether England might be invaded again. It seemed unbelievable, and yet the French had once carved up this land for themselves, and the Austro-Hungarian Empire might yet do the same. He leaned on the wall of the bridge and stared fixedly at the water below; no, it was impossible. It must be impossible.

He and Kent had arranged for the shoot in the last week in August, but it had been done in a low-key fashion. They had no idea how many men they might call on for beaters; Kent had reckoned that ordinary men might enlist. "You'd be in a pretty pickle then," he had observed. "So would we all."

"How so?"

Kent had smiled. "Where do you think they'd come from?" he had asked. "Do you think they'd only volunteer in the cities?"

"I can't see recruitment reaching us here."

"Can't you?" Kent had said, surprised. "How many have you got at Rutherford? Forty? Fifty? Counting the farms too. You think they would kick their heels at home when there's an adventure to be had? You think they'd continue to be happy polishing your silver? There's no glamour in that when they might have a chance to drill a hole in a fat German and have a sweetheart thank them for it."

"Glamour, indeed!"

"That's how any red-blooded boy would see it, old man. You know that as well as I do, and Harry's no exception. Mark my words. They'll be cramming the recruiting stations before Christmas."

"Perhaps it will be over by then," William replied.

Kent made no comment, other than once again eloquently raising an eyebrow.

William pushed himself away from the wall now, and began to walk. It was a sharp rise from Green Bridge up to the castle, and when he reached the walk he was out of breath. *I am getting old,* he thought, and it surprised him, for he was not a man to dwell on age. He had always been remarkably fit. And yet, next to Octavia . . .

The idea of Octavia brought him to a complete halt. Octavia was a young woman still, and he thought that he had never seen her look as lovely as she did now, this summer. It was strange how a man could be married for twenty-odd years and

315

lose sight of that one simple thing: his wife's beauty. In the spring, after Charles had come, the light had gone out of her face, but he was pleased to see that Rutherford had restored it, even if it had not restored any warmth in her for him. He had felt a pang of envy as he had seen her talking to the young American before dinner yesterday evening; she had looked almost girlish again. It was a blessing that Gould had arrived here to lift her spirits. The man was all charm and deference to them both, and his presence had softened what might have otherwise been a very frigid atmosphere. Octavia smiled again, even if she did not exactly smile in his direction. Gould was a valuable distraction.

He had said as much, in passing, to Hamilton Kent.

"Extraordinary combination, wealth and humor," Kent had said mildly. "One doesn't often get it, especially in that sort of family. In my experience, the self-made man is a dour blighter, eyes fixed on gain."

"Gould isn't the self-made man. That is his father."

"And another jolly sort, so they say. They all rather break the mold. It's said that your man Gould will take up the reins of the business."

"He hardly seems the type to sell hat ribbons to New York matrons," William said, amused at the thought.

316

"From what I hear of him, he could sell ice to the Arctic. Rather a charmer. Clever too."

"Yes," William agreed. "That's true."

William had rested after lunch yesterday afternoon, and then taken himself to see March and Gray, his land steward. Octavia had not, after all, gone walking; she had kept herself in her room after they had spoken. He had left her to her own devices, not wishing to disturb her any further, and the first he had seen of her again was when she had come down to dinner.

She was perfection. Not that he had said so.

No, that had been left to the American. "Perfection," he had heard Gould murmur to himself as Octavia had come to the sitting room door.

She was dressed in something that William did not recognize; it was some sort of brocade with a deep V-shaped neckline. The material of the skirt was caught up at the sides, and there was a pattern of bright pink and yellow fans on it. He did not make it his business to comment on her gowns usually, but in this she was especially pretty. "Rather Oriental," he said, as she took a seat.

"I have had it since 1910, William," she'd replied. "But at least you have noticed it now." She had smiled; he had nodded. And he suddenly felt himself to be very formal in the presence of Octavia and Gould, for they were both so much younger than him. He had been, truth to tell, too warm in his woolen suit; Gould was lounging in something that might have come from the Continent—white linen; William supposed that it was fashionable. And the man wore a silk bow tie folded very loosely—some kind of silk, at least, rather bright. William had taken his place by the mantelpiece, feeling like an old schoolmaster surveying a class of teenagers. Octavia and Gould were turned towards each other. He had felt awkward in his own home, an intruder. When they went in to dinner, he had pointedly offered his hand rather than his arm to Octavia, but the fingers that she laid in his were dead, inert. All through dinner, the silk bow tie and the drooping fingers had irritated him beyond measure. He could not explain why that should be. He kept looking at Gould, unmoved by his boyish stories of New York, whereas Octavia was rapt. William had gone to bed early; she had followed. They had left Gould smoking a cigarette on the terrace, obscure in the twilight and his wreaths of blue smoke.

William had allowed an hour to pass before he got out of his bed, opened his own door, and went across the corridor to his wife's room. The lights were out, but he could see her in the four-poster. As he got to the bed he could hear that she was breathing deeply, seemingly asleep. He had put out his hand and stroked her arm; she had woken immediately, and whispered, "My God. It's you."

"Of course," he'd said, somewhat piqued. He had started to turn back the bedcover.

To his surprise, however, she had gripped his wrist. "I'm not prepared," she had told him. "That is . . . I am not well."

He had stopped his clumsy attempt to kiss her, understanding her meaning rather late. "I see," he had answered. She was so very close, and he could feel her warmth. It had been months, but he would not force her; that would be beneath them both. He had stepped back. There was a little chair next to the bed, and he had pulled it towards himself and sat down. Octavia had wriggled more upright in bed and gathered the sheets to her as if for protection. He fought down this rebuff and his solitariness; he knew that he was being selfish, but he would have liked very much just to lie next to her and hold her in his arms—yet the message that came from her was that this was the last thing she wanted. He was caught between need and the old, old precept, learned so long ago, that he must keep his dignity, that he must not beg or fawn. That he must respect her, treat her with rigid courtesy. Still, his body ached.

From his pocket, he took the gift that he had hastily bought in London. He had put it on the cover between them. "This is for you," he said.

She made no move towards it. He tried to see her expression in the dim room, but could not make it out. He picked up the box again and

319

opened it. "Would you wear it?" he asked. "As a token of forgiveness?"

She had paused for some time, but had not touched the necklace and pendant that had cost him fifteen hundred pounds. "Sapphires," she had murmured finally.

"They suit you, darling."

She had nodded. "Thank you."

"Will you wear it?"

"Perhaps tomorrow," she had told him. "Perhaps then."

He had paused. He had been turning the issue of her proposed visit to Blessington over in his head all day. It seemed churlish to refuse her; it might, after all, bring her out of herself more and make her more cheerfully disposed towards him. And what harm could it do? The mill manager would no doubt, on William's discreet instruction, make it quite clear to Octavia that there were all kinds of reasons why new housing was inappropriate. In fact, he might go over there himself before their joint visit and draw up some kind of map to show that the land she had suggested using was water-logged, or too stony, or some such thing. Or say that building there would only make things worse farther down the hill, or perhaps interfere with the proper running of the mill's own water supply. There were a dozen reasons that might be conjectured to throw in her path, and she was woefully inexperienced. Gould would soon be gone, and that would be her only ally removed, if ally he was. William was confident that it would all be a flash in the pan; he thought that perhaps she had thought it up only to annoy him. And he had been pleased when he had come up with the answer. He would placate her with a little independence over money.

"I've been considering your idea at Blessington," he had said then. "I shall instruct the bank for an account. I shall arrange for money to be paid into it."

But Octavia didn't gush out her thanks, as he might have expected. Instead, her hands relaxed on the gathered sheets for a passing second. And then, "I am glad, William, not to argue about it," she said. "You're most kind."

He looked out now at the lovely prospect from the castle, down to the bridge, past the little town, out to the fields and hills. He had made the account arrangements today as promised, but he didn't particularly care for being called kind. Kindliness was a quality for grandmothers or maiden aunts. He wanted to be loved, as he expected a wife to love him. But there was something different in Octavia; that soft sense of fragility had gone, and he realized now with some depression that he had always liked that in her. Thinking about it objectively, he supposed that was rather feeble of him, wanting a merely docile wife. A woman had to have some character, of course. But he had never valued her character as much as her obedience, the submissiveness that she afforded him because she saw no other choice. He felt himself to be in the process of losing something, but could not fathom exactly what it was.

Louisa must come home, he thought. That would make all the difference. It would help them; it would tie them together again. He expected both Charlotte and Louisa tomorrow, traveling up by train; that had been his instruction by letter earlier in the week. It was wrong that they had all been parted for so long, even if both girls had seemed to prefer their friends and—in Charlotte's case—their chums from school over their own family. Still, at least they had been protected from the iciness between himself and Octavia. Unconsciously, he now straightened his shoulders. The issue that had threatened to break Octavia and him apart must be put aside; it must be forgotten; it must be mended. He must make his peace somehow with Harry. The family must work as one; Rutherford had to present a united front—now, more than at any other moment in his lifetime, it was their duty to keep together.

Standing there at the great height above the river, he had a momentary sensation of falling, and he stepped back suddenly from the unguarded edge, until his back was against the mighty stone wall of the keep. For a second or two, he could not understand where this awful sensation had come from; he was not afraid of heights. And then he realized that it was something else he feared, something that had been at the back of his mind while he wrestled with the idea that a stranger's hand might take everything he owned from him.

He had a memory of Octavia, entirely fresh, as if it had happened yesterday, turning to him as the old landau had come into Rutherford Park for the first time after they were married, all those years ago. She had looked at him with such pleasure and excitement. In the mornings of that first week she had always wanted to cling to him, trying to hold his hand even at breakfast or as they walked through the house. He had not seen that look for years; he thought she had lost it with her youth; he had never expected to see it again.

But he had seen it. He had seen it yesterday.

He had seen it as she gazed at John Gould.

Octavia was at that very moment sitting in her own bedroom, with Mrs. Jocelyn in attendance. It was an hour before dinner, a fact that the house-keeper had already seen fit to point out to her.

"I shan't put you to any more trouble than is necessary," Octavia had said, sitting facing her looking glass while Amelie dressed her hair. "I simply wanted to tell you that Louisa and Charlotte are arriving at lunchtime tomorrow."

Mrs. Jocelyn stood with her hands crossed in

front of her. "The rooms are ready, ma'am, as usual."

Octavia inclined her head to one side so that she might catch Mrs. Jocelyn's expression; the tone had been abrupt. "They are coming on the morning train, so Lord Cavendish tells me."

"I'm sure his lordship knows best."

At this, Octavia turned to face the older woman. "Mrs. Jocelyn, is something wrong?"

"Not at all."

"You seem preoccupied." There was no reply; the housekeeper kept her gaze steadily on her mistress. "Is it one of the staff?"

"No, ma'am."

"Are you well?"

"Certainly. And there is nothing amiss with the staff."

Octavia paused. "We ought to discuss the summer fair tomorrow, I suppose," she said. "I shall see March about the marquees, and Mrs. Carlisle—"

"With respect, ma'am," Mrs. Jocelyn interrupted. "Mrs. Carlisle and I have always managed the food to your satisfaction. We have not changed the menu for the children for some years. And his lordship speaks to Mr. March about the rest."

It was said with absolute finality. At her back, Octavia heard Amelie give a sharp intake of breath. She could think of nothing to say. The housekeeper gave a short nod, turned on her heel, and went to the door. Here, she turned back again. "If you don't mind, your ladyship," she announced, "I should be obliged if you would not call me when dinner is being prepared."

Octavia brushed away Amelie's hand from her hair and turned around. "I shall call on you whenever I please, Mrs. Jocelyn."

The other woman did not flinch. "Then I must speak to his lordship," she said stonily. "I have my role and I know my duties."

"No one is questioning your duties or your ability to perform them," Octavia countered. "And his lordship won't thank you for bringing domestic arrangements to his attention." She began to frown. Under the housekeeper's steady, obdurate gaze, she felt herself inexplicably blushing.

"There is a right and a wrong way to do things," Mrs. Jocelyn told her. "I'm sure that I have never had cause for complaint, and I'm sure that I know right from wrong."

"*Mon Dieu*," Octavia heard Amelie whisper.

Octavia stood up. "I'm afraid I have quite lost your meaning, Mrs. Jocelyn," she said. "You must explain it to me."

She caught the housekeeper's glance in Amelie's direction. "Do you have something to say about Amelie?"

"Not Amelie," Mrs. Jocelyn replied.

There was a frozen second of silence; Octavia walked a step, and then stopped. "If you have something more to add, I am interested to hear it," she said.

Mrs. Jocclyn opened the door. "I have always discussed my concerns quite freely with his lordship when necessary," she said.

"You mean that you used to before I came here."

The older woman nodded. "That is precisely what I mean," she said. "I shall always have concern for his best interests."

"His lordship's interests are not your concern," Octavia said. "They are mine. Your concern is this household. That is your business, and nothing else."

Mrs. Jocelyn said nothing.

"Is that perfectly clear?" Octavia asked. "Do you understand me?"

"Yes, ma'am," the other woman replied finally. "Yes, indeed. I understand you."

It was late when William returned; he arrived just in time for dinner. It irked him to see Gould already at the table looking so much at his ease, and he deliberately let the conversation fall flat, sulking, making little contribution. At one point, he caught a complicit look pass between the man and Octavia, one of puzzlement at his own silence. Harry was eating, head down, disinterested. William took a mouthful of wine, and then slowly put down his glass.

"I've been speaking to Kent about getting you a commission, Harry," he said.

His son's head whipped up; he stared at his father, astonished. "A commission? In what?"

"The Princess of Wales's Own. The Green Howards."

Octavia's knife and fork clattered on her plate. "You've done what?"

"It's a fine regiment."

"Have you discussed it with Harry?" Octavia asked.

"He has not," Harry said. He pushed back his chair. "It's all very well, Father," he began. "But I don't want to be a foot soldier."

"There's no need to be in the army at all, is there?" Octavia objected. "You were never an officer yourself, William. There's no precedent. Your father abhorred the military."

"My father wanted me in Parliament," William pointed out. "And I have discharged that duty, and I discharge it to my country in other ways still."

"Harry has no duty to be in any regiment at all."

"You are wrong, dear," William answered. "We must be prepared. The country is going to war."

"No," Octavia said, her voice quavering. "But that is nonsense, surely."

Harry threw his napkin onto the table. "May I be included in this conversation?" he asked. "May I have an opinion on my future?"

"You don't have to do anything at all," Octavia told him. "You can stay here."

"I don't want to stay here," Harry said. "I'm going to Upavon to get my pilot's license."

Both parents now stared at him; Gould too. Though the American was the only one who was smiling. In fact, he gave Harry a small thumbs-up gesture. "Well done, Harry," he murmured.

William glared at Gould in fury; then, "Where the devil is Upavon?" he demanded.

"Wiltshire," Harry said. "Harold Blackburn is going there. He's going for his Cert B from the Central Flying School. His Royal Aero Club license won't cut the mustard, he says. Not for the Flying Corps."

"And who is Harold Blackburn?" William was in a rage.

"He's the maker of a new kind of aeroplane. He has a works setup at Filey, on the beach. He's a flier, a mechanic, an engineer. And he's a jolly good sort."

"You seem to know a damned lot about it."

"I've flown with him," Harry said. "I went to Bradford and I went up in his Type One and it was the most thrilling thing in the world. It's what I shall do."

William looked accusingly at Octavia, but she appeared to be as horrified as he, and had put her hand to her mouth. "It's not going to be such a jolly jape when war breaks out," he said to Harry quietly. "You will be a sitting duck. You realize that, I suppose, boy? In reach of the artillery."

"No, sir," Harry replied. "I shall not be a sitting duck, and I shall fight any war you care to mention."

"Harry," Octavia murmured. "It's not a game."

Harry slammed a fist on the table. "You see, this is the entire problem," he said. He turned to William. "You call me a boy, sir, but it seems to have escaped your notice that I am not a boy. I may not, of course, be quite as old as the other son of yours, but I am certainly able to know my own mind." He then looked at Octavia. "And Mother, you must realize that I can't hole up here like a rat. I must do my part."

"I don't think you are a child at all," Octavia said. "You are a man, Harry, with responsibilities."

William let out an exasperated sigh. "What responsibilities? He has done nothing but spend money like water for the last eight months! He doesn't understand the word!"

Octavia began to speak, then stopped herself. "He has more than you may imagine," she said.

"I don't see my responsibilities as slogging in a ground regiment, no matter how honorable."

"It is preposterous, "William said. "These are fledgling machines."

"I think you'll find they are very sophisticated," Gould ventured.

William looked at him with icy contempt. "I

329

don't recall asking for your opinion," he said. "In fact, I don't recall inviting you to stay here indefinitely, let alone take part in a private family discussion."

Gould stared back; then he laid his napkin slowly on the table.

"Don't be ridiculous," Octavia exclaimed to her husband. "John has kept me company. He has been the perfect guest."

"I'm glad to hear it," William told her. "But just at this moment it's not convenient to have guests."

"I don't see why not," Octavia objected.

"Because the girls are home tomorrow." William couldn't frame the explanation as to why he wanted his children and wife here, and no one else. But that was his conviction.

"The girls don't occupy the guest rooms," Octavia pointed out. She turned to Gould. "I'm very sorry, John. William doesn't mean to be rude. You're welcome to stay, of course."

William was on his feet. "I shall decide who stays under my own roof," he told her.

"Under *your* roof?" she echoed. "It's the family's roof. We all live under it."

"It is my house and my decision," he said.

Gould now got to his feet. "I'm sorry to have been the cause of any trouble," he said. "I shall go, of course."

"No," Octavia said.

The single word fell like a stone. William saw

Gould smile at her, and make a face close to sympathy; the other man raised one hand slightly, as if to say that now was neither the time nor the place. It was an intimate gesture, the kind passed between friends who understood each other. William felt his temper boil. In response, Octavia had raised her hand a little, and now Gould took it and raised it to his lips.

"You've been wonderful to me," he said. "And I thank you very much." He turned to William, after placing Octavia's hand gently back on the table. "And you have been very kind to me also, Lord Cavendish," he said with frigid formality. "I've outstayed my welcome; that's clear. I apologize for it."

Harry had crossed his arms; he was looking at the three of them with amusement. "I say, Gould," he murmured. "Want to come flying?"

"If you would try not to be a perfect idiot for two moments together," William snapped.

Harry now shot to his feet. "An idiot?" he asked. "Why, thank you, Father."

"Stop it," Octavia pleaded. "This isn't necessary. None of this is necessary. Harry, you don't need to fight in a war. There won't be a war. But . . . but, you know, you may fly. Of course you may. I'm sure your father really doesn't mind your flying. You can even go to Wiltshire. That will be all right."

Harry paused, looking at his feet, a small smile

on his face as if he were considering the most polite way to reply to her. "Mother," he said at last, "I'm sorry, but I really don't need your permission. I shall do this with or without it."

William fumed. "You might be civil, at least!"

"I'm being civil," Harry pointed out with exaggerated calm. "I don't believe I've raised my voice, Father. I've simply stated a fact."

Octavia seemed to be on the verge of tears. She was not looking at William; her gaze switched between Gould and her son. "Perhaps Mr. Gould could go with you to Upavon," she suggested at last. Her voice quavered. "To keep you company. To see how things are. As a favor to me. That is, to his father and me. Both of us."

"I don't need a nursemaid, for God's sake," Harry retorted. "This is too damned extraordinary for words. I'm nineteen years old, Mother."

"I think I should know that," Octavia replied.

William walked around the end of the table, towards Gould and his wife. "You want this man to accompany our son," he said. His tone was dangerously low. "A stranger? To give me advice on my own son?"

Gould glanced at Harry. "Harry," he said quietly. "Why don't you let me talk to your father for a while."

Harry threw his hands in the air. "Good bloody luck," he exclaimed, and walked to the door. Harrison, the footman, sprang forward to open it, and Harry paused next to him before he turned on his heel to address them. "Do you know," he suddenly said to his parents, "I'm pretty bloody fed up with people opening doors for me. For anything. Why should Harrison here open any door? Why should Gould open a door for me at Upavon? I'll find my own way." And he turned again and stuck out his hand towards Harrison; with almost comical hesitation that seemed to approach disdain, Harrison shook it. "That's a fine fellow," Harry said. "Don't open a door again, though. Don't come and lay out my clothes. I'm sure you have better things to do in life." And he was gone.

The footmen, Harrison and Nash, looked at William. In the same instant, Bradfield's footsteps could be heard in the great hall; he had gone to ensure that the drawing room was properly lit for when dinner had finished. They heard Harry almost collide with him, utter a curse, and then his footsteps on the stairs. Bradfield came into the room with an expression of inquiry on his face.

"Bradfield," William said, "would you mind leaving us alone here. Nash and Harrison may go too." The three servants stood undecided, confused, in the doorway for a moment; then Bradfield ushered them out. The doors closed with an echoing thud.

Octavia stood up. William looked from her to Gould and back again. "Is it necessary for me to ask what has been going on here while I've been away?" he asked.

There was an awful silence. John Gould opened his mouth to speak, but Octavia held up her hand to silence him. "I think you ought to know that, when the girls come, I'm going to take them abroad," she said. "And Harry too, if he will come. There are aeroplanes for him to fly in other countries."

William stared at her, aghast. He had been expecting all kinds of replies to his question, but this was not one of them. "Abroad?" he said. "You can't go to Europe, for God's sake."

"I don't intend to go to Europe," she replied steadily. "I'm going to America."

For a moment, William said nothing at all. His face betrayed utter astonishment; then it collapsed in a smile. He began to laugh. "America," he repeated. "America?" He shook his head.

"It's not a joke," Octavia told him. "And it will take Harry out of harm's way, at least."

William stopped laughing and gave a sigh of exasperation. "He wouldn't want it," he said. "You just heard him. Even if it were a thing to be countenanced, which it is not."

"Then I'll take the girls."

"You'll . . ." He stared at her in complete bewilderment. Then he pointed at Gould. "This is your doing," he accused.

Gould returned his stare. "I don't deny it."

"You don't deny it!" William shouted. He strode around Octavia, brushing away her hand, oblivious to her attempt to restrain him. "You damned dog."

Gould had not flinched; he stood his ground. William, losing all control, suddenly lunged forward, catching John a blow to the face. The younger man made no effort to deflect him. There was a horrible moment while William tried to land several blows, some of which struck home, but most of which caught Gould on the shoulders or chest. It made William seem monstrously clownish. He had never been aggressive, never a fighter. It showed now. His punches had no weight, no effect. Pity crossed Gould's face, and, seeing it, William grabbed Gould by his jacket and pulled him close. For a second, the two men were face-to-face. Then William dropped his hands. He pushed Gould once in the chest, forcing him to take a step back, and then turned to Octavia. "This man?" he said. "*This* man?"

Octavia said nothing at all. She was trembling, but she looked him in the face unflinchingly.

William walked away; he looked out through the windows at the long green sweep of grass and the road of beech trees. "No," he whispered. "No, no, no." He turned back; Octavia and Gould were now standing side by side. He saw Gould's hand drop from his wife's waist, and her head incline slightly as if acknowledging the touch. "Do you mean to tell me . . ." he began. But he couldn't go on.

Outside, somewhere past the garden, came the faint sound of a dog barking, and of voices. William put his hand on the sill of the open window, clutching it for support. Octavia watched him; then she walked over to him. "William," she said quietly. "I'm very sorry."

"Sorry!" he echoed. "You can't do this."

"I can leave whenever I want," she corrected him. "I can go and live in Blessington until the details are arranged. I can supervise the beginning of the work there. When John decides, we will go to New York."

"When . . . when John decides," William repeated, as though trying to work a meaning out of it.

"He is going to build a house on Long Island," she explained. "I'll take the children there. I see what is in Harry's mind; I see what he wants to do. But he can do that just as well in America. And Louisa may marry just as well . . . New York society . . ."

William was apparently listening. He bowed his head and closed his eyes.

"And of course," she added, "I do see that Harry and Louisa both will be adults in three or four years. Their lives are their own. They may return. I would not stop them." There was no response. "William," Octavia prompted. "This war. If there is to be a war. I must take them away if that is really to happen. You must let me take them." There was still no reply. "William," she prompted. "William."

A deep sigh came from him at last. He opened his eyes, lifted his head, and gazed at her. "It's all very quick," he murmured.

"It's not quick at all," she told him gently. "Not to me. I've wanted to love you, but you have never loved me, William. I realize that. But now I have a chance of it. Would you deny me what you won't give me?"

He was looking at her intently, taking in every detail of her face. Very slowly, he began to smile; she took it as acceptance. But behind her, John Gould saw something different. He started forward. "Octavia," he warned.

William suddenly gripped both her shoulders. "Leave whenever you want?" he said. "House on Long Island? What a nice little plan. How purposefully you've spent the summer." Octavia tried to disengage his grip, but his hands slipped downwards and took her by the wrists. He bent both of them back until, gasping, protesting, she slipped to her knees. "You'll leave me?" he said. "By God, you won't leave this house! And as for the children . . ."

John Gould was quickly next to them; he put his own hands over William's, trying to prize them away. William froze; his face was an inch from his rival's. "If you don't take your hands off my wife, I'll kill you," he muttered.

Gould stepped back.

William looked down at Octavia; then he let go of her. She scrambled back against the skirting board under the window. William stared at her uncomprehendingly for a moment; his mouth trembled; he clamped it shut and sidestepped them both and walked to the door. There he paused and looked back at the table—the vast table with its beautiful arrangements of summer flowers and its silver, the long white cloth where the soft evening light was reflected in the glasses. The table where he had sat alone for those long empty years until he married. The table where he had sat so many times since with Octavia. It was a lovely picture, but to him, with all its color and light, it seemed like a ruin.

He turned around. "You are wrong, quite wrong, to say that I've never loved you," he said, his voice breaking despite himself. He opened the door to the shadows of the great hall. "And it's not the only thing in which you're mistaken, Octavia." He looked away from her, unable to bear the sight of her on the floor, and Gould's hands outstretched. "You can go wherever you wish," he told her. "To . . . America . . . or wherever you wish."

He glanced back at them both. "But you won't take the children," he said. "By God, you won't. I shall make sure of that."

Chapter 8

The house was silent the next morning. Breakfast had been laid as usual, but no one came down for it. After waiting for some time, Bradfield went back downstairs and knocked on Mrs. Jocelyn's door.

"Come in," she called.

He stood on the doorstep. "Have you seen her ladyship?"

"I have not," she said. "She sent luncheon menus directly to Mrs. Carlisle. And dinner."

"To Mrs. Carlisle?" he echoed, amazed. "But you see her each morning."

"I've been asked not to attend." Mrs. Jocelyn did not meet his eyes; she was sorting linens, counting them in the huge cupboards to one side of the door. On the table next to her lay the sheets and counterpanes for Louisa's and Charlotte's rooms.

Bradfield watched her a moment; then, glancing along the corridor, he stepped in and shut the door behind him. She looked up at him critically.

"Is it true?" he asked. "All this with the American?"

"I'm sure it's not my business."

"Why doesn't she want to see you?"

The housekeeper laid her hands on the sheets

and sighed. "Then it is," she admitted. "There, and be satisfied."

"What, all summer?"

"So I believe."

"My God. Harrison is saying as much in the kitchen. He says they've been seen in the parkland, the woods. Some of March's boys saw them. And the maids told you?"

"The maids don't need to tell me. I've seen it for myself. It's not the house it was. The devil is in it."

Bradfield frowned. "And what of his lordship?"

Mrs. Jocelyn turned to face him, hands on hips. "You'll stand by him?"

"I was here before she came." He considered in silence for a moment, then: "He ordered us out of the dining room last night. There was something then between the three of them."

"The maids say she went to his lordship. They saw her cross over the gallery; she threw open the door. They heard them inside. Her weeping. Voices raised. They could hear it as they went up the stairs, past midnight."

"What has Cooper said?"

"Nothing. Cooper went with him to Paris this last time, but he tells me not a word."

"Amelie is the same." The pair of them, identically but unconsciously, drew their mouths down in distaste. The valet and lady's maid were a law unto themselves, rarely mixing with the other servants. "They think themselves too high," Mrs. Jocelyn added.

Bradfield shook his head, stared at the floor, then straightened. "Thank you, Mrs. Jocelyn."

"It's a bad day," she told him as he opened the door to go. "I'll not believe this story of Madame de Montfort. I'll not believe it of his lordship. Her ladyship was hysterical in London; she's of that type. You know that as well as I. A nervous hysteric from the first, not a shred of dignity. Running about after him and the children. Barefoot in summer. Laughing at dinner. You've seen it; you've seen the way she's always been. The young master, now . . ." She paused. "Well, I won't say he's cut from the same cloth. He's sown his wild oats, I daresay. He shall regret it, but then that is men. But the young mistress, Louisa . . . there's one like her mother." She was now furiously, blindly folding and refolding the sheets. "The fact is, her ladyship's beneath this house. I don't mind saying it. I *shall* say it. I've said as much to her. She knows my mind. She's brought bad behavior into it from the first. She's not aristocracy; she's never been right."

Bradfield did not comment. He was regarding Mrs. Jocelyn with mute horror; when she looked up at him, he hastily rearranged his face to show its usual emptiness. "It will blow over," he murmured. "It will pass."

"Pass?" she repeated. "*She'll* pass. She'll go

341

with him, the American. You mark my words."

"I hope it won't come to that." Bradfield stepped out into the corridor. Looking back, he saw her wagging her finger in his direction.

"God sees," she told him, and there was a glint of triumph in her eye. "God sees, and he takes His vengeance."

Harry had gone out at first light, taking the Metz.

It had been months—probably almost a year—since he had driven it, yet it had started the first time. He supposed that he had Jack Armitage to thank for that, although he was under no illusion that Armitage would do it for him—it was more likely that he did it for the love of the car. It took Harry one or two miles before he adjusted to it, and he started to sing as he bowled along the empty lanes in the summer morning—something he had heard from *Hello, Rag-Time!*—a stupid song that got into a fellow's head; he put back his head and shouted, "'All they do is talk like babies, Hear the way they bill and coo! Poogywoo, poogywoo . . .'" He started to laugh. The road whipped out along the river and then rose a little; in a moment he could look back to Rutherford, just its chimneys above the trees. He put his foot down and was through the village in seconds; he saw a boy wandering through a field with a stick urging on the dairy cows; in a house by the church a woman was hanging out washing.

The world went whipping by. " 'All night long he calls her snooky ookum, snooky ookums. . . .' "

It was a silly song. It was a silly morning, spent in glorious gadding about. But as he came back through the gates of the park, he slowed down, stopped laughing, stopped singing, and drew up in front of the house. He couldn't help thinking that no matter how much life there was out here, there was none in there anymore. Anyone could see that his mother and father were at loggerheads; probably it was still over bloody Charles de Montfort.

Harry got out and slammed the door. Well, the blighter could go hang, he thought to himself. Harry would often conjure up Charles de Montfort's face simply in order to imagine himself spitting in it. He hoped fervently that what Father said was true, and that there would soon be a war in which Charles de Montfort would be obliged to fight. The French would call up all their reservists; de Montfort would be out of Paris before he knew what had hit him. And Harry hoped that something would hit him. Some bloody great Austrian bullet between the eyes. It never occurred to him what his Father would think of that, but in all honesty he didn't care.

He would go to Upavon and get his license, which was all that concerned him. Mother and Father must work out the whole damnable mess on their own, though he pitied his mother being cooped up here. She was no better off than the prize pigs down at the tenant farm; she would be trotted out at the summer fair and made to give out prizes for the best bloody potatoes, or some such rot. He would try to be kind to her today, he decided. She had little enough attention as it was.

He opened the front door and stood for a while surveying the great hall. He remembered sliding down here, the whole length of the hall, on some sort of Indian mat when he was three or four years old, and Bradfield blustering about it. Mother had just laughed. Father had never known; he had been a distant presence. He had memories of being in his mother's lap, and of her stroking his hair by a fireside in the nursery, comforts that were absent when his father was home from Parliament. The world would suddenly become more formal then, and he and his sisters would be paraded before Mother and Father before dinner—three in a row: "My little crop of flowers," Mother would say. He recalled Father always telling him to stand up straight. And he would—yes, he would, such was his hero worship of his father then—he would stand as tall as he could, and earn himself a pat on the head. The kisses would come surreptitiously behind his father's back from Mother as she shooed them away back upstairs. He would lean into her for a snatched second, inhaling the delicious scent of vanilla and roses that always identified her.

Mother and flowers, Mother and flowers. He smiled now to himself as he stepped inside and shut the door.

As if she'd been summoned by the power of thought, he saw Octavia come out of the drawing room door. She was holding a letter in her hand. "Where is your father?" she said.

Harry walked forward, taking off his gloves and throwing them on the reception table. "I don't know," he told her. He smiled, but then saw the expression on her face. "What's the matter?"

She looked down at the piece of paper that she was holding. "It's Louisa," she said dazedly. "It's from Louisa." She held it out to him; he took it.

"I thought she was coming up today?"

"She is. She was. With Charlotte." Octavia was staring behind her. "The library," she murmured. "He must be in the library." As she went to look for William, Harry looked down at the letter.

Dearest Mother,

it began. It was written in a hurried scrawl.

Please, oh, please, darling Mama, would you speak for me to Father, and forgive me? I shan't be coming with Charlotte. I have met a man and he has asked me to marry him in Paris. It is all so hurried and I am so sorry, but we do hope to come back as soon as we can. His mother is all

alone and if a war is to come we must marry. . . . Mama, please see, won't you? It's impossible to leave him. I am to be Mrs. Maurice Frederick. Oh, please be happy for me! Be as happy as I am, Mama. Please find it in your heart to give us your blessing and make Father understand. I am still your
Louisa

Harry read it twice. "Dear God in heaven," he murmured. His hand dropped, holding the letter loosely, and he tried to remember the conversation he had had with his sister all those weeks ago. She had told him that she had met a man who was French. She had told him the name. And he had made a joke of it. He looked again at the letter, and saw that the date was yesterday.

His mother came running along the hall, with his father behind her. She held out her hand for the letter and, when William reached her, passed it to him. A deep color suffused the older man's face as he read it; then he looked up.

"Did you know anything of this?" he asked his wife.

"No, of course not."

William nodded. "Because you were not there," he said.

Octavia stared at him; she gasped a little, and then bit down on her lip. Cutting as it was, it was the truth, and was said simply as a fact, not as an accusation.

"Louisa told me, not Mother," Harry said.

Both of them gazed at him.

"She told *you?*" William demanded. "When?"

"I don't mean that she told me she would run off with the blighter," Harry replied indignantly. "I mean that she said she had met a man who claimed that he knew me. A Frenchie."

"Whose name was . . . ?"

"Frederick," Harry confirmed, nodding towards the letter. "But I knew no one called Maurice Frederick. I told her so."

"And she was seeing him?" William's tone was completely scandalized. "How could that happen?"

"I got the impression it was by accident somehow."

"While she was in the care of the de Rays." Fury contorted William's face; he turned on his heel and strode back in the direction of the library. Octavia and Harry followed him, Harry holding the studded leather door for his mother when it swung hard back on its hinges and almost slammed in her face. William was already lifting the telephone receiver, asking for the London number of the de Ray house. There was an agonized minute or more of silence while he was connected and he waited for the number to be answered. He asked for de Ray himself, but, by the inflection of voice that answered him, it was evidently his wife. William listened with twitching impatience, holding the receiver slightly away from his ear. Then, "Please put her on," he said.

"What is it?" Octavia whispered.

"The daughter," William told her.

Octavia held her hand out for the receiver. "William," she said. "Please."

He hesitated, and then handed it to her. She pressed it to her ear. "Florence," she said. "It's Lady Cavendish."

"She didn't tell me," she heard Florence say at once. "I've only just discovered the note. We were about to ring you. She said last night that she would get Devenish to drive her at six, and that we weren't to bother seeing her off because it was so early. But I did get up, and she was already on the step. She seemed so excited; I thought it was that she was at last going home to Rutherford. Devenish said he dropped her at St. Pancras and got a porter for her bags. But she didn't get Charlotte's train, Lady Cavendish. She just simply didn't turn up for it."

"And Charlotte? What has happened to Charlotte?"

"The Gardiners took her to the railway station at seven. They waited for Louisa; when the time came, Charlotte insisted she would go by herself."

"Oh, my Lord!" Octavia exclaimed.

"It's all right," Florence told her. "Mr. Gardiner got on the train with her himself, rather than let her be by herself. He has property in Leeds. He told his driver that he was quite happy about it. The driver came around here just ten minutes ago. He brought a note saying that Louisa had missed the train. And then I ran upstairs to her room. I don't know. . . . I just had an awful presentiment then . . . about her excitement. It suddenly seemed . . . not quite right . . . and I found the note, addressed to us all."

"Read it to me," Octavia instructed.

The content was much the same. "Who is this man?" Octavia asked. "Do you know him?"

"He . . ." She heard Florence stop and begin to weep. There was a shuffling sound, and muffled voices. Then Hetty de Ray's voice came loud, clear and furious along the line. "Octavia," she said. "My dear, I feel so responsible, but I had no idea at all. We can barely believe it of Louisa."

"It's no one's fault," Octavia replied. She heard William hissing his disagreement. "But what does Florence know?"

"She says that Louisa spoke of him; she believes she met him secretly. Four days ago she went with Louisa to Hyde Park to meet him. I promise you, Octavia, I was not told about this; I would have absolutely banned it. Louisa said that it was to bid good-bye to this man. He was leaving the country."

"But she has not said good-bye. She has gone with him."

"Yes," Henrietta de Ray replied. "I cannot think how; I cannot think why. . . ."

"Who does Florence say he is?"

"He worked at the French Embassy. He is Parisian."

"Parisian?" Something very cold entered Octavia's bloodstream and chilled her to the core. "What age?"

"Her own age, I think. Florence says perhaps a little older."

"Please let me speak to Florence again, Hetty."

The telephone was passed back. "Florence," Octavia said. "What is this man like? What did he say?"

"I don't know what he said, other than good-bye," Florence whispered. "Louisa told me they had parted."

"Is there an address on the note, a place where she is going?"

"No, Lady Cavendish."

"But it is Paris."

"She said . . . she said his mother lived near Montmartre. He said that she was . . . that she knew painters. . . ."

"She's a *painter?*"

"No, no. I can't think how she phrased it. Perhaps it was just an impression. But she kept saying as we walked home that his mother was alone and that she would keep her company if

Maurice went to fight. That they would help each other because he would be gone."

"Oh, God," Octavia whispered. She covered the receiver and stared at William. "She's gone to this man's mother. Because he was going home, she went with him." And then an expression of complete and utter horror crossed her face. She reached blindly behind herself for a chair and dropped into it, the receiver still in her hand. "Montmartre," she whispered.

"Where?" William echoed.

"What is it?" Harry said.

She looked up at her son. "Did you ever see him?" she asked. "This Frederick?"

"No," he told her. "I thought nothing of it. I thought it was just some passing fancy. . . ." And as he said the words, he realized how stupid they sounded. He blushed.

William caught hold of his son's arm. "You left her to the predations of this person?" he asked. "You never asked who it was, demanded that you see him? Your own sister, and some stranger who claimed that he knew you?"

"I . . ." Harry could think of nothing to say in his own defense. He dropped his eyes from his father's face. "No," he muttered guiltily.

"Florence," Octavia said slowly into the receiver. "What did this man look like?"

There was a pause at the other end of the line. In the background, Octavia could hear Henrietta

351

de Ray exclaiming loudly that some servant should leave the room. "He was rather ordinary," Florence began hesitantly. "That is, he was dressed in a rather ordinary way: a black suit, a grey waistcoat . . . cheaply, I suppose. Louisa said that he had not much money, and that her parents . . . that you, Lady Cavendish, and Lord Cavendish . . . that he said that you would not be pleased that Louisa knew him. That you would not approve of him addressing her. He told her that he and his mother had been left alone when he was young. That his father had left them. I think, from what she confessed to me the other day, she had seen Maurice often. She would sometimes say that she was ill, but I think . . ."

"You think she went out alone to see him?"

"Yes," Florence admitted. "I'm so very sorry."

"What is it?" William demanded. "What is she saying?"

Octavia glanced up at him. "That she went out alone with him."

"My God!" William thundered. "What the hell has got into that household!"

Octavia turned away from him. "Florence," she said quietly, "what did he look like?"

"He was rather tall . . . over six feet tall, at least. He had fair hair. But I only ever glimpsed him from a distance. She said he had been outside a theater once, and spoken to her at the races, and I recalled someone who moved away as we walked towards them."

"You never heard his voice?"

"No . . ." She paused. "But there is one thing. Louisa said he . . . that he had a slight . . ." Octavia heard a prolonged sigh. "She thought it was endearing. I'm sorry, but that was her word. Evidently he did not say 'Louisa' quite right. He prolonged the S. It made a kind of hushing sound. He lisped it. She rather liked it."

"Oh, God," Octavia murmured. "Oh, God."

"What is it?" William demanded.

She let the receiver fall into her lap. Down the line, far away, she could hear both Florence's and Henrietta's voices asking whether she was still there. She gazed up at her husband. "It is someone a little older than Louisa," she said. "He has fair hair; he claims that his father left him and his mother all alone when he was a small child. That the mother lives near Montmartre . . ."

"Christ, no," William muttered. "It can't be."

"And that he can't say her name," she added, and her voice broke. "He can't say the name 'Louisa' properly."

Harry looked from one parent to the other. "What is it?" he asked. "Do you know him? Do you know Maurice Frederick? Who is he?"

William had lowered himself slowly to the chair on the other side of the desk, and stared at the books laid out there, the books belonging to his own father that he had been preparing to read that morning. "He's not called Maurice Frederick," he whispered with incredulous horror. "His name is Charles de Montfort." He was still staring down at the desk, thunderstruck. "Helene's father . . ." he muttered.

"What about her father?" Octavia asked.

He looked up at her. "His names. His Christian names, that is. *Maurice Frederick* de Montfort."

In the ensuing silence, Harry put a hand on his mother's shoulder. "Oh, Christ. Surely not. Louisa is . . . I mean, she's . . ." But his sentence faltered to a stop.

Octavia stared at William. "You do not know?" she whispered. "Truly, you don't know if he is your son?"

"I've never known for certain."

"Would Charles know . . . for certain?"

"How can he?"

"Would Helene have told him something she would not tell you? That you were his father, in truth? Is that why he came to London and demanded so much? Now is the time to tell me if you know, William."

"I . . ." William stopped, frowning. "Helene could not say."

"She impressed it upon you all these years when it suited her."

"Yes, she did that."

Harry stood, perplexed, trying to catch the

354

meaning of the conversation. "There's a chance that . . . it's all lies?"

"No one knows for sure except Helene herself," William replied.

"But all this fuss this year . . . you mean, it might have been for no reason? You mean that he came asking for money when he may not be your son?" Harry began to laugh in an exasperated way, then stopped. "You're telling me that I may have a half brother but that, on the other hand, I may not have a half brother? By jingo! What a farce." His voice was loaded with sarcasm.

"Don't speak to your father in such a way," Octavia said.

Harry started to reply, then saw her unhappiness. "I'm sorry," he relented. He looked at his father. "Good God," he observed. "This woman has you over a barrel. She's strung you along, and that's the truth of it, got you dancing to any old tune she cares to play." William opened his mouth to reprimand him or deny it, but evidently he could not. It was perfectly true, after all. "Well," Harry decided. "One thing's for certain, at least. We can't just let this bloody chancer take Louisa away. Making the poor kid believe . . ." He paused, and his face blanched. "He's taken her to defy you, to get his revenge on you," he said to William. "That's all it is, isn't it? Because you threw him out. Because you wouldn't give him money, or a name."

"Perhaps," William admitted.

"It is too cruel, if so," Octavia murmured. "Poor Louisa."

Harry's brow furrowed in concentration. "I mean, if he doesn't know what she is to him, and if he doesn't know if she's really his half sister or not . . . he wouldn't really marry her? Not actually?"

Very quietly, with muffled sobs, Octavia began to cry.

"I don't know his motives," William said. "I can't imagine what they might be."

Harry shook his head. "But Louisa says they're to be married. How could he break it to her in Paris that it was all a ploy, and expect her to stay there?"

"She couldn't get back alone," Octavia murmured. "She wouldn't know how."

"Then he's going to abandon her," Harry answered. "If that woman's told him that Louisa's his sister, he's simply done it to get revenge, for spite. He's done it to break her, to reject her."

"Just as he's been rejected," Octavia said.

William shook his head in abject despair. Octavia looked at her husband. "Did she know the father or not?" she said quietly. "Did she lie to you, her son, herself? Which?"

"I don't know," William told her again. The endless repetition of it did not make it any easier.

"You don't know much," Harry observed. He

waited for his father to admonish him, threaten him, but instead was rewarded by the despair only increasing on William's face. It surprised Harry so much to see this weakness, this inability to act in his father, that he couldn't speak.

"All these years," Octavia murmured, holding William's gaze. "She has played with you."

William said nothing at all. He dropped his eyes.

"And here is where we all suffer for it, Louisa most of all," Octavia continued, her voice very low. "Either she'll be part of an incestuous marriage, or abandoned. Or she'll live in some desperate situation with Helene." She screwed her eyes shut as if to close the image in her head. She thought of her daughter in Helene's sphere, dominated by her. Louisa was no match for Helene's twisted character, and it suddenly came to her that this was what it all might be about: Helene wanting Louisa, getting Charles to lure her to Paris, to claim her, to wrench her away from her parents—to mold her, change her, corrupt her.

"Why would she be so vengeful, if Charles was not really your son?" she said. The truth of the remark, so awful in its consequences, fell between them into silence.

Harry spread his hands, trying to find an answer. "Perhaps it's nothing to do with her," he suggested. "Perhaps this is just about Charles trying to hurt us. He's trying to get to you by destroying Louisa. Just because of the money. Just because of refusing him the Cavendish name. Perhaps he's done this of his own accord, and his mother knows nothing at all about it."

William glanced down with a desperate sympathy at the sight of Octavia's distress. He wanted to reach out and comfort her, but his heart seemed to be knotted inside him, and he felt a sudden, crushing pain in his chest. Taking a breath, he watched Harry put his arm around his mother's shoulders. "Don't cry, Mother," Harry was whispering. "We shall find her. We'll go to Paris. We'll bring her home."

"I should have stayed in London," Octavia whispered. "I should have stayed."

Harry straightened up, and father and son looked at each other for some moments without speaking. At last, William nodded.

"We'll go together," he confirmed. "And at once." He walked to the door and opened it for Harry. As his son passed him, William looked back at Octavia. She was white-faced, lost for words, a host of conflicting emotions crowding into her expression.

"Don't leave me, I beg you," he said.

It was done so quietly and with such pleading grace—barely a whisper—that she thought she might have misheard him, even when the door closed and his footsteps echoed along the flagstones of the hallway outside.

• • •

John Gould had been in his room all morning.
Breakfast had been taken up to him while he
wrote letters to his parents. He had told them
that he would be coming home, and that he
wanted the release of the funds that he had
invested, asking his father to see to it. He hinted,
though he gave no details, that he would not be
arriving alone, and inquired about the status of
the land at Long Island.

He had then sat for some time staring out
the bedroom window at the green lawns of
Rutherford, allowing himself the fantasy of a
home with Octavia, of perhaps their own children
running down the long slopes of some equivalent
paradise that would end in a beach, the ocean, a
jetty with a sailboat moored. He would have a
boat built especially, he decided. It would have
Octavia's name on its side.

And then, just after breakfast, he had heard
the commotion downstairs. He went out onto
the gallery and listened to Octavia's and Harry's
voices in the great hall below, catching the drift
that there was some crisis with the daughter
Louisa. He heard William's stride, his muttered
exclamations, and then the door to his library
opening and closing.

John had leaned on the gallery balustrade,
intrigued. He had never met Louisa; she had only
been described to him as the darling child favored

by her father. Of the two daughters, John had surmised that he might like Charlotte better; for all her youth she reputedly had the spark of rebellion that he felt himself. He had fantasized that he might win the older daughter round with all the thrills of New York, and the run of the great towering enterprise that was his father's retail empire, but the younger of the two, Charlotte, he hoped he might mentor—might teach or encourage to be different, to travel the wider world.

And in all this he had never given William Cavendish a thought, other than to pity him as a generation past. Harry, he guessed, would stick by his father eventually; he would stay in England and join the Royal Flying Corps; nothing was likely to deter him from that. Then, after the war . . . well, the mills were waiting. He would be another Cavendish, another Beckforth wielding power. He couldn't escape it; it was in his blood. It was the way the world went—this world, at least, where land and fortunes were preserved, nurtured, passed down. Harry Cavendish was part of a chain that could not be broken.

John had gone back to his room and was surprised, after he had dressed, to see the Napier brought to the front of the house and William and Harry getting into it with a single piece of luggage between them. He had rapidly stepped out of his room, gone down the gallery and watched from the east window as the car went out along the drive. William's valet was one of the staff watching the car go. There were others there—Bradfield, Nash, Harrison; they talked briefly to one another in a huddled group. John frowned, puzzled. William and Harry had only just got home; where would they go again so soon, and with luggage?

He made his way downstairs.

He found Octavia in the drawing room. She was standing in front of the large Parisian looking glass that hung over the fireplace; she didn't appear to hear him come in, and he walked stealthily over to her, putting his arms around her waist and kissing her cheek. She jumped as if an electric charge had gone through her, turned around and gave him a watery smile.

"What's the matter?" he asked.

"Louisa has eloped with someone," she said tonelessly. "She's gone to France."

He raised his eyebrows in amazement. "Do you know the man?"

"It . . . We think it may be Charles de Montfort."

He gasped, and then began to laugh. "William's son? How can that be?"

"We don't know," she replied, putting a hand to her head. "We aren't sure. About him. About anything."

"Is that where William's gone?" he asked. "I saw him and Harry get in the auto."

"Yes," she murmured. "They've gone to Paris."

He shook his head. "That'll be a tall order," he told her. "France mobilized thirty-six hours ago." She gazed at him uncomprehendingly. "They're going to war," he explained. "Didn't William tell you? It's in this morning's paper. Russia started massing its troops, Germany copied them; they demanded French neutrality; France thumbed their nose and mobilized. Yesterday morning, Germany declared war on Russia."

She was staring at him. "William knew," she murmured.

"He did if he reads his newspaper. But he'll have known last night, with his contacts."

"But what about here; what about this country?"

"Well, the *Times* says that Germany will declare war on Russia today. That's their guess. Russia's your ally; Russia and France both. Austria's got its head down like a warhorse—they want to obliterate Serbia. The Russians have got troops on the Austrian border. . . ."

"My God," Octavia said. "It's a bad dream."

"My father wrote me only yesterday saying there was talk of closing the stock exchange because of all hell breaking loose in Europe."

Octavia closed her eyes momentarily, then walked to the couch and sat down. "What will France be like now?"

"One terrible mess, I should think. I give it forty-eight hours before Germany declares war on

France too." He shrugged. "It's a line of dominoes. They fall together."

"And then . . ."

"If Germany's declared war on your allies, what choice does Britain have?"

Octavia put her hands to her mouth briefly. "He was right," John heard her whisper to herself. Then she lifted her head and asked him, "But in France, now . . . there'll still be transport, trains?"

"I should think there'll be a whole city trying to get out of Paris, going south. Panicking."

"They would leave their capital?"

"Wouldn't you?"

"I don't know," she murmured. "Louisa has gone to this man's mother there. Would they leave too? Go somewhere else?" She paused. "Bergerac?" she wondered softly. "Somewhere like that?"

"Maybe," he agreed. He sat down beside her and took her hand. She seemed to be very cold; he chafed her skin in an effort to warm it. "Don't worry," he said. "Try not to, at any rate."

She glanced at him as if seeing him for the first time. "Don't worry?" she echoed.

He smiled at her. "I've been making plans," he said. "Would you like to design your own house? We can arrange it. We can hire someone very good. Modern, if you like. A nice sprawling seaside house with a view of the ocean. Would you like that?"

"You're talking about America?"

"What else? Our future."

Abruptly, she stood up. "I can't think of that," she told him.

"Why not?"

"Why *not?*" she exclaimed. "Didn't you hear a word I said? Louisa is in danger. More danger than I even knew a half hour ago."

"Well, I guess this boy will protect her. And then her father will arrive, and that'll be that. Fur will fly. They'll be home." He spread his hands to express this fait accompli, smiling.

Octavia's mouth dropped open in shock. "That's all you have to say?"

He stood up now next to her and tried to grasp her hand again. "They'll be all right."

"But you just said—"

"William will get to her if anyone can. Of course he will. It's a foregone conclusion. He knows the right people; he can cut through any red tape. Diplomatic immunity, special passage. They'll be back in three or four days."

Octavia's eyes narrowed. "You're placating me."

"I'm trying to reassure you, darling."

"Don't you care?" she demanded. "It's my daughter, my husband, my son. We don't even have an address for Louisa in Paris, other than Charles's mother."

"Then they'll go straight there, won't they?" John replied. He smiled slowly at her. "And as for caring . . . if something concerns you, it concerns me. Your children too."

She broke away from him and took a couple of uncertain steps. "They're not *my* children," she said. "They are William's and my children."

John drew himself up warily. "Yes, I heard him say that," he responded. "I heard the threats."

"Well, I . . ." She began wringing her fingers. "I don't know that I can leave. I mean, if I have the authority to take them. He may be right. Does a woman have any say at all? Can I go?"

"Of course you can go," John said, astonished. "You have a right to do whatever you want, whenever you want. You could leave right now."

"No," she said. "I don't have a right to leave my children. I must be here for Louisa when she comes back."

"Well, of course for that. I meant figuratively. You are free."

She shook her head uncertainly. He walked up to her, took her hand, kissed it lingeringly. Then he wrapped his arms tightly around her and pressed his cheek to hers. She dropped her head onto his shoulder and he could feel her shaking. He began to stroke her hair. "It's our world," he murmured. "Can you feel that, our world? Just waiting out there. Louisa will come back, and you can distract her, take her out of herself. Let her see New York. Charlotte too. It's no disgrace what's happened to her, is it? She's let herself be swept away by some scoundrel, that's all. She's only young. In a year or two, no one will remember it."

"They'll remember it here," Octavia said. "In society. In London."

"All the more reason to go to New York," he told her. "It won't be a scandal there. No one will remark on it. No one will care. She'll be able to hold her head up. You'll want that, won't you? For her to be able to go out and meet people, find friends—new friends, new people who won't judge her? Let the girls come and I'll show them my city. I'll show them what room there is, love. Room to breathe." His voice was soft, beguiling, lilting. "It's a big country. It's wide, full of air. No boundaries, no traditions, no histories. It'll be our history instead. We'll write our own."

She lifted her head and looked at him.

"It will all come right," he said. He stroked the flat of his thumb across her face, following the cheekbones and then drawing down the length of her neck to the soft base of her throat, and farther downwards. She made a small movement, as if she would break away from him. "I promise you that," he said, holding on to her tightly. "I promise you and the girls everything you want, everything you need. And I keep my promises."

Chapter 9

*J*t was four in the morning two days later when William was woken by the noise outside the hotel in Rue Théodule-Ribot. For a second, he stared around himself, disoriented; he and Harry had been traveling for nearly forty hours when they had finally arrived in Paris. He got up and went to the window, and opened it onto a small balcony; standing there, he could hear the sound of vehicles along the Boulevard de Courcelles—a relentless, unaccustomed noise of blowing horns.

Stepping onto French soil had been akin to stepping from the warmth of summer to the cold of winter; mobilization notices had already been posted, and the trains had largely been taken out of service. William and Harry had stood on the French dockside with the three-hundred-foot length of the steamship behind them, and it had taken two hours to hire an automobile, and that at an extortionate price. In the early hours of August third they had driven down to Paris through villages where almost every shuttered shop was scrawled in chalk—*Called out for service in the army*—and where the women stared at them. It was only when they reached the outskirts of Paris that they realized what the stares

367

meant, for in front of Les Invalides were five hundred requisitioned cars, and everywhere they passed, anything wheeled that could be moved was piled with rifles and ammunition. They passed one drooping-headed horse, asleep on its feet, tethered to a market cart full of guns, and all around the city they stopped, they started, they stopped—pulled over all the way and were asked for their papers.

Eventually, William stopped the car and bought a flag from the roadside, an American flag. It was all they could find; God only knew why the newsagent kept that. Perhaps it was the only nationality he had left, but it gave them a kind of peculiar passage through the crowds. As he had fastened the Stars and Stripes to the windscreen, William had felt his heart give another lurch of protest—he thought of Gould's hands on Octavia's shoulders. They motored past the Gare d'Orsay, and a group of St. Cyr cadets stopped to salute them; beside him, Harry was slumped down in the seat, saying nothing, staring at the buildings and the sea of faces.

The streets by that time had been getting dark. In the summer twilight they saw more flags and yet more flags, until the streets became fringed with French, British and Russian insignia. The reservists passed in groups, going to their assigned stations, sometimes with a phalanx of supporters singing the "Marseillaise," and sometimes carrying the flowers that midinettes, the sewing girls of the couture houses, threw from upper windows, but more often with ashen-faced wives and perplexed children at their sides. At one corner, the car was forced to stop again for the crowds, and right alongside them a man clutching a waxed-paper parcel of food gently prized his wife's fingers from his own to kiss her good-bye. He turned and walked away, and the woman looked straight in at them and back at the flag on the glass; she gave a little salute, a kind of trembling shrug, and the baby in her arms had begun to cry.

At the reception desk of the hotel, the concierge had spread his hands when William had asked what rooms were available. "There are many rooms," he had explained. "People are leaving Paris. Have you not seen?"

William had apologized, agreed, and signed the register. He and Harry carried their own bags to a suite overlooking the street and had stood together looking at a Paris devoid of light. William had turned to his son. "It's inconceivable," he had murmured. "Paris in darkness."

"What shall we do?" Harry had asked. "Where do we start looking?"

"At Rue de l'Abreuvoir," William had decided. They had not even taken off their coats; now they turned together for the door. "It's her town house," William explained. "Or was, three years ago."

William had closed and locked the room door. Down the corridor, they could hear a man singing drunkenly in his room, while a woman's voice pleaded with him to stop. William had pocketed the key. "I've not had cause to go there recently," he said.

They had walked. There was no other way. Several times they were lost in the darkened alleys approaching Sacré-Coeur; they almost felt their way along the cobbled route. Above them, glimpsed every now and then on the top of the steep hill, the massive newly finished Basilica glowed grey in the moonlight. They at last found the little restaurant that marked the corner of the right street, and they turned off Rue des Saules. Harry, despite the sultriness of the night, was shivering. He was hoping that Charles would be with his mother, and that Louisa would be with them both. He couldn't decide which to do first: punch Charles in the face, or wrench his sister away. He felt sick every time he thought that she might actually have been married, and in ignorance. He kept thinking of her, with her brightly lit and trusting face, walking into Helene de Montfort's house and being told the truth of the matter. Whatever that was, of course. That Charles was not her half brother, and had married her to spite her father nevertheless, and had no love at all for her? Or that he was indeed her relation, and had no intention of being either lover or husband? Harry tried not to consider the third alternative: that perhaps de Montfort really loved Louisa, and could legally marry her, or already had. And that they were happy, and that Louisa, in a city at war, would never come home again.

He voiced this last fear as they felt their way along the high-walled gardens of Rue de l'Abreuvoir. "If they've married," he began, "if that's possible—if they've done it, and if they're staying . . ."

William stopped and turned back to him. "Then we will have to go home and tell your mother," he said. "And God help us in that."

"Louisa's children would be French," Harry mused out loud. "Their grandmother would be Helene."

"If Germany won the war, then Louisa's children would be German," William pointed out. "Living in a German state. As well might we all."

"It won't come to that."

"No," William said, drawing a long breath. "No, that is a most ridiculous notion."

At last they came to a halt at a gate with two large stone pillars. On one of them was the number 15. "It's here," William said. There was a bell in the wall; he pulled it. They could hear nothing. In the darkness, William glanced farther up the road. "Helene always wanted to live in this street," he mused. "A painter called Renoir lived five houses away."

371

"Renoir?" Harry echoed. "She knew him?"

"In the 1880s," William replied. "She knew them all. It was a different place then. So many artists and poets. I recall that little restaurant back there . . ." Then he stopped, caught by the memory. "Never mind." He pulled the bell again.

"Perhaps it's disconnected," Harry suggested.

They tried the gate, and it fell open; warily, they made their way between high shrubs to the front door of an imposing mansion. When William knocked on the door, the sound could be heard echoing through the house, and eventually there was a pattering of footsteps. A diminutive maid opened the door.

"May we see Madame de Montfort?" William asked.

"There is no one here of that name."

"Oh, for God's sake," Harry muttered. "Open the door."

"What is it, Francine?" called an elderly man from along the hall. He edged forward and eyed the two Englishmen suspiciously.

"We are looking for Madame de Montfort and her son," William explained.

The man made a typically Gallic noise of dismissal. "She has not lived here for some time."

"But she owned this house."

The man laughed. "Owned?" he echoed. "She took the upper rooms. She owned nothing."

William looked shocked. "And her son?"

"Wherever they go, they go together."

William and Harry glanced at each other. "Do you know where she is now?" Harry asked.

"Past the church somewhere," the old man replied vaguely, waving his hand. "On Rue de Foyatier, so I'm told."

"Which number?"

"How should I know?" The maid began to close the door. Behind it, they heard the old man hiss, "Foreigners."

William tried to put his shoulder to the panel, but the door was locked tight in his face. "We are your allies," he called loudly. "If we are foreigners, then we are foreigners who will fight for France." There was no reply. They heard the retreating footsteps of both the maid and her employer, and another door closing within the house. Briefly, William rested his forehead on the door. "And will die for her in our thousands," he muttered to himself. Then, abruptly, he seemed to remember that Harry was at his side, and he straightened up, catching his son's arm. "Rue de Foyatier," he instructed.

They climbed the hill; it was by then past midnight. In the barred shadows cast by the moonlight they looked down the long, long drop of steps and the dark houses alongside.

Two gendarmes materialized from the shadows of the street. "Papers," said the nearest man.

William took out their passports. "I am with the British Embassy," he said.

They peered at him and Harry. "Permits, if you please."

"I have none," William confessed. He gave his name and explained that Harry was his son.

"What is your business at this hour?"

"I have come from England to find my daughter. She is missing."

There was much sucking of breath and shaking of heads. "M'sieur, the streets must be clear by eight at night. You understand? You must go back to your hotel."

They saw that further protest was useless. Turning away, Harry said, "No one in their right minds will open up to us now anyway, and we don't know which number."

William conceded defeat. "We'll try again in the morning."

The fourth of August dawned cool and showery, with a brisk wind blowing in the street.

William and Harry breakfasted quickly in an almost empty restaurant; on one of the pavement seats a raddled, florid-faced woman cuddled her dog and blew it kisses. When they got up to leave, she blew them a kiss too. "English?" she asked. "I very much love English boys," she called after them. "For many years." And she laughed.

At the tobacconist's where William stopped to

buy cigars, the man serving them was wringing his hands with anxiety. Many of his shelves were empty. "I have to go and register," he told them. "I was born in Trieste, but I was brought here as a child. They can't make me go back there."

"Do they have that power?" Harry asked.

The man almost squealed in despair. "They have power!" he exclaimed. "We have to go home. That's what they call it. But I'm Parisian, you understand? I don't know Trieste, you see? I know no one there—it is absurd!"

They left him voicing his same complaints to the next customer. People were crowding the street, some with pinched and worried faces, others with expressions of superior fortitude. They heard more than one murmured conversation recalling the last Prussian invasion of Paris. "I shall raise another barricade," an old man cried to a circle of younger friends on the pavement. They closed around him, and a middle-aged soldier, wearing a greatcoat hung with medals, curled a placatory arm around his shoulders, but the teenagers in the group glanced at William and Harry with fearful, confused faces.

William frowned. "We must call on the embassy. We must ensure our permits," he told Harry.

"Now?"

"Not now. Helene now."

They trudged back the way they had gone the night before, the mere four hours of sleeping telling on their pace. At Rue de Foyatier, they knocked on half a dozen doors before anyone had heard of Helene. They were pointed down the hill, where the large houses became smaller, and to a green door behind a dilapidated railing.

It seemed an age before the door opened to their repeated knocks. But eventually Helene herself stood before them, a shawl clutched to her, her eyes red rimmed. Her mouth dropped open in shock when she saw who it was. "William!" she said. "What are you doing here?" She edged past them and looked along the street as if she had been expecting someone else, and was fearful of that person now appearing. Then she plucked the shawl closer around herself and raised her chin in the old head-tilted way with her smiling, mocking expression, as if she were the center of attention at some garden party, and not standing with uncombed hair and slippered feet at the street door.

William was not in the mood for conversation. "Where is Louisa?" he demanded.

"Louisa?" she said. "How should I know?"

"She's in Paris," Harry interrupted furiously.

"She is?" Helene looked from one to the other. "Why?"

"Let us inside." William barged past her into a gloomy hall. He walked forward, opening doors into rooms empty of furniture. At the end of the corridor, just before the steps to the kitchen, he turned to face her. "What is this?"

She shrugged. "It is my refuge."

"From what?"

She looked away from him. "It is temporary."

"I see," he said. "You have been let down."

"You might say so." She gave a tremulous smile. "And if you don't mind, William, I should prefer that you leave. I am expecting someone." William nodded. He looked her up and down, raising an eyebrow; she blushed a deep color and turned away. "Well," she said. "You have a little victory. I am as you see me, alone."

"I wish no kind of victory," William told her. "I only want my daughter. Where is Charles?"

She turned back to him. "You've come through Paris, I suppose. Can't you guess?"

"Has he been called up?" Harry asked, suddenly realizing what she meant.

"All reservists are called up."

"But he was working in London."

She frowned in puzzlement. "Yes, that is what I mean," she said. "He came back because he is a reservist. He came back two days ago and stayed here, and he left this morning."

"This morning? To go where?"

She looked from one to the other again. "I don't see why it is your business. Why in heaven's name do you care where Charles is suddenly?" She stared at William pointedly. "You've never cared where he is until now, have you?"

Harry stepped forward, eyes bright with anger.

"Your son took my sister away. He met her in London and he proposed to her."

Helene caught her breath, and then began to laugh. "Why, that's absurd," she said. "Louisa was not here. He didn't bring her. He didn't mention her." Her eyes narrowed. "It's a lie, a joke."

"There is no joke," William said. "Louisa left a letter saying that she was coming to Paris with him. That they were to be married."

All three stood silently; at last Helene walked away, through a small door to the back of the house. Here, in what should have been the servants' kitchen, she sat down at a small table where a pitiful breakfast had been laid—bread and coffee and a small bowl of figs. There were two plates, two cups. She waved her hand over them. "He got up at four this morning," she murmured sadly. "We sat here. He had his orders. He had to go." She showed them a piece of paper on which she had written the name of his regiment and the time of the train, holding the sheet tenderly and then, with an unhappy moue of disgust, throwing it across the table towards them. William picked it up.

"There was no mention of Louisa." Helene said the name with heavy sarcastic emphasis. She looked up at them both. "Perhaps she has made up a story," she opined, shrugging. "She's gone away with someone. But not Charles."

"It's not a story," Harry burst out.

She raised a sardonic eyebrow. "How does she know him?"

"They were together in London."

"Oh, yes? You saw them together?" She glanced at William. "Either of you?"

"No," William said. "But it's his description. And he called himself Maurice Frederick." She frowned, but did not reply.

He put the piece of paper with the train time and the regiment name in his coat pocket. Then, after a moment's hesitation, he drew out the other chair and sat down opposite her. "Helene," he said quietly, "in all these years, you have never given me the answer to this question. But you must give me the answer now. Much depends on it. Is Charles my son?"

She looked at him steadily. "I do not know."

He shook his head. "I think that you do. I think that you have allowed me to be in ignorance. Perhaps it has been amusing for you. Perhaps you amuse yourself this way with others. But I must know."

She remained silent, mouth set in a determined line.

"Good God," Harry muttered, and he turned away and walked to the window, looking out onto a yard filled with decaying, sun-starved trees.

"Helene," William prompted, "Louisa has no idea whom she is with. She believes she may marry this man. She is in love with him. Have pity on her."

A kind of glittering fury came into Helene's face. "Pity?" she echoed. "For your child?"

"She is only eighteen."

Helene barked out a cynical laugh. "Darling," she replied, "when did you show *me* any pity?" She waved her hand as if to brush away his questioning, confused expression. "I know your opinion of me, in truth," she continued in a harsh voice. "Oh, you have extended hospitality, I suppose. You have allowed me into your home, though an invitation was not exactly forthcoming. And, although you found me certainly diverting when we met, when we discovered we were of the same blood so long ago—yes, then you found me good enough company, is that not so? The outrageous woman in Paris. Where men of your kind came to have women who would do what Englishwomen would not do. Oh, yes, *then* I was your darling, William. And you cannot deny it."

"I do not deny it," William said in a low voice.

"Nor should you," she exclaimed. She took a moment, and tilted her chin again. "But then, I was not good enough to marry," she added bitterly.

"You never wished to marry!"

She leaned forward, arms on the table. "And would you have married me, William?" He said nothing, but dropped his gaze from her face. She smiled coldly. "No, you would not. You married that whispering besotted child, that girl with a fortune instead."

Silence fell. Harry, hearing his mother described this way, turned slowly back to face Helene. Ignoring his baleful glare, she continued looking at William. "You deserved to be punished," she said finally. "For treating me with such carelessness."

At this, William, despite himself, crashed his fist on the table, making her flinch. "With carelessness?" he exclaimed. "I have supported you. You have done all but blackmail me. You have implied that Charles is mine. Tell me the truth."

A small triumphant smile came to her face. "And now you have lost your daughter," she said. "How apt. I have lost my son to a war. I may not see him again. And you have lost your child to disgrace."

Their eyes locked, and at last William saw the truth in her. "He was never mine," he said.

"No," she admitted. "Never yours."

"And all these years . . ."

"You would not marry me."

"You never wanted to be married!"

"Did you ask me?" she demanded. "Did you?"

He stared at her in complete bafflement. "You always told me . . ." he began. "Other men . . ."

"You did not ask. You married *her*."

Suddenly, shocking them both, Harry began to laugh. They looked up at him. "It was some other man's son," he said. "But none of them would marry you. So you got your revenge on some

381

poor devil in Bergerac by driving him to his death, and you got your revenge on my father by stringing him along for money."

Helene had sprung to her feet. "You don't know!" she said. "So do not insult me!"

Harry smiled coldly. "It is not possible to insult a woman like you," he said.

Helene gasped, and then, after a few seconds, her expression completely crumbled. She slumped back again into her chair. "My son is all I have ever had," she said, and tears came to her eyes. "He is the one constant of my life. And now he has gone."

They watched her weep.

"Helene," said William softly after a moment or two. "Did you tell Charles that I was his father?"

She had pulled a handkerchief from the depths of the dressing gown, and wiped her face. "No," she murmured. "I told him the truth. He has known for some time. His father died when he was young."

Harry looked at William with sudden deep sympathy; instinctively, he put his hand on his father's shoulder; then, in a moment of mutual embarrassment, he dropped it again.

"He was an artist. He died of tuberculosis," Helene whispered. "He was my love in a way that you were not, and never could be. I met him a month after you had left Paris in 1892; we were together all summer. He died in December, and

Charles was born two months premature soon after. So premature that you were able to believe the possibility that Charles might be yours."

"And allowed me to believe."

"Yes."

Harry had been shaking his head in disbelief and disgust. "For money," he said. "For revenge."

She made no reply; she leaned her head on one hand and looked past them to the pale morning light from the window. "You have no idea what it is to be alone, and to be a woman making her way alone, and you have no right to condemn me," she said. She drew herself up a little in her chair. "Revenge is a very tawdry emotion. I have merely been pragmatic. I have done what had to be done to survive."

"And Charles?" William asked. "You sent him to me, to Octavia, to cause trouble between us."

"I did not," she said quickly. "He has told me what he did, but I did not approve of it. He has no claim on you."

"He wanted an inheritance."

"I told him he was not entitled to it."

"And yet he tried."

"Yes . . . he tried."

Harry let out a breath of exasperation. "He learned it from you," he said. "Deception. Envy."

"Envy of a family?" she said quietly. "Of being an accepted son? Yes, perhaps. Perhaps he had always wanted that."

"And came to me to find it, when he could find it nowhere else?" William asked.

She shrugged listlessly. "To be part of that . . . to have what he had never had, what he thinks was denied me? It is possible. These things go deep." It was said with tragic self-pity.

William leaned across the table and touched Helene's arm. "Helene," he said, "he made Louisa believe he would marry her. But while knowing that she was not related to him?"

"He knew. But he said nothing about her to me."

"He did not say he had proposed to her?"

"It's preposterous. He would not do such a thing."

"He has done it!"

"I don't believe it. He is incapable of it."

William got up and turned on his heel, looking about the small room as if he were trying to find something to hit in frustration. He calmed himself, and turned back to her. "He has done it," he repeated. "She's in Paris somewhere with him."

"No," Helene insisted.

"How can you be so sure?" Harry demanded.

"Because . . ." She folded her hands very carefully together in her lap. "He does not like women . . . in that way."

The two men stared at each other.

"Helene," William said, "we have every reason to think that he has done this. Please tell us where he is." She glanced up at him, and a ghost of the old coquettishness came to her face. Looking down at her, William had every confidence that her present crisis would pass. There would be some other patron; Helene could not be extinguished, not even by war. She would rise again, and at some point in the future, traveling in Paris or London—if either city could survive—he would see her again, dressed in high fashion, on some other man's arm, as if war and deprivation and disappointment could never touch her.

"He was called to Gare de l'Est," she murmured. "At seven o'clock. But you will not find him. The trains were for eight. He will have gone."

Defeated, they turned to go. Harry did not look back and was at the street door in an instant, but William turned again halfway along the corridor. He looked back at the woman he had known for so long. "Helene," he said, "have you seen Louisa at all? Do you know if she was with him, in truth?"

"She was not with him," Helene replied. "He would have told me. I know my son."

"None of us truly know our children," William replied.

Her answering gaze was as cold as the grave. "You are wrong," she said. "Charles may occasionally act in a way I have not foreseen. But in the end, my son's heart and soul belong to me."

They left her, shutting the door firmly behind them.

• • •

In Rutherford, the morning was deathly still. Belowstairs, the servants were gathered at breakfast with all the solemnity of a funeral.

"It'll break up the house," Harrison was saying.

"It will not," Mrs. Carlisle replied testily. "His lordship lived here before by himself. He can do it again. But it's not going to come to that. This is something and nothing, this American."

"There'll be no breakup," Nash agreed. "Her ladyship won't leave. Not this place. Not here."

"She's sitting in his lordship's library, by the telephone," Mary said. "She came down just after I swept the room."

"It's because of Miss Louisa."

"What is it she's done?" Mary ventured.

"Never mind," Nash told her.

Harrison laughed to himself, and was rewarded with a scathing look by the cook. "If Mr. Bradfield hears any of you, there'll be merry hell to pay. So eat, and don't speak," she told them.

Harrison flung down his knife. "I'm tired of being told to keep quiet," he said. "Sitting here like scared cats. Can't say this, can't do that. I'm going to the Border Regiment when war's declared. I'm going to my brother in Carlisle and we'll join together."

"Is it really war?" Cynthia asked, trembling. "Where's it come from? Why are we fighting?"

"We're not fighting yet," Mary reassured her.

"But we will," Harrison said. "And do you know what? It'll be a jaunt in France. Give me that any day. We'll chase 'em off by Christmas, and I want some of it. Better than pressing tailcoats and carrying plates."

The door opened. Bradfield stood on the threshold; he was holding a newspaper in his hand. He walked around the side of the table and sat down heavily at its head in the Windsor chair reserved for him. "You'd desert us?" he asked Harrison. "That is a comfort to us all, I'm sure."

Harrison smiled. "I'll be a war hero, Mr. Bradfield. I'll plug a hole in the Kaiser for you."

Mrs. Carlisle gave him a withering look, and leaned forward to point at the newspaper. "What does it say, Mr. Bradfield?"

He spread it out flat on the tabletop. "The Belgians have refused the Germans free passage. The editorial claims that Germany will invade the Low Countries this morning. If they do that . . ." He paused and read from the newspaper. " 'It is the duty of every British subject to defend the sovereign rights of Belgium and our allies.' "

"I told you. It's war," Harrison said. "It's war out there, and it's war in here." He paused. "Wonder if Mr. Gould will want a valet when they set up house together? I fancy America after the war's over."

"Wash out your mouth!" Mrs. Carlisle exclaimed. "Ungodly talk!"

387

"Now you're sounding like Mrs. Jocelyn." And Harrison began to laugh.

Bradfield struck the table with his fist, and the staff turned as one to stare at him; he was a man never known to show aggression of any kind. Cynthia began to whimper; under the table Mary pinched her leg. "Hush," she whispered.

"Mrs. Jocelyn is unwell," Bradfield intoned, his voice booming. "Respect will be shown." He looked at Harrison. "Do you hear me?"

"I'm not disrespectful, sir," Harrison countered. But there was a look of challenge in his eye. Bradfield was looking down a table where every face was unsettled; the old man shifted uncomfortably in his seat.

"Nash is right. Her ladyship won't leave," Mrs. Carlisle said firmly. "And I won't hear anything to the contrary in my kitchen."

"Why not?" Harrison asked. His voice was even, reasonable; he felt Bradfield's thunderous look on him, but continued all the same. "A handsome man with a fortune. What woman wouldn't want him? And there's more reason than just Mr. Gould. She'll take the children to America because America isn't at war, and isn't likely to be. She'd be protecting them, that's what. Wouldn't you, wouldn't any mother, given half a chance?" A murmur, a sense of uncertainty, rippled round the table. "Read out the rest of it, Mr. Bradfield sir, if you please. For the ladies."

Harrison crossed his arms and leaned back in his chair. "Read out the part that says America will declare neutrality as soon as we declare war."

Silence fell on the room. They finished their meal, eyes down, not meeting one another's glances.

When it was over, Nash got up and went out into the corridor and walked towards the outer door. When he got to the yard he stood taking in great gulps of the morning air, looking up at the vast roof of Rutherford: at its pretty lines of Tudor chimneys that reminded him of barley sugar-canes, at the dappled color of the brick, at the line upon line of windows all catching the morning light. He felt a tug on his sleeve.

He looked down at Mary beside him. "Will you fight?" she asked. "Will you go, like Harrison?"

"I'll do my duty."

"And what is that?" she asked. "Dying for them? Dying for this?"

"Yes," he said. "If need be. For them. And for this."

Octavia had been sitting in William's library for more than two hours. It was very unlikely that the telephone would ring if William and Harry were in France, but all the same the faint possibility kept her within sight of the receiver on his desk. Last night she had spoken again to the de Rays, and heard only that William had sent a note from

Folkestone that they were about to catch the ferry to cross the Channel. Since then, there had been nothing at all, except the rumors that France was in an uproar.

John had gone out first thing that morning to Castle Howard; he could not, he told her, miss the opportunity to see Vanbrugh's great house. She had at first begged him not to go—it was not open to the public, and she did not want him to be invited in and reveal that he had been staying all summer at Rutherford. There would be comment already locally about his prolonged visit, she knew, but it was unwise to fan the flames farther afield. She dreaded their relationship becoming common knowledge before it was settled, and until they were ready to go, and she thought that John might show his feelings in his face if he were engaged in conversation. He was alight in every fiber of his being—anyone could see that—and desperate to take her away. But for her part, she felt rather like a child who was swept along on some dreadful and thrilling dare, and whose fingers clung to the nearest support, betraying her misgivings.

"I shall stay today if you would rather," he had offered earlier.

"No . . . go. It would be pointless for us both to wait by the telephone."

"You'll be all right?"

"Yes, of course."

He had gone, swearing that he would not breathe a word of who he was. "I'll walk in Ray Wood, at least; I hear it's a fine plantation. And then spend the afternoon in York," he had told her. "I've not seen it yet. I want to be able to say that I have when we're back in the States."

In truth, now she was glad that she was alone; she could not have borne to see John's impatience waiting for news of Louisa. John always wanted things settled at once—he was used to simply having his way, and making sudden decisions; in that, he was so different from William's steady, obdurate pace. But patience—yes, exactly that— William's steadiness and patience were what was needed now. Patience to find Louisa. Patience and steadiness to bring her back.

She sat staring out into the orangerie and, past that, onto the terrace. She felt curiously empty and dislocated from reality. In the music room, far down the great hall, she could hear Charlotte practicing on the piano. She strained to listen; Charlotte had every ounce of William's calm— nothing stirred her resolve. Everyone always took to Louisa—of course they did; she was so pretty, so bright. But perhaps it was Charlotte who, in the future, would prove to be the real treasure. And at the thought of Louisa, Octavia's stomach rolled. She felt momentarily sick; she knew that she ought to have taken breakfast that morning, or at least tried to eat something. But she could not eat, and she had barely slept. Louisa must come back. *She must come back.* That was all that was in her mind, the only thought that she could keep in her consciousness for more than a few seconds at a time.

She glanced again at the windows of the orangerie. The weather had taken a turn for the worse; a strong wind was blowing and the sky threatened rain; far down the lawns on this north side she could see white ripples on the lake. She leaned her chin on her hand. They had once had a small boat, she and William, that they took out there on the glassy water. They had once had a party when lanterns were sent out in little paper yachts onto the lake. It had been a great success, like so many picnics and parties here. And they had once . . . but she abruptly closed her eyes. It was no use thinking of what had once been. It was all over. She had been living in a locked cage for so long that she had failed to see the bars that enclosed her. Now the door was flung open. She had only to step outside.

She stood up and began to pace the room, trailing her hand along the spines of the books. The ones that William kept in here were more personal, not the great gilt-bound volumes of the next room. He kept his accounts here in little leather notebooks, just as his father and grandfather had done. She opened one now, seeing his modesty and care in every line: repairs to the house, bills for dinners while he was traveling, reminders about meetings.

She noticed that, tucked in the back, was a well-worn piece of paper, sepia at the edges with age. Carefully, she opened it, and found that it was a receipt for a brass-bound collar that he had had made for a mastiff, a great fawn-colored dog that had been his constant companion when he and Octavia had first been married. He had adored that dog, she thought, but it had quietly lain down and died one morning while William had been walking the estate. Missing it, William had retraced his steps and found his faithful hound stretched out beneath one of the beech trees. He had even tried to carry it back to the house, until Armitage had seen him, and taken the burden from him. Octavia shook her head sadly now at the memory. And here was the receipt, kept safe. On the outside, a much younger William had written, *Collar for Bridgetown.* All the dogs at that time had been named for part of the Beckforths' Caribbean estates. Sighing softly, she closed the notebook and replaced it, and looked at his desk.

There was the large silver inkwell and stand that had been given to him by his colleagues when he retired from Parliament. There was the daguerreotype of his parents. On the desk blotter, his writing papers were neatly arranged. She touched each one of them warily, and then picked up the fountain pen. He had sat here before she came; he would sit here after she had gone, trying to make sense of it, no doubt. Trying in vain to arrange his life as tidily as the inkwell and the blotter and the lamp and the daguerreotype. She thought of his hands on the long polished mahogany surface; the desk had been made from wood brought back from India four generations ago. Everything in this room—like all the other rooms—had a story, a history. And no doubt in the years to come, her name would be expunged from Rutherford's life. She would be the black shadow in the family, the empty space. No one would mention her name; the Singer Sargent portrait would be taken down from the stairs.

Biting her lip, Octavia sat down in William's chair and opened the drawer of the desk. She was, perhaps, looking for something of him, or about him, to take with her, but she was surprised instead to see a large green leather ledger. Frowning slightly, she took it out and opened it.

To her amazement, it was a record of all the family portraits that had been taken since William and Octavia had been married. All these same images—larger ones—were framed and kept on the piano and on the occasional tables through-out the house, but she had not realized that William kept his own copies here. On the very first page was Rutherford itself, looking rather more prim and manicured than she could ever recall. On the second page was their wedding portrait, taken in 1893. She put her finger to the page. That dress had been stifling: so much lace, so much satin. And here, on the next page, were some little cartes de visite: photographs of William that had been made when a photographic visiting card was all the rage. He must, she thought, have been too embarrassed to use them; she had never seen them before. On the succeeding pages was the record of their married life together, among the photographic portraits, Harry as a small boy with his arms around the neck of his pony, and a formal pose of Octavia herself with all three children. The date was 1909—Harry was trying very hard to look grown-up by the side of Louisa, who was suppressing a naughty smile; Charlotte was wide-eyed and serious. And then here, on one of the last pages, was Louisa again, in the garden, surrounded by roses.

She turned back the pages to the beginning. And then she noticed the small envelope tucked behind one of the prints. She took it out; it was a flimsy, opaque piece of folded tissue paper. She opened it carefully and revealed a pressed flower and a scrap of lace. She stared at them in astonishment for some seconds; the flower had once been a lily of the valley, and even from the scrap of lace one could tell that it was finest Brussels. It had a familiar pattern of entwined vine leaves. Slowly, Octavia looked back again at their wedding photograph. In the image, she sat below William and his hand was on her shoulder. She carried a small bouquet of lilies of the valley, and around them both swirled the train of antique Brussels lace decorated in a pattern of vines.

Octavia took a deep, shuddering breath. She never knew that he had kept them. She never knew in all these years that the day had really mattered to him at all. He had never spoken of it, never reminded her of it, even as an affectionate aside. She thought that the marriage had been something merely contractual to him: the settlement of his financial future, the choosing of an eligible, malleable bride. But she had been wrong. At some point William had taken a flower from the bouquet, and pressed it, and kept it to cherish. He had wrapped it in tissue paper and preserved it, as one would preserve a precious memory.

And it was here, all here, she realized. Here within the pages of the green leather book. All that she and William had achieved, and all that they had created.

And all that they were about to lose.

With her hand still on Louisa's image, she put her head on the desk and wept.

It was almost eleven o'clock by the time William and Harry managed to make their way to the Gare de l'Est. There were no cabs to be had, no omnibuses; someone along the way had told them that even the bicycles in the Peugeot showroom in the Avenue de la Grande Armée had been requisitioned, all three hundred of them. On street corners they heard other rumors: that forty thousand Americans were stranded in Europe that week, and the same number of British, that the ports were scenes of mayhem, and that already overloaded ferries were being overrun by hysterical crowds. "Running like rats," they had heard one drunken man say. "You have a *permis de séjour*?" he had asked threateningly, eyeing William's figure and clothes—his unmistakable aristocratic bearing—from head to toe. "You live here? Here in Paris, eh?" They had moved on quickly. "You're a spy, maybe!" they had heard the man call.

"Don't answer," William had murmured to Harry. "Don't look back."

They arrived at the Gare de L'Est at eleven. The place was seething with people, men and their families crowding into the station under the wrought-iron balustrades and vast semicircular window of the entrance lobby. A large Avis sign within the station concourse announced the closure of the French-German border. Here and there children were caught up in the throng, stamped on, pushed, herded towards the platforms, where, no sooner had they arrived, than they were forcibly separated from their fathers.

Flowers were pressed into hands, arms thrown around shoulders, babies held up to be kissed. Here and there elderly parents looked on. Women turned away, some weeping, some gazing disoriented into the middle distance.

"Which company is this?" William asked, catching hold of a porter. "Which regiment?" He held up the paper that Helene had given him, and the man scrutinized it.

"M'sieur, they have left long ago," he said, throwing up his hands as if to show William's hopeless ignorance.

"To where?" William insisted, running alongside him for a few paces. "Do you know where?"

The man grimaced, rolling his eyes. "To war!" he shouted above the voices of the crowd. "To war!"

William dropped back. He and Harry stood while the tide of humanity flowed around them. In a few minutes, the train whistle sounded and a hundred doors slammed; the wail of distress mounted as the carriages began to move. The train gathered speed, and the faces of the men looking out the windows rapidly disappeared. When at last the train was gone, an awful silence descended on the platform. No one moved for some time, and then began shuffling back the way that they had come, back under the huge railway clock, back out past the railings and into the drizzling rain that had begun to fall.

"Perhaps she's here," Harry suggested. "Perhaps she stayed here after he left."

They walked the length of the station, looking in every kiosk, on every bench, and in every café. But there was no Louisa.

"It's hopeless," William said. "She might be anywhere at all."

They stood at the front of the station, gazing out at the 10th arrondissement and down the street towards the Jardin Villemin. "This has always been the station for war," William murmured. "In the 1870s they built a hospital over there for injured troops. That was the last Prussian war. It seems we go in circles; we tread the same steps. We make the same mistakes."

They walked out aimlessly towards the gardens. The rain gradually seeped through their overcoats. It was hard to believe that only a few days ago they had been in England; William could not help thinking of his walk by Richmond Castle. He had not known about Louisa then. He had not known about Octavia and Gould. As they went through the old military gates of the gardens, his steps began to slow, until he finally stopped dead, staring at the ground. "I have failed my family," he said.

Harry looked at him, astounded. "No, sir," he replied. "That is not true."

William looked up at him bemusedly. "It *is* true," he said quietly. "I have not paid attention. I did not pay attention to your wishes. I did not pay attention to my wife. There you have it. Whatever is happening, I am the architect of it. I have constructed it. I have let you down."

"It's the reverse, if anything," Harry told him. "If you want to censure anybody, you might as well censure me."

William waved his hand dismissively. "You've only wanted to break from tradition. Every young man thinks the same. You are no different."

"I am different," Harry answered. "I broke my word to you."

"Broke your word? When?"

"At Christmas," Harry said. His face was pale. He stumbled over his words. "You asked me a question. You asked me for the truth, and I lied to you."

"What question?" William asked. "What lie?"

Harry was trying to hold himself straight, to keep command of himself, but the effort of it made him shake. "I gave you my word that I didn't know the girl who died," he stammered at last. "The maid who was taken from the river. Emily." His voice broke; he bit his lip, took a breath. "But I did know her. It was my fault. I abandoned her. The child was mine."

Father and son stood face-to-face for a while, each trying to see the truth, the reaction, in the other's face. And then, despite his efforts, Harry began to cry. William made no move towards him.

"The fellows at Oxford . . ." Harry began in utter misery. "They said . . ." He stopped. "But it wasn't their concern. I ought not to have listened to them. I cut her off. I told her that she was a wonderful girl, and then I wished her well, or some such brutal thing, and I left her. That night, at Christmas. The same night that she walked to the river. She never told me about the child, but then, I never gave her a chance." He looked away from his father, too ashamed to meet William's gaze. "And I made a nice bloody show of the whole thing by lying to you and Mother. And I went down to London and drank it away." He paused, shaking his head. "But it doesn't go away. I might as well have murdered her. That's what a fine son you have. I try to tell myself that it didn't happen. I forget about it sometimes for days at a time. But it did happen. And the reason it happened was me. My own selfish bloody callousness." He managed, finally, to look back at William. "And that is the person you have for your son, sir. And I'm very sorry for it."

Harry began to walk on, shoulders hunched. After a few seconds watching him, William started out after him. All around them, the soft greens of the gardens stretched away; William had a surreal sense that the world, so close to crumbling, and in such throes of despair all around them, actually meant nothing at all. All that mattered was his son. "Harry!" he called. "Harry!"

Harry's steps faltered; he looked briefly over his shoulder. William caught up with him. "You mean to say that you've carried this secret all this time?" he asked. "Alone?"

"It was hardly something to speak of."

"But, Harry . . ." William faltered. "Did you never think of confiding in me?"

"In you?" Harry echoed. And the meaning of it was clear: Harry had never thought that he could confide in his own father. He had expected punishment, rebuke, loathing. Nothing else.

William's heart gave a few staggering beats. He put his hand to his chest, and then held out his arms and wrapped Harry in his embrace. "I am sorry," he said in a whisper. "I am sorry for your loneliness. I am sorry for the poor girl. But more than those things, I am sorry that you could not come to me."

The rain fell heavier as they made their way an hour later to the embassy, anxious to obtain the permits that would allow them greater freedom of travel. William was still carrying the passports and his letter of introduction from the Prime Minister that was always with him, so it was with horror that they saw the vast queue stretching all the way down the street. "This will take all day," Harry said.

"I don't think so," William told him. They walked onwards, past the lines of people, some obscured by umbrellas. In places the line was three or four deep, groups who knew one another. They heard the same conversations over and over again as they walked; sterling was not acceptable; no foreign currency was acceptable. Without money, tickets could not be bought or accommodation paid for. There was an atmosphere of barely concealed panic; homelessness, rootlessness and loss of identity showed in the faces that were turned towards them.

At the door of the embassy, William gave his name. They waited while an official disappeared into the depths of the building. "Who are you?" the first man in the queue asked William. He was ruddy faced, bowler hatted, and sweating inside his suit. "We've been here since eight o'clock, old man." He stepped forward, as if he were ready to push Harry out of his way.

"Hold on," Harry warned. "My father's known to the ambassador."

"I don't care if he's known to the King himself," the man retorted. "We all want to go home. It doesn't make you better than the rest of us."

The door miraculously opened just as the curious crowd surged forward behind their interrogator. William and Harry were admitted into the gilded gloom of the hall. The same official who had let them in paused. "Lord Cavendish?" he said. "Of Rutherford Park?"

"Yes."

"Of Rutherford in Yorkshire. I'm not mistaken, sir?"

"You are correct."

The man nodded, smiling. "The ambassador sends his greetings; he asks to be excused at the moment."

"I understand."

"Rather busy, you know." He gestured back towards the entrance, as if the declaration of war in the last few days had been a minor disturbance to the eternal implacability of diplomatic life. "But we've been expecting you, naturally. I must say, your response has been remarkably rapid, sir. You were here in Paris already, I assume? And now you're seeking onward travel, of course."

"Not yet. I need a permit. We intend to stay in the city, at least for the time being." William stopped, suddenly realizing what had been said. "Expecting us?" he echoed. "Response? I don't understand you. I am here to find my daughter. My son and I have come to look for her. It may take some time. We are trying to find her address in Paris."

"But . . ." The man stopped. "There is some confusion," he said. "Your name, of course, at the door. I thought that you had answered our message."

"What message?" asked Harry.

"Our telephone message to the embassy in London this morning."

They stared at him; he smiled in return. "But I see that is not so. Please follow me."

They walked behind him, glancing in puzzlement at each other. Halfway along the first corridor, the man opened a small door. "It is the most private room we could find," he said. "We thought it more appropriate, in the circumstances."

William and Harry stepped inside. The sitting room was sumptuously furnished; heavy drapes shielded it from the street. By the window on a low couch, with an untouched tray of coffee before them, sat two women; one, in a spotless grey dress of unmistakable Parisian lines, was holding the younger woman's hand alongside her.

This woman, young as she was, looked as if the weight of the world had fallen on her. Her hair was pulled back from her face severely; she wore a crumpled coat over a traveling dress, beneath which her once-pretty pale shoes were stained with dirt and dust. Louisa had been crying, perhaps for days, and she looked lost, like a bereaved child, stunned with shock. At their entrance, she gasped and gripped the other woman's hand tighter, then got hesitantly to her feet.

"Don't be angry with me, Father," she whispered.

William walked forwards at once. For a moment he put his hands on her shoulders and held her at arm's length, looking her over; then he pulled her close to him. She buried her face in his shoulder; one hand covered her face. Then she pushed herself back and looked at him. "I don't understand what I did wrong," she said. She was shaking now from head to foot. "I came with him to be married. I came to live with his mother. But he took me to an awful hotel and left me there alone. And then he arrived this morning . . ."

"It doesn't matter," William murmured.

"It does matter!" Louisa exclaimed, tears springing to her eyes. "As soon as we were in France, he barely spoke to me. Why would that be? I never saw his mother at all. All he would do was look out of the train window once we got to France. We got off in Paris and we went to a hotel. . . ." She colored deeply. "I thought . . ." Shuddering, she plucked at the collar of her coat as if to cover herself more tightly. William stroked her hair.

"It was then," she whispered. "Then that I first thought . . . Well, it was wrong, you know. Not speaking to me, putting me in a room in a hotel. I asked him what was happening; he wouldn't say. He just . . . he *smiled* at me. Such a cold, horrible smile. I asked to see his mother. I asked when . . . when we would be married . . . and he . . ."

Harry stepped alongside them both. "It's all right," he said consolingly. "Just tell us, Louisa."

Louisa looked at him, and a small twisted smile came to her face. "He laughed, Harry. He said that

I would soon see the joke." She looked at her father and brother both, as if the answer might be written in their faces. "It wasn't a joke, was it?" she said. "How could it be a joke? Such a thing isn't a joke, is it?" Her voice dropped to a whisper. "Not to me," she said.

Above her head, William and Harry exchanged despairing and angry looks. Louisa was staring at her feet, continuing her mumbled explanation. "And then he went away. And I stayed there all night. I didn't dare have anything to eat; I stayed in my traveling clothes. I thought he would come back. But he didn't. He didn't come back that evening, or the next day. I walked down to reception; I asked if they knew him. They just shrugged their shoulders, and they looked at me as if . . ." She paused. "As if I were stupid, which I am. I am." She wiped the streaming tears with the back of her hand. "He came back this morning, and he just took my arm and walked me to a railway station. And it wasn't until we got to the station that I saw . . . I realized."

Her voice broke; she took a painful breath. "There were soldiers; he said he had to go. I had no money. I begged him. Was it wrong to beg him?" Her pitiful look was directed at her brother. "Was it, Harry? And he said he had a message. I don't know what it means." She put a hand to her head. "I don't know what any of it means."

William put his arm around her and guided her

again to the chair. They waited around her while she brought her sobs under control and the Frenchwoman patted her hand in consolation. Harry looked at his father, and then leaned down to Louisa. "What was the message?" he asked gently.

She looked from him to William, where her eyes rested. "He said it was for Father," she replied slowly. "You see, but that is what I don't understand. He said that he had met my father in London this year." She frowned. "But it isn't right, is it? Because whenever I talked about meeting you, Father—I wanted him to meet you—he told me that it was not to be. Not yet. He told me that you would not approve of him. But then, at the station . . ." Her voice drifted away. She looked from them both as if replaying the scene in her mind. "He was standing on the steps of the train, and he said that I was to tell my father that . . . that he had kept the promise he made to him in London."

She dragged her gaze back to William, her expression vacant, her mouth trembling. "He said," she added in a low voice, "that my father would understand now what it was to be ruined."

Chapter 10

*I*n the final week of August, the last field of hay was cut on the fields below Rutherford.

In the heat of the afternoon, a loaded wagon traveled from the village with a towering load of the dry, sweet-smelling grass. Jack Armitage sat with the reins held loosely in his fingers, watching the road ahead of Wenceslas's slow, steady pace. He was eyeing the progress of the horse, but his mind was not on what he could see: it was up at the house, beyond the trees. It was in the orchard where the white canvas of the tents was stretched out to form a cool roof against the midday sun; it was at the long tables where he had seen Louisa this morning, sitting with the child on her lap.

He had seen the master and his son come back three weeks ago; seen the hired car from the station with its windows closed. He had stood unnoticed at the edge of the terrace as Louisa had been hurried into the house, almost carried along, like the invalid she was. The doctor had pronounced it to be nervous collapse; the maids said she kept to her room and that her mother and father were constantly with her. One night a few days ago, she had at last come down to dinner, and been seen walking about the house. She was not what she was, the maids had told him. She was quiet; she did not smile or sing or run about as she always used to; she had to be coaxed into her clothes. He had asked whether she cried, but they could not tell him. He hoped very much that she did not cry, but then perhaps silence would be worse.

The baby girl had been brought by the woman from the pub in the village; it was the local womens' job to dress the tables while the men set up the barrels of beer for the summer fair. Little Cecilia had been put down on a blanket, and no one had been paying attention as she reached out a tiny hand and gripped the edge of the nearest long tablecloth. It had been Louisa, pale and apparently listless, walking silently through the marquee, who had seen the movement and leaned down, and discovered the little face looking back at her.

Unbidden now, Wenceslas turned the last corner into the park, and began the long approach to the house. Jack leaned back and looked up at the beech trees, seeing the blue sky between the high branches. The air above him was where Harry Cavendish would be, somewhere in the south of England, in Wiltshire; it was said that he was learning his trade fast, and would be enlisted in the Royal Flying Corps and go to France. The thought trailed across Jack's mind, as idle as the sway of the trees, as slow as the tread of the shire horse. He felt nothing at all when he thought of

Harry Cavendish now. He wished him Godspeed, he supposed. He wished them all Godspeed, and safe passage. The first of the planes had already gone, and British troops had landed in France on August 12; now all that anyone talked about were the places that had been unknown to them a few weeks before—places with romantic-sounding names like Liege and Louvain and Dinant.

The newspapers said that the German army had massacred six hundred people in Dinant as they passed through it; they said that they burned villages, and libraries of medieval manuscripts, and churches. Jack didn't know what to believe; he couldn't imagine it. He couldn't imagine an army marching through the village at Rutherford's gates and burning the church, or the priest, or a child like the one Louisa held in her lap. It seemed not to be possible, but he supposed it must be. And Harry Cavendish would be in the air above it, looking down on men killing one another. That didn't seem possible either.

He looked ahead at Wenceslas's curving neck, at the patient nodding of the horse's head as they made their way slowly along the road. His father had told him that horses were being requisitioned, that the Kents had already sent some to Carlisle, that people in London were even offering the hunters that they rode each morning on Rotten Row. Jack had scoffed at the very idea; no, that was beyond belief indeed. A highly strung horse like a hunter would never stand work, and could not be made to pull wagons; they would shy at the least noise, never mind guns. No, the kind of horse . . . Thinking of it now, he instinctively tightened his grip on the reins. Wenceslas would never be taken. Ridiculous. He was needed LORD, like all the horses. He was not so much an animal as a solid, softhearted boy; he knew Jack's voice; he would take orders from no other. And to think of all those miles, and crossing the Channel? Of putting a shire like Wenceslas into a train, or a ship—how could that be done; how could the poor beast be cajoled into such a thing? It would be frightened to death; it would not understand what was wanted. Besides, he would personally fight the man who laid hands on this horse. He would kill the man who suggested putting the shire behind an artillery carriage in the filth of someplace in Flanders or Paris, or wherever it was they were supposed to go. No man was going to take Wenceslas away; he would make sure of that. And that was the end of it.

Jack determinedly turned his mind to other things. He thought of Harrison, who had gone to Carlisle just as he had promised. He would not be coming back to Rutherford anytime soon. Two of the gardening boys had also gone to the recruiting office in Catterick. Posters had gone up in the windows of the shops in Richmond in the first week of August: posters headed, LORD

KITCHENER'S APPEAL, and asking for volunteers, and Harrison had up and left the very same afternoon, without giving any notice to Lord Cavendish, to Bradfield's horror.

In the same windows in Richmond, there had been orders about restricting "aliens," though no one was entirely sure what an alien was. And then someone set fire to de Reszknak's shop in York, and it went up in a torrent of flame, and afterwards de Reszknak himself came out on the pavement and wept, and put a Union Jack over the charred shutters. They said that de Reszknak was an alien, but he had lived there all his life, and his father before him, and he had protested that they had come from Hungary eighty years ago. Nobody in the servants' hall knew where Hungary was precisely, but they knew that it was closer to Germany than England.

As Rutherford came now into view, Jack twitched the reins so that the wagon would be steered to the side lane. Normally he would never go in the front gate as he had done, but it was necessary to get the hay close to the marquees. It was baled into seats, and would be laid down next to the tables. He well remembered previous years, when by the time darkness fell, the children would be scratching from all the insects that came out of the grass, but by evening not one person would care. There would be dancing, and the flickering fairy lights of the orchard, and there would be music.

But he doubted . . . yes, he doubted very much . . . that Louisa Cavendish would dance at all.

Octavia was not in Rutherford that morning.

She had left at first light, driven to the station by her husband. Neither of them had said a word as William had parked the Napier on the railway forecourt, and they had sat in silence together while they waited for the train. When it had come Octavia had got out and walked to the platform alone.

She was now in York, standing under the Great West Window of York Minster, waiting for John Gould. She glanced up at it, hearing the clocks outside strike midday. The window was seven hundred years old, and known as the Heart of Yorkshire, but at this very moment she felt as if her own heart had turned to glass, as ultimately fragile as the window itself. She had been told that all the stained glass of the cathedral would be taken apart and put into storage, and that it would be put back together only when the war was over. It seemed a job of torturous, unbearable delicacy. But then the unbearable must become bearable; certain tasks now had to be done. There was no alternative. And, glancing down, she saw John coming towards her.

He kissed her cheek and stepped back, his eyes ranging over her face. He had been staying in York ever since the news of Louisa's shock and illness had been related to Octavia; he had thought it politic to take himself away while Octavia and William dealt with the immediate crisis. He had been patient, waiting alone all this time. "Is it done?" he asked. He was smiling anxiously.

"It can't be done," she told him quietly.

"My God," he said. The hopeful optimism that had been on his face as he walked up to her drained suddenly away. "So that's all? You've come all this way to tell me that? To tell me it can't be done?" She said nothing. He took hold of her hand and gripped it tightly. "Anything can be done. I can arrange it."

"No, John," she said softly. "You can't arrange this. I can't take Louisa from her father, and I can't leave without her."

"I'll get her whatever you want. The best doctor. She'll recover, darling."

"Yes," she agreed. "She will. But not away from home. She needs to be at Rutherford, and William wants her there." She looked at him, and then down at their joined hands.

"And that's it?" he said. "And that's all?" He had raised his voice; one of the vergers of the church looked over at them, frowning. John pulled on her hand. "Walk with me," he said. "Come outside."

They went down the great nave and out into the city. Sun streamed along the narrow streets.

"I'll wait another few weeks," he offered

eagerly. "She'll be better then." They had come to a few benches along a quiet promenade; after a moment of urging she obeyed his plea to sit down. "Octavia," he said, stricken. "Please talk to me."

She shook her head. "I don't know what to say."

"Say you'll come out at Christmas. Say you'll come out in the spring. I'll wait here, or in London. I'll wait anywhere." Tears had come to his eyes; he looked away from her in an effort to compose himself.

She gazed at the other walkers who passed them by. She envied their worlds, their seeming peace and calm. The pain was knotted inside her, an inanimate obstructive thing; it was as if it had invaded her, taken possession of her. "If I went anywhere, I would have to go with Louisa and Charlotte. And I would want to have Cecilia." She looked directly at him. "It's one thing for us to go together," she said. "It's quite another to take three others away, and one of them a tiny child who has never known her father."

"William has told you this. You're following some sort of order."

"No," she said. "William has said nothing at all. But he . . ."

"He what?"

"I'm not sure that he's well. He seems to be in pain from time to time."

"What kind of pain?"

"His heart, I think. He won't admit it."

"Then perhaps he doesn't feel it. Perhaps it's you who feels it. Perhaps you think you've made him ill. It's guilt, Octavia. Your guilt, that's all."

She was frowning hard. "I can't be sure."

He was trying to read her expression. "You don't love me," he murmured. "You don't want me. This talk of William being ill is just an excuse."

She turned on him, eyes blazing. "You think that I don't want to live as we lived this summer?" she said. "You think that I want to lose that, to never have it again?" She made a fluttering gesture of helplessness.

"Then let's go now," he urged her. "This week. I'll book a passage for you and the girls. They'll want for nothing. I'll book the best suite. I'll build that fine house." He made a pathetic attempt to be jaunty and to smile. "I'll hire a nursemaid; I'll buy a piano. I'll be domesticated, if you like. I'll clean the grates; I'll haul in the coal." His feigned cheerfulness lasted only a second, however. As he saw her face, his expression dropped through a thousand degrees of grief. "It's no use, is it?" he asked. "You won't come with me."

She couldn't reply. She wasn't able to form the words.

"Don't you know how I love you?" he asked. "Tell me what to do. Tell me."

A long moment passed. "I can't tell you what I don't know," she whispered.

They watched the people pass by; at last, they heard the clock strike the half hour. She looked long and hard at him, as if to remember every detail. And then she stood up. "My train is at one o'clock," she said.

He got to his feet. "I'll walk you to the station."

When she looked back on those thirty minutes, she tried to reconstruct how they passed the time, what they saw, or how the crowds were, or how long they waited, side by side in a desperate caricature of normality, until they heard the steam engine coming along the track. She tried to remember whether she had said anything at all as he handed her into the carriage of the train. But there was nothing left, only his own words.

"I will come back," he said. "Don't be under any illusion about that, Octavia. I will come back for you."

It was not the last scene that Octavia had to endure that day. On the way back on the train, she set her mind firmly to what she had to tell William. He met her again at the station, searching her face just as John had done and with the same intensity.

He started the car and they drove in the direction of Rutherford, but just before the village Octavia put her hand on his on the steering wheel. "Will you stop the car for a moment?" she said. When they came to a stop, she nodded towards the church. To his puzzled frown she made no answer, simply getting out of the car, and when he followed her, she went through the church gate and around the churchyard, picking her way through the ancient stones until she came to a flat piece of grass with no marker and no monument.

"Do you see this?" she asked him.

He looked around. He could see only a slight mound with a few sparse green weeds growing over it. "Can I ask what I might be looking for?"

"A grave with no marker," she said. "It belongs to Emily Maitland. The girl who tried to drown herself. The girl who died last Christmas."

William looked at the ground. "You want there to be a stone of some kind?" he asked, perplexed. "Some memorial?"

"Yes. That would be appropriate."

Of all the things that William had expected to discuss this afternoon, this was not one of them. "But we do not raise memorials to the staff," he pointed out. "That is the responsibility of their own families."

Octavia looked at him steadily. "Precisely," she said. "This girl was the mother of your grand-daughter. The child she bore was Harry's. The child is alive; she's at Rutherford this after-noon."

If William was shocked, he did not show it. In fact, something in his face told Octavia that it was a long-buried suspicion. "Harry told me in

Paris . . ." he began. He put a hand to his forehead. "But only that he had known the girl, and . . ." He looked up. "The child survived, and you never told me?"

"I asked for her to be taken care of. I went to see her in the New Year. I simply knew. . . . I didn't have to ask Harry. The moment I heard that Harry had been at the river, and that Jack Armitage had struck him, I knew it in my heart. And if further proof were needed, one has only to look at the child. She's the image of Harry at that age, William. There can be no doubt."

"Does Harry know?"

"Not yet."

"My God," he muttered. He began to shake his head bemusedly. "And you never felt that you could tell me?"

"There were so many things we could not discuss," she said levelly.

"But you could not even discuss this at all with Harry?"

"Harry? In the condition he was in while we were London?" she asked. "How could that be broached?" She shook her head. "I could not tell Harry before I had told you. It was something that you and I together would need to present to him, and reconcile ourselves to. It is still." She paused. "It might have been possible then if we were close, William. But we were not."

"You blame me."

She considered him calmly. "I don't censure you, necessarily. But Harry, once his word was given, could never discuss it with us. We have both failed him, in fact." She looked down thoughtfully at the grass. "We have tried to set an example, but we have both failed."

"And I transgressed my own rules of behavior. I suppose you think that." Octavia gave no reply, and William made a confused, almost desperate gesture. "Charles was never my son. I have told you all that Helene told me in Paris. What more reassurance can I give you?"

"Not that reassurance, certainly," she told him. "I accept that. It was never the issue of his being your son or not that divided us. It was that you had not told me; it was that you allowed Helene de Montfort to come between us, in however circumspect a fashion. And through it all . . ." She gave a little shrug. "I was very much the loose cannon who must be taught how to behave." Her voice was full of sad irony.

"You have never for one moment embarrassed me, Octavia."

"Oh, I think I have," she said. "And we have each hurt each other, William. We've done that most efficiently." They allowed the silence to develop between them, each with their own thoughts. Then, "I shall stay at Rutherford and carry out my duty to my children," she said. He

421

noticed acutely that she did not say she had any duty towards him as her husband. He wondered whether her heart was quite closed to him, whether there was any chance of her love returning to him. "I'll stay here to see Louisa well, and Charlotte grown," she continued. "And I'll be here when Harry comes home. There will be continuity for them. There will be security."

A flush had come to William's face. "And John Gould . . . ?"

She looked away, at the church, at the lane beyond. "I don't know what John Gould will do," she murmured. "I won't see him again."

Despite himself—despite his wish to keep his dignity—the relief showed eloquently in William's body; he slumped slightly, and the impenetrable expression—the face of superior calm cultivated over a lifetime—momentarily vanished. As the mask slipped, a man was revealed in the throes of relief: desperate, barely contained heartfelt relief and thankfulness. But he did not move. He gazed at Octavia, and then, very slowly, very hesitantly, he smiled. "I feel that I have had rather too many pieces of news recently," he said. "I wonder if there might be a limit to them."

She returned the smile sadly. "At least in that we feel the same, William."

She walked back, swiftly, in the direction of the car. It was only after some moments that he felt able to follow her.

• • •

The daylight began to fade in the orchard at around nine o'clock that evening. Paper lanterns hung from the branches of trees among the apples and leaves, the breeze that had been blowing all day died, and the brass band from the village began to play.

At first, the dances were formal. Octavia and William, as was the custom, danced the first. Octavia was dressed in pale yellow, an old-fashioned dress that fell to her feet, tied with a broad white sash. Dancing with her, William thought that she looked so much younger than her age; her shoulders were bare and she wore no jewelry at all. He wondered what the war might bring them; whether she would ever again look like this, or whether they both might bear signs of anxiety, or terror, or grief. He tried not to think of it. Instead, he looked across at the staff lining the edges of the orchard, clapping their hands to the music and at the same time dutifully applauding them.

He saw Nash take hold of Mary's hand; saw him lean down to whisper something to her. Years ago, when William had first inherited Rutherford, such a thing would be unheard-of; no footman talked to a maid, and certainly not in the sight of the master of the house. William smiled to himself at Mary—fair, short, square shouldered; she and Nash, who was so tall and dark and lean, were hardly a match. But then, he wondered, what did match in these strange and darkening days? A man to a girl, a hand to a task; no one knew. The world he understood, the world that he thought he knew, was blowing away like husks blown from corn in a mill. Each one of them was inside that mill, and the grindstones were rapidly turning.

William and Octavia stepped from the floor; it was the time-honored signal that the staff could begin their own celebrations. For a turn or two, William encouraged Charlotte to dance with him, but his daughter, laughing at her own two left feet, turned back towards the knot of women who were fussing over Cecilia; as she reached them she pointedly stared at her father and then at Octavia. William smiled as the boys of the village rushed in, each with a girl on his arm, and the musicians began to stamp time on the board stage on which they stood. He followed where Octavia had gone, to the door of the canvas tent.

They walked out onto the close-mown grass under the apple trees; Octavia, glancing over her shoulder, saw Louisa look up from her lap to the hand extended to her. She saw her daughter gaze into Jack Armitage's face. He was standing solicitously over her; she shook her head but did not take her eyes from him, and her own hand fluttered to the empty seat alongside her. Jack sat down slowly at Louisa's side, and then the dancers obscured them from Octavia's sight.

"Will Harry come back before he is sent to France?" she asked William.

"I shall ask that he does," William said. "Although, my dear, what influence I have now is hard to imagine."

"He must come," she murmured. "He has someone to meet."

They looked at each other. Keeping silence, they walked a little farther, until the dancers, and the apple trees, and the swaying lanterns, now bright against the shadows, were left behind.

"Do you remember the time when Harry was a boy," William mused, "and you were with him on the banks of the river? And you came back across the grass here, and I walked out to meet you?"

Octavia did. It was the day that her husband had lectured her for walking barefoot. He had told her that she had a role to play, a place to keep, a reputation to protect.

"Yes," she said. "It was hardly something to forget."

In the darkness, she could see that he was smiling. He dropped her hand. "I have walked across here a thousand times," he said. "Perhaps five thousand—ten thousand—who knows? But I have never touched the grass."

To her surprise, he suddenly stretched down and untied his shoelaces, and took off his shoes and socks. Then, with one shoe in each hand, he began to walk, slowly and self-consciously at first, feet lifted exaggeratedly. She suppressed a smile. He picked up his pace, hopping comically from one foot to the other. Eventually, out there in the warm green darkness, he dropped the shoes and began to run. After a few more yards, he looked back at her. He was out of breath, and laughing. "Quite extraordinary," he called. "You really ought to try it."

Even if it had been broad daylight, he would not have been able to read the expression on her face. She was standing stock-still; he saw her framed against the great tawny-colored walls of the house that rose far behind her.

His overriding instinct was to go back, and grasp her around the waist, and force her to walk with him. But he resisted the temptation.

Instead, he walked on, his head thrown back, and, looking up into the vast darkness, he prayed that she would follow him.

Readers Guide to Rutherford Park

1. The novel opens at Christmastime with the tragic story of Harry's relationship with Emily, their daughter's birth, and Emily's death. How does Emily's fate affect Harry's relationship with his parents, and with himself, as he grows into adulthood?

2. Louisa is portrayed as an innocent, a naïve young woman who aims to please her family and live up to society's expectations. However, when she is being fitted for her Presentation dress, Louisa feels a strange urge to step on the seamstress's hand, and "to hear the girl squeal" (p. 103). What do you think this brief scene reveals about her true character?

3. Mary and Emily are both mill town girls, yet they are polar opposites in character. Emily is timid and runs from her troubles, while Mary is outspoken and tackles obstacles head on. What do you think this says about the extent to which personality is affected by situation?

4. The women in the novel seem to consider it a fact of life that men will cheat on their wives, and Hetty had "not even seemed surprised" that William had had an affair (p. 172). Octavia, though, has an affair of her own with John Gould. Do you think Octavia's affair is justified? Going further, do you think her affair represents empowerment while William's signifies weakness? Discuss.

5. John Gould finds, in going through William's paperwork, a note that someone wrote in the margin: "Honesty is no match for villainy" (p. 151). To what extent does the novel support this theory? What are some examples?

6. Throughout the novel, Helene is portrayed as a caricature of sorts, representing a modern, independent and promiscuous woman. However, when William and Harry confront her in her Paris home while looking for Louisa, she is not the fashionable flirt she usually appears to be, answering the door in a shawl and slippers. Do you sympathize with her and her situation, or do you think she deserves her fate?

7. Octavia says to John that she longs to "do anything at all" (p. 242), and even somewhat envies the servants for their work. At

Christmas, William looks out at the laborers and considers them more "real" (p. 71) than the monuments he and his wife symbolize. Do you think William sees his privileged life as a blessing or as an obligation?

8. Helene is the catalyst for Octavia and William's marital troubles. However, she is also the epitome of a free and modern woman. Is Helene the villain in the novel who causes the Cavendish's downfall, or is her affair with William a blessing in disguise for Octavia, opening her up to new possibilities for happiness?

9. John believes that human beings are taken down by "not giant chaos, but trivial mistakes" (p. 198). To what extent do you think this is true? What trivial mistakes have brought down the characters in the novel?

10. Like Helene, John has a reputation as a charmer and a flirt. These characters bring up the idea of reputation versus the truth. How are Helene and John similar, and how are they different in terms of living up to their scandalous reputations?

11. John expresses that he considers himself an adventurer and explorer who is not ready to

settle down, doubting that he could ever be faithful to a woman. However, he daydreams about a future in America with Octavia and the children. John himself "didn't know what he was, and that was the truth" (p. 251). Who, do you think, is the real John Gould? Give examples that show his true character.

12. Throughout the novel, William expresses a very traditional view of women, believing they should be obedient wives who are "protected from reality" (p. 313). Do you think that William's attitude toward women has changed at all by the end of the novel? If so, how?

13. How would you describe Harry and William's relationship at the end of the novel? Do you think they have reached a sort of truce, or will their differences always create tension?

14. Why do you think Octavia stays at Rutherford at the end of the novel? Is it purely for the children's sake, as she suggests, or are other motives involved?

15. At the end of the novel, do you think Octavia will follow William in his bare feet? If yes, do you think that signifies weakness or strength in her character?

Center Point Large Print
600 Brooks Road / PO Box 1
Thorndike, ME 04986-0001 USA

(207) 568-3717

US & Canada:
1 800 929-9108
www.centerpointlargeprint.com